PRAISE

Gina Detwiler has again pulled her readers into her great series about a hundreds of years old Nephilim teenage boy, and the constant battle between good and evil that rages around and in him. Forlorn and Forsaken were awesome reads, but the author cranks it up in Forgiven. The suspense of what Jared and his friends are going to face brings a constant mix of excitement and dread. The book does not disappoint, and was as hard to put down as the two previous books. Forgiven has Tower of Babylon type moments as man shows there is no depth he won't go to as he strives to make God irrelevant. In Forsaken, the battle for Jared is ramped up, and it is again shown that no one is ever truly forsaken by God, and forgiveness is always possible. Forgiven pulled me in so well, that I reached the last page and was surprised when there were no others to follow. Forsaken and the other two books in the series are an excellent, Christian, and wholesome substitute to the vampire books that are so popular among teenagers today.

—Mark Buzard, Blogger, *Thoughts of a Sojourner*

Grace Fortune is back, and she and Jared are up to their necks in angels, antichrists, and a billionaire playing God. Throw in a marriage made in Heaven and a weapon powerful enough to open the Gates of Hell, and the third book in the Forlorn Series reaches apocalyptic magnificence. The pace is blinding, the twists are magnificent, and the ending...WOW! Never saw that coming. Who but Detwiler could blend Faith, Science, and Romance so perfectly? There is no justice in the world if Forgiven doesn't become an instant bestseller!

—D.L. Rosensteel, Author of *Ionic Attractions* and the *Psi Fighter Academy Series*

FORGIVEN

Forlorn Series
Book III

GINA DETWILER

Vinspire Publishing
www.vinspirepublishing.com

For my daughters, Dani, Nikki and Sami

May angels always watch over you.

Then they said, "Come, let us build ourselves a city
and a tower with its top in the heavens,
and let us make a name for ourselves,
lest we be dispersed over the face of the whole earth."

Genesis 11:4 (ESV)

ALSO BY GINA DETWILER

Forlorn

Forsaken

WRITING WITH PRISCILLA SHIRER:

The Prince Warriors

The Prince Warriors and the Unseen Invasion

The Prince Warriors and the Swords of Rhema

The Winter War, a Prince Warriors sequel

PART ONE

BLACK HOLES
AND
REVELATIONS

1

Going to Mars

Angel

I might be in trouble again.

I am summoned to the Assembly of the Seven. They gather at the top of a tall mountain, surrounded by seven more mountains and blanketed by clouds. They wear armor unique to their dominions in service to the High Lord, Elohim. I wonder at this earthly setting, at their human shapes formed of Light, at their blazing swords and shining armor.

This can mean only one thing.

War.

In their presence, I am no more significant than a grasshopper in the company of eagles. I am a Guardian, the protector of a girl named Grace Fortune. No doubt, this is why I have been summoned. Grace has come to the attention of the Seven before, along with her friend Jared, who happens to be a Nephilim. Yet, after years of grappling with their many enemies, they have retreated from the battlefield, content in their love, their families, and their newfound peace. Their band, Forlorn, no longer makes public appearances. They still play their music, and they write and sell songs through a publisher who keeps their identities a secret. They are happy to be out of the spotlight, away from the world's madness. I have enjoyed the respite.

I bow before Gabriel, the revealer, usually the one to speak. Michael, the protector, glowers at me with withering disapproval, as usual. Uriel, the destroyer, stands in fierce silence. Raphael, the healer, is the only one to convey any hint of empathy. The last three—Saraquel, Remiel, and Raquel—remain ever quiet, although I believe they communicate with each other in sendings I do not hear.

"Guardian," Gabriel says. "Something is happening that concerns your charge."

Surprising. Grace's world is now very small. But the archangels are members of the Council—they stand before the Throne. They know things I cannot.

"Has she done something wrong?" I ask.

"Not yet," Michael grumbles. "Although I'm sure it is only a matter of time."

Gabriel throws him a warning glance. "It will be better to show you. Uriel will take you. It is important that you understand. For Grace's sake. And...the boy's as well."

The boy. They once referred to Jared as "the creature." At least they acknowledge his humanness now.

"Go now," says Gabriel.

Uriel's hand touches my shoulder and my Light flows into his. I find myself on earth under a cloudless sky. Before me is an enormous dome made of brown wooden slats, tilted like a globe. Situated in a green space, the structure is surrounded by low, nondescript buildings against a backdrop of sleepy, white-capped mountains.

"What is this place?" I ask.

"This is CERN." Uriel's voice rumbles like thunder. "A global center for nuclear research. It contains the largest particle collider in the world, seventeen miles in circumference."

"What is it for?"

"For men to discover the secrets of the universe." Uriel lets out a sigh like a north wind.

"They spend billions smashing particles while children starve and wars rage on."

"Don't they know how the universe began?"

"They reject the words of Elohim. They seek their own explanation."

Uriel takes me inside the globe, where giant video screens surround large white resin balls suspended in a sea of midnight-blue, meant to represent particles in an atom. We slip through the blackened ceiling to a space above, a lecture hall under the arched dome. People in white coats with name badges gaze in rapt attention at a man standing on the platform. He is tall and lank, with thinning dark hair, pale eyes, and protruding ears. His arms and legs are unusually long and his shoulders broad, making him appear out of proportion to himself. He speaks with an air of humor and humility.

"Thank you for inviting me," he says to the crowd. "Wow, this place is truly amazing. It has always been my dream to be a part of what you folks are doing here. Until now, my interest has been in outer space, searching for new worlds to conquer. But lately, I have come to realize that the true frontier, the one yet to be explored, is right here in the subatomic world. To discover what we are truly made of and what we can become. To discover, in effect, our past, which will lead to our destiny."

The crowd applauds. A lone whistle shrills through the room.

"This is where the whole world comes together." The speaker gains momentum. "Twenty-two nations united for a single purpose—to advance the cause of science in our world. To create a global society, a global order, to meet the needs of future generations. And I want to be a part of that. We will do great things together. You and I both know that the LHC is in need of a major upgrade. It must be bigger and run at higher energies in order to reveal the secrets of the atom—secrets we must learn in order to move forward. That's why I'm here. And that's what I'm going to do."

The room erupts in riotous applause.

"Who is that man?" I ask.

"His name is Darwin Speer."

I have heard the name before.

~

Time moves backward into night. We hover above the courtyard of the CERN campus. In the center of the courtyard, an enormous statue of the Hindu god Shiva performs the dance of destruction inside a ring of fire.

"They pray to Shiva now?"

"They don't pray. But this god is their symbol for what they want to achieve."

"Which is?"

"Creation. And destruction."

Spotlights shine on Shiva from different angles, casting huge shadows on the surrounding buildings. Dark Ones dance in the shadows—they glom together, form a ring around the statue which comes to life…its fires flicker, its arms and legs take up the dance.

A line of black-robed figures parades through the curtain of Dark, their shadows long against the hovering buildings so they seem like giants. They circle the statue in tightly choreographed procession. Suddenly they stop and face the dancing statue, raising their arms in worship. They begin to chant, droning in an ancient, unknown language.

One of the worshippers steps out of line and approaches Shiva. Three others follow—they remove the first one's robe to reveal a woman with blonde hair dressed in a long white gown. As the chanting intensifies, she lies on the ground and Shiva dances in a frenzy around her still form. A black-robed priest raises his hand and a knife flashes in the spotlight. He bends over the woman and stabs her through the heart.

It is day again. The courtyard is empty.

"Was that real?" I ask.

"It does not matter. What matters is that it was done. This is war, Guardian. The Dark Prince stands ready. It is only a matter of time."

2

Where We Come Alive

Grace

It's weird, being back in New York. I didn't want to come, but I also didn't want to disappoint Ethan. His video game, *The Wrath of the Watchers*, is being launched at GAME-ON, the biggest video game convention on the planet—or so he says. And since our quest to kill a Watcher was the inspiration for the game in the first place, Jared and I decided we had to be there.

We drove to New York in the "new" PsychoVan, Ralph's latest customized Chevy that might be a decade or two newer than the last one. It's been a long time since Ralph let us go to such a public event. Maybe he trusts us more now. Or maybe our enemies have moved on to easier prey.

Ralph—always concerned about our safety—booked us rooms at a funky little hotel in the Meatpacking District, near where the convention is being held. Ralph is sort of Jared's dad but not really. He knows the hotel owner, who promised to keep our presence a secret. That's necessary because a lot of Forlorn/Jared Lorn nut jobs are still out there. There have been Grace Fortune and Jared Lorn sightings on every continent since the demise of Lester Crow and Blood Moon, except maybe Antarctica. But I'm sure that's only a matter of time.

The hotel is pretty bizarre. The furniture in the lobby is straight out of a turn-of-the-century brothel. A giant disco ball hangs from the ceiling. The bellhop wears a monkey hat like in the old movies, and the wooden calendar behind the counter reads "May 35." The May part is right, anyway. We're far enough away from my mother's old stomping grounds on the Upper West Side that I feel relatively safe—even though my mother now lives on the West Coast with her mega-preacher husband Harry Ravel.

The event is scheduled for tonight at six p.m. The guests are encouraged to dress as characters from their favorite video game. Jared and I will be disguised as Watchers.

Go figure.

Bree and Ethan were already checked in when we arrived this afternoon. It's been months since I last saw my best friend, Bree. She transferred to Ithaca for her sophomore year. She said she did it because they offered a better program in Music Education, but I knew she wanted to be closer to Ethan, who attends Cornell. Those two are pretty serious about each other, despite the fact that they don't seem to get along.

We hugged a lot and caught up on each others' lives. Bree has graduated from Disney princess to preppy college girl, and Ethan is no longer a high school dork with frizzy hair and coke-bottle glasses. His hair is short and a smudge on his chin threatens to become a beard. Compared to them, Jared and I haven't changed at all. Except I've dyed my hair black, more for camouflage than anything else.

"What's with the hair?" Bree asked, staring at me. "It seriously doesn't work with your complexion. Way too Goth."

"What color should I do?"

"IDK. Pink? Blue might be nice."

"I like it." Jared defended my choice.

"You would, weirdo," said Bree.

I've missed her. And yet there is something strange between us too, a chasm too wide to cross. She's moved on with her life, made new friends, had all kinds of new experiences. I have stayed where I was. No college, no real job, other than writing music. No plans either. I worry we won't have much to talk about, once the "catching up" part is over.

We order up our favorites from room service—chicken nuggets and fries, salad for Bree—still a vegetarian—and a hamburger for Ethan. But he can't eat, he's so nervous about the launch.

"They have this huge screen," he says. "And they made this awesome trailer and there's a band and everything. People from all over the country—the world—will be there. Every gaming professional. Journalists. Bloggers. Reviewers." He puts both hands on top of his head. "What if it sucks?"

"It doesn't suck," I say. "How could it? You're a genius."

"I'm a fraud!" Ethan throws himself face-down on the couch.

"Oh, for crying out loud." Bree drops her French fry and goes to talk to him. I've never seen this side of Ethan before.

"He's having a nervous breakdown," I say.

"He's always been wound a little tight." Jared shakes his head and smiles.

Once Ethan calms down, Bree and I go to our room to change into our costumes. Mine is classic Grim Reaper—a long black robe with a wide hood. Not terribly creative. Bree' silky black gown with wide lace sleeves makes her look a little like a very pretty and fashionable Bride of Frankenstein.

"This won't fool anybody." I stare at myself in the mirror. "Shouldn't we have masks?"

"Makeup is better. I found a great design, and I brought all the supplies."

"I'm not sure this is a good idea, wearing a demon costume. It seems like it would invite the wrong sort of spirits."

"Hiding in plain sight, remember? Your demon friends won't be able to tell the difference between you and the rest of the crowd."

"Still…"

"Relax, Grace. It'll be fine. You should quit worrying about all that angel-demon stuff, anyway."

Quit worrying? Has she totally forgotten all that's happened to us? Maybe she has. She lives in a different world now.

"How's your dad?" she asks as she does her makeup at the bathroom mirror. I stand in the doorway and watch—Bree's an artist with an eyebrow pencil.

"He's okay. Cancer's in remission. The doctors say it could last for months. Years even. He goes for scans every three months. That's nerve wracking. But so far, so good."

"Cool. I saw that your stepdad Harry Ravel is running for governor of California."

"Ugh. Don't call him that. But yes, that's true." The thought of my mother becoming First Lady of California turns my insides out.

"He's leading in the polls too. Everyone says he'll win."

"Yeah. He promised to balance the budget, and she promised to kill all the vampires."

We both laugh.

"You and Jared…okay?"

"Oh yeah. Sure."

"Any…plans?"

"Like what?"

"To get married?"

"Are you kidding?"

She turns to face me. "No, I'm not. Haven't you talked about it?"

"We can't get married. He's a…you know what he is."

"What difference does that make? You love each other, right?"

"Yeah, but think about it. In twenty years, I'll be forty

and he'll still look like a teenager. Not to mention all the other issues."

"What other issues?"

"You *know* what other issues! We could never have a *normal* marriage like other people."

"Why not? I mean, what if you're wrong?"

"Excuse me?"

"About the curse. What if all those bad things you think will happen don't? I mean, things have changed. Jared's not the same as he was. Neither are you."

I don't tell her how often I've thought of it. Jared and I married and living together in some cottage in the country with a couple of kids—adopted, of course—a dog, a cat, maybe even a goldfish. But then I get to the part about me being an old lady and him still being young and beautiful, and it grosses me out.

So where does that leave us? I try not to think about it. I pretend there is no future. I'm only twenty. Plenty of time.

"I heard your new song." Bree starts to apply glittery black makeup to my face. "*Only Human*. Great title."

"How did you know it was ours?" Jared and I don't perform our own music anymore. We like being anonymous songwriters now.

"It's obvious. You guys have a certain style. And theme. Everyone knows."

"They do?"

"Of course, silly! Don't you pay attention to social media?"

"I try not to."

"I miss Forlorn," she says wistfully. "Hey! I have an idea! We should do a reunion concert. Like the Stones."

"We only did one concert in our whole career."

"So?"

I laugh. "Sometimes I want to. But no, it would be impossible. Too much...collateral damage."

Bree sighs and focuses on my makeup again. "How's

Penny?"

"Okay. She still has some trouble from the injury. It's hard for her to remember things. She's going to night school to finish her GED. Ralph wants her to go to college. She's really smart, and she studies like crazy. More than I ever did."

"And you still don't want to go to college?"

"I've thought about it. But going to a school, to actual classes with all those people…it's not for me. Maybe I'll try an online course in something."

"Grace, you're becoming a hermit." Her voice drips reproach.

"Hey, I'm here, right? In New York City, about to attend a public event?"

"In disguise."

"Well, I'm still going."

She sighs, gives up the argument, and finishes my makeup. I look in the mirror and gasp. She's painted huge silver wings around my eyes and doused my lips in black paint.

"I'm a nightmare."

"That's the idea. Come on. Let's go see our demon boyfriends."

3

God Only Knows

Jared

I put the demon mask on and stare at myself in the mirror.

Maybe this isn't a disguise. Maybe this is the real me.

"Looks good." Ethan's voice is muffled by his mask of the current President of the United States. We both wear black capes with the ends attached to our wrists so they flare when we raise our arms. Like Dracula. Ethan enjoys flapping.

"Is this how it feels to be you?" He's trying to be funny.

"Sometimes."

"This mask is as hot as Hades." He takes it off and runs a hand through his damp hair. Sweat pours down the side of his face—a combination of heat and nerves. He tosses the mask on the bed. "Where are the girls? We're gonna be late!"

We aren't, but I don't say so. "I'll check." I text Grace and report her reply. "They'll be here in a minute."

"A minute? How long is a minute for those two?"

"Relax, Ethan. I'm going outside." I head to the balcony to avoid his incessant fretting. The wind is brisk and cool, speckled with rain. I take my mask off and let the fresh, misty air bathe my face. My gaze drifts to the sidewalk below. Only four stories, an easy jump. I suppress the urge to fly from this balcony to the sidewalk below.

"Don't jump." I whirl around. Grace stands in the doorway, shivering. At least I think it's her. She's all in black with the most ridiculous makeup. She smiles and extends her arms to make her cape flare. "Like my new look?"

"Not particularly."

She stands beside me at the rail, glances down, and swoons a little.

"Want to go down that way?" she whispers.

"Not tonight." I push back her hood and touch her hair. I'm still not used to the color. She rests her head against my shoulder and her arm slides around my waist under my cape.

"Don't get makeup on me."

"Ha. You're really warm. Are you sure you'll be okay? No…flare-ups?"

"I have it under control."

Her hand creeps under my shirt and rests against my skin. I feel the familiar twinge, half pleasure, half pain, and my body becomes an electric current running through us both. Her heart beats in sync with mine.

"Maybe we shouldn't go," I say. "Maybe it's too soon…"

"We have to go. Come on, it'll be fun. We only have to stay for the presentation. Okay?"

I sigh and kiss the top of her head.

"Hey, lovebirds! Let's go already!" Ethan's annoyed voice breaks us apart.

"We're coming."

~

The Meatpacking District, once a block of slaughterhouses, is now a neighborhood of trendy, retro shops and lofts. We walk to the convention hall in our silly costumes, drawing curious stares and muffled laughter. Bree capitalizes on the attention by belting her version of the Bee Gees' "Stayin' Alive," with all the requisite disco moves. She coaxes Grace to join in. They dance down the sidewalk like goofy teenagers. Even Ethan has to smile.

"Stayin' Alive." The song brings Azazel to my mind. My father. Not my biological father, who died over a hundred years ago. But Azazel the Watcher is still alive, despite the fact that Grace and I had gone into the Abyss and killed him. Or we thought we did. Turns out we were wrong.

I can sense him now. Whenever he is awake, when he is active or excited, the sensation starts as a faint tremor at the base of my skull and radiates down my spine to the tips of my fingers. I hear him whisper my name in that broken pipe voice of his. *Jared. Jared. Jared.* Just that.

Nothing else.

The convention hall resembles the slaughterhouse it once was—a low, long brick building with a corona of windows under the ceiling. Did I work in one of these places a long time ago? It's familiar—unnervingly so.

Already, a long line of gaming enthusiasts wait at the door. When we reach the entrance, we show our tickets and receive a pat-down from brusque security guards. I balk when one of them asks me to remove my mask. When I reluctantly acquiesce, he grunts and waves us through. He doesn't recognize me.

Grace sticks close as we enter the main hall, her clammy hand clasped to mine. Over the past two years, she's rarely left her loft except to come to the Hobbit Hole, where I live with Ralph. She says she doesn't like leaving her dad alone, but I know that isn't the whole reason. I understand her fear. Every time either of us steps out into the world, bad things tend to happen. We can't escape the sensation of being hunted.

Roving beams of colored light pervade the hall, accompanied by the pulsing bass of electronic rock music. Huge posters of video games cover the weathered brick walls. Trusses crisscross the ceiling, revealing broken expanses of blue-black sky. Hundreds of chairs are set up before an enormous video screen. The crowd converges on food tables and the bar, which extends down one whole side of the room. Medieval warriors and wizards intermingle with futuristic soldiers, and demons of many varieties. There are plenty of angels too. Several of the costumes have their own lighting and one seems to be on fire.

I look around for real angels. Usually, I can see them, but not always. Only if they choose to reveal themselves. Demons—the real ones—are prevalent. The whole building hums with death—it was once a killing place, after all. We've barely arrived, and already I want to leave.

Ethan and Bree had gone in before us to alleviate suspicion. Speculation on social media suggested Grace and I would come to our friend's big night, so even masked, we thought it prudent to stay separated as much as possible.

"Look. A Loganberry fountain!" Grace points to a silver fountain flowing with purple liquid. "Ethan must have requested that." An homage to his hometown and Grace's personal obsession. She holds a plastic cup under one of the fonts, slurps down the contents and offers me a taste, but I refuse. I can't stand the stuff.

We stroll past the vendor's booths where people can demo the games. The *Wrath of the Watchers* booth is mobbed. A huge poster looms above the display depicting a big, blond guy and a red-haired girl bulging with muscles wearing in souped-up battle armor. The guy wields a gigantic sword, the woman sports a high-tech bow. Their faces are set in grim determination, hardened and self-assured as only video game characters can be.

"Is that supposed to be us?" Grace giggles.

"You look badass."

"Where'd that bow come from? I didn't have a bow."

"It's a game, Grace."

"Ethan said there was this whole team of designers that came up with the characters based on his description. But I guess you can make whatever character you want in the real game."

The music intrudes from the live band, hard-core metal that jangles my nerves. I turn to the stage and my spine stiffens. The lead singer wears an angel costume identical to the one I wore when I played with Blood Moon.

Grace sees it too. "No way. I hope that wasn't Ethan's idea."

I'm surprised at the memories that costume brings back, not all of them terrible. But mainly, I think of Daniel Crowder, aka Lester Crow, the man who blackmailed me into joining his band, who abused me and threatened me and drove me nearly crazy...and probably saved my life.

"Hey!" Bree and Ethan come up behind us. Grace jumps. Bree laughs. "See that? You didn't know how famous you were, did you? I mean, after Blood Moon and then the Shannon wedding thing."

"I was hoping everyone would have forgotten about that by now," Grace says.

"Are you kidding? It's not just a story anymore. It's a legend."

"I didn't have anything to do with that." Ethan points to the band. "Just so you know."

A voice comes over the loudspeaker, announcing that the presentation is about to begin. Everyone scrambles for a seat. Bree and Ethan sit in the front row, but I pull Grace to the back. She protests. "I need to get a good picture!"

"It's safer."

A handsome, bearded black man takes the stage and speaks into a microphone.

"Welcome, everyone, to the fourth annual GAME-ON Launch Party!" The crowd cheers. "I'm Ross Chapman, as you probably already know. Tonight, we will show you the trailers for some incredible new games that will literally knock your socks off!"

Applause. Grace leans over and whispers, "Literally?"

What follows is thirty minutes of high-tech explosions, weird creatures, pseudo-humans getting murdered in every imaginable way, weaponry that has yet to be invented, superheroes and monsters destroying whole cities—in short, Azazel's world. No wonder he is awake and alert, whispering to me. After each trailer there is raucous applause and the designer is invited on the stage to talk about his or her work. Ethan is probably having a heart attack right now, preparing to get up on stage in front of all these people.

The Wrath of the Watchers is the last trailer to be shown.

Grace digs her nails into my arm as a verse from Genesis appears on the screen:

> The Nephilim were on the earth in those days, and
> also afterward, when the sons of God came in to the
> daughters of men, and they bore children to them.

The screen lights up with the image of a boy and girl running through a cave filled with enormous, spear-shaped crystals. I almost laugh. In the film I am clad in futuristic body armor while in reality, I had worn a pair of fleece longjohns. Grace's character wears a skin-tight outfit that's nothing like the actual parka and fleece pants she had on in the Abyss. But I guess that wouldn't have looked nearly as cool.

There is a moment when the two heroes are together, frozen, and their faces are in close-up. They *do* look like us. Right down to the angel pendant my character wears. Grace sees it too and her fingers go to her neck, where the pendant now rests.

The music up to this point has been rumbling and ominous, but then, with a thunder of drums, the Watchers appear, one after the other, huge angel-demon creatures in a variety of colors. Some of them look startlingly realistic with their twisted limbs and blank white eyes. The heroes fight each of them with lightning swords and martial arts and a bow that shoots little flaming bombs. None of that actually happened, except for the sword. It was an angel sword and pretty awesome.

The trailer ends as the two humans and the angels come upon the lair of Azazel. Just before they go through the crystal maze that would reveal the enemy they had come to destroy, the screen goes to black.

Grace lets out a breath, her body going limp. I take her hand, relieved the trailer didn't show the rest of that scene. Azazel had lured me with his flattering lies into nearly killing Grace, and in the end, my father and I went into the pit of fire together.

Except we didn't.

The crowd applauds with surprising enthusiasm.

"That wasn't so bad, was it?" Grace whispers.

"Actually, it was kind of cool."

"That was literally incredible," says Ross, retaking the stage. "Let's talk to the designer, who was only seventeen years old when he created this game. Literally! Seventeen! Incredible!"

Ross continues to talk, but I no longer listen. The room grows darker, the overhead lights dimmed by some unseen presence. I look up just as a shadow passes over the skylights, moving stealthily. Then another. My unease deepens.

I survey all the entrances. Security guards stand motionless, their hands folded before them as they gaze without interest over the crowd. I scan the room for any suspicious activity, people who don't belong or who might be hiding guns. Or bombs.

Then something hot presses against my back. I spin around but nothing is there.

I hear a voice, clear as day:

Leave. Now.

It's Ariel.

—

I grab Grace's arm. "Let's go."

"We can't! Ethan is about to go on stage! I need a picture for Ralph and Silas and Penny." She holds her phone up as Ross introduces the game designers.

"Please welcome the seventeen-year-old wunderkind, now a sophomore at Cornell University, Ethan Ellerman!"

Ethan climbs the steps to the stage and shakes hands with Ross and the GAME-ON sponsors. Cameras flash. Ethan smiles awkwardly as the crowd cheers.

Go!

I nudge Grace again, but she ignores me.

"Ethan!" Ross traps Ethan in an over-eager side hug. "That trailer literally took my breath away. So, what are these Watchers, anyway?"

"They're fallen angels…" Ethan stammers, his face bright red. He stares at the audience with a deer-in-the-head-lights expression.

"Whoa, angels. Bad angels, even better. We are all getting a little tired of zombies." Ross laughs. "What inspired you to come up with the idea?"

"Well… I…uh…read about the Watchers and how they were bound in this underground prison called the Abyss…"

"That's awesome." Ross cuts him off. "While I've got you up here, everyone is dying to know what's happened to your friends Jared Lorn and Grace Fortune. You all were in that band together, right? And then there was all that fuss with Blood Moon and Jared coming back to life and all… But since then, they seem to have literally disappeared. So what happened to them?"

"Oh, they're fine." Ethan's voice squeaks.

"Any chance they're here tonight?"

Murmurs erupt. People start looking around. I stiffen, my hand on Grace's arm. She lowers the phone.

"Uh, no. They couldn't come."

"Oh, that's too bad. Tell me something, though. Did Jared and Grace have anything to do with this game? I mean, did they help you at all with its creation? Because I couldn't help but notice that your two heroes look an awful lot like them. I figured they must have inspired you in some way, right?"

"Yeah, I guess."

"Well, the game is literally amazing. Okay, gamers, let's hear it one more time for all these amazing designers!"

Once the applause starts, I pull Grace out of the seat and steer her toward the exit, brushing past the guards and the ticket takers.

I push the main doors open just as a woman comes in.

"Excuse me." I move around her.

"Jared Lorn, I presume."

I stop cold.

Probably in her mid-thirties, she's slim and regal, with large dark eyes and hair swept into a complex twist. I don't know her.

"I'm so glad I ran into you." She keeps her hand on the door to block my path. "I have a message for you."

Grace steps in front of me. "You've made a mistake. Would you excuse us, please? We're in a hurry."

The woman ignores Grace and continues to stare at me. "Please don't be alarmed. I won't expose you or ask for your autograph. But I have a close associate who is anxious to speak to you." She holds out a business card—black with a golden spear emblem above a name and phone number. *Darwin Speer.* "Call as soon as you can. He is available any-time you are. He asked me to tell you that it is a matter of life and death."

I take the card. The woman spins and disappears into a black limo idling at the curb. The car pulls away without a sound. *Electric.*

"Darwin Speer?" Grace takes the card and reads the name. "The Mars guy? This must be a joke."

"I don't think so."

Music starts up in the hall. People begin to stream into the lobby. I take Grace by the arm and pull her outside, walking fast.

"What about Bree and Ethan?" she asks. "They'll wonder—"

"Send a text. We'll meet them at the hotel."

4

Poison in the Water

Grace

I take off my makeup, change into sweats and go to Jared's room. He's agitated, pacing up and down like a panther in a cage. His costume is strewn on the bed, his mask crumpled in the trash can. Ethan's laptop sits on the desk, open to the Wikipedia page for Darwin Speer. I slide into the chair and read, digesting the highlights of the piece.

Darwin Speer was born in Switzerland and emigrated to America as a teenager, leaving his widowed mother behind. He received a scholarship to UCLA, dropped out after a year and took a job at a tech startup. When only twenty-one, he developed online financial software for self-service investors and sold the company for millions. He's started several companies involving space travel, electric cars, solar heating, medical research, and nanotechnologies. His stated interest is 'reducing the risk of human extinction' by fighting global warming and colonizing Mars. He's also reclusive, rarely appears in public, and often uses a cartoon version of himself rather than an actual photo on websites and social media. When I do find a photo, it's of an awkward looking thirty-something man with thinning hair and prominent ears.

"Have you read this?" I ask.

"Yeah."

"I don't see any connection to you. What do you think he wants?"

"I don't know. I need to talk to Ralph."

I dial the number on my cell phone and put it on speaker. When Ralph answers, Jared tells him everything that happened at the launch. Ralph is quiet for a moment, and I wonder if we've lost the connection.

"Ralph?" I say. "What do you think?"

"Hmmm, I'm not entirely sure. The only way to find out what he's after is to ask him."

"You want me to call him?" Jared is as surprised as I am.

"He obviously knows something, either who you are or what you are, or he wouldn't want to speak to you personally. And there's another thing. I'm not sure of this, but Darwin Speer might be a distant relation of ours."

"What?"

"I remember my mother mentioning a branch of the family with that name in Switzerland."

"If he's in the family, then he could be...like Jared?" I ask.

"I doubt he is quite like Jared, but he could be a carrier. Most of our family members are. I need to look into this further. In the meantime, call the man and see what he wants. But don't tell him anything."

"What if he wants to meet?" Jared asks.

"Then meet with him. But keep it casual. I must say I'm more than a little curious." Ralph pauses. "You say this woman at the launch knew who you were? Even with the disguise?"

"Yeah."

"And you're sure she didn't follow you from the hotel."

"I think I would have noticed."

"Well, there's nothing to be done about it now. See this through and get home as quickly as you can."

After we hang up, Jared goes out on the balcony. I know

he wants to be alone, so I continue to search for more information on Ethan's laptop. Why had I insisted on staying at the launch? Jared wanted to leave—he must have known something was wrong. I should have listened.

Bree and Ethan arrive a few minutes later.

"Oh, man, you really missed it." Bree bursts through the door chattering. "Everyone was looking for you. It was a madhouse."

"Yeah, we thought when that guy mentioned us, it might get hairy," I say. "But it was so cool to be there, Ethan. I'm so proud of you."

"I'm glad it's over." Ethan shudders. "Remind me never to do that again."

"Did you win?"

"Second place." Bree's disappointment is obvious. "What's with him?" She points to Jared on the balcony. "Is he okay?"

I tell them about meeting the woman with the business card for Darwin Speer.

"Seriously?" says Ethan. "Wicked cool."

"Why is this cool?" Bree turns on him. "The one time these two try to go out in public and they're ambushed!"

"Yeah, but it's not as if Darwin Speer is some lunatic Satanist like Lester Crow. This guy's the real deal. A mega-genius. He's doing things other people only dream about." Ethan grabs the laptop from me and sits on the bed. "Let's see what Mr. Speer has been up to lately." He clicks the keys. Bree and I lean in on either side. "The guy launched an unmanned rocket to Mars, for Pete's sake. I mean who does that? Whoa. It looks like he joined the board at CERN."

"What's CERN?" Bree asks.

"It stands for…European Something Something for nuclear research. It's where the LHC is."

"LHC?"

"Large Hadron Collider. Don't you people read?"

Bree lets out a huffy breath. "Okay, Brainiac, what's that?

Since we're so dumb."

"It's the biggest particle collider in the world. You've heard of them, right? They smash protons together at the speed of light, create new particles, anti-matter, black holes—it's the last frontier. Who knows what they'll find. Maybe other dimensions."

"Other dimensions," I say slowly. "Like, *spiritual* dimensions?"

"Well, they don't call it that. They use words like 'multiverse' and 'supersymmetry.' See, most of the universe is made up of dark matter and dark energy, and scientists really have no idea what that is. The LHC could help them figure it out."

"Break on through." Bree hums the tune.

"Exactly! You see, there's this thing called the Higgs Boson, according to the Standard Model—"

Bree holds up a hand. "Slow down, Rocket Man. Speak English. What's all this got to do with Jared?"

"I'm not sure. But if Speer is interested in finding other dimensions, and if he knows that Jared might be able to do that and *has* actually done it…well, this is like the new frontier of quantum physics—"

"Jared doesn't know anything about quantum physics."

"Jared *is* quantum physics." Ethan is really excited now. "He's like this singularity, a human being with angel DNA. He's not only been to the other side, he *is* the other side."

"Grace has been there too. And she's totally human."

"Yeah, you're right." Ethan rubs his stubbly chin. "But if the Abyss actually exists in that other dimension—that fifth Dimension, so to speak—then Grace going through shouldn't have been possible. But if Jared was the portal, and if Grace, a human, could go through with him, then Speer might think that he can do it too."

The sliding glass door opens, and Jared appears, staring at us. I can tell he's heard every word. I go over and tug on his shirt so he looks at me.

"It'll be okay. He can't know what's really going on. He's a science nut. He probably doesn't even believe in the spiritual realm, anyway." I touch his face. "Don't worry. We're protected."

"*You* are."

"We'll be right there with you." I glance at Ethan and Bree. "You guys are coming, right? Ethan, you're dying to meet this guy. And Bree, you love celebrities."

"Of course we'll come!" Bree claps her hands together like a little girl.

"See?" I lean into Jared. He's so tense. "So, you call the guy and tell him that if he wants to see you, he has to see all of us. We're a team. We're Forlorn. Right?"

"Sure, we're a team." Bree glances at Ethan, who shrugs and nods.

"Yeah. Go team."

Jared cracks a smile. "Thanks, guys. I'll need all the help I can get."

"Literally," I say.

5

Play With Fire

Jared

A sleek electric limo with tinted windows picks us up at the hotel the next morning. It's a Speerhead Model Z, one of Speer's latest designs. The driver, a young middle-eastern man wearing dark sunglasses despite the cloudy sky, opens the door for us to get in. The car moves away from the curb, smooth and silent. Soft classical music plays through the speakers. A video screen in the ceiling plays a running commercial for the Speerhead line of electric cars.

When I called last night, I expected to hear the voice of the woman who accosted us at the launch or some other assistant of an assistant. Darwin Speer himself answered.

"Jared! Let's get together. When are you available? I'll send a car for you." He spoke with a barely detectable German accent. He never said hello, like he already knew it was me calling.

I told him that I was leaving the city but I could meet for an hour around nine a.m., and that my friends would be with me.

He agreed without hesitation, but I still felt uneasy.

"This is awesome," Bree whispers. She runs her hands over the lighted buttons on the door. "What do all these lights do?"

"Don't touch anything," Grace says.

"I can't help it. Have you ever ridden in an electric car before? It's like a space ship."

The car turns onto 10th Avenue and speeds up, heading south over the river.

"We're going to New Jersey?" Ethan sounds nervous.

A glass partition separates us from the driver. Bree pushes the intercom button.

"Hey, where are you taking us?"

"Manhattan Yacht Club," says the driver.

Bree giggles. "He has a *yacht*!"

We pull into the marina where several yachts and sail-boats are docked in the shadows of skyscrapers. The driver directs us to the biggest one there, a monstrous, sleek white vessel that looks a little like a UFO. "Lucille" is painted on the hull in a fancy cursive script.

"*Holden Caulfield*," Bree says under her breath. She and Grace have developed a system of using literary and celebrity names instead of actual swear words.

A dewy-faced young man in a white outfit meets us on deck.

"Welcome! I'm Owen, Mr. Speer's personal assistant." He flashes a friendly smile and shakes hands with each of us. "Come on in. He's finishing up some work and he'll be right with you."

Owen leads us into the main cabin area which is bigger than most houses. Two long sofas in beige and brown sit at right angles to each other in the sunken center, facing a ma-hogany bar and a giant-screen TV. Enormous cubist-style paintings of fish hang between the windows. A raised plat-form beyond the seating area holds several pinball machines. Speer must be a collector.

Owen asks if we want drinks. Bree and Grace ask for cokes. I ask for water. Ethan is too busy eyeing the pinball machines.

"Go ahead and try them," says Owen, seeing his interest. "You'll find tokens on the bar."

Owen hands out drinks and leaves us alone. Bree and Grace wander around touching things while Ethan plays a pinball machine. Discordant pings and buzzes fill the air.

"This is freaking amazing." Bree's eyes are wide. "I wonder if he'll give us a tour."

I take a sip of the water. I must have gripped the glass too hard because it shatters in my hand. Blood pours from between my fingers.

Grace grabs a towel from the bar and runs to me. "What happened?"

"I don't know...the glass broke—"

"What a mess!" Bree says. "We're here five minutes and we've already ruined the place." She grabs another towel and gathers broken pieces of glass. "Ethan! Get the trash can!"

He grabs one from behind the bar and brings it over.

"I'm fine." I hold my hand up. The bleeding has stopped. One of the perks of being not quite human is that I heal quickly.

"You still don't know your own strength." Grace wipes the rest of the blood from my hands and throws the towel into the trash. Bree adds the broken glass and puts the lid back on. "Everything will be okay."

With the crisis averted, Bree returns to gawking. Ethan puts the trash can back behind the bar and resumes his pinball game. Grace sits beside me on the couch and rubs my back.

"Why are you so nervous?"

"I don't know. This seems strange."

"Let's just go with it," she says. "Relax. It might be fun."

"Welcome, Jared and friends!" Speer bursts through the doorway with arms wide open in greeting. He's tall and skinny, with large floppy ears and pale, watery eyes. He wears a black t-shirt, skinny jeans, and white Converse sneakers. The whole effect is of a grown man trying his best to look like a kid. His eyes cross a little like he might be near-sighted but refuses to wear glasses.

Ethan stops playing pinball and stares. Speer glances at him and laughs.

"That one's my favorites. *Attack of Mars.* 1995. They've made some reissues since then but none of them beat the original." He goes to Ethan and puts his hand out. The gesture is somehow awkward, as if he's trying too hard to be hospitable. "You must be Ethan. I heard about your kick-ass video game."

"You...heard?" Ethan takes his extended hand.

"Hey, I'm a gamer too. I designed a game when I was twelve. SpaceStar. Not nearly as good as yours, but the technology wasn't quite where it is now, am I right?"

"I guess not." Ethan seems unable to speak—he's utterly star struck. Bree steps in to rescue him.

"I'm Brianna." She offers her hand. "You can call me Bree."

"Oh, Bree. Like the cheese?" Speer takes her hand, laughing at his own joke. He reminds me a little of Ralph.

"Your boat is really nice," Bree says. "Thanks for inviting us."

"No problemo. I hope Owen took good care of you."

"Oh yes. Were you named after Charles Darwin? I mean, it's an unusual name."

"Yeah, my parents hated me." Speer laughs again. His laughter has the cadence of a wheezing donkey. "No, seriously, my parents were both scientists, so we all got science names. My brother's name is Newton."

"Really?"

"No." Speer laughs again. "I don't have a brother. Only a sister. Lucille. I tell her she was named after the early *afarensis hominid* found in Ethiopia. She hates that." Speer turns his attention to me, and I catch the brittle intensity of his unblinking gaze. "You met her last night."

His sister? They don't look much alike.

"So! Jared Lorn. Back from the dead." He steps down into the seating area and grips my hand. The pulse of his palm runs into mine, like a static shock when you touch a doorknob. He feels it too but doesn't pull away.

"This is Grace," I say, disengaging my hand. He glances at Grace and smiles with disinterest.

"Hey, Grace. How's it going?"

"Uh, fine." She shakes his hand and seems about to ask something, but Speer has already turned back to me.

"Well, you're probably wondering why I asked you here. But before I tell you, there's someone who's dying to meet you. Maddie!"

A girl skips down the spiral staircase. She's ten or eleven years old with pigtailed hair and shy eyes. She clasps something in her arms I can't make out.

"This is my daughter, Madeline," says Speer. "She's a huge fan of yours, Jared. Come on in, honey, don't be shy. He won't bite. Will you?" Speer laughs again—a nervous habit.

"No." I start to relax. Perhaps Speer only brought me here to meet his fan-girl daughter.

The girl walks up to me, her face frozen in a smile. "Hi."

"Hi. It's nice to meet you, Maddie."

She giggles. "Can you sign this?" She holds out the item—a framed picture of me onstage in the angel costume, performing with Blood Moon.

"Uh, sure." I glance at Grace, who rolls her eyes. Speer produces a marker and I sign the picture.

"Maddie told me all about you, Jared," Speer says. "How you died and returned as a rock star, and then you disappeared again. I promised her I would find you." He takes the marker and snaps the cap back on. "I like to keep my promises."

"How *did* you find me?"

He shrugs. "I have my ways." He gives me a mischievous grin.

"Okay, well, if that's all you wanted—"

"Hey, you just got here! You can't leave without taking a tour of the boat."

"Sounds great!" says Bree.

Speer takes his daughter's hand and leads the way through a door. Bree and Ethan follow. I hesitate.

"What's wrong?" Grace asks.

"I don't know. I don't like this."

"I'll protect you, I promise."

She takes my hand and coaxes me into the formal dining room.

"I never thought I would be one of those rich guys who buys a yacht, but I've got to admit, I love traveling by sea. It's so much easier to come and go unnoticed. To slip in and out of places whenever I want. Such a sense of freedom. Wouldn't you agree, Jared?"

I don't answer. The way he keeps saying my name gets on my nerves. We continue the tour through five sleeping cabins, each with its own bathroom, a spacious, wood-paneled bridge where we met the captain and first mate, a high-tech kitchen, and the upper deck. His sister Lucille is there, lying on a wide, cushioned chaise lounge next to a sunken hot tub. She wears a sheer, black cover-up over a bathing suit and holds a book in her hands. Her eyes are invisible behind dark sunglasses, but I sense she's watching me.

"Hey, sis," Speer says. "Say hi to my new friends."

Lucille smiles. "Maddie was ecstatic that you were able to come, weren't you, Mads?"

The girl nods with another burst of giggles. I want to ask why she said this was a matter of life and death.

"Want to come with us, Luce?"

"No thanks, I'm comfortable here." She smiles and raises her book, although I'm pretty sure she's not reading.

When we return to the main cabin, I hurry to start the farewells. I need to get out of here. "Thanks for the tour. But we need to go—"

"Not yet, surely. I thought we could talk for a minute." He turns to his daughter. "Maddie, why don't you go for a swim? I'll let you know when lunch is ready."

The girl nods obediently and leaves. Speer plops on the couch and puts his feet on the coffee table. The rest of us join him.

"I have to admit, after Maddie told me about you, Jared, I was curious," Speer says. "I started following your press. There certainly have been a lot of crazy rumors about you."

"That's basically how rumors work."

"Oh, I know. There have been plenty of rumors about me too."

"Do you really believe we're living in a computer simulation?" asks Ethan. Bree jabs him with her elbow.

Speer laughs loudly. "That's a whole different conversation. Anyway, Jared, I'm the type of guy who likes to get to the bottom of things. So I did a little digging about you. Imagine my surprise when I learned that you and I are actually related."

My chest tightens. "Really?"

"Yes. It turns out our great-great-great grandfathers were brothers, Lucas and Jean-Claude Laurent. In the mid-nineteenth century they grew up in Saint-Genis-Pouilly, a tiny French hamlet on the border of Switzerland."

"That's where the LHC is," Ethan blurts.

"Ironic, right? Anyway, Lucas—your ancestor—went off to join the circus in France at age fifteen, but Jean-Claude, *my* ancestor, joined the army and went to fight in the Crimean War. It did something terrible to his nerves, and he ended up at the convalescent home in the Alps. He met a pretty Swiss nurse there, got married, settled in St. Moritz, and had five daughters. One of them married a Swiss watchmaker named Otto Speer, my great-great-grandfather. So, you see? That makes us cousins four times removed." He waves a hand in the air. "Or something like that."

"Wow," says Bree. "How did you figure that out?"

"It wasn't easy, considering the Lucas side of the family kept changing their name. Lucas had two children, a daughter Noelle and a son, Jean-Luc. Lucas died young, and his wife Charmaine remarried and moved to Bordeaux but she kept her own surname. I found marriage and death records for both Charmaine and Noelle, but no death record exists for Jean-Luc." Speer's eyes bore into mine. "Don't you think that's odd?"

I shrug. "It was probably lost somewhere."

"Possibly. But there's more. Around 1938, a woman named Colette Laurent emigrated to Canada with two children, Jean-Luc and Raphael. Neither of them were her own children, as she never married. Colette had two brothers, one of whom, Raphael, was killed in the war, so I assumed that the younger Raphael must have been his son. As for Jean-Luc, well, I figured he must have been the son of her other brother. That is, until I found his passport photo. Oh, wait—I have it on my phone."

He swings his feet off the table and digs his phone out from his back pocket. He scrolls through it for a moment before he shows it to me.

"Does he look familiar?"

I try not to react.

Bree gasps. Grace's fingers dig into my thigh.

"It looks exactly like you, don't you think?" Speer says.

I shrug. "A family resemblance."

"Right, that's what I thought. I was still curious about Charmaine's son, the first Jean-Luc. I mean, what happened to him? Why was there no record of his death? So, I did more digging. I found some letters, correspondence from Jean-Claude indicating that his brother's son Jean-Luc suffered from a genetic disorder that was the dread secret of the family. The letter talked of an ancient line of giants that once roamed the earth and so on. It seemed like a lot of nonsense—you know how superstitious people were back then. But it got me thinking. Maybe Jean-Luc never died at all. Maybe he was still alive."

I freeze, barely able to breathe. His gaze lingers on me, reading my thoughts, knowing things he should not know. He continues, savoring his tale.

"Well, once I started down *that* rabbit trail it was hard to stop. Fast forward to about five years ago, a man named Ralph Lorn and his 'son' Jared emigrated from Canada to Buffalo, New York. That would be you, right?" Speer smiles. "I looked for your birth certificate and discovered it had been somewhat—how would you say—doctored? The names of your parents were fake. I began to put two and two together. And the sum of it seemed impossible, but it was the only explanation."

Grace is silent beside me. Bree and Ethan exchange glances, too stunned to speak.

I should deny it. Pretend I have no idea what he's talking about. But I sense it would be futile. He wouldn't have brought me here if he wasn't sure of himself. Besides, his perseverance has made me curious.

"What exactly do you want?" I ask.

Speer's grin broadens. He leans toward me, his elbows on his knees. "I want to know how you do it."

"Do what?"

"Travel through time."

6

Dangerous Game

Grace

Time travel? That's what he thinks?

I don't know whether to be relieved or panic-stricken. Ethan turns his head away as if he's trying not to laugh. Bree's breath catches.

Jared straightens, confused. "What do you mean?"

"Come on, we can talk about this, can't we? The cat's out of the bag, as you Americans say. Look, Einstein proved that time is relative. Astronauts have actually traveled seconds into the future. We know that gravity can bend time. That's one of the reasons why I'm fascinated with space tech. I believe a time will come when we will be able to slip through worm holes—dimensional tunnels, as it were—and go back and forth in time. And I think you know all about that, my friend."

Jared shakes his head. "I'm not a time traveler. I don't know what you're talking about."

"Yes, he is," Ethan blurts out. We all look at him and his face reddens. "Sorry, Jared, but you have to come clean. You're right, Mr. Speer. I didn't believe it at first either, but it turns out he has this genetic mutation that makes time travel possible. When he disappeared in Norway, we figured it was best to pretend he died, since we never thought he'd come back in our time. We were all surprised when he reappeared."

My jaw almost drops to the floor.

"So you can control it!" Speer's voice rises in excitement. "Jared, I know I may sound a little crazy, and many people have called me that, but you of all people know what I'm talking about. I need your help."

"My...help?"

"My daughter, Madeline...she's sick. She has a genetic disease, Huntington's. Onset is usually early twenties—it causes degeneration of nerve cells in the brain, total loss of muscle control, mental breakdown, and eventual death. There is no cure. Yet." Speer gets up and goes to the bar. He pulls a Diet Coke from the mini fridge as he talks. He's become fidgety. "She got it from her mother—I didn't even know she had it until it was too late. There have been advances in gene therapy that could save her, but researchers say they are still decades away from being able to implement them. We don't have decades. I need it now." He returns to the sofa and sits, but he doesn't open the can. "Please, Jared. Help me save my daughter. I need you to help me travel into the future and get that cure."

Bree nudges Ethan and glares. Ethan clears his throat.

"Uh, wait. I didn't say he could do that. He doesn't actually choose the time—"

"There's got to be a way." Speer sets his jaw. "And I will find it. If you would allow me to study you and learn more about you, we could work together to figure this out—"

"I'm sorry." Jared is on his feet. "But what you are talking about—it's not possible."

"But would you at least consider—"

"No. Whatever you think of me, you have it wrong. I can't help you." Jared turns to me. "We need to go."

We say hurried goodbyes. Speer looks crushed beyond words. Maybe Jared shouldn't have been so harsh. Speer's grasping at straws and Jared definitely isn't a time traveler, but still. The man wants to save his child. Any father would go to the ends of the earth to do that.

Owen escorts us to the end of the gangway where the driver waits, still as a statue, in the electric car. Has he moved at all the entire time we were on the yacht?

"Oh, my gosh, that poor man," Bree says as we leave for the city. "That was so sad. Are you sure there's nothing you can do for him?"

"There's no point in giving him false hope." Jared's voice is hard and distant.

"You could have done that healing thing you did with Ethan," I say. "You could have offered." I can't hide the irritation in my voice.

"The guy's a scientist. Do you think he'd go for that faith healing stuff?"

"He was going for the time travel stuff. Is that so much more believable?" Bree snorts in disgust.

"Why did you even say all that, Ethan?" I ask. "About time traveling. You know Jared isn't a time traveler."

"Don't you think it's better for Speer to believe Jared's a time traveler than for him to know the truth?" Ethan lowers his voice in case the driver is listening. "And anyway, it might be true."

"What do you mean?"

"Time is different for Jared than for the rest of us. He ages ten times slower, which means time moves ten times slower for him. Plus—and this is something we've never actually talked about—do you have any idea how long you were in the Abyss?"

I glance at Jared. "I don't know—a few hours?"

"A few hours." Ethan shakes his head. "Try three days."

"Three days?"

"Ralph told us not to mention that to you. When you went into the Abyss, you passed through a time barrier. And I think…" Ethan hesitates before continuing. "You might still be in it."

"*What?* What are you saying?"

"It's too soon to tell. But suppose that when you went into the Abyss, you entered a different time path from the rest of us. Maybe it's Jared's time path. I'm not sure."

"How could that be?"

"Imagine time is like a river, okay? A river ebbs and flows depending on where you are. Sometimes it runs fast and sometimes it runs slow. In space, time runs slower the faster you travel, which makes time travel theoretically possible, exactly like Speer said. If you were near a supermassive black hole, for instance, time would slow down—"

"Okay, my brain is starting to hurt." Bree rubs her temples. "Why don't you two click your heels together and chant, 'There's no place like the future.' Maybe you'll be magically transported there on a rainbow."

"This is not a fairy tale," Ethan retorts. "Didn't time stop in the Bible? More than once?"

Jared shrugs. "Stopping time is one thing. Traveling through it is another."

"Actually, there is time travel in the Bible."

"Where?" I ask.

"Do you know that story where the disciples are in a boat in a giant storm? And Jesus shows up walking on water? Well, it says that as soon as Jesus got into the boat, it immediately reached the shore. I've done the math on this one. The boat was only halfway across the lake at the time Jesus appeared in the middle of the night. At least two miles from the opposite shore. But as soon as He got in, the boat arrived in Galilee. *And* it was morning." Ethan folds his arms in triumph. "Time travel."

"Whoa," Bree says. "Have you been reading the Bible?"

"That's totally not the point. Angels travel back and forth through time, right? Heaven is outside of time, and so are the heavenly places. And Jared is half-angel, so that means he might have the capacity to do the same thing."

Jared shakes his head. "You're forgetting I'm also human—*mostly* human—and the human part of me would prevent that other part from going off on its own. Have you ever seen me disappear or walk through a wall? I can't do that stuff." He leans back in his seat and looks out the window. "We should stop talking about this."

We ride the rest of the way in silence, but I am stuck on what Ethan had said about me. Was it possible I had entered into a different time path too? After all, an angel—an actual heavenly being—had resuscitated me with his breath. I went into the Abyss virtually dead, and Ariel brought me back to life.

So the question is, if an angel gives you CPR, does that make you something more than human?

PART TWO

ORIGIN OF SYMMETRY

7

New Born

Angel

Darwin Speer lies on a surgical table. Several attendants hover around him in the white, sterile operating room. One bolts a steel frame to his head while another covers him with blue sheets. Speer is awake and smiling, telling jokes that make the attendants laugh. A doctor puts the mask over Speer's face and administers anesthesia.

A moment later, a surgeon enters, accompanied by nurses and a few observers. He drills six tiny holes into Speer's skull, inserts a catheter into each of the holes and injects something into them with a large syringe.

"What is happening?" I ask Uriel. We have gone forward in time, two months from Grace and Jared's encounter with Speer on the yacht.

Uriel speaks. "Speer is having Jared Lorn's DNA injected into his brain."

"Jared's DNA? How could he have that?"

"Do you not remember? Think about the events on the yacht."

I go back to the boat. And then I see it—the broken glass and the blood—and I understand. Speer's tale of time travel was a ruse. What he really wanted was Jared's blood. His genetic material.

"He said it was his daughter who was sick."

"That was a lie. The girl isn't even his daughter. She is his niece, borrowed for the occasion. Speer is the one who has the disease."

"So Speer believes in the family legend, after all? He's knows Jared is a Nephilim?"

"Of course not." Uriel scoffs. "But he knows Jared has a genetic mutation that allows him to live far longer than the average human. They injected the DNA with a virus that will attach to Speer's cells and alter his genetic makeup."

I am amazed and appalled at these humans, at their daring, their ingenuity, and their blindness.

"Can we stop him?"

"No," says Uriel. "We are here only to observe. Elohim will not allow us to interfere."

We watch the surgeon complete his work, remove the catheters, and close the holes in Speer's skull with special plugs. He is whisked away and the surgical team disperses. Maintenance crews come in to clean up.

—

The surgical room recedes, zooming out through the walls. Now, we are outside a medieval castle shaped as an irregular square with tall towers in each corner. The massive structure sits atop a ridge overlooking a narrow lake. The courtyard hums with activity. Armed guards in black uniforms patrol the area while others drive electric jeeps up and down the winding road to the castle gate.

"This is The Ark," Uriel says. "It contains Speer's labs and his hospital unit. It is also the headquarters of the Interlaken Group."

"What is that?"

"An organization of powerful men and women, giants in their chosen fields. They provide the funding for Speer's various experiments."

In the distance, I see the massive wooden globe that marks the site of CERN. They have already started digging, tunneling under the earth to make the collider twice as long and four times as powerful.

"Shouldn't we warn them?"

Uriel glances at me. "Do you believe they would listen?"

8

A Beginner's Guide to
Destroying the Moon

Jared

I'm glad to be back home, even if "home" is a bunker built beneath the charred remains of the Mansion. We call it the Hobbit Hole, the brainchild of Ralph's "housekeeper" Emilia. I was absent when the Mansion burned and Ralph and Emilia went underground, so I'm still not sure how they managed it.

The large main room has three openings. One leads to three tiny bedrooms, one to a galley kitchen, and the other to the Lair and the music studio. The Lair is Ripley's domain, a cramped space chocked with computers sitting on pizza boxes, unidentified gizmos, Snickers wrappers, and three years' worth of Mountain Dew bottles. Ripley, a former student of Ralph's, is now his "research assistant." He works and sleeps in the Lair, so we avoid going in there as much as possible. It has a peculiar smell.

Emilia greets me with a hug and a large mug of hot chocolate.

"We're certainly glad you're home in one piece," she says with a wink. "We never know with you, do we?" I've come to think of Emilia as a weaponized Mary Poppins. She spends most of her time filling us with food and hot chocolate, but she has other skills we know little about.

"I always come back in one piece," I say.

"There you are!" Ralph's jovial voice echoes down the bedroom hallway. He appears in a Hawaiian shirt, pajama pants, and slippers. He used to be a professor at the local college, but since going underground, his only occupation is reading and studying my origins. He told me he's working on a book, a mammoth study of the Nephilim race. I doubt he will ever finish it.

He pats me on the shoulder—his usual greeting—and then settles into his wingback chair. I sit on the sofa.

"I'll make a pie." Emilia hurries off to the kitchen.

"Pumpkin!" yells Ripley from the Lair. The only time we see Ripley is when he heads to the kitchen or the bathroom.

"Pumpkin it is!"

"So." Ralph crosses his legs. "What was he like, this Darwin Speer?"

"He was…interesting. A little bizarre." I shrug. "I mean, if this guy is such a genius, could he really believe in time travel? Seems more like science fiction than science."

"The two grow closer every day. Twenty years ago, a mission to Mars was science fiction. Today, it is a reality."

"I suppose. But Speer has secrets. How is it no one knew he had a daughter? And his sister is a piece of work. Has Ripley found out anything about them?"

"He started investigating Speer but was sidetracked by the Interlaken Group."

"The what?"

"One of those groups that meet in secret to decide the fate of the world. It's better if he explains it. Rip! Can you come out here, please?"

Ripley appears, his headphones around his neck and a half-eaten powdered donut in one hand. With the other he wipes sugar off his Guardians of the Galaxy T-shirt.

"Pie ready?"

"Explain to Jared what you learned about the Interlaken Group."

"Oh." Ripley stuffs the rest of the donut in his mouth. We wait for him to finish chewing. "Okay, so the Interlaken Group meets every year in Interlaken, Switzerland—hence the name—in this big old castle on top of a mountain. It was founded by William Hyde, the techno-billionaire who funds many of Speer's projects. You've heard of the Hyde Foundation? That guy."

"Who's in this group?" I ask.

"Oh, the usual suspects from the military-industrial complex, but also, a lot of high-profile scientists and technocrats, including the Director of CERN."

"Okay so it's like a think-tank of some sort." I shrug. "What's the big deal?"

Ripley's eyes nearly pop out of his head. "What's the big deal? Jared, these secret societies have tried to run the world for centuries! Have you seriously never heard of the Illuminati? The Freemasons? The Bilderbergs? The Club of Rome? The Trilateral Commission—"

"Okay, I get it." I raise my hands in surrender.

He takes a breath, calming himself. "Hyde is an uber-rich psychopath, in my opinion. He knows that when it comes to world domination, science and technology are much more useful tools than politics. No messy, expensive world wars; no tolerating megalomaniacs like Hitler and Stalin. The goal of the Interlaken Group is globalization. It's the New World Order."

"I didn't know people took conspiracy theories like that seriously."

"That's the problem," says Ripley. "Most people don't take them seriously *enough*. They don't realize that there are people who have their hands in every pie, behind the scenes, dictating our lives—"

"Okay, Rip, I think that will do for now." Ralph cuts in

with a chuckle. "Thanks for filling us in."

"Fine." Ripley stands to leave. "Oh, by the way. The Interlaken Group publishes a list of attendees before their annual meeting. And guess who's on the list this year?"

I shrug. "Who?"

"Harry Ravel."

I blink. "Harry the preacher? Shannon's husband? He's not a technocrat, is he?"

"No, but he's rich, and he's running for governor of the biggest state in the US, with TV-ready good looks and support from the Christian Right and the Progressive Left. He's a big proponent of environmental causes too, which is the Holy Grail of the Interlaken Group. Wanna bet he wins? I wouldn't be surprised to see him on the ballot for president in the next four years." He puts his headphones over his ears. "Let me know when the pie is ready."

After Ripley returns to the Lair, I look at Ralph, who smiles grimly.

"Where Harry Ravel goes, Shannon won't be far away," he says. "I have a feeling Azazel is behind this."

"I have that same feeling."

9

Who Will Save You

Grace

Harry Ravel is elected governor of California.

I break my longstanding rule of not watching the news to see his acceptance speech on election night. My mother stands beside him, a stilted smile plastered on her face. She looks...bizarre. Too thin, too much makeup, her eyes too wide, unblinking. She fidgets constantly and strokes her neck like she has a rash.

"Does she look strange to you?" I ask my dad, Silas, who's framing cabinets for the new kitchen. Between bouts of chemotherapy, he throws himself into the grueling project of renovating our loft.

We bought this old building on the east side, mainly because it was in such a run-down part of town that no one would bother looking for us there. Plus, it was cheap and according to Silas, it had "good bones" with its weathered brick façade, exposed ductwork, and decorative windows. It was known as the Lighthouse because it had once housed a light bulb business, light bulbs being a big thing in Buffalo at the turn of the century. But when the population of the east side moved to the suburbs, many of the businesses died and left these mammoth Art Deco skeletons behind. The

Lighthouse stands alone on the block, exactly like the Mansion used to. Maybe, I had thought, we could be part of its resurrection.

Silas joins me, his hammer in hand. He's lost a lot of weight and hair from the chemo so he wears a knit cap. With his one earring and myriad tattoos, he looks like a hipster lumberjack. I glance at his drawn but still handsome face and wonder what he's thinking as he stares at the woman on TV—the woman who had once been his love, his obsession. He'd wanted to marry my mother and spend his life with her. But she had betrayed him and tried to erase his very existence.

"Is she on something?"

"Could be," Silas says.

"What's going on?" Penny climbs down the ladder from her room in the "Hayloft"—Silas built it just for her. She has a Bible in her hand, her thick glasses perched on her nose. The glasses are the result of the brain injury she'd sustained when we were kidnapped by Satanist drug lords—long story. She spends hours in the Hayloft reading, which is difficult for her now. She has to pore over each word before its meaning becomes clear. Her hair is still a vivid shade of purple, and her clothes are always black. She accessories mostly with piercings—several in each ear and one in her nose.

"Shannon's on TV," I say.

Penny joins me on the couch. Silas remains standing, his arms folded, his face stern. Harry Ravel gives a rousing speech punctuated by loud cheering. It is only because my eyes are on Shannon, at the corner of the screen, that I see what happens next. Her eyes flutter and her head rolls. She twists violently as her fists rise to strike Harry on the side of his head. Someone jumps in front of the camera, so all we can see are secret service men trying to drag Shannon away while Harry is hustled off the stage. Penny gasps out loud.

The flustered TV announcer tries to fill in the gaps. "It

seems that Mrs. Ravel has had an episode of some kind...perhaps she fainted."

"This has happened twice before on the campaign trail," says another voice. "The campaign has stated only that Mrs. Ravel has been suffering from a lingering cold. But they haven't given any more details about her condition."

"I guess the rigors of the campaign have worn her out," says the first announcer, although he sounds doubtful.

The two voices prattle on, speculating on what happened to Shannon, as the camera pans around the room and finally cuts to a commercial.

I stare at the screen in total shock. "What was that? Is she sick?"

"That ain't no...disease." Penny's speech is halting as she struggles for words. "That's...Lilith."

The name sinks like a stone into the pit of my stomach. *Lilith*. The demon that Jared said was living inside my mother. Lilith is still there.

Penny stands with her hands on her hips. "Grace, you gotta...go help your mama."

"Help her? How can I help her?"

"You gotta get that...thing...out of her."

I liked it better when Penny couldn't talk at all.

I look at Silas. "Well?"

He shrugs. "I don't know. Maybe you should talk to Harry first. See what's up."

~

Getting hold of Harry Ravel is not easy. When I call his campaign office, a staffer reports he's already left for Sacramento to begin work with his transition team. I tell her who I am, and she gives me the number for Melanie, Shannon's personal assistant.

I haven't seen Melanie since New York four years ago, when I moved in with Shannon for the summer. I remember her as a sharp, efficient, perpetually texting young woman who rarely looked up from her phone. I'm surprised she still works for Shannon in her post-movie career.

Melanie answers after seven rings.

"Hello?" The voice is clipped and impatient.

"Hi, Melanie. This is Grace Fortune."

"Uh…yes." I can tell from her tone that she's remembering how I left New York, after the huge blow up at the disco. She probably blames me for what happened that night. "What can I do for you?" Her voice is cool and guarded.

"I'm calling about my moth…about Shannon. I saw what happened at the speech last night. Is she okay?"

Awkward silence. When Melanie finally speaks, her words are stilted. Guarded. "Yes, she's doing much better. Her doctors are monitoring her closely."

"Melanie, please, be straight with me. I won't go to the media. I just want to know what's going on. We've had our issues, but I'm still her daughter and I want to help."

Melanie sighs deeply. "Okay, well, to be honest, no one knows what's wrong with her. She's been erratic and more unstable than usual."

"Was she drinking?"

"I don't think so. Not last night anyway. She's been having these episodes. We've tried therapy, medication. Nothing seems to work. Harry is at his wit's end. We've managed to keep the reporters away, but I'm not sure how long we can do that, considering that fiasco last night. Social media has gone crazy."

"Why isn't she in a hospital?"

"Harry says it's not necessary. Personally, I think he's afraid of the publicity. He has her at the house on lockdown. We've had to hire extra people to keep an eye on her, especially at night. She's gotten out a few times."

"During the night?"

"Yes. She's disappeared in the middle of the night. But she's always come back in the morning. Once, she was all bloody, like she'd been clawed by an animal. But the doctor said...he said she had clawed herself."

A vein throbs in my throat. "I'd like to come to see her." *Why had I said that? Please, tell me not to come.*

"I don't know—anytime I mention you, she has a fit." There's a pause on the line. "On the other hand, we don't know where to turn, so maybe...maybe you *should* come. Harry sent his daughter Sally to some relatives so Shannon would have time to recover. But do it soon. Before...something else happens."

I take a deep breath. "Okay. I'll text you my flight plans."

"Great. I'll have Richard meet you at the airport."

I hang up and face Silas and Penny. "I guess I'm going out there."

"I'll come too." Silas's face is set and determined. I wish he would put the hammer down.

"Are you sure you're up to this?"

"I think—don't ask me why—that she needs me too."

I hug them both. "I need to call Jared."

10

Hard Love

Jared

"Grace wants to go see Shannon."

Ralph stands at the kitchen counter, bobbing a tea bag in a cup of hot water. Emilia must be out running errands because he rarely makes his own tea.

"I'm not surprised. I have kept up with Ms. Snow—or Mrs. Ravel—ever since the last run-in we had with her. I've watched her deterioration, as least what has been evident from her public appearances. Clearly, Lilith is taking control."

"She wants us to go with her."

"Of course we will. If there is to be a procedure, she will need a team."

"You mean an exorcism?"

"I hate that word. So loaded with innuendo. But yes, I suppose so." Ralph takes a cautious sip of his tea. "We have always known it would come to this."

I had hoped we were finished with Shannon Snow. After what happened in California, I'm surprised Grace would even *want* to see her again.

"Nothing good can come of this," I say. "It's a bad idea to go there."

"You might be right, but it is what Grace wants. Tell her to find out the name of Shannon's therapist, if she has one. We will need to clear this with him or her first."

～

Two days later, we are on a plane for California. I am still plagued by doubts. Facing the demon Lilith will be much tougher than the deliverances we've done in the past. I've assisted Ralph on many of those, including Lester Crow. But while Lester had been severely oppressed, he had not been possessed. His demons hadn't inhabited his soul and taken over his personality. I believe Lilith is so intertwined with Shannon's soul that it might be impossible to separate them. It would be like trying to separate powdered lemonade from water.

I don't want to deal with demons at all anymore. For the past two years, my life has been almost normal. Demon-free. I have Grace, I have a family, and I no longer live in fear of my angel father, the Watcher Azazel, who has tried to lure me back to him so many times. Yet for all I know, Azazel is behind this resurgence of Lilith—it would be like him to use that demon to draw me from my safety zone.

The plane surges for the take-off. Grace holds her breath, bracing herself. She hates flying. I put my hand over hers and her fingers relax slightly.

"Did you tell Bree?"

"I left a message but haven't heard back. I saw on Instagram she has a sorority thing this weekend, so she's probably busy."

"Bree's in a sorority?"

"Yeah. It's a new thing at Ithaca and she's one of the organizers. Of course. Social butterfly Bree."

The plane hits a bump as it ascends. Grace gasps softly and closes her eyes. I can't help but smile.

"Relax. No plane has ever crashed because of turbulence."

"Not yet, anyway."

I put my arm around her and draw her into me, her head pressed to my shoulder. There was a time when I couldn't do this, couldn't touch her without pain. That was the result of my resistance to the evil inside me, the evil that slumbered within and waited for an opportunity to awaken. But I broke that bond and had a measure of victory—or so I thought.

We land in Oakland late morning. Shannon's driver Richard meets us in the terminal and guides us wordlessly to the white Cadillac Escalade, probably the same one that chased Grace over half of California last time she was here. Ironic.

That part of my life seems more like a nightmare now—traveling all over the country with Blood Moon, playing to twenty thousand delirious fans every night. And then the disaster on Magick Mountain that turned us into fugitives for three days. Yet there had been moments of blessing, when I had experienced the presence of God like never before. Me, a Nephilim, a cursed one. Moments when I did not feel quite so forsaken.

I forgot how beautiful this land was. The mountains rise in every shade of purple, the blue bay as still as a mirror, and the seamless sky so different from the rainy, cold Buffalo we left this November morning.

The car turns up a steep hill, and Grace grips my arm. Is she thinking of her last visit here?

I put my hand over hers. "Are you okay?"

"I'm scared out of my mind."

"There's nothing to be scared of," Ralph says. "You've been through deliverances before, even your own."

"Yeah, but this one...this demon—"

"It may take longer, but the procedure is the same. There are no ritual incantations like in the movies. This is not magic. This is a battle. And yes, the demons are powerful. But we have the greatest Power. We must never lose sight of that."

"When you tell the demon to come out, it does, right?"

"Not necessarily. Shannon herself must release it. That may not be so easy. These demons have been with her for years. They made her who she is. To lose them might be to lose herself."

To lose herself. I am reminded of my own twisted self, the two halves of me at war with each other. If there was a way I could free myself of the angel half, how I would jump at the chance to be wholly human...truly free.

"*These* demons?" Grace says. "I thought there was only one."

"There is rarely only one. They glom together, like cells in a tumor. And they are adept at hiding. My hope is that they will all go with Lilith."

"What if it doesn't work? Has that ever happened?"

"Yes," Ralph says. "It's happened."

"So how will we know?"

"I'll know." I hope I will.

11

Control

Grace

The house is as ugly as I remembered it—a clunky, rambling Mediterranean in white stucco at the top of a narrow, winding drive. It's an eyesore, but the views are spectacular. Being here again is like returning to a nightmare and forgetting how beautiful it had seemed at the time.

Melanie waits on the driveway when we pull up to the entrance marked by a portico that runs the length of the house. She looks up from her phone and smiles stiffly as I get out of the car.

"Grace. Wow. You're all grown up."

"Yeah, guess so." There is this awkward moment in which we don't know if we should shake hands or hug, so we both laugh and wave. Her expression changes when Jared gets out of the car, eyes widening so I can actually see their brown color. People always react like this when they see Jared up close for the first time.

"Are you…him?"

Jared smiles. "Hi." He puts his hand out to shake.

"It's nice to meet you, finally. I've heard a lot about you." She might actually be blushing. I half expect her to ask for a selfie.

Ralph and Silas soon join us. I introduce them to Melanie who mumbles a greeting, barely noticing them.

"Did you tell her we were coming?" I ask.

"No. I thought it might be best if it were a surprise. She's not even up yet—another bad night. Come in, Richard will take care of your luggage. Carla is making lunch."

Jared grabs his guitar and slings it over his back. I get the impression he might need it. We follow Melanie inside. She leads us through the wide foyer to the kitchen.

The kitchen might have come straight out of a Tuscan villa, with weathered cabinetry and a wood-beamed ceiling. Melanie introduces us to Carla, the cook and housekeeper. She must be new—I don't remember her from before.

"You help Missus, yes?" She catches hold of my arm. She's tiny but her grip is fierce, her eyes red-rimmed as if she's been crying.

"We'll try."

Melanie invites us to sit on stools around the large center island and offers us iced tea. A plate of cookies sits on the counter. I wonder if my mother knows there are cookies in her house. The old Shannon would never allow it.

"I try to get her to eat but she eats nothing," Carla says as she stirs something spicy-smelling in a huge pot on the stove. "She so skinny. You can see right through her. She like a skeleton!"

"Do you want me to get her up?" Melanie sounds rather reluctant. I suspect getting Shannon out of bed can be an ordeal.

"Not yet. Let's talk first," says Ralph.

I stir sugar into my tea, wishing it was coffee. Jared, sitting next to me, doesn't touch his. His arms are folded his face very still. His eyes glow faintly, which usually means he senses danger. I wonder what sort of spiritual activity he sees. The guitar leans against his leg. I half-wish he would take it out and play something to drive away whatever demons lurk nearby.

"Why don't you tell us a little about what's been going on with Shannon," Ralph says. "So we can get a clearer picture before we talk to her."

Melanie sets her phone down. I'd never seen her do that before.

"Where do I begin? I was still in New York when Harry called, about three months ago, looking for a new assistant for Shannon. He offered to pay me way too much money, and for the chance to live out here...well, I took the job. Once I got here and saw the condition Shannon was in, I understood why he was willing to pay so much. Several assistants had quit over the past year." Her phone buzzes and she pauses peek at the screen.

"What exactly did you observe?" asks Ralph.

"At first, it was erratic behavior like the old Shannon, only worse. She'd be angry when she didn't get her way and scream at everyone. She always did that. But there was a new edge to it now, something a little too crazy. Her doctor said she was stressed out because of the campaign, so he prescribed Xanax. For a while, it seemed to help, but then the fits started again and they grew more and more violent. She'd go crazy over the littlest things and throw valuable vases, statues, ashtrays—whatever she could get her hands on. I can't even tell you how many lamps we've had to replace. But then, five minutes later, she would laugh about what she'd done, and make jokes or even apologize.

"Harry thought it was the alcohol—she was drinking a lot—so he took it all away. We have standing orders not to let her drink. Somehow, she still manages to get her own supply. We don't know how. Maybe she bribes the gardener or something. I've found bottles stashed in the fireplace, under couch cushions...Carla found one in her underwear drawer.

"She hardly sleeps at night, and when she does she has terrible nightmares. She wakes the whole house with her screams. When Harry's not home she begs me to sleep in her room. She's terrified of being alone. But then she ends up sleeping most of the day."

"And her spells, like the one on election night?" Ralph asks.

"They aren't fainting spells, that's for sure. She was tested for epilepsy, but the results were negative. The brainwave tests came out normal. There doesn't seem to be any explanation."

"And therapy has proved ineffective?"

"So far. Dr. Lewis is the best—she treats all the celebrities in the Bay Area. But she told Harry she can't make real progress with Shannon. Shannon either lies outright or recites nursery rhymes instead of answering her questions."

"You mentioned that she harmed herself." Ralph has taken a small notebook from his jacket and is scribbling notes. "Have there been other incidents like that? Self-harming?"

Melanie blanches. "The day before the election, I pulled up in the driveway around noon and saw her walking toward the pool. I was surprised—she never went near the pool. Then she just walked right over the edge into the water—fully dressed. I ran up because I thought maybe she'd accidentally fallen in but she wasn't swimming. She was sinking. I had to dive in and get her out. And when I did, she was angry with me, shouting and spitting at me in this voice that was...well, not her voice. It was awful." Melanie takes a deep breath. "That was the last straw."

"She should have gone to a hospital," I say.

"That's what I said." She laughs darkly. "I told Harry once the election was over, I was done. But then you called." She looks at me. "Maybe it was...a sign."

"Does Harry know we're here?" I ask.

"Yeah. He wasn't too happy about it, but he's at his wit's end. He'll try anything. As long as we keep your visit quiet. If you know what I mean."

"I get it." I send Ralph a quick glance. "This is all totally confidential."

Melanie breathes out a sigh of relief. "Grace...this is awkward but...you're sort of religious, aren't you? I mean, I don't know if I believe in God, but honestly, what I've seen her do these past few months...there's something so weird about it, so..."

"Demonic?" Ralph asks gently.

"Yeah, maybe. I know it's crazy."

"Not as crazy as you might think," murmurs Silas.

"In fact," Ralph says, "we need to tell you that it is our intention to find out if Shannon is demonized. Perhaps even possessed."

"Possessed?" Melanie's eyebrows lift. "That's a real thing? Like The Exorcist?"

"Well, not quite like that. But yes, it's a real thing. Does Shannon, by any chance, consult a medium?"

"She used to. For years. Myrna Priven. She lives in West Hollywood."

"That's good to know. What about other 'spiritual' pursuits? New Age? Astrology? Anything like that?"

"Oh, yeah. Shannon used to go to those New Age seminars and met with gurus and all kinds of spiritualists. She had her charts read twice a year. Everyone does that in the entertainment business. But after she married Harry, she became a mega-Christian, leading women's studies and preaching and everything. So she must have stopped all that stuff."

"Hmmm. Not necessarily. I'm not convinced Shannon has truly accepted Christ. In any event, Christians can also be demonized, a little-known fact. Especially if they have spent time dabbling in the occult. Can you check her cell phone? See if there've been any calls to Myrna in the recent months?"

"Sure," Melanie says. "Have you talked to the shrink...I mean, Dr. Lewis?"

"Yes. I explained what we plan to do. She was quite skeptical, but I referred her to some literature and now, she is willing to allow us to work with Shannon under her super-vision."

"I want to see my mother." I stand and face the others. "Alone."

Melanie gives me a queasy look. "I'm not sure what she'll do. I take it you and she didn't part on the best of terms."

"That's true," I say with a sigh. "She almost had me killed, and I almost had her arrested. But I still want to see her. And don't worry. I'll be safe."

"I'll come with you," Jared says.

"No. You will only antagonize Lilith. She hates you even more than she hates me."

"Lilith?" asks Melanie, confused.

"It's what the spirit calls itself." I turn to Silas. "Can you come with me?"

He rises and nods for me to lead the way. Jared looks unhappy, but he doesn't voice an objection.

"Stay calm, whatever you do," Ralph says. "That's the most important thing. If the entity starts to speak, don't en-gage with it at all. Talk only to Shannon. And if she gets violent—"

"I know what to do." I turn and head upstairs to my mother's suite.

~

The room is dark. It smells musty, like old clothes in a thrift shop. That's weird. Shannon is a neat freak with a bionic nose.

I glance around. The walls are painted a deep gold and the furniture is heavy, dark wood. Not Shannon's style at all. Her apartment in New York had been sleek and modern. A heaviness weighs on me as I step into the room, made worse by the oppressive darkness. There's no movement from the large, rumpled bed.

Leaving Silas in the doorway, I go to the window and

open the slatted blinds. I want to open the window as well, but it's sealed shut. So she can't jump out?

Bars of light stream across the bed where my mother lies. Her eyes snap open. I freeze and clutch the shade pull. I half expect her to open her mouth and reveal ugly fangs.

She turns over and buries her face in the pillow.

"Carla? What are you doing? Close the friggin' blinds. I'm trying to sleep."

A grumpy, normal Shannon voice. I let out a breath.

"Hey, Mom," I say. "It's me. Grace." I take a few steps toward the bed. Shannon slowly raises her face from the pillow and, squinting against the light, peers at me.

"Grace? What are you doing here?" She glances around the room as if she isn't sure where she is. Her fingers clutch the bedsheets. "What time is it?"

"Around noon."

"Oh my. Why didn't Melanie get me up? I have to do something about that girl. So irresponsible." She sits up and tries to straighten her hair, turning away, averting her face. "Why are you here? I thought you would never speak to me again."

"I was worried about you. I saw the news and I thought you might be sick."

"I'm not sick." Her voice sharpens. "I'm fine. Just fine. Did you come alone?"

"No. Ralph and Jared are here. And...Charles." I use Silas' first name.

"Charles..." Her lips form the word slowly, her brow furrowed. "I don't...know who that is. Please go away. I'm not up for company."

"Mom." I cross to the bed and sit down beside her. "I came to help you."

"Help me? I don't need help."

"Yes, you do. You know you do. There's a spirit inside you, and it needs to come out."

She jerks upright and her eyes snap open, so I can see

white all around the irises. Then she emits a harsh, mocking
bark of laughter.

Lilith.

"Are you still into all that demon stuff? There's nothing
wrong with me. I'm a *Christian* now, for God's sake. My husband is the most famous preacher on the planet! *And* he's
the governor of California. If anyone here has a demon, it's
you!"

"Mom, please listen—" I put my hand over hers. She re-
coils as if I my touch burned her skin.

"No! Go away. Please. Go away." Her voice becomes
thin and reedy, a little girl's voice. "Go. Please. Go. I can't.
I can't. Don't. Go." She buries her face in the pillows.

I glance at Silas, who motions for me to leave.

"Okay, I'll go. Why don't you shower and get dressed?
Then you can come down to the kitchen and eat something
and we can talk more."

She doesn't answer. I rise and leave the room. Silas closes
the door after me. He is quiet, his eyes glassy.

"Are you okay?"

He nods. "I just…I haven't seen her in so long."

"What do you think?"

"I think—we have our work cut out for us."

12

Rescue Me

Jared

From the moment I walked into this house I felt the resistance. The oppression almost stopped me in my tracks. For me, such darkness is as alluring as it is repellant. It is not a place I should linger.

But I have to stay for Grace's sake.

She is calm when she returns from her mother's room, Silas at her side. She doesn't speak as she sits next to me on the stool. I glance at Silas. *Not good?* He shakes his head.

"How is she?" I ask.

Grace sighs. "Pretty awful."

Carla sets a large bowl of paella on the table along with a basket of crusty bread and a pitcher of iced tea. Ralph says the blessing and we eat silently for a few minutes. Grace does not eat with her usual enthusiasm. She takes a few bites and pushes the plate away.

"No good?" Carla rushes over. "I get you something else?"

"No, it's delicious. It's just...my stomach doesn't feel too good right now."

Melanie comes in from some other room, brandishing her phone and grinning.

"I got a hold of Myrna!" she announces. "When I told her who I was she almost hung up on me. She didn't want to talk about Shannon at all. She seemed—spooked."

"Interesting." Ralph exchanges glances with me. "Melanie, that story you told about the pool—I believe it might have been a positive sign."

"Oh?"

"At first, I thought that Lilith actually tried to drown Shannon. But that wouldn't make sense. For one thing, demons hate water. For another thing, I don't believe Lilith is done with her yet. No, the more I think about it, the more I believe Shannon might have been trying to drown Lilith. She would have drowned herself as well, of course, and so it was a good thing—or perhaps a *God* thing—that you were there to pull her out. But it shows, at least, that there is a part of her that wants to get rid of this demon."

"Then Shannon's in real danger," I say. "Demons don't like it when their hosts try to renounce them. Lilith will retaliate."

"I believe she already has."

Melanie interrupts. "You know, I remember a few years ago when Shannon had to do a beach scene for a movie. There was a part where she had to go into the ocean, and she absolutely refused to do it. She threw one of her famous fits and the writers had to re-do the whole scene. I thought she'd had some bad experience in her past that still haunted her."

"What do you know of her past? Her childhood?"

"Next to nothing. She never talks about her family."

"I read her Wikipedia page," Grace says. "But I have a feeling it's all made up. It doesn't sound like a real life. Maybe she doesn't even remember her own life. Maybe she's erased it."

"Or Lilith did," I say. "Lilith could manipulate her memories like she manipulates everything Shannon does. Or block them completely."

"Perhaps we should talk to her now," Ralph says. "Melanie, can you get her down here?"

"It might take some time."

"We'll wait."

Melanie heads for Shannon's bedroom. Grace and I go for a walk—we both need to get out of that house. I hold her hand as we stroll through a rambling wildflower garden. The air is cool and sweet and the pool and grounds quiet, peaceful. On the outside.

"It's like Paradise," Grace's comment comes out low, almost a whisper—as if she's afraid of disturbing the stillness. "With a serpent sitting right in the middle."

"That about sums it up." I glance at her. "Were you scared? When you went to see her?"

She tilts her head and her eyes narrow almost to slits. "Not scared."

"What then?"

"Just… sad. I felt…pity for her. She looked so pathetic. So lost."

"She *is* lost."

Grace's phone buzzes in her pocket. She takes it out to see who's calling.

"Blocked number."

"Maybe you shouldn't—"

But she's already hit the accept button.

"Hello? Oh…hi, Harry." She shoots me a panicked look. "Yes, we're here at the house. She's not up yet—what? Tomorrow night? Uh, no, I don't think she'll be able to make it. You need to give her some time to… yes, I understand, but tell them she's been ill and her doctor doesn't want her to travel. Well, I know, but there's no way… Harry… Maybe you should come here to be with her…" She pauses, listening, then sighs. "Okay, I'll tell her." She hits "end." "What's wrong with that guy? He's totally clueless."

"He's blind," I say. We sit on a bench.

"So, what sort of activity is going on in there?" She

glances back at the house.

"A lot."

"How many?"

"I don't know. Too many to count."

"So it's like a party? A demon party?"

"You could say that. Most have been here a really long time. Something bad happened in this house. The people left but the spirits stayed."

"Is that normal?"

"It can be when there are no opposing spirits. They get comfortable and hang around."

"But we have opposing spirits?" I nod. "Thank God for that." She puts her head on my shoulder. I pull her into me. "I wish, sometimes, that we could be normal people."

"You mean clueless like Harry?"

"Yeah. Wouldn't that be nice?"

It would.

"What'll happen to us, Jared?"

"What do you mean?"

"I mean, Bree asked me about the future. You know. *Us.* And I couldn't imagine it. Right now is fine, and tomorrow will be fine, and next week, and next year, but what about after that? What happens then?"

I have no answer for her. Perhaps because I know where this will end, and I can't face it myself.

~

We return to the house to find Shannon sitting at the island, a bowl of steaming paella in front of her. She wears a pale pink, loose-fitting sundress, her hair pulled back into a ponytail that accentuates her sunken cheeks and the shadows under her eyes. Her once legendary beauty has withered to a haunted shell.

The Dark Ones around her are quiet but watchful, fearful of our presence. Lilith is well hidden. She would not give herself away unnecessarily.

Carla sits beside Shannon, trying to get her to eat. Ralph watches from the table.

"There you are," Ralph says.

I go to stand by Silas, near the stove, out of Shannon's view. He gives me a wan smile.

Grace takes a stool beside her mother. She speaks cheerfully as if to override the gloom in the room.

"Hi, Mom. You should try the paella. It's great. Carla is an awesome cook."

I'm surprised to hear her call Shannon "mom."

Her mother doesn't seem to hear. "Melanie, get me my cigarettes." She speaks calmly, formally.

"Perhaps later," Ralph waves Melanie off. He stands, moves to the counter and leans toward Shannon on his elbows. "Do you mind if we chat a bit? Get caught up?"

"Caught up on what?"

"On your life. The campaign. Has it been a difficult time for you?"

"It's been fun." She glances around at all the faces staring at her. "Why are you all here? I don't know any of you."

"You know your daughter Grace."

"Yes. I remember her. Where's my stepdaughter? Where's Sally?" Shannon's head twitches in an odd manner as she looks around the room.

"She's away," Melanie says. "Remember, I told you. She went to Harry's parents for a visit."

"Sally hates me." Shannon's tone changes, becomes more sly. "Harry does too. He wants to put me in a looney bin."

"Why do you think that?" asks Ralph.

"He tells me so. I tell him he'll have to catch me first." She laughs. "After he begged me to let him run for governor. He knew I would be useful to him for that. But now, he doesn't need me anymore." Her fingers tap on the counter, insistent, desperate for a cigarette.

"It's not true," Grace says. "I just talked to him. He's very worried about you. He wants you to get well."

"Oh, does he? That's hilarious." Her leg bounces under the counter. Her agitation puts me on guard. "He thinks I'm a danger to Sally. But I'd never hurt her, despite what she did to me."

"Did to *you*?" Grace says.

"She put those texts on my phone and made it look like I had something to do with those drug people. It was all Sally's doing."

"No, it wasn't!" Grace is appalled. "How could you accuse a nine-year-old girl of—"

"Oh, you don't know Sally like I know her. She's a little devil like her father."

I almost laugh. Nothing like the pot calling the kettle black.

Ralph straightens and clears his throat. "Perhaps we should move on to—"

"It's really your fault, Grace." Shannon jerks her head to look squarely at her daughter. "It's because you left me. You abandoned me after all I did for you."

"You mean like conspiring to have me killed?"

"Why would I want to kill you? I loved you, Grace! But you could never love me back, could you?"

13

Spiritual War

Grace

I don't know how to respond. I admired her once. I even wanted to be like her, to please her. But had I ever loved her?

Besides, I know Shannon's claim that she loves me is a lie.

"Excuse us for a moment." Ralph rises and summons Jared, Silas, and me. "We'll be right back."

Leaving Carla and Melanie with Shannon, we go into the butler's pantry to talk.

"We've seen what we need to see," Ralph says. "The signs are all there. Nightmares, self-harming, deflection, delusion. But I suspect the main demon—Lilith—is hiding very deep. It will take some time to draw it out."

"How much time?" I ask.

"Hours. Days perhaps."

"Days?" I make a face.

"Let's not get ahead of ourselves. We should fast and pray the rest of the day and get plenty of sleep so we can start fresh in the morning. We already suspect the spirit we are dealing with, but we must prepare for more than one. Jared will discern the spirits. Grace, can you provide music?"

I nod. "And Silas, I will need you as an intercessor. Can you do that? I know there is history between you and Shannon…"

"Yes," Silas says. "I can pray for her. I've never stopped praying for her."

Jared and I spend the rest of the day singing in the sun-room. I play the gorgeous white piano left in the house by the previous owner, some rock musician. What happened to him—was he a victim of the spirits in this house as well? Playing takes my mind off demons for a while. And food, since Ralph said we should fast.

We go to bed early. Melanie and I sleep in the same room that night—neither of us wants to be alone. I lie in the bed, listening to the sounds of the house and Melanie's gentle snores. It takes a long time to fall asleep.

A thump on the wall jerks me awake, my heart pounding. Melanie continues to snore. I hear shuffling in the hallway and slip from bed. My legs shake as I creep to the door and open it a crack. The hall is dark and silent. I let out a breath. My imagination is getting away from me.

A muffled scream breaks the silence.

I throw the door open and run onto the landing. Jared trudges up the steps, Shannon in his arms. She is limp, her eyes closed.

"What happened?"

"Melanie said she wanders at night, so I stayed down-stairs in case she tried to escape. I heard a noise on the land-ing and came into the foyer…and there she was, standing on the top of the railing."

"Standing on top?" I gasp.

"I got there just as she fell." He carries her to her room.

"She tried to kill herself?" I trail behind him as I try to imagine my mother standing on a railing about to throw her-self to a marble floor. What if Jared hadn't been there?

"I don't know. But Lilith knows what's going to happen tomorrow. She can't be too happy about it." He places my mother on the bed. We both draw the covers over her. She seems to be asleep, although her lips move slightly.

"Maybe I should stay with her."

"I'll stay. I can't sleep in this house anyway." Jared doesn't sleep much at all. The spiritual activity in this house must make it even harder.

"How am *I* supposed to sleep?"

"Try. It'll be a long day tomorrow."

He smiles at me. Jared doesn't smile often, but when he does, it's like a burst of sunlight on a cloudy day. I slip my arms around his waist. He leans down and kisses me but pulls away quickly, like always. He knows his limits and refuses to cross them. I understand. But I still want more of him.

I go back to my room. Melanie is still snoring. Must be nice... I slide beneath the covers and pull them up to my chin, then stare into the darkness and sing the AngelSong—softly. I don't want to wake Melanie. From somewhere in my heart and soul, Ariel's voice joins in, singing with me.

Go to sleep Grace.

~

"Grace. Wake up."

I open my eyes to Jared shaking me gently. Had I actually slept after all? My mouth is dry and sticky and my head hurts. "What time is it?"

"Almost seven."

"Why do we have to start so early?" I roll over. Melanie is gone, her bed made. She probably thinks I'm a slug.

"We have to prepare. There's coffee in the kitchen."

"Thank God."

"I'll meet you downstairs."

I wait till he's gone before I get up, shower, and put on a sweatshirt and jeans. Is this appropriate dress for an exorcism? Doesn't really matter—it's the best I can do right now.

I brush my teeth and hair and put some makeup on to hide the under-eye circles. My reflection in the bathroom mirror stares back at me, bleary-eyed, freckly, ghostly pale. Ready for a long day of demon battles? Not exactly.

Down in the kitchen, I grab the biggest cup I can find and fill it with coffee followed by huge amounts of cream and sugar. Fully armed, I head to the sunroom where the others are gathered. I hope coffee is permissible at exorcisms.

Ralph, Silas, and Jared are gathered together. Ralph is praying. I join them and let the prayers wash over me. Then, Silas reads from Ephesians 6:

> "Finally, be strong in the Lord and in his mighty power.
> Put on the full armor of God
> so that you can take your stand against the devil's schemes
> for our struggle is not against flesh and blood…"

Ralph reminds us that this is a battle. "Remember, Shannon Snow is not the real enemy. Remember also that Christ's authority is higher than any demon that can come against us. Never, ever believe otherwise. Demons usually gain the upper hand through intimidation and confusion. Be prepared."

Good to know.

Melanie appears, accompanied by a slim, stylish, middle-aged woman with auburn hair pulled neatly into a bun and oval glasses that make her look both pretty and smart. She holds a notebook tucked in one arm, the other stiff at her side.

"This is Dr. Muriel Lewis," Melanie says. "Shannon's therapist. She's here to observe."

"Pleased to meet you all." The doctor smiles stiffly and

we all shake hands in that uncomfortable way you do when meeting someone who isn't that thrilled about meeting you.

"Are you a believer, Doctor?" Ralph asks her. No beating around the bush with Ralph. He comes right out with it.

"I think of myself as a secular Jew. But I will try to keep an open mind."

"An open mind is all we ask." Ralph clasps his hands together. "Melanie, if you'd like to bring in Shannon now, we're ready for her. But only if she comes willingly. Don't force her."

"Okay." She heaves a big breath and leaves the room.

I sit at the piano. Jared picks his guitar up and pulls the strap over his head. We start to play softly.

Jared's eyes are fixed on his strings. I know it helps him shut out everything around him and prepare himself for battle. He's better at it than I am, although he still doesn't trust himself. He knows there's a corner of his soul he can't control. I've seen him lose that battle before. I hope I'll never see it again.

I start to sing, and he joins in.

When peace like a river abandons my way
And sorrows like sea billows roll
Whatever my lot, thou has taught me to say
It is well, it is well with my soul.

The music works its way into my bloodstream and slows my racing heart so I can breathe easier. I sense Jared relaxing as well, the glow in his eyes softening to a radiant warmth. I picture us clearing the room of demons as we sing, preparing the way for victory.

We continue until Shannon appears, Melanie behind her. She stops in the doorway and stares at us, her eyes widening, clearly off-guard. Then she smiles broadly, and a familiar mask fall over her face—the Shannon Snow movie star mask, the face she presents to the world. Luminous, gently mocking, oblivious to pain.

"A party? For me? You shouldn't have."

"Shannon." Dr. Lewis approaches. "How are you feeling today?"

"Do I know you?"

Dr. Lewis reddens. "Shannon, you know who—"

"Who's that?" She turns from the doctor and focuses on Silas, who rises and smiles.

"Hi…Lily. It's me. Charles."

Lily. The name Silas knew her by long ago. The name of the girl he loved.

"Charles?" Her voice sounds different, young and gentle. Her face morphs again, the mockery and cynicism gone. This is neither Lilith nor Shannon. It's someone else.

Shannon moves toward him as if in a trance. She studies his face for a moment, her mouth softening, forming an O. She reaches up to slide his hat from his head. "Charles— what happened to your hair?" She frowns. "You had such beautiful hair." It's like she's gone back in time, to the day she first met Charles Silas on the movie set.

"I lost it."

She frowns and drops her arm. "You look—old."

"I am old. I'm forty-five."

"No, you're not."

"'Fraid so. But you're still as pretty as I remember." He indicates the chaise lounge in the corner. "Do you want to sit? So we can talk awhile?"

I expect Ralph to interrupt this reunion, but he stays quiet and simply watches the two of them. Silas takes Shannon's hand and leads her to her seat. Silas, Ralph, and Dr. Lewis sit around her. Melanie stays in the doorway as if she might bolt at any minute.

I start to play again, although my fingers fumble over the keys. My father gazes at Shannon, his eyes lighting up in a way I don't like one bit.

"Has it been so long?" Shannon is focused on Silas if no one else in the room exists anymore.

"Yes, it's been a long time," Silas says. "Do you remember when we met? I was the security guard who saved you from zombies."

"I remember." She laughs, a sound of pure delight. "You were just a painter, weren't you? But the actor didn't show up and so you got the part. You were so much better."

"Do you remember what happened before that?"

"Before what?"

"Before you got to Hollywood. You never told me about your family. Your mom and dad."

"Mom and dad?" Shannon's mouth flattens. "They're dead. I want a cigarette."

"I don't think that's a good idea," Ralph says.

"I need a cigarette." Her voice sharpens. "Now. I'm not talking until I get one."

Ralph sighs. "All right, but only one."

Melanie leaves and returns a minute later with a pack of cigarettes and a lighter. She gives them to Silas, who taps a cigarette out and puts it to Shannon's lips. He lights it for her. She inhales deeply. I want to protest that Silas has lung cancer and shouldn't be around the smoke. Not to mention the rest of us. But he doesn't move away, and she visibly relaxes.

"Thanks," she says. "That's better."

"What was your mother like?" He strokes her knuckles with one finger. "You never mentioned her before."

"My mother...she cried a lot."

"Why did she cry?"

"She wanted to go home."

"Where was home?"

"Russia."

"Your mother was from Russia?"

"Yes."

"Was your father Russian too?"

"No."

"So how did they meet?"

"My father bought her…I mean he *brought* her…to Philadelphia."

Bought her? I stop playing and glance at Jared. His eyes begin to pulse. He puts a hand on my shoulder to steady me.

Ralph takes over the conversation. Silas continues to stroke Shannon's hand.

"What did your father do for a living?"

Shannon puffs on the cigarette and blows the smoke out her nose. Her manner shifts again, becomes guarded as she turns her attention to Ralph. "He was a doctor. A pediatrician. The best in the city. Everyone loved my father."

"Did you love your father?"

"Of course I loved him. He was very good to me." She draws another deep puff.

"Good to you how?"

"He gave me gifts. He bought me expensive clothes. Anything I wanted. He always told me how beautiful I was. How proud of me he was. Especially after."

"After what?"

Shannon's mouth pinches closed. Ralph leans in, his brows knitted.

"What did your father think of your movie career?"

She rolls her eyes. "He hated Vinny."

"Vinny?" Ralph looks at Silas for an explanation.

"Vince Valero—her director."

"Ah!" says Ralph. "So your father didn't like 'Vinny' because he took you away from home?"

"He made me a star," Shannon says. "My father didn't like that."

"He didn't like that you were famous?"

"He thought Vinny had bad intentions. But he didn't. He just wanted to make money. He didn't love me. No one loved me."

"I loved you," Silas says. My heart nearly stops beating.

"You?" Shannon searches his face as if trying to remember. "You saved me. From those awful zombies."

He laughs. "That was only a movie. But we had something real. Don't you remember?"

"I remember…walking on the beach with you, holding hands. Did we do that?"

"Yes, we did."

"You made me go to the beach. I never liked it there. But I felt safe with you, didn't I?"

"I hope so."

This is not Shannon and Silas—this is Lily and Charles. Her head drops toward him, her eyes soft and liquid. I can't play anymore. Tears stream down my cheeks.

But when I look at Jared, his eyes are fire-white, his whole body rigid. He can see something I can't.

"What is it?" I whisper to him. He doesn't answer.

"I had always hoped we would get married," Silas says. "Have kids."

Shannon stiffens, pulls away from him. Her voice changes again, crystallizes. "Children would ruin my body and my life."

"Does the thought of having children make you angry, Lilith?" asks Ralph.

And then everything blows up.

14

Demon in Profile

Jared

The mask falls from Shannon's face. Her skin becomes shiny and smooth as plastic, her eyes dilated until the green dissolves into black. Her mouth twists into a grotesque caricature of a smile.

"Excuse me while I throw up." Lily is gone. Shannon sits straight, imperious and commanding, and gives Silas a withering look.

"You were so weak," she says. "You would never amount to anything. A painter! A drug addict! Did you think I would actually spend my life with you? Give up my freedom, my body, my career—for you?"

He leans back, saddened. "I wouldn't have asked you for that."

"Ha. That's what it amounts to, though, doesn't it? I saw what it did to my mother. I could never put myself through such…horror."

"I loved you Lily. I thought you loved me too."

"Lily." She spits out the name. "Lily is dead to us."

"What do you mean?" Ralph asks.

Shannon blows smoke. "She was such a fool. She betrayed us. Refused to get rid of it."

It, I realize, was Grace. I look at her and see the shock in her face, the realization that her mother had wanted to abort her. Only Lily had managed to stand up to her—to them.

"Who's we?" Ralph asks.

"We is me. Me is we." Shannon puffs frantically on her cigarette. The ash breaks off and smolders in her lap. She ignores it.

"So you mean Lilith? Or are there more of you?"

"What are you talking about?" she snaps. "You aren't making any sense."

"I want to know to whom I'm speaking."

"I want to know to whom I am speaking." Shannon repeats the words in a mocking sing-song. "Good luck with that." She smashes her cigarette into her arm. Everyone gasps. Her nostrils flare, her mouth twists, and her eyes blacken. Her head jerks sideways as her face changes, distorted like a cubist painting. Another face appears, beaked and beady-eyed—a bird's face.

This is Lilith.

Melanie and Dr. Lewis rush to her to check her arm. Ralph holds up a hand to stop them.

"She's here," I say.

"Who's that?" Shannon's head swivels toward me, eyes blazing.

"It's Jared," I say. "Lilith...I see you. You can't hide from me."

Although Shannon doesn't move at all, Lilith comes at me like some deranged fury, scratching and pecking, screeching at me to leave her alone. I have the sensation of claws raking my skin, I can actually see bloody grooves down my arms and across my chest. I am not afraid, only confused and unable to respond. My body feels stiff and unresponsive. I let her rip by flesh to ribbons, doing nothing to stop her.

Grace starts to sing the AngelSong. Instantly the claws retract and Lilith coils up, sliding back into some corner of

Shannon's consciousness. I look at my arms. There is no blood, only the usual flashes of lightning under my skin where the Light rises to the surface. I let out a breath I've been holding for minutes.

Shannon clutches her arm and moans softly.

"Get some ice," Ralph says. Melanie runs out.

"I think that is quite enough," Dr. Lewis stands and smooths her skirt. "This…procedure…must stop."

"Let's talk outside, Doctor," says Ralph. "Jared, you need to come too. Silas, stay with her. Grace, keep playing." Silas gathers Shannon in his arms. She collapses against him as if she's in a swoon.

Ralph ushers Dr. Lewis out of the room. I squeeze Grace's hand and follow Ralph as Melanie rushes past us with an ice pack and a first aid kit.

We go to the kitchen and close the door so we won't be overheard.

"I see clear evidence of dissociative personality disorder," says the doctor. "She has hidden this from me. I believe 'Lily' has not been allowed out for many years. I must admit that your methods, while unconventional, did reveal something I had been unable to detect. Be that as it may, I cannot allow this to continue. Shannon is a danger to herself and others and needs to be in a secure medical environment. I will recommend her immediate transfer to a facility—"

"Dr. Lewis, I realize that giving her the cigarette was a mistake," Ralph says. "We will restrain her from now on, in case the entity chooses to manifest again. I should have taken over—that was my fault. I thought it best, at the moment, to let the conversation with Silas play out."

"Entity?" Dr. Lewis rolls her eyes. "The entity is a construct of her own mind—"

'No," I say. "Lily may be an alternate personality, but Lilith is a demon. I saw her—it."

Dr. Lewis takes off her glasses and pinches the bridge of her nose. "This is nonsense."

"What happened to your open mind?" Ralph asks. "We have barely begun this process. It would be counterproductive to stop now. We merely need to take necessary precautions. Once her burn is dressed, we will begin again."

"As her therapist, I must insist you stop this at once."

"Dr. Lewis, you are a very learned woman—the best in your field, no doubt. But what you and so many other professionals fail to understand is that humans are not only psychological and physiological beings. They are also *spiritual* beings. Modern science has chosen to ignore the spiritual, just as the Church chose to ignore the physical and psychological for centuries. Both avenues of thinking are wrong. We are here to address Shannon's spiritual issues only. We will leave you to deal with the others, something you cannot do as long as these spirits block her true self from you."

The doctor opens her mouth to speak but closes it again. Finally, she says, "Very well, but at the first sign of trouble, I will intervene."

"Let me tell you, doctor, when there are unclean spirits involved, a sign of trouble means we are finally getting somewhere."

Dr. Lewis sighs and puts her glasses back on. "I want it on record that I was strongly against this proceeding."

"Understood."

"And I would like to administer a sedative—"

"No, we can't do that. We need her to be as clear-headed as possible."

She agrees reluctantly and we return to the sunroom.

Silas holds the ice pack over Shannon's wound as she rests her head on the back of the chaise, eyes closed, humming tunelessly. Melanie stands by with a bandage and ointment. Grace sits at the piano, playing a single note at a time, her head down so I can't see her face. I sit beside her and put my hand on her back.

"I saw what she did to you," she whispers. "She attacked you."

"You saw that?"

"That's why I sang."

"I wondered." I study her profile. "Are you okay?"

"I just heard my mother wanted to abort me. How do you think I feel?"

"You can't listen to that. It's the demon talking."

"That doesn't make it untrue."

"Even if it is true she considered it, remember that in the end she didn't."

Grace nods and lets out a long breath. "Okay."

Silas puts the ointment and a bandage on Shannon's arm. Ralph whispers something to Melanie and she hurries out of the room again. Ralph opens his Bible and reads some passages from Psalms. Grace starts to play a hymn. I keep my hand on her back as if I am holding her up.

Melanie returns with two long scarves. Ralph takes them and gives them to Silas, who uses them to tie Shannon's wrists to the arms of the chaise with infinite care. She rouses at his touch and watches what he does with amusement.

"You want to play?" She giggles like a little girl.

Silas averts his eyes, embarrassed. "I don't want you to hurt yourself again."

"Oh, is that all?" She sighs, disappointed.

"Shannon, do you understand why we are here?" Ralph's voice is not as gentle as it was before.

She gives him a sideways look and yawns. "You think I'm crazy. So does Harry." I see movie star Shannon now in all her shimmering theatricality.

"You aren't crazy. You are under the control of a very powerful demon. It calls itself Lilith. Do you know who I am talking about?"

Shannon starts to laugh. "You're one of those nutty Jesus freaks, aren't you?"

"Yes," Ralph says. "Do you know who Lilith is?"

"You must have me confused with someone who cares. Why am I tied up? I need a cigarette." Her legs bounce against the chaise lounge. She draws her knees up and straightens them again as she tugs on the restraints. "Give me a cigarette."

"No," Ralph says. "Not unless you talk to us."

"Fine, fine. What do you want to talk about?"

"Do you believe in God?"

"God?" She raises one eyebrow. "I *am* God. We are all God."

"Who told you that?"

"I forget his name. Egbert something or other."

"A spiritual teacher?"

"A god. I was the goddess. They worshiped me. All of them."

"Who are they?"

"They." Confusion clouds Shannon's face.

"Tell me about your father," Ralph takes an abrupt change of direction.

"My father?"

"You said he was a doctor."

"Yes." Shannon continues to bend and unbend her legs.

"Was he...*your* doctor?"

Shannon's legs freeze, then slowly straighten. She smiles slowly, and I see glimpses of the bird face again as Lilith awakens.

"Yes..." Her gaze darts around and her head starts to twitch. "There's nothing wrong with that, you know. It happens all the time."

"What was your father's name?"

Shannon hesitates, like she can't remember. "Sova. Peter Sova."

Ralph leans over and whispers something to Melanie, who starts typing on her phone.

"So, your real name is Lily Sova," Ralph says.

"My name is Shannon Snow."

"Shannon Snow is not your real name. Not the name you were born with."

"I was never born. I told you. I'm a god."

Lilith doesn't like that Shannon has revealed her real name. She's moved in to block the conversation. Ralph knows it. He stands. "Okay, fine, if that's how you want it."

"What, you're quitting? Already?" Shannon seems alarmed.

"You cannot continue until you are ready to tell us the truth. We will give you some time to think about it."

She sighs dramatically. "Fine."

"Can I get you something to eat? Drink?"

"How about a whiskey? Make it a double."

"Water or tea."

"You're no fun."

15

Unstoppable

Grace

I need a break.

Ralph tells Silas to stay with Shannon and the rest of us go to the kitchen for a conference. I grab a cup of coffee from the machine and load it with sugar and cream. My hands tremble as I stir the coffee. Jared touches my shoulder. I look at him and his smile reassures me.

I try to think of some reason why I can't continue with this. I don't want to even be in the same room with my mother. My chest tightens so it's hard to breathe.

"I've got you, Grace."

I glance up at Jared. He knows what I'm thinking. Funny how he said the very same words Ariel spoke to me when he saved me from the fire.

Melanie wiggles her phone. "Peter Sova," she says. "I found a newspaper report about him in the Philadelphia Inquirer from the early nineties. He was accused of molesting several of his pediatric patients but he settled out of court, voluntarily gave up his license and moved to Wisconsin."

"Are we sure it is the same man?" Dr. Lewis asks.

"It seems so."

"What happened to the wife and child?" Ralph asks.

"This article doesn't say."

"I'll have Ripley follow up. Do you have a phone?"

"You can use mine." Melanie holds out her phone.

"No, thanks. I never touch them. Is there a house phone?"

"In the butler's pantry." Melanie turns to me after he leaves. "He never touches phones? Is he like…Amish or something?"

"He doesn't like cell phones. It's a thing with him." I grab an apple from the bowl on the center of the island and bite into it, making a loud crunching noise. Everyone looks at me.

"Sorry." I shrug. How do they expect me to eat an apple quietly?

Dr. Lewis sighs and goes to the coffee pot to pour a cup. Carla appears with a plate of muffins and I grab one. I feel the need to stay busy, to keep my mind off my mother's words. Eating seems to be my only option.

Dr. Lewis cradles her coffee as she approaches us, her gaze on Jared. "You said earlier that you *saw* this demonic spirit." Her voice is carefully neutral. "Tell me—what did it look like?"

Jared glances at me before answering. "Kind of like…a bird. A big bird. With a thick beak and long talons."

Her eyes narrow. "An owl, perhaps?"

"Yes, it could be."

"How…curious."

"Why?"

"Because the name Sova is Russian for owl."

"Whoa," says Melanie. "Freaky."

"Lilith is usually portrayed as a screech owl," Jared says.

Dr. Lewis's eyebrows rise above the rim of her glasses. "A night hunter."

"No wonder Shannon's up all night," I murmur. No one else speaks.

Ralph returns. "Ripley will check into Peter Sova and his

family and get back to us as soon as he can. Well, where were we? Okay, next steps. We will talk to Shannon some more and see what else she can tell us about her relationship with her parents. This will be helpful in learning her pathology as well as the nature of her possession."

"Nature of her possession?" Dr. Lewis raises an eyebrow.

"How complete it is. There are different degrees, as in stages of diseases. Since this demon has been with her a long time, I would say the stage is very advanced. But we need to know for sure."

Dr. Lewis nods thoughtfully.

I toss the apple core and the remainder of the muffin in the trash as we head back into the sunroom. My stomach, at least, feels more settled. But then I see Silas cradling Shannon's head on his shoulder and it starts to churn again. I turn away quickly and go to the piano.

Ralph restarts the interview. He probes deeply into Shannon's childhood, urging her to tell us more about her father. But she continues to speak of how much she loved him and wanted to please him. On the other hand, she seemed to despise her mother. She admired strength, even if it was abusive strength, and she hated weakness.

I bristle when she starts to talk about her pregnancy—how it made her feel fat and ashamed and how she wanted to get rid of that 'thing' inside of her. She was barely nineteen when she had me.

"Did you try to get an abortion?" Ralph asks.

"Of course I did. Every time I went to the clinic, something happened. Once, I got horribly sick and threw up all over, so they told me to go home until I felt better. I was sick for weeks, and it wasn't morning sickness. It was all day sickness. Then I tried to go back another time but there was a thunderstorm and the clinic lost power and shut down. When I went back the next day, the sonogram machine wasn't working—it had been zapped in the storm and they had to wait for a repairman which they said would take days.

It was one thing after another."

Ralph glances at me and smiles. "Perhaps God was protecting your child," he says.

Shannon doesn't hear him. "After that, it was too late. That's when Vinny took me to Paris."

"You didn't go back home?"

"My father refused to take me back. He was still angry at me for leaving him. And for getting pregnant. He felt...betrayed."

"That must have been very hard for you."

She shrugs. "I learned. Never allow anyone to leave you. Always leave first."

I glance at Silas, who closes his eyes.

The conversation continues in a desultory fashion. Shannon often goes off on tangents about her movies or things she remembers from living in France. Her love of vampires, which isn't surprising. She'd had an obsession with vampires since she'd read the Anne Rice novels and had hoped, in going to France, to find the vampire Lestat. She watched the Tom Cruise movie a hundred times and seemed to think there were actual vampires in France. When the Hollywood studio called her back to play *Katrina Kross, Vampire Killer*, she thought it was her destiny.

"So you went from loving vampires to killing them," Ralph says.

"You don't understand. In the vampire world, those two things are the same. Love and Death. All the same."

After a while, she starts to yawn and says she's very tired and wants to take a nap. With Ralph's consent, Silas unties her scarves and helps her to her feet. She leans heavily on him as he leads her out of the room.

The rest of us go into the kitchen and grab sandwiches from a platter Carla set out.

"We'll give her a couple hours to rest," Ralph says. "You should all rest as well. Once we begin again, it will be harder, as we will need to call the spirit out. There will be a lot of opposition. We will meet for prayer before she returns to us."

Jared and I take our food outside to the lounge chairs by the pool. I wolf the sandwich down and guzzle a glass of iced tea.

"I'm exhausted," I say. "And I didn't even do anything."

"Lilith didn't come out at all this last time," he says. "Shannon sounded normal. Rational even."

"Lilith's biding her time." I switch to a Wicked Witch voice. "But just try to stay out of my way, just try! I'll get you, my pretty! And your little dog too!" I cackle and reach over to poke him in the ribs. He pushes my hand away.

"Not funny."

"Sorry." He's really on edge. "What has you so wound up?"

"I don't know. Just…something. This house. Shannon. Everything."

"Is that all?" I try to make my voice light and breezy, but he's starting to scare me too. "Is Ariel here?"

"I haven't seen him."

"Me neither. Not in a while. It's not like it used to be. Maybe he has someone else to watch over."

He glances at me and the corner of his mouth tilts up slightly. "I'm sure he's still watching. They're all watching."

"Who? The angels?"

"And the demons."

"Awesome." I pick my phone up. Having a real iPhone is still a new experience, and I already have an unhealthy attachment to it. Plus, I need to get away from this place. Nothing like a smart phone to help with avoidance issues.

I text Bree with an update, but she doesn't respond right away. So I open the Twitter app and scroll through the news feed.

"Hey, there are a bunch of tweets about Darwin Speer. He's disappeared from social media. No one knows where he is. Rumor has it he's gone back to Switzerland for a sex change operation or something."

"Let's hope not."

"There's a picture posted of his yacht."

"We aren't in it, are we?"

"No. Speer's not either. That woman is though. Morticia."

"I thought her name was Lucille."

"Whatever. She's cruising around the Mediterranean, and claims Speer is fine—that he's taking a much-needed vacation." I put the phone down. "Why does that worry me?"

"That Speer is taking a vacation?"

"Yeah. I mean, he didn't seem like the kind of person who takes vacations."

"Maybe he found someone to treat his daughter."

"Yeah, maybe. Why is there no mention anywhere of him having a daughter?"

"He likes to keep his private life private."

"That bothers me."

"What does?"

"People who keep secrets."

"You mean, like us?"

"Exactly."

~

I must have fallen asleep because the next thing I know, Jared is calling my name. I rouse, still on the lounge chair, to see the sun already dipping behind the bay. The air has turned much cooler and a stiff breeze has kicked up. I shiver.

"What time is it?"

"About four."

"Wow." We dump our plates in the kitchen sink and head to the sunroom where Ralph leads us in prayer and scripture reading. Then Silas goes to get Shannon. Dr. Lewis reappears looking composed and takes her usual seat with her notebook like a lecture is about to begin. Melanie stays in the doorway, peering out anxiously, awaiting Shannon's return.

"I want you to remain calm, no matter what happens," Ralph tells us. "I remind you again that if Lilith or any other entity tries to speak to any one of you, do not respond. You may experience a great deal of confusion. That's normal. These spirits seek to rule by invoking chaos. Do not engage them. Do not speak to them. That is paramount."

I glance at Dr. Lewis, who is writing in her notepad, avoiding eye contact with any of us. What is she writing? How crazy she thinks we all are? Melanie clears her throat several times and drums her fingers against the doorjamb. Jared leans against the glass wall with his arms folded. His body is relaxed and rigid at the same time—he's on full alert but trying not to show it.

Silas finally arrives with Shannon on his arm. She leans on him like a lover. He settles her on the chaise lounge and gently ties her wrists again. She doesn't resist. Her head flops to one side, her eyes half-closed.

I start playing to distract myself from this little scene—one of my favorite old hymns.

Softly and tenderly Jesus is calling,
calling for you and for me;
see, on the portals He's waiting and watching,
watching for you and for me.

I play it at half speed, drawing out each note like a lullaby. *Keep calm.* Didn't David use music to calm Saul's demons? I hope for the same effect.

"Shannon," says Ralph in a commanding voice. She raises her head and looks at him blankly. "How are you feeling now?"

"I want a cigarette."

"Not until we talk. Tell us about Grace."

"Grace?"

"Your daughter."

A slow smile spreads across her face. "I didn't name her Grace, you know. I named her Mallory. It's French. It means Unfortunate." She laughs. "Can you imagine if Helen Fortune had kept that name? Mallory Fortune! Mal Fortune."

Little Mis-Fortune.

I stop singing. The words scream accusingly in my mind. My mother never wanted me, hated me from the moment she knew about me, and lured me back into her life only to destroy me.

I was not meant to be born.

This thought—while I know it is a lie—drives me to my feet. Why had I come? Why did I want to help this woman who wanted to kill me even before I was born? Jared is suddenly beside me, his hand on my shoulder, gently pressing me back to the piano bench. I look into his eyes and see love there—his love for me. A memory flashes of my adopted father, Henry Fortune, tucking me in one night and kissing my forehead. Whispering, "Love you, Pumpkin." He called me that because of my hair. It's the only memory I have of him.

Shannon's laughter breaks in. I don't know what she's laughing at—me or something in her own head.

"But you asked Grace back into your life," Ralph continues with the interview. "You wanted to adopt her."

"That was my publicist's idea. I needed something to get back into the news. You're nothing if you aren't on BuzzFeed. No one cared about Katrina Kross anymore. But the studio still had to sell tickets."

"You used her."

"I used her, they used me. Everyone uses everyone. That's how the game is played."

Jared puts his lips to my ear. "It's all lies. Don't pay attention."

That doesn't make the words hurt any less.

Ralph leans in close to Shannon, his eyes focused and unblinking.

"Who am I speaking to?"

She leans toward him, mocking his gesture. "Have you forgotten already? Maybe you're the one who needs a shrink."

"I want to speak to Shannon."

"I am Shannon."

"You're lying."

She laughs and throws herself backward against the chaise. Her eyes close, her body stiffens, and her back arches. Her head jerks from left to right and her gaze roves maniacally. She looks like a totally different person. Or, rather, not a person at all.

"Go away!" Her voice is high and shrieking. "Leave us alone."

"Lilith? Is that you?"

"Go away!"

"No, Lilith, it is you who must go away," Ralph says, louder now.

"Ha. If I go, she goes with me. We go together."

"No, only you. In the name of Jesus, I order you to come out of this woman. Now."

I grip Jared's leg. His arm tightens around me. This is happening too fast. I want it to stop.

"Shut up! Shut up!" Shannon shrieks in Lilith's voice.

"Stop that," Ralph orders. "You will not manifest, do you understand?"

She goes still.

"Now," says Ralph in a calmer voice. "I want to speak to Shannon."

Her words come out in desperate pants, like she's hyperventilating. "No. Leave me alone. You're a fool. We hate you. We'll kill you."

"Shannon…speak to me, Shannon. In the name of Jesus, speak."

Shannon's body seems to collapse, her chest sinks, and the muscles in her face slacken.

"What do you want?" Her voice is very weak.

"You need to renounce Lilith and make her leave."

"She won't go."

"She will if you command her in Jesus' name."

"Jesus? Jesus? I don't know Jesus."

"Shannon, do you want Lilith to leave?"

"Yes. No. Yes. No."

"She's trying to hurt you. She will destroy you. Is that what you want?"

"No."

"Then tell her to leave in the name of Jesus."

Ralph says this over and over in a chanting rhythm.

Shannon's legs slam against the chaise lounge and her head pounds the headrest repeatedly.

She lets out a blood-curdling scream.

It goes on and on. Her face turns red, then purple. It pierces my brain and shoots down my spine like a sword or a bolt of lightning. If not for Jared's arms around me, I would slide off the bench and fall catatonic to the floor. Never in my life have I heard such a sound.

Dr. Lewis half stands, ready to intervene. Ralph holds up a hand. We wait, motionless, for Shannon to run out of breath. Finally, the scream dies away. Her head drops to her chest and she makes a rattling sound. Then she's quiet, perfectly still.

I pray it's over.

But it isn't.

Her back arches, her arms fly up and break the ties. One fist swings in a wide arc. Silas manages to dodge the blows, but Ralph is too slow. Her fist smashes into his face. He tips backward on his chair and falls against the window, holding his nose. Blood seeps through his fingers. Dr. Lewis jumps up and holds her clipboard like a shield. Silas tries to grab Shannon's arms, but she slithers away from him to the floor.

Jared pulls me away from the piano and shoves me behind him as Shannon scrambles over furniture and jumps on top of the piano like some rabid cat. Her eyes shine yellow as her gaze fixes on me. Silas grabs her leg, but she twists away and launches herself at me. Jared stops her in midair and throws her off. She sails into a low table and smashes it to pieces. I rush to her, thinking she's hurt, but she springs up and comes at me again, her fingers curled like claws and her mouth yawning open, her teeth bared.

Jared tackles her and pins her to the floor. She continues to fight and flail, screeching and spitting. If he wasn't supernaturally strong, she'd be unstoppable. I start to sing. I cry, too, and my soul splinters with every one of my mother's screams.

As I sing, I begin to see what Jared saw. The bird-creature takes over Shannon's face, screeching at me, the fingers elongated, bent into talons, desperately trying to free themselves. I sense Ariel's presence falling on me like fresh snow. Suddenly, I'm not afraid anymore.

I take a step toward my mother. "In the name of Jesus, I order you to leave!"

Shannon responds with guttural screeches.

"In the name of Jesus, I order you to leave my mother alone! Get out of her, you filthy, evil, rotten, disgusting demon. Get out!" I yell, over and over despite the horrible words she speaks, the spitting, the snarling, and the inhuman cries. I shout over her as strength returns to my limbs and my voice. Jared's body radiates light that blinds Shannon, who shuts her eyes and cries out in agony.

"In the name of Jesus, leave this woman alone!"

Shannon's screams dissolve into whimpers. The bird image fades. I repeat the words in a continued litany, softly now and gently, like a lullaby. Her mouth goes slack, her body limp under Jared's grip.

No one moves for a long time. All I hear is my heartbeat—and Jared's, beating as loudly as my own.

"Let her go," I tell him. He hesitates, uncertain. But then he does as I ask. Shannon doesn't move. For a moment I fear she might be dead. Did I kill her? Did Lilith?

Silas kneels beside her and brushes the hair from her face. He lifts her wrist and feels for a pulse, then he glances at me and nods. Wordlessly, he picks her up and carries her from the room.

I collapse to the floor, exhausted, emptied, and sad, as if something irretrievable has been lost.

"What in the world..." Dr. Lewis speaks from the corner of the room, her notebook clutched to her chest. She stares at Jared, who still glows, although not as brightly as before.

"He has a condition," I say. And then I start to laugh. I can't stop. Dr. Lewis practically runs out of the room.

I look at Jared. "Is it gone?"

He nods slowly.

"It's gone."

16

Don't Dream It's Over

Jared

Ralph resets his nose himself, much to Dr. Lewis' horror. I help him, using bandages from Melanie's first aid kit.

"I shouldn't have let things get out of hand." He straightens his glasses and rests them gently on his swelling nose. "Rookie mistake. After all my preaching about staying calm."

"You know these demons are unpredictable," I say. "Especially ones as old and deep as Lilith. But…Grace did well."

"Grace was magnificent. She is more than a match, for the demons and her mother."

Once Ralph is bandaged, I return to the sunroom where Grace has stayed, seated at the piano, idly playing random notes. I sit beside her.

"Is Ralph okay?" she asks.

"Yeah. He has a broken nose, that's all."

"Silas?"

"He's fine. He's keeping an eye on her."

She nods and releases a breath.

"You did it," I say. "It's over."

"Her face, Jared. I can't get it out of my mind. It was like that time—"

"In the Abyss," I say. "It's what you saw in me."

She nods. "Not the same face, but similar. Inhuman. Pure...evil. She came at me the way you did. What is it about me that makes these...things...want to kill me?" She looks at me and her eyes spill tears that streak her cheeks. I touch her face and wipe them away.

"It's the good in you," I say. "The power in you. You're a threat. But you saw today, didn't you? They have no real power over you. You defeated me. You defeated Lilith. You're stronger. God's bigger. I'm thankful for that. It's what keeps me going and gives me hope."

"Hope?"

"That if it ever happens again...you will live."

I gather her into my arms, her face pressed to my chest, and her heart beats next to mine.

"I love you, Jared. And what happened in the Abyss...it'll never happen again. Never."

I want to believe her. More than anything.

We eat a quiet dinner of leftover paella—Carla is too upset to cook—and go to bed early. Ralph is in pain and Grace is beyond exhausted. I hope she will sleep. I won't even try. The spirits are too alive and now Lilith is among them, perhaps, looking for a way back in. It won't find one. Silas sits at Shannon's bedside, praying over her. He will stay up all night, protecting her—Lily, his first and only love.

In those long, dark hours, I do nothing but mull over the events of the day before. I can't shake the notion that we missed something. But there's so much spiritual activity around us, I can't distinguish them all. We need more time. We'd need to do this a dozen more times to get them all. But we won't. We have to get out of this house as soon as possible.

Morning comes with a weak sun struggling to break through a gray sheaf of clouds. The first cloudy day I've seen in this place. I climb the stairs to see Silas coming out of the Shannon's room. His eyes are red-rimmed from lack of sleep.

"How was your night?" I ask.

"Peaceful. She didn't wake up. She slept through the night. From all we've heard, it might've been the first time in years." He yawns.

"That's a good sign."

"Yeah. How's Grace?"

"I hope she slept too."

"She's tougher than she seems." He rubs his face. "Thank you for...looking out for her. I couldn't—"

"No problem," I say. "I'm glad to be able to help you for once." Silas got me through that awful time with Crow. He had been my guardian angel. I owed him a great deal. "You still have... feelings for Shannon, don't you?"

He laughs a little. "Usually when you meet an old lover, you wonder what made you ever love them," he says. "When I saw her, all I could remember was how much I *had* loved her. Isn't that crazy?"

"You know she's not that girl anymore. Maybe she never was."

"I know. But still. Nothing is impossible with God, right?"

~

I return to the bedroom to take a shower and then head to the kitchen. Dr. Lewis is already there, talking to Ralph. Despite his bandaged nose and blooming black eye, reminders of yesterday's events, he and the doctor chat pleasantly and share notes.

"Jared!" Ralph's voice is nasally. "Good morning! Muriel and I were talking about you!"

Muriel? "Morning." I acknowledge Dr. Lewis before heading to the coffee pot.

"When I mentioned your name to my daughter, she was quite ecstatic," she says with a laugh. "I had no idea you were so famous. She begged me to get your autograph. Do you mind?" She holds out her notebook.

"Uh, sure." I scribble my name. "Is no one else up yet?"

"Apparently not," Ralph replies.

"How was Shannon's night?" Dr. Lewis asks.

"She slept through. Silas stayed with her."

"Ah. Good. *Very* good."

I sit at the counter and listen to them converse. Dr. Lewis asks many questions and writes often in her notebook. She's clearly intrigued, whether she believes in the whole demon thing or not.

"Have you seen this kind of possession before?" she asks Ralph.

"Every situation is unique. But this is probably the closest to perfect I've seen."

"Perfect?"

"When exorcists speak of a person being perfectly possessed, it means the demon has achieved total control. In such cases, the person is considered without hope. But in Shannon's case, she—and Lily—were still able to assert themselves. I'm thankful we were here in time."

"So you're saying a person who is perfectly possessed is purely evil?"

"Perfectly controlled by an evil spirit."

"And such a condition is irreversible?"

"Well, nothing is impossible, but for the most part, yes. The demon spirit and the human spirit have become one."

"You know, many in my profession would say that such people are simply psychopaths."

"There are overlaps, which makes diagnosis all the more difficult," Ralph says. "Like two diseases that have virtually the same symptoms. Sometimes, it is a process of elimination. Most psychopaths, for instance, are non-violent. Violence is often an indicator. Psychopaths lack empathy, which make them prime targets for demonization. The more narcissistic a person is, the more easily they can be manipulated.

Demonized people usually have certain things in common—voices speaking to them, for instance, nightmares, self-harming. Things that probably wouldn't affect a true psychopath. So you see, it is never simply one thing but rather a series of things."

Melanie comes into the kitchen, freshly showered and wearing a heavy coat of makeup. "She's up," she announces. "Silas is with her. I peeked in the door but didn't want to interrupt. They were...talking. Shannon seemed calm."

"Good! I will go and see her." Dr. Lewis gets up from the table and turns to look at Ralph. "Would you care to accompany me, Ralph?"

He glances at me with a wink and follows her out.

Melanie goes to the coffee pot. "It looks like the good doctor has a thing for your dad."

I laugh a little. "Is Grace still sleeping?"

"Yeah." She sits down opposite me and smiles nervously. I can see in her eyes all the questions she's afraid to ask. "Do you guys do this often? Like what you did yesterday."

"No. Not often."

"Well, that's good. I guess. I mean...I never saw anything like that." She takes a gulp of her coffee.

"It's rare, actually—what happened yesterday."

"Oh?"

"Normally, the spirits don't manifest like that. This was an extreme case."

"Wow."

I listen for noises from upstairs, the sound of breaking furniture, screams. But all is quiet.

"So is Shannon cured now?" Melanie asks.

"Far from it. This is only a first step. There is a lot of healing that needs to be done. Demons are like rats on a pile of garbage. You can get rid of the rats, but if you don't get rid of the garbage, they'll come back."

"Oh, you mean garbage like all that stuff from Shannon's past."

"Yeah. That stuff's festered for a long time."

Melanie sighs. "I don't know if I could do this again. I'll call Harry and resign. This is way out of my league."

"Do you believe in God, Melanie?"

She looks at me and blinks. "Well, I honestly never thought much about it. But now...I don't know. Something's going on, for sure."

"Something *is* going on. But you also have to know that God is stronger than any demon, even stronger than all of them put together. If you stay—and I hope you do, because Shannon needs someone on her side—you can rely on His power. It's all you need."

"Oh. Well. Thanks. I really should see where Carla is. We need breakfast." She jumps up from the table and out of the room.

I go for a long walk. When I return, the aroma of frying bacon fills the kitchen. It's a comforting smell. A *normal* smell. Carla stands at the stove, wrapped in a robe. She smiles when she sees me.

"All better? Missus is all better?"

"She's better," I say.

Carla does the sign of the cross and kisses her fingers. *"Gracias a Dios."*

Grace, Melanie, Ralph, and Dr. Lewis are eating pancakes. Grace has a big stack in front of her, which makes me happy. She looks at me and smiles a smile without shadows. I sit beside her and grab her hand under the counter.

"I am quite amazed at the difference," Dr. Lewis says. "Even when I asked questions to which she would normally react by shutting down, she answered me. There is much work to do, of course. She still has a rather unhealthy memory of her father and doesn't understand that what he did to her was not love at all."

"That was the first lie," Ralph says.

"What do you mean?"

"The day she believed that lie—and she knew it was a

lie—that her father did those things because he loved her and cared about her, that was the day that Lilith entered her soul."

Dr. Lewis's eyebrows lift slightly. "I would agree that such a trauma would have a lasting effect."

Ralph nods. "I wish we could stay longer, but we must leave tonight. I know Shannon is in capable hands." He and the doctor share a smile. Graces glances at me and rolls her eyes, mouthing the words, "Oh, brother."

~

Ralph books us on the red-eye back to Buffalo. We lounge in the sunroom, playing music, and resting. Shannon stays in her room with Silas. We don't see either of them all day.

Harry returns in the afternoon. Dr. Lewis fills him in on what transpired. He thanks us for our "great work" and says he is looking forward to having some time off to spend with his wife and daughter before the inauguration.

"We're going to Belize," he tells us. "A little vacation. The campaign has been hard on all of us. It'll be great."

"Belize is not a good idea," Ralph says. The color rises up his neck. I can see he's genuinely irritated with Harry Ravel. "Although I would suggest getting her out of this house. Permanently. Even a hospital, for a short stay. Shannon needs time to heal and to sort through her issues. And she needs counseling in the true faith before she can fully recover."

"True faith?" Harry's pleasant facade begins to crack. "My wife is—"

"Very confused," says Ralph. "She has lived a lie for most of her life. Even her Christian faith has been a lie."

I'm certain Harry is about take a swing at him. Instead, he smiles and nods indulgently. "Thanks so much for your advice. I'll take it under consideration. I will have Richard take you to the airport."

We pack hastily and say our goodbyes. Melanie hugs Grace, clinging to her like she doesn't want her to leave.

"Call me anytime," Grace says. "Let me know how she's doing."

"I will."

Carla gives us a container of cookies to take with us. "Bless you, bless you," she says. Dr. Lewis shakes each of our hands and lingers a little on Ralph's.

"Are you going to say goodbye to Shannon?" I ask Grace. She shakes her head.

We pile into the car. Grace dozes off with her head on my shoulder. Silas stares out the window. No one speaks.

We get to the airport and check into our gate. Since we have three hours to kill before our flight departs, I go to one of the public computer terminals and look up information about the Ravel house. Surprisingly, there are several posts and even a few news stories. The house had a nickname— The Suicide House. It had been built by a dot-com millionaire for his wife, but the owner died in a freak accident shortly after the house was finished. His wife, overcome with grief, held several séances in the house to raise his spirit and speak to him. In one séance, the spirit of her husband apparently told her to commit suicide so they could be together "on the other side." The wife complied by throwing herself from the house's balcony to the rocky hillside below. The house, tainted by this story, was on the market for years until an up-and-coming rock star bought it. He sold the house to Harry Ravel less than two years later and left California altogether.

Who knows if this story is even true. But it does fit the spiritual mayhem I saw in that house. And makes me wonder what happened to the rock star.

"What are you doing?" Grace asks over my shoulder.

"Oh, nothing," I close the browser and turn to her. "Why didn't you want to say goodbye to Shannon?"

She shrugs. "I just want to be done with her. I'm tired of

her drama. I'm tired of her…inflicting herself on my life."

"And on Silas?"

Grace looks away as tears well in her eyes.

"I get it," I say.

"Am I a bad person? For being jealous of my own mother?"

"Maybe a little." I smile and pull her into my lap. "It was Lily he loved and Lily's gone. He knows that."

"It's sad, though. I felt like Lily might have been someone I would have liked to get to know."

"Me too."

PART THREE

SIMULATION THEORY

17

Feeling Good

Angel

We move forward several more months to August. The Ark brims with activity.

Two armed guards are stationed at the bottom of the winding pebble drive that leads to the castle. They check the IDs of each car waiting to ascend—there's a long line of them, mostly black sedans with tinted windows. A small group of humans gather at a distance, held back by more armed guards. They carry mobile phones and cameras and try to get a glimpse of the people inside the cars.

—*It is the gathering of the Interlaken Group*, Uriel says.

We move into the sanctuary of what was once the chapel, dominated by huge marble columns. Tall, narrow stained glass windows allow muted shafts of light to pierce the gloomy space. Aged frescoes in sepia tones cover the walls—images of martyrs burned at the stake, crucified upside down, and fed to lions—bizarre adornment for such a place as this.

There are no electric lights. Candelabra line the pews and surround the altar. The air is smoky. There is no table in the altar space, only a raised platform backed by a large screen.

—*Why are we here?*

—Wait and see.

We wait. We watch. For three days, the attendees of this conference meet in this room and listen to discourses on science and technology, delivered by pragmatic men and women in arrogant, monotonous tones. There are sessions between where topics are open for discussion, and sometimes, the debate is quite lively. The main topics focus on global problems—climate change, population growth, poverty, and pandemic disease. The people in this room are leaders in their fields, scientists, engineers, government bureaucrats, army generals, think-tank intellectuals—the world's elite. They belong to a small and exclusive society of those who believe they have the knowhow—and the power—to move the world in whatever direction they choose.

There are a few among them who surprise me.

Harry Ravel is one. His wife Shannon Snow is another.

But Darwin Speer is absent.

"Where is he?" I ask Uriel.

"Wait."

On the third day, the attendees gather as usual, cradling their coffee cups and thick leather-bound folders, and take seats. The billionaire William Hyde, the leader of this gathering, rises to speak. He's in his eighties, with scant hair covering his mottled pate and small, slitted eyes. His attempt at a smile appears more like a sneer.

"Welcome my friends." His voice scours like steel wool. "I know this is the day you've waited for all week. A close associate of ours has been absent for a while, working on a new project that has consumed all his energy. But he's back, my friends, and he has something astounding to share. Without further ado, I give you the one, the only, Darwin Speer."

The hall erupts in applause and then in shocked gasps when Speer emerges from behind the screen. He is markedly changed. His hair is now pure white and abundant, perched like a patch of snow on top of his head. His once gangly limbs are thickly muscled and well-proportioned. Eyes that were a toneless gray, have turned a brilliant, vivid blue. He stands before the crowd, nods to the cheers and applause, and finally raises his arms to silence them.

"It's great to see you all again." Speer beams from ear to large, protruding ear. "It's been a while, right? Do you like my new look?"

He does a little runway spin to ripples of nervous laughter and applause.

"Yep, it's really me. *Really*. As you can see, I didn't have a sex change operation, despite the rumors on social media. But I'm sure you are wondering where I've been for the last year, right?" Murmurs of assent. "Well, that's why I'm here today. I wanted it to be a surprise. Surprise! Are you surprised?"

Titters of laughter follow.

"Cool. I love surprises, don't you? And I have a doozy today, let me tell you. This last year has been what I can only describe as an Incredible Journey. With capitals. It was a journey of discovery. And what I have discovered will blow. Your. Mind." He speaks the last three words very slowly and pauses after each one. "I won't keep you in suspense any longer. To put it plainly, I have discovered the secret to perfect health and eternal life."

I turn to Uriel. "He has discovered faith in the Risen One?"

He scoffs.

Speer pauses, waiting for the murmurs to die down before he continues. "I see I have your attention now, right? I mean, who doesn't want to have eternal life? Or perfect health. Some of you are looking at me now and thinking, 'Okay, he's finally gone completely crazy.' I get where you are coming from. But what I am about to tell you is the complete and honest truth, and I have plenty of evidence to back it up.

"Let me start at the beginning. A couple of years ago, I

was diagnosed with a rare and fatal congenital disorder called Huntington's Disease." The audience gasps. "You already know what that means, I'm sure. I also learned that this disease was the reason my father committed suicide when I was four years old. My mother kept the information from me, hoping, I suppose, that I wouldn't develop the disease. She finally did tell me about my father, just before she passed away. Needless to say, I was in total shock. I got tested immediately, and I was positive."

He pauses to let that sink in. The audience is quiet now, on the edge of their seats.

"The disease can manifest anywhere from age twenty to forty. I'm thirty-five. I figured I didn't have much time to come up with a cure. You and I know there is no cure for Huntington's, and most treatments have proven ineffective. But I stand before you now, completely cured."

Excited murmurs sweep through the crowd. People look at each other, mouths dropping open.

"So you're wondering how? Well, through the wonders of science. There have been incredible advances in gene editing these past few years. We've talked about them in this very room on many occasions. I tried all the known therapies but none of them worked for me. Most can only be administered at the embryonic level anyway. I needed to go further. I needed to be able to edit my own genome. With the help of the Hyde Foundation, I was able to find a way to do it. What I needed, though, was a perfect host. Someone with a unique genetic makeup able to correct almost any disease or condition. Such a person doesn't exist right? Well, he does exist. And I found him."

More murmurs.

"But before I go into all that, I want to bring out my own personal physician, Dr. Len Wilder, to explain more details of the procedure. Len?"

Another man joins Speer on the platform, a handsome, silver-haired man with an ageless face. He explains, using marvelous moving images on the screen, how Darwin Speer had been cured of his congenital disease.

"We injected Darwin with the DNA of the host using an advanced gene editing technology similar to CRISPR. I won't go into all the details here, but you can find it in the report you will receive after this session is over. This new DNA did an astonishing thing. It actually repaired the mutated gene in Speer's body, thereby curing him of his disease.

"We believe," Dr. Wilder concluded, "that this particular DNA strain has the potential to cure any genetic disorder known to man, as well as many other diseases. To test our theory, we injected Darwin with a well-known and quite deadly virus. Don't worry, he signed all the necessary forms ahead of time. It was his idea, in fact. Well, an amazing thing happened. His immune system defeated the virus in a matter of hours."

There are hands in the air and a flurry of commotion in the crowd.

"We have also discovered that Darwin's healing process has sped up exponentially. We'd like to do a little demonstration to show you what we mean."

Wilder nods to Speer, who rolls his sleeve up and holds out his arm. The doctor hands him a scalpel, and he proceeds to make a deep cut in his own arm. People gasp as blood pours from the wound, then whisper in amazement as it begins to heal right before their eyes. The man smiles through it all, apparently not even in pain.

"Don't try this at home, kids," he says and holds his arm up high so everyone can see. In a few minutes, the wound is completely healed.

The chatter in the crowd becomes so loud, Wilder is forced to raise his voice to be heard.

"We believe this treatment will also slow down the aging process, allowing a person to live on well into their hundreds and perhaps even longer. There are still more tests to be done, but we have seen in Mr. Speer a regeneration of brain cells as well as rapid regeneration of many other cells in his body."

"I literally feel like I'm twenty years old again," Speer says.

"So this is a miracle cure?" asks a woman in the audience.

"We don't like the word *miracle*. This is a genuine scientific breakthrough. The only side effect I can see is that my hair has turned completely white and I've put on a little weight. But I think it's not a bad trade-off, don't you?" Laughter ripples through the crowd. "It's like being a vampire who can enjoy the sunshine and eat a good steak. The best of both worlds!"

A portly, older man rises to speak. "You said the original source of the DNA strand was a perfect host—what do you mean? Who is this perfect host you are talking about? Is it human?"

"I cannot divulge any specifics at this time," says Speer. "In fact I must insist on absolute secrecy until we are ready to go to market. This is why I have had all the doors of this room blocked. No one can leave here without signing a binding nondisclosure agreement. I know I can count on all of you to comply. You are privileged members of this group, so you understand that confidentiality is paramount. I must warn you that any leaking of the information discussed in this room will not be tolerated."

His friendly tone now carries a distinctly threatening edge. Alarm sweeps the assembly as people notice male and female guards stationed at every doorway. They wear black jumpsuits with the golden spear logo on the breast and carry assault rifles.

"My assistants are passing out the forms now," Speer says. "Once you've signed, you are free to leave. Only don't go yet. I've barely begun. We haven't even scratched the surface. There is more, so much more! Stay, my friends, and let me tell you how I will assure you all, every one of you, a kingdom of your own."

I turn to Uriel. "What does he mean, a kingdom of their own?"

"He means the war has begun."

18

Clearly

Grace

We celebrate Jared's 495th birthday at the Hobbit Hole with Emilia's special beef stroganoff and an enormous birthday cake. 495 is not Jared's actual age—we pick a random number every year. He's been as old as 2,578. After he blows the candles out—as many as we can fit on the cake—we quiz him on what growing up was like 495 years ago. He tells us he lived in a little thatched house with three pigs and two cows and that he had a job on the "graveyard shift" listening for the "dead ringers." Back then, people were buried with strings attached to their arms leading to a bell above ground. If it turned out they weren't actually dead, they could ring the bell and get dug up. Being buried alive was fairly common apparently.

We have the party a week early so that Bree and Ethan can attend before they head back to school for their senior year. I can't believe they will actually graduate from college next year. They're focused on the future and on what they'll do after graduation. Ethan's video game is doing so well that the company offered him a job. His dad isn't too happy, but Ethan is ecstatic. All he's ever wanted to do is make video games.

Bree will be a music teacher. But first, she wants to travel through Europe and maybe hike the Appalachian Trail. Ethan has no interest in Europe or hiking anywhere. I wonder what will become of those two.

I envy them their choices and their freedom. I have trouble leaving the house. But I'm not unhappy. I have Jared and we can be together whenever we want. Besides, I have to take care of Silas. He's still sick and needs me. And Penny, still recovering from her brain injury, needs me too.

"Has Darwin Speer ever tried to contact you again?" Ethan asks Jared, jarring me back to the present.

Jared shakes his head.

"He's still AWOL," says Bree. "It's been like a year and a half. No one's seen him. But his boat is docked in the Mediterranean somewhere."

"Monaco," Ethan says. "Which means he's probably in Geneva. Maybe working on the CERN expansion. What I wouldn't give to be there when they fire that thing up again."

"Sure, and blow up the world," Bree says with a toss of her hair.

"They won't blow up the world. They're doing important work."

"Important? Name one thing they've done to improve life on this planet."

"The World Wide Web." Ethan doesn't miss a beat. "That was invented at CERN."

"Oh." Bree closes her mouth. "I guess that's kind of big." She turns to me and changes the subject. "What's new with Shannon? Have you heard from her since the—you know—thing?"

"No."

"Really? That's weird."

It *is* a little weird. Melanie texts me occasionally but Shannon has been silent. Maybe now that Lilith is gone, she has no more use for me.

"She must be very busy being First Lady of California,"

says Ralph. "She's thrown herself into the job, shows up everywhere, kisses babies, visits homeless shelters, and talks about Clean Water projects, non-GMO food, and urban renewal. Ravel's popularity rating is nearly seventy percent—thanks to her, some say."

"A marriage made in heaven," says Ethan in a fake falsetto.

I look at Silas, who stares at the tablecloth.

"So she's like…a normal person now?" Bree asks.

"We hope so," I say.

When Bree and Ethan leave, I drive Silas home in the Mini Cooper. He never learned how to drive. When he feels good, he rides around the city on a bicycle.

"Maybe you should call her?" I need to air out the unsaid thoughts that always linger between us. "To see how she's doing."

He shakes his head. "Nah. She's married. She's happy. I'm happy for her. Besides, I'm dying."

"You are *not* dying."

He laughs a little. "Well, anyway, I suppose what I feel is a longing for something that could never be."

I know that longing because I have it with Jared. Even though I can see him, talk to him, and even touch him, I can never *have* him. But I've gotten used to that familiar ache in the pit of my soul, something I cradle and nurture and protect from the outside world.

We find Penny already home, sitting on the couch with her head in her hands.

"I thought you had class tonight," I say. She has finished her GED and recently started night classes at the community college. She doesn't respond. Her body trembles like she's cold. I rush over to her. "Penny, what happened?" I notice a terrible smell.

"Jamel…" she whispers.

"What?" I grab her shoulders. "Talk to me, Penny."

"He…he came out of nowhere…"

"Jamel?"

She nods and bursts into tears. "I was leaving school and felt someone following me. I could…*smell* him." She pauses and wipes her eyes. "I will never forget how he smells. Like incense. Like smoke. I started to run. He followed me. I ran and ran—he followed. I ran into an alley and climbed into a dumpster. I stayed in there until he was gone."

That explains *her* smell.

"Did he talk to you? Say anything?"

"No."

"So he didn't touch you."

"No."

I look at Silas, who stands over us, listening. His face is drawn in worry. He's thinking what I'm thinking. Jamel. Also known as Manuel Torega, the drug lord who had kidnapped and almost killed Penny. He's back.

Penny doesn't remember much about the night of the kidnapping. Before that, Jamel had been a friend, a fellow student, someone who'd taken an interest in her and seemed to really like her. She was used to having people betray her, but it was never as bad as that had been.

"Penny, I need to ask you, are you *sure* you saw someone following you? I mean, a real person?"

"Yes, yes!" she says emphatically. "I'm not imagining it. He was there."

"Okay, okay. We'll figure something out. I'm going to tell Ralph. He'll know what to do."

I help her into the shower. After she's gone to bed, I send a message to Ripley with instructions to have Ralph call us.

"Do you think we should call the cops?" I ask Silas.

He shrugs. "I don't know. I could go to the station tomorrow and talk to the detective who handled the case…see if Torega is still in the area. But it might have been anyone. Or *anything*. With her brain injury, Penny could have imagined the whole thing."

"She said it was real. I believe her. It had to be Torega.

Penny's not afraid of anyone except him."

A few minutes later, the doorbell rings, making me jump. Silas goes to the intercom.

It's Jared.

"That was fast," I say.

Silas buzzes him up.

"What happened?" Jared says when Silas opens the door. "Are you okay? Is Penny okay?"

"Yeah, she's fine. Just scared."

"Maybe you should all come to the Hobbit Hole for a while."

"We're fine here. He doesn't know where we live."

He sighs. "Okay. I'll stay here tonight. Just in case."

"Jared, there's nothing you can do—"

"I can stay awake and keep watch."

Keep watch. I can't help but think of his lineage.

The offspring of a Watcher.

19

On Fire

Jared

I stand in front of the window in Grace's loft, looking out on the darkened street. Watching for lurkers—Dark Ones and drug dealers. It's quiet.

Then something moves, shifting from shadow to shadow, swift and silent. Demon? Human?

It stops in front of the building. Gloved hands rise to throw off the hood.

Torega.

No.

I grip the window sill. The head glows and eyes of flame rise to meet my gaze.

Ariel.

I leave the window, race down the stairs, and go out to the street. Although I half-expect him to be gone already, a figment of my imagination, he's still there. Not as tall as he appeared in the Abyss, his seven-foot frame is shrouded in a black cloak. He looks real, material—solid. I resist the urge to touch him and see for sure.

"What is it?" I ask. Why would he come this way? Why not appear to Grace? He's her guardian.

But his words are meant only for me.

"Darwin Speer has become like you."

"He's a distant relative," I say, uncertain about his meaning.

"Not anymore. He is your son. Your brother."

"What?" He makes no sense.

"Listen and watch," he says. "You will see." He removes one of his gloves to reveal a hand, shining as if it had been dipped in light. He places the hand on my head.

He's gone, everything around me disappears into a gray void. Then an image emerges out of the gray—Darwin Speer on the operating table, a steel frame attached to his head and tubes running into his brain. More images come in rapid succession: Speer on a treadmill for hours, hooked up to nodes to monitor his heart rate, Speer lifting thousand-pound weights effortlessly while men in lab coats stare in awe.

His hair has turned snow white.

The images shatter and Ariel is there again, standing on the dark street.

"Do you understand now?"

I nod.

Another vision intrudes. Speer stands on a platform overlooking a giant machine seven stories tall, a circular kaleidoscope of metal in spiraling colors that glow and shift.

—Ariel speaks in a sending. —*The detector at the Large Hadron Collider.*

—*What does this have to do with anything?*

He takes my shoulder and lifts me with him into the sky. We pass through several shifting curtains of air and soon we speed down a long, circular tunnel of huge metal tubes. For some reason, I can see inside the tubes. Streaks of pure light—millions of beams—smash together to create monstrous explosions, more powerful than any nuclear bomb. A shower of tiny, glittering particles spray out in all directions and disappear as rapidly as they appear. It is like a fireworks display in fast forward.

The next thing I know, I am back on the street, alone.

Ariel is gone.

Had I dreamt it?

Maybe it was all the cake.

I hear Ariel's voice in the darkness.

—*Go and watch.*

Go where? Watch what? I return to the loft. The house is quiet. *Watch.* I stare out the window. Nothing happens. Watch...TV? I turn the television on and flick through the channels until I come to a news station.

There it is.

A shaky video, as if taken on a phone, depicts a night sky dominated by a weird blue light that pierces heavy clouds creating an eerie, spiraling halo. The caption scrolls below: *Strange blue lights over Tromsø, Norway.*

Tromsø. My stomach lurches.

An anchor narrates something about the possible explanations of this weird light. The spiral grows into several thin rings and dissipates slowly into a black hole in the sky. The hole widens and the spiral lights gather around its rim until it fills the entire screen. When it seems to be over, the screen flashes with rapid bursts of light, like a strobe. The camera shakes as if whoever is holding it has started to run. The screen goes black and the whole thing repeats again.

I watch the rerun several times. The way the spiral of light dissipates into a hole looks very much like a...portal. Ariel's words return to me...Darwin Speer and CERN...the collider...the Abyss. They all come together in my head like a collision of atoms.

Numb, I pull my phone from my pocket and search for Speer's number. I hit "call."

"Jared!" He answers immediately. "Great to hear from you."

"What have you done?"

"Why don't you come see? I'll have a plane at the Buffalo airport in four hours. Don't forget your passport."

He hangs up.

I stare at the phone for a long time after. Dread snakes through my limbs, freezing my muscles.

He was expecting my call. How could he have known?

I spend the rest of the night considering what I should do. I scribble a note on a scrap of paper in the kitchen: "Got something to do. Call you later. J."

I leave the loft quietly and run the whole way to the Hobbit Hole. No one is up yet, not even Ralph, usually the first to awaken. I throw some clothes and my passport in a backpack and grab the keys to the PsychoVan. Before I leave, I write a hasty note and leave it on the table where we keep the car keys. *Be back soon.*

⁓

I drive to the FBO adjacent to the main airport. A private jet painted black with the golden spear logo waits on the tarmac, its engine whining. I go into the building and hand the van keys to the attendant at the desk. I give him Ralph's name and number.

"Are you Jared?"

I turn to see a woman approach. She wears a white shirt with blue epaulettes and a pilot's winged badge.

"Yes."

"I'm Jen. This way. We're fueled up and ready."

I follow her out to the plane. A man sits in the co-pilot seat, looking at an iPad. I climb the steps and take in the sleek interior done in blue and gray.

"Have a seat. Buckle up."

I sit and fasten my seatbelt.

"Where are we going?"

"Newark. That's where Mr. Speer is docked."

"Oh." The yacht. But in New Jersey? Not in Monaco? Or Norway? I had left so quickly, I hadn't given a thought to where I was actually going.

"We should be there in under two hours. There are

snacks and water in that compartment if you get hungry."

The engines roar and the plane taxis down the runway. I stare out the window, wondering what I have done.

~

We land in Newark airport a little after nine a.m. I spent the flight rewinding the events from the night before. In the broad light of day it seemed like a waking dream, a working of my own imagination. Ariel had come to me—but how do I know it was really him? It could have been a demon, an agent of Azazel, in disguise. I curse myself for not looking closer, for not questioning him and making sure.

And the blue halo—had that been real? As soon as I get cell service I check my phone, but I can't find any reference to the event on the news. Maybe I'd imagined that too.

But the phone call to Speer, that was real. He had known why I was calling. He was prepared. I'd played into his hands.

The screen blinks—phone call coming in. Grace. I silence the ring and let it go to voicemail. How can I explain any of this? I text her: *Sorry, can't talk. Everything's fine, be home soon.*

"All set?" Jen smiles at me, opens the hatch, and lowers the stairs.

I turn the phone off and shove it in the backpack. "Yeah. I'll need to go back in an hour or two."

She looks at me, surprised. "Oh, okay. I'll check with Mr. Speer."

A black car idles on the tarmac. The driver doesn't come out to greet me. I get in the backseat and he picks up a phone. "On the way." He pulls out of the airport onto a nearly empty expressway. It's strange that there's no traffic. The driver plays country music and I stare out the window. We drive over the bridge, and twenty minutes later pull into the marina in front of the yacht named *Lucille*.

Speer stands on the deck as if he's been there for hours. Three crewmen in white uniforms flank him.

"Jared!" He waves.

I blink and stare at him. This is not the Speer I met before. He's muscular and white-haired. The vision I had was true. He *has* become me. Or something like me, anyway.

I climb the steps and stand before him. "What have you done?"

"Did you enjoy the show?" He cracks a mischievous grin. "I arranged it just for you."

"What?"

"Come inside. Breakfast is ready."

I follow him into the cabin with a glance back at the three guys watching me. They don't look like ordinary deckhands. They're burly and menacing, more like...bodyguards.

We walk through to the dining room where the table is set for three. There's a huge amount of food in the center— waffles, pastries, fruit, and bacon.

"My sister's not up yet," Speer says and seats himself. "It's a little early for her. But I'm glad you were up last night. It's so much better when you can see it as it happens."

"What did you do to yourself?" I ask again. "How did you do it? And what was that blue halo?"

Speer ignores my questions, lifts his napkin with a flourish, and sets it on his lap. "You might as well sit down, Jared. This may take some time."

Reluctantly, I sit and place my backpack on the floor between my feet. He helps himself to several waffles and douses them with butter and syrup.

"It's really I who have a lot of questions," he says. "But I knew you wouldn't respond in the normal way. I needed to get your attention. And lo and behold, it worked. Who would have thought? Waffle?"

I shake my head.

"The blue halo—that was nothing. Merely a little movie magic with the help of some rather large antennae and a whole lot of imagination." He digs into his waffle and talks between bites. "I don't sleep much anymore, but I'm constantly hungry like I can never eat enough. I used to have a problem keeping weight on, but not anymore. I wake up every morning and find a new muscle has popped up. Look at this." He flexes his fork arm to display his bicep. "If only the bullies on the playground could see me now." He laughs and grabs a handful of bacon from the platter. "Are you sure you don't want anything?"

"Are you saying that the lightning and the blue beam in Norway were manufactured?"

"You thought I'd opened the Abyss, didn't you?" Speer gives me a lopsided grin. "That's what I hoped you'd think. Pretty good, huh?"

I stand up. "I'm leaving."

"I don't think so."

At that moment, I hear a low whir of an engine starting up and the big boat shifts under me. Speer grins.

"We're going for a little ride."

I grab my backpack and race out to the deck to see we have pulled away from the dock. The three deck hands are lined up, facing me with their arms folded.

The dock isn't that far gone yet. I can jump it easily. Before I can move, I hear a voice behind me.

"Don't leave yet."

I spin around. It's Lucille. Pointing a gun at me.

"You're not going to shoot me." I turn to make a dash for the gunwhale. There's a loud noise like a crack and a burning pain in my back. I go down, confused by my sudden weakness. Heat courses up my neck to my face. My vision blurs, my right arm feels unnaturally heavy.

She shot me. But it wasn't a bullet. It was a tranq dart.

As I struggle to regain my footing another dart hits me in the leg. I ignore it, intent on escape. I'm on my feet but it's like running through molasses, I can't seem to get anywhere. The rail seems too far away, the dock receding. I stumble on, reaching for the rail as another dart hits me in the shoulder. My blood is on fire, a heavy weight crushes my muscles. I fall. Can't get up again.

Everything around me spins as if I've ridden on a very fast merry-go-round for too long. Through bleary vision, I see the three men gather around me. Two of them hold me down, while the other one binds my hands and feet. Between their faces, Lucille appears and finally, Speer himself.

He speaks, his voice coming to me as if through a deep sea. "Jared, you don't look well. Seasick? I have a patch for that."

He laughs. I try to respond but my mouth doesn't move. My body is frozen.

"How much Quelicin did you use?" he asks Lucille.

"Enough to put down an elephant. Len wasn't sure how much it would take, but we didn't want to kill him, either."

"Ha! That's amazing. How long does it last?"

"Five minutes, perhaps."

"Okay. Get him below."

The guards pick me up and manhandle me down a steep staircase to below-deck. I try to fight, but my attempts have no real effect. Quelicin must be a paralytic. They carry me to a windowless cabin.

"Over there." A man with silver hair points to a bunk. The men dump me onto the mattress and strap me down. The silver-haired man looks into my face and smiles.

"Hi Jared, I'm Dr. Wilder. Relax now." He wraps a tourniquet on my arm and prepares an IV. He intends to inject me with something else. I focus all my energy on the arm and manage to raise it, snap the straps, and jerk out of the doctor's grip. The men are on me in an instant and force my arm down to the bunk.

"Whoa, there, Thor, relax," Wilder says. "There's no point in fighting it. This won't cause any long-term damage, I promise."

"What's…" I can't form any more words. The needle

pinches my arm.

"Don't try to talk. I'm hooking you up to a sedative, along with a paralytic, to help you stay calm. For your own safety." He checks that the IV is working and hooks the bag to a pole beside me. I flex my arm but I can't dislodge the needle.

"I wouldn't do that if I were you," says Wilder in a confidential tone. "The paralytic works on a trigger mechanism. If you try to move too much, it will release another dose. Too much might cause cardiac arrest, even in you. So try to stay as still as possible." He pats my shoulder. "Good man. I'll check on you later."

He exits the room with the three men leaving Lucille alone with me. She sits on the bunk and runs her hands up and down my arms, my chest, and my face.

"How beautiful you are," she whispers.

"What...do...you...want..." I struggle to speak, but the words come out as grunts, gibberish.

Lucille smiles and bends over to brush her lips against mine. My heart quickens, though I can do nothing. In all my life I have never felt this helpless, not even in the Abyss. "How I've wanted to do that since I first saw you." She straightens with a small sigh. "I'll be back soon. Don't go away."

She gets up to leave. Her laughter echoes until the door closes and the lock clicks into place.

I am alone to ponder what a complete idiot I have been.

20

Giant

Grace

Sorry, can't talk. Everything's fine, be home soon.

After calling all morning, this is the only response I get. After that, his phone goes straight to voicemail.

Something is very wrong.

I drive to the Hobbit Hole to find Emilia pacing with worry—highly unusual—and Ralph hunched over Ripley's shoulder in the Lair, also unusual. The blood drains from my face.

"Where is he?"

"Grace." Emilia gives me a hug. "We don't know. A man from the airport called and said the van was there and Jared had left the keys."

"Airport?"

I break away from her and race into the Lair. It's a place I avoid, mainly due to the smell. But right now, I don't care. Ripley and Ralph are staring at the computer screen with anxious faces.

"What's going on?"

Ralph straightens. "That's what we're trying to find out. The FBO says that a man matching Jared's description flew out early this morning on a private jet headed to Newark."

"That's insane. Why would Jared do that?"

"I checked the tail number," says Ripley. "It's owned by a company called Agro Solutions, which is the entity that owns Silo City. And guess who the major shareholder is?"

"Darwin Speer." I whisper the name.

"Nope. William Hyde. As in the Hyde Foundation. As in the Interlaken Group."

"So William Hyde is the secret "bigwig" who owns Silo City, where Jared lived for nine months, unknown to anyone."

"Yep. They're all tied in together. I told you this was a conspiracy."

"I still don't get why Jared got on that plane without telling any of us where he was going. This doesn't make any sense."

"Maybe this is why." Ripley points to the video on the screen. It's dark and grainy, a night sky with a spiraling blue light in the center.

"What is that?"

"It appeared last night over Tromsø. Right before a massive electrical storm that caused dozens of fires."

Tromsø. A stone's throw from the Abyss.

"Whoa, that's weird," I say. "What caused that?"

"There are a million theories. But I think it could have something to do with EISCAT."

"What's EISCAT?"

Ripley clicks his mouse to display what looks like a forest of tall antennae in the middle of a remote valley. "This is EISCAT, near Tromsø. It's basically a very advanced radar system. The antennae broadcast high-wattage beams of electromagnetic energy into the ionosphere. These beams are so powerful, they can actually push out the envelope of the ionosphere which could lead to all sorts of problems I don't even want to think about. I mean, the ionosphere is our shield, the bubble around the earth that keeps us from being destroyed by cosmic rays. Messing with it is simply asking for trouble if you want my opinion."

"Is this what caused the lightning?" Ralph asks.

"Well, it could be. There are all sorts of speculation as to what they're actually doing there, like changing weather patterns and conducting experiments for military uses. But see, these beams could deflect back into the atmosphere in bolts of electricity a million times more powerful than natural lightning."

"What does that have to do with Jared?" I demand.

"I have a theory." Ripley changes the screen to an aerial photo of CERN. "EISCAT's radar system can detect tunnels and underground metal reserves a thousand miles away. If the LHC at CERN happened to produce a super-massive particle collision at the same time EISCAT was beaming… Well, it's possible that energy could have surged into the beams and been deflected back to earth. Those beams can go through solid rock and directly to the earth's core, with enough power."

"In the earth? You mean, into the Abyss?" Waves of heat shoot through my veins.

Ripley shrugged. "It's only a theory. But if Jared saw this and thought that's what was happening, well…"

"And he would have thought Speer had something to do with it?" I take my phone out and press Jared's number. Again, it goes straight to voicemail. I want to throw it on the floor and stomp on it. Instead, I scream at the screen.

"Jared! Stop this craziness. You'll get yourself killed. Come home right now so I can kill you myself." Ralph takes the phone from my hand. "Where he is now? Does he have a bracelet like me? Can you trace him?"

He shakes his head.

"Darwin Speer's yacht left the marina shortly after that plane landed in Newark," Rip says. "I'll bet you anything Jared is on it."

"Why didn't he tell us?" I cannot make sense of any of this. All I had was one text. *Be back soon.* Now, even that seemed to be a lie.

I spin and run out of the Lair to collapse on the couch. My mind goes in crazy circles, unable to grasp what is happening. Unable to believe it.

Jared has left me—left all of us.

Ralph sits beside me and puts a hand on my back. "We'll find him," he says in his soothing voice. "Ripley has ways, I assure you."

Emilia sits on my other side. "We have to trust Jared now. That he knows what he's doing."

"Why didn't he tell me?"

"My guess is he wanted to protect you."

"From what?"

Emilia sighs. "You'd know better than anyone, wouldn't you?"

I wipe my eyes. "Yesterday, we had a birthday party. Today…everything is crashing around us. Why is this happening? Is God mad at us?"

"Just because bad things happen, doesn't mean it's God's will," Ralph says. "What we do know is that none of this is a surprise to Him."

"But Jared—"

"Can take care of himself. He's a grown up, older than all of us." Ralph sighs. "Sometimes, even I forget how much living he's done. Whatever he's doing, I'm sure he has a good reason. And he will be fine."

"How can you be so sure?"

"Because I know him. And I trust in the Lord—as you should."

"But Jared is not—" I stop short of using the word. *Protected.*

"This is the time to *trust*, Grace. When we have no other answers." Ralph pats my shoulder.

"I have an idea," Emilia stands. "Come into the kitchen and I will make you a nice cup of hot chocolate. It always makes you feel better."

I don't want hot chocolate, but I can't think of anything better to do. I follow her into the kitchen, where she starts warming milk on the stove. I reach for the jar of her "secret" mix.

"Whipped cream is in the fridge."

I find it and spray a huge mound into a mug before I sit at the table. The kitchen is like a cross between the Flintstones and the Jetsons with a rustic stone arched ceiling and ultra-modern electric appliances. I still haven't figured out how Ralph and Emilia managed to get the Hobbit Hole built in the first place. It is one of the many mysteries of this peculiar family.

Emilia pours the chocolate into my mug of cream and sits opposite me. She hasn't changed at all from the day I met her at the Mansion, right after the shooting. She's short and a little on the plump side, with her hair always in a tight bun, and wears round glasses reminiscent of Mrs. Piggle-Wiggle. And like Mrs. Piggle-Wiggle, she looks like a benign grandma with untold powers of intuition and maybe even magic.

"So I suppose you aren't worried either." I sip the hot chocolate, and for some odd reason, it does make me feel better.

"Worry does not add one day to a person's life. Jesus said that."

It isn't exactly a "no."

"What do you think is going on, Emilia?"

"I'm not sure, of course. But all this reminds me of something. Do you know the story of Nimrod in the Bible?"

"Uh...the guy who built the Tower of Babel?"

"Indeed. A great grandson of Noah. A very proud man, a ruler, a mighty hunter, a king. Nimrod considered himself greater than God."

"What happened to him?"

"He tried to build a tower to heaven. But God did not care for that idea." She purses her lips. "He confused the language of the people so they couldn't communicate with each other. They scattered all over the earth and the tower was never finished. Nimrod ended up the ruler of no one."

"Yeah, so…what's your point?"

"All giants will fall."

"But Jared is a giant too." I say. He may not look like one, but he is a Nephilim and they were literal giants, back in the day.

Emilia smiles and pats my hand. "He is a giant on bended knee."

"I have the impression you and Ralph know what this is all about, and won't tell me because you think I'll freak out."

"Grace, the best thing you can do for Jared now is to pray for him. Pray the Lord will be merciful. And just."

Two things that don't seem able to coexist.

"It's not enough," I say. "We have to find him. We have to help him. I won't sit around here like I did the last time he was gone. I can't go through that again. I have to do *something*."

"Like what?"

"That's what I have to figure out." I stare into my hot chocolate and try not to cry.

Emilia puts her hand on mine. "Sometimes it is necessary to simply…be still."

21

Houdini

Jared

I am learning to be still.

I lie in the dark and will my body not to move. My legs and arms burn from the paralytic flowing through my veins. I fight sleep, but the drugs are strong. My dreams are horror stories.

"How are you today, Jared?"

I open my eyes. Dr. Wilder stares down at me, a broad smile plastered on his face.

Is he kidding?

"I guess that was a dumb question." He chuckles a little and listens to my heart with a stethoscope. "Very strong. That's good. I'll unhook the IV now. You will be able to move around in a few minutes, but be careful. You'll be weak and dizzy for a while. Take a shower. There's a change of clothes here for you. We will be back in about twenty minutes to take you up top."

"What time is it?"

"Ten-thirty in the morning."

I've been here for over twenty-four hours.

"Are you hungry?"

"No."

"Well, you need to eat. I'll see you in twenty minutes."

When he's gone, I test my legs and arms. I can move, although my muscles still burn. After a few minutes, I put my legs over the side of the bunk and stand slowly, wavering a little. My vision blackens, then clears. I hold onto the wall and creep toward the bathroom. In the shower, I let the water blast my face and body. It feels like needles on my skin, but I welcome the pain—it reminds me I'm alive. I dry off and put on the clothes left for me. Khakis and a black T-shirt with Speer Enterprises' golden-spear logo on the breast.

I sit on the bed and wait while I try to get my bearings. My backpack is gone. I have no phone. Grace and Ralph are probably going crazy by now but I have no way to contact them. Why had I not told them where I was going?

Dr. Wilder returns accompanied by two of the bodyguards from day one. They look prepared for a fight but I don't have the energy to give them one.

"All set?" The doctor smiles. "Follow me."

I stand and follow him with the two guards close behind. I barely have the breath to climb the steps, and I pause at the top, actually dizzy. Weakness is a new sensation for me.

"Easy there," Wilder says. "Take your time."

When I'm ready, he leads me to the dining room. The light is too bright after so long in the dim bunk room. I blink several times, convinced I must be seeing things.

Seated at the table with Speer are Harry Ravel and Shannon Snow.

What are *they* doing here?

"Hey, Jared," Speer rises to greet me. He's smiling but there's a hint of nervousness in his eyes as he gauges my reaction. "Glad to see you're feeling better. Seasickness is a bear, right?" He barks out a laugh. "Sit down. Sit."

Wilder guides me into a chair at the far end of the table. The guards strap me to the chair with a belt around the waist and zip ties around my legs. My arms are free. I'd like to turn the table over, but I know better than to waste my energy on futile gestures.

Owen places a plate heaped with eggs and bacon in front of me. The smell makes me nauseous. Two other people—an older man and woman—sit at the table across from Harry and Shannon. The woman moves her fork absently around her plate. The man leans on the arm of his chair and watches me intently.

"Eat," Speer says. "You must be starving."

Harry shifts in his chair, but Shannon smiles and lifts her coffee cup to her lips.

"Jared Lorn," she murmurs. "Now it's your turn to be tied up. How do you like it?"

Harry looks at her, confused.

Speer continues. "You've met Len, of course. And you already know Harry and Shannon. Small world, right? And this is Marta Keller." He indicates the woman. "The Director of the Global Initiative on Biotechnology based in Geneva and one of my closest friends."

"I'm pleased to meet you." She is middle-aged and slight, with a thick German accent. Her eyes dart quickly away from me. She's disconcerted by the way I was brought in.

"And this man," Speer continues, pointing to the other man, "you probably already know too, because he's more famous than I am. William Hyde, Founder of the Hyde Foundation, the largest philanthropic organization in the world."

Hyde's eyes are cold and assessing. Unlike Marta, he seems unmoved by the way I am being treated. I sense a very disturbing presence around him.

"Bill and I co-founded the Interlaken Group."

"I've heard of it," I say. "Kind of like the Illuminati."

Speer erupts in wheezy laughter. "No, no, not like that. This isn't one of those weird secret societies where rich old men dance around a fire half naked and worship a giant owl. The Interlaken Group is totally different. This is the most forward-thinking group I've ever had the privilege to be a part of. The members are devoted to the one noble purpose of saving mankind. They know that our true salvation must come through knowledge. Utilizing advanced technologies to deal with the problems we face in the twenty-first century."

"And so, in the interest of science and saving the world, I am tied to a chair."

"Sorry about the restraints. I wanted to do this another way but we figured you wouldn't be cooperative right away. And knowing your unique abilities, it was necessary to...disarm you."

I glance at Lucille, seated next to Harry, whose eyes rake me with single-minded purpose.

"Why are they here?" I point to Shannon and Harry. As I do so, I look around for something within reach I can use as a weapon. I have been given only a plastic spoon.

"Harry's a member of the group, of course," Speer replies. "The Ravels have been generous investors and spiritual guides to me personally. I'm not the religious type, but I do like their brand of religion. It's self-empowering without getting bogged down in boring theology. It's what the world needs."

I want to laugh.

"You see Jared, we aren't the bad guys here," says Harry Ravel. "We're the future, sitting right here at this table. The work we do will unite the world to solve our shared problems. We pool our resources, our knowledge, and our faith, in the spirit of mutual cooperation. And you are a part of this. Your gift could save the world."

I stare at him in utter disbelief. *Save the world? Is he insane?*

"It's not a gift," I say. "It's a curse."

"All I know is that a year ago, I was doomed to die a painful and humiliating death and now, I am completely cured," Speer says. "I'm better than I was before. Even Marta couldn't believe it. That's why I wanted her to meet you, to prove you were real. You see, Jared, your genetic 'mutation' is actually an un-mutation. Your DNA, for some reason, has not been corrupted by the constant thinning of the gene pool for a millennium. You are how men were supposed to be. How they were in the beginning before entropy set in. Shame on you, for keeping it all to yourself for so long."

"You have the power to cure hundreds, even thousands of people," says Harry. "Not only genetic diseases but cancer, heart disease, and any number of terrible ailments."

"And now we have the technology to make it happen," adds Speer. "Well, *I* do. As soon as my treatment is approved."

"So you are going to...sell my DNA to the world?" I ask.

"Of course!" Speer waves a forkful of eggs in the air. "You'll be richly rewarded, I promise you. Look, I can't simply give it away. This technology is expensive. It requires seed money. The Interlaken Group and the Hyde Foundation have provided the startup costs, but making this procedure available to the world will require a lot of capital."

"So you will steal my DNA to make yourself and these people rich."

"Jared! My friend! You have it all wrong. I have no intention of stealing your DNA. That would be illegal and immoral. I need your permission to proceed."

"My *permission*?" Have I been propelled to an alternate universe? "I'm sitting here, tied to a chair and drugged, and you expect me to give you permission to use my body for your science experiment?"

Harry speaks. "Jared, you believe in Jesus Christ, don't you?"

"Yes—"

"What did Jesus do? He helped people. He made the blind see, the deaf hear, the paralyzed walk. He offered his body as a sacrifice for many. Don't you want to do what He did?"

The question blindsides me. I see, for an instant, a possible path to redemption. Could this be it?

I lower my gaze and shake my head. "My condition...comes with a price. A very heavy price. And I'm not talking about money." I stop to catch my breath. Even talking exhausts me. "There are side effects—"

"You mean for people who aren't in our genetic line, right?" Speer doesn't let me finish. "You're worried about a compatibility issue. Marta here is working on that hiccup. But we can't proceed further until we have enough of your DNA to start manufacturing the serum. We need your blood, Jared."

"And you are seriously asking me to give it to you?"

"Of course. Did you think I would take it without asking?"

I look down at my restraints. "Yes."

Speer chuckles. "I admit I could have done that when you were sedated. But I don't want to do things that way. This is not an illegal operation. We're not mad scientists here. We've prepared a contract. Take a look." Hyde hands him a sheaf of papers, which he places before me. "Read it before you sign."

I look through the papers. The writing is small and it's hard to focus. The words jumble on the pages.

"Do humanity this service, Jared," says Harry. "You are a good man. I know you are, deep down."

"And if I don't sign it?"

Speer's pleasant smile disappears. "If that's your answer, we will let you go—with the knowledge that you could have saved thousands of lives but you chose not to. Because you were too selfish."

Am I being selfish? I've always looked upon this condition of mine as a curse. But is it, in fact, a blessing? Had Ariel led me here and shown me these things so I would agree? Is it God's will that I participate in this plan to save the human race?

Save the human race. What a lie that is, the mother of all lies. I know what signing this paper and agreeing to this scheme will really do to the world. I stare at it as if staring my destiny in the face. Speer won't let me go, if I refuse. He'll keep me here until I agree. Or he will just take my blood anyway. But maybe I can control his ambition a little.

I look at Speer. "Add wording that neither my genetic material nor your treatment will ever be turned over to the government or the military."

Speer looks surprised and pleased. "Absolutely."

"And that you will never, *ever*, tell anyone about me."

"Of course. One hundred percent confidentiality. You have my word."

"Fine, then. Make those changes, and I'll sign."

Speer's whole face splits into a grin. Everyone else exhales a collective breath.

"The world will thank you, Jared," says Harry. "Even if they don't know your name. God will bless you."

A flash blinds me like a thousand camera bulbs going off at once. A familiar voice speaks aloud in the room, although I am the only one who can hear it.

—*What are you doing?*

—*I'm giving them what they want.*

—*You know where this will lead.*

—*Yes.*

—*And you don't care.*

—*No. I don't.*

I have nothing but rage in my bones now, rage against these people and their schemes, their grand plans to make the world as they want it. Rage against the thing that made me what I am, a cursed being, forlorn, forsaken, and unredeemable. Unforgiven.

—*What about Grace?*

That stops me cold. What *about* Grace? What would happen to her? And Ralph? And Silas? I don't know. But they are better off without me. Through these past years, I have started to have hope that I might be saved. But now I understand my purpose. It is not to save the world but to assist in its destruction.

I can rest in knowing that Grace and the others are covered. They are in the Spirit. They will be there at the dawn of the New World, the true New World Order. Not one made by men, but by God.

The light fades.

Hyde returns a short time later with a new copy of the contract. He puts it in my hands and I read while the others watch in expectant silence. Having read the contract, I hold out my hand, and someone places an ink pen in my palm. I sign, and Speer scrawls his signature as well.

~

"You might be interested in how this works," Wilder says as he prepares the blood donation kit. Actually, I'm not, but he doesn't wait for my reply. "We'll extract the DNA from your white blood cells. The technology works much like cut-and-paste on a computer. We use RNA to target the defective gene sequence, cut it apart, and replace it with your DNA sequence. We've been doing it for years in mice and embryos, but Darwin was the first adult human to receive the treatment. We weren't really sure if it would work, but as you can see, it worked beautifully."

Yes, I can.

"We'll take two pints at a time. I'm supposed to wait a week between donations, but since your blood regenerates at a faster rate than an ordinary person, I'd say every other day will suffice. After the donation, we'll give you an injected sedative to keep you calm. But no more of the paralytic. You should be able to move about on your own."

"Move about?"

"Of course! You are our partner now, Jared. You can go anywhere you want on the yacht. Enjoy it. It's a beautiful boat."

Is it big enough that I won't run into Harry or, worse, Shannon? I doubt it, but I am glad for the freedom. As my strength returns, I need to move.

"How much blood will you need?" I ask Wilder as he straps the tourniquet on my arm.

"We'll start with twelve pints. That should be sufficient. Our team is working on a way to synthesize your genome."

"You mean you're going to clone me?"

"In a way. But don't worry, there will not be little Jareds jumping out of Petri dishes anytime soon. Our treatment is strictly for therapeutic purposes. Here, hold this." He puts a ball in my hand. I grasp it as he sticks the needle in my veins. The attached bag starts filling up with blood. "We are all shocked by the speed at which Darwin's condition reversed. It's a momentous breakthrough. Think of all the young people stricken with Huntington's who will be able to lead normal lives. You are doing the world a great service, Jared."

I say nothing.

"No one at the lab can get over it. Your genetic makeup, I mean. They'd never seen anything like it. You are the most unusual human specimen we've ever encountered."

That's one way to put it.

He continues until two bags of blood are filled, then he pulls the needle out and presses a gauze bandage over the hole in my arm.

"All done. Take it easy, now. Two pints of blood is a lot, even for you." He puts the bag of my blood in a cooler and tosses the needle in a bin. "How are you feeling? Any nausea?"

"No."

"Good. Rest here for a few minutes." He snaps off his latex gloves. "I'll have Owen bring you some food. I noticed you didn't eat your breakfast." He pats my shoulder in that fake-fatherly way of his and leaves. Owen appears with a tray of food—some sort of creamy soup and saltines. I ignore him and he goes away without speaking.

Twelve pints. Twelve days. Then I will be free.

22

A Demon's Fate

Grace

Days pass with no word from Jared. I press his number on my phone over and over, unable to accept the fact that he doesn't answer. By the fourth day, even voicemail doesn't respond anymore.

Speer's yacht doesn't show up on any of the ship-finder sites, despite Ripley's repeated efforts. I call everyone I can think of, including the U.S. Coast Guard. No one can give me any information. I'm shocked that a private yacht can simply disappear, but they say once a boat is out in the open ocean, there really isn't any way to locate it unless it sends out a radio signal. And this boat clearly does not want to be found. This boat belongs to Darwin Speer. If he wants to disappear, he will.

Meanwhile, the news from Norway isn't nearly as bad as we had thought. The media reported that the weird blue light in the sky was the result of a failed rocket test from Russia, which had, purely by coincidence, occurred at the same time as an unusually ferocious lightning storm.

"Yeah, it usually takes them a day or two to come up with some plausible explanation for the weird stuff that happens," Ripley commented. He never believed anything the

media or the government said, preferring to get his information from conspiracy websites. But even the conspirators
couldn't seem to agree. Theories went from alien invasion
to secret government projects to military testing of new and
more horrifying weapons. A few even believed the Abyss
had been opened.

We've watched the news incessantly, looking for signs
that the Watchers might be on the loose. But no strange
sightings have been reported of giants rampaging the earth,
other than the usual reports of Bigfoot and Sasquatch. Ralph
even calls his friend Enok, the boat captain who had taken
us to Seiland, to see if he had heard anything.

"Not a thing," Enok tells him, "but you know, people up
here see all sorts of things and most everyone ignores them."

That was certainly true, as Enok himself had told us
about his mortal battle with a giant kraken in which he lost
an eye, and I never could tell if he was joking.

Silas and Penny try to help but neither of them can offer
any solution, short of chartering a boat or a plane and physically searching the Atlantic Ocean for Darwin Speer's yacht.
Silas distracts himself by working on the loft. Penny tells me
to keep praying. It is the best thing we can do for Jared.

I try. But my prayers turn into rants against Jared and
against God.

One day, at the bottom of my despair, I take the Mini and
drive to Silo City.

I need to be close to him, to feel his presence near me
again. Jared had "lived" in this place for nine months.
Knowing now that Silo City was actually owned by William
Hyde makes me wonder about the mysterious ways of God.

I drive down Ohio Street to the entrance. The complex
of grain silos has a "No Unauthorized Access" sign on the
gate. I rattle the chain link fence, but it's locked. I can barely
see the corner of Jared's silo at the end of the gravel path.
For a moment, I try to conjure his face, imagine him leaping

through the silos, racing down the conveyors and monkey-ing up and down the marine towers. But I can't get there.

Instead, I follow the fence down the embankment to the river's edge. I wade through the tall weeds and sit on a bro-ken chunk of concrete in the shadow of the silos, watching the river flow below me. There is no sound but dragonflies buzzing on the surface of the water. I close my eyes and try to imagine him again—where he is now, what he's doing. I even ask Ariel, but he doesn't answer.

I try praying. I remember that the apostle Paul said that sometimes, we don't even need words, we simply need groans. So, I groan.

It occurs to me as I sit there with my knees bent up to my chin, how easy this position is. I never used to be able to sit like this. My legs, which had been crushed in the car ac-cident that killed my adoptive parents when I was six, now bend and straighten easily. When had that changed? I try to remember. Ever since the Abyss...

The Abyss. Although I still bear the scars on my neck from my encounter with Azazel, my legs have been healed. Was this the result of going to the Abyss and being resusci-tated by an angel? Was I different now, like Jared, a being with superhuman strength?

I stand and walk over to a tree with high limbs. My gaze settles on a limb above me, well out of my reach. I brace myself to jump, to spring into the air and grab hold of it and swing around like a gymnast.

I spring and miss by a mile. Nope, no super strength, but I still wonder. If I'm not a Nephilim and I'm not a com-pletely normal human, then what am I?

A noise, a rustle of grass, catches my attention. I whirl, expecting to see a deer or a rabbit. Something dark, defi-nitely not an animal, shifts behind a tree.

My chest tightens, heart racing. How could I be so dumb to come here all alone? I practically run up the embankment.

At the top, I glance back to see the black shape again—definitely a person in a hoodie following me. *Torega*. He had gone after Penny. Now he was coming after me. Panic takes over my brain and I start to run toward my car.

"Wait up!"

The voice doesn't sound threatening. It sounds—desperate. I freeze as the hooded figure climbs up the embankment after me. His movements are clumsy and slow, as if he's very tired.

"Wait. Grace. Please."

He knows my name. I shove my hand in my pocket and grab my phone. I wish it was a gun.

"Stay away from me!" I yell. Now would be a good time to scream. Or sing. I can't manage either.

He's panting. "Don't run away. I won't hurt you. Please."

He pulls his hood off.

What?

I have a flash of memory, like a movie playing out before my eyes—those black eyes staring down at me, full of lust and hatred, giving praise to Satan while the knife in his hands is poised to rip my heart out.

"Mace?"

"I won't hurt you. I need to talk to you. Please."

He says it over and over. His hands are up in surrender. His face is wan and thin. His eyes plead. Not the Mace I remembered.

"Why aren't you in jail?" My heart thuds in my ears, but I fight to keep my voice steady. *Don't let him see your fear.*

"I got out."

"You escaped?"

"No. They released me."

How had that happened? Why wasn't I informed? *Go*, a voice in my head says. *Run away.* But another voice follows with, *Stay. Listen.* I don't know which one to obey.

"Come any closer and I'll call nine-one-one." I dial the numbers on my phone and hover my finger over the send key.

Mace doesn't try to approach me. "Please, let me talk to you. I'm clean. I promise."

He's not shaking or wild-eyed and doesn't appear to be high. The viciousness and the lustful evil I had seen before are gone.

"I'm listening."

He lowers his hands slowly and his shoulders relax. "Man, I could not believe I saw you here. That you would come back. It was like…an answer to prayer."

"Prayer?"

"I've been praying. Asking God for a miracle."

"God? I thought Satan was your guy."

"No more Satan. I've been here for days, talking to God. I didn't think He was listening. And then you showed up." He smiles and I see he's missing most of his teeth. He couldn't be more than nineteen. Only a kid. He was a follower of the Sodality, the Satanic cult that worshipped Satan and the band Blood Moon. The same cult that performed ritual killings for Manuel Torega.

"That night, during the ritual, I heard the singing. It was your voice, wasn't it? And I saw…I saw something glowing…covering you. I tried to stab you with the knife, but I couldn't do it. I couldn't kill you because of that glowing thing. It was an angel, wasn't it?"

I lower the phone, amazed. "You saw that?"

"Yeah. I thought it was the drugs, at first. But when the others ran away, I couldn't. It was like I suddenly realized everything I had done—my hands were covered in blood, not only animals, but people too. I felt…ashamed." His body sags, like he's about to fall over. "I wanted to die. I tried to kill myself in jail. I didn't eat for over a month. They put me in a hospital, force fed me until I was stable. Threatened to put me on a feeding tube.

"When I went back to jail, they moved me in with a new cellmate. His name was Randy. He'd sit around reading the

Bible all day. I started making fun of him and his religion. He didn't get mad or nothing. One day, he gave me this." Mace pulls a small, tattered Bible from his pocket. "He told me what he'd done to get locked up. He was a murderer, like me. Worse than me, maybe. Until Jesus saved him. He said God forgave him for what he done. And that He'd forgive me too." The Bible shakes in his trembling hand. "So I read this. I read about Jesus—about His story and what He did. It pierced me like a knife."

"That's great, Mace." I am moved by his words but still do not trust him. "Maybe you should go to a church. They'll take you in, give you a meal—"

"They'll find me."

"Who?"

"Torega. The cartel. They are looking for me 'cause I turned on them."

"A church would be a safe place. They wouldn't look there."

"You don't know. They have spies everywhere. Informants. No matter where I go, they will find me."

"I can't help you," I say. "I mean, I'm glad you're clean and all, but there's nothing I can do for you—"

"Yes, there is." He pauses and licks his cracked lips. "You can get this demon out of me."

I freeze. This is it. He'll kill me.

"I tried to get rid of it. But I can't do it alone. I need help." He looks at the book in his hands. "I feel like that guy—Legion? In this book. This demon won't go away. Torega will kill me. But I don't wanna die with this demon in me."

I peer at him. "How do you know you have a demon?"

"Randy told me. He said it was why I felt the way I did. I thought he was crazy but now..." Tears well in his eyes. "I don't want to kill anymore. But sometimes, I can't help it. I can't stop it. Please. Help me. I know you can."

He starts to cry, drops to his knees, and clutches the Bible to his chest.

I sigh. "Fine. Come with me."

～

I make him take off his jacket and prove he has no weapons. He obediently puts the garment on backwards and I zip it up so the hood covers his face. He doesn't fight me.

I guide him into the passenger seat and buckle his seat belt. Then call Ralph and tell him I'm coming over with someone who needs his help.

"Don't move a muscle." I start the car, and turn to give him a stern look, even though he can't see it. "Or I'll dump you on the side of the road and leave you there for Torega to find. Got it?" He nods, even though he probably knows this is an empty threat.

Mace sits still as a corpse while I drive to the Hobbit Hole. In the underground garage, I help him out of the car, and lead him, still blindfolded, to the entrance of the Hobbit Hole. Ralph and Emilia are waiting in the main room when we come through the door. I unzip Mace's jacket and take it off.

Emilia draws in a quick breath but doesn't speak. Ralph sighs.

"Come and sit, both of you." He offers Mace a seat in his own wing-backed chair, which surprises me. I sit on the couch with Emilia. Mace looks really small in that big chair. His legs twitch and his fingers twist around each other restlessly. Whatever demon is in him is probably alert and afraid.

"What is your name?" Ralph asks. "Your *real* name."

"Mason...Watkins." he says in a choked voice. I'm no discerner, but I realize the demon is trying to stop him from speaking.

"Mason." Ralph clasps his hands together. "Tell us about this demon of yours."

23

Gold Plated Lie

Jared

It should be hard to bear, this mere existence. But it isn't.

Between blood donation sessions, I stay on the top deck at the bow and stare out at the endless ocean. The wind plasters my face and hair and the cold digs into my bones. Wilder gives me a sedative every night and I sleep. I don't fight it. I want to sleep now, to stop my brain from thinking, ruminating on the past and rehearsing the future.

My dreams are vivid but no longer frightening. I dream of jumping off the tops of mountains, high cliffs, or out of airplanes flying through the sky. I do a lot of flying in my dreams—real flying, and it's exhilarating. I don't want those dreams to end.

I avoid the others on the boat. No one seems interested in me anymore. I saw Shannon only once, hanging over the deck rail and gazing down at the water. I had the impression she was thinking of jumping too. I detected fear lurking behind her gaze. A mixture of dread and longing. The water— she still hated it, even after the exorcism. She glanced at me but didn't move and didn't look away. She simply stared at me.

I refuse to eat meals with the others. I assume Speer and

Hyde and Marta spend their times in some secret room, plotting how they will take over the world.

One day, Owen comes to me with a message that Speer wants to have dinner with me—alone. I want to refuse, but in the end, I agree. Speer has kidnapped me and drugged me and forced me to partner with him, but I can't seem to resist him. He draws me to himself with gravitational force, like the moon to the earth.

Owen leads me to a luxurious stateroom, ringed with windows that curve around the rich dark woodwork. The bed is extra-long, obviously custom-made for Speer's frame.

"Jared!" Speer greets me in his usual manner, and we sit at a table beside the window. Attendants bustle around us, serving plates of lobster and filet mignon. Speer gets two lobsters and two thick slabs of steak. Owen presents a bottle of wine. Speer glances at me.

"Red or white?"

"Neither."

"I won't tell anyone."

"I don't drink."

He exhales his disappointment and points to the red. Owen fills a big glass.

"How are you doing?" Speer picks up his lobster and breaks it in two. Water spews out and splatters his shirt. He wrenches off a claw and cracks it open with his hands. His movements are savage, almost animalistic. He attacks the lobster with gleeful viciousness.

"Okay," I say.

"Awesome. I told Len not to overdo it. I mean, you may be somewhat superhuman, but everyone has their limits, right?"

"How did you know?" I can't help but ask. "About me."

"You mean about your genes? Well, to be honest, I didn't. Not until I got your DNA."

"How did you get that?"

"Well, you remember. On the boat. The broken glass."

I stare at him.

"Ha! I got lucky there. See, I knew there was something about you that wasn't normal, based on the ancestry research I did. I'd bought this set of crystal tumblers in Murano years ago, but they were so fine they kept breaking. They were probably defective. I told Owen to serve you from one."

"So you planned that too."

"Well, it was my only shot. I knew you wouldn't go for the time travel thing. If you didn't break the glass, I'd at least get your saliva for a DNA test. I needed more than that to create the serum, however. I took a risk, and it paid off. That happens a lot for me." He laughs. "But seriously, I really owe you a lot, Jared, and I won't forget it, I promise. I'll make you rich."

"I don't want your money."

"Then give it to your girl—what's her name?"

"Grace."

"Grace. Right. Or give it to your favorite charity. I can see you're a guy with principles. I have principles too, you know. That's why I didn't want to steal your DNA. I mean, I know I stole a *little* of it, only for myself, but if you had said no, I would have ended it there."

I put my fork down. "Are you kidding? You consider luring me on this boat and tying me up and drugging me having *principles?*"

Speer pretends he doesn't even hear. "People don't understand that nothing can get in the way of progress. That's what I'm about. Progress. Moving the human race forward. That's why I do everything I do. Before I die, I'll have every house running on solar energy. An electric car in every garage. A colony on Mars. I'll reduce the carbon footprint of every human being on this planet to 8.5 metric tons. And, because of you, I'll cure every disease known to man." He pauses to wipe the butter off his chin. "Like it or not, Jared, I *will* save the world." He smiles at me, still chewing. "And also because of you, I'll have a lot more time to work on those things. I rarely need to sleep anymore—I can practically work around the clock. And I'll live to be what, two hundred? Three hundred? It's awesome, being you."

"You haven't been me long enough to know that."

He ignores the comment and launches into a long discourse I can only call "Speer's Personal Theory of Everything."

"You know what really ticks me off? That for the last twenty years, all the best minds in the world have focused on one thing—software. It's like the world is ruled by apps. People seem to care more about how to get more followers on Instagram than they do about solving the world's problems. What happened to real innovation? NASA hasn't invented anything new since freeze-dried food. They're hopelessly behind on Mars exploration. Why should a private citizen like me spearhead that, anyway? NASA should have done it a long time ago. Oh yeah, they discover a new planet now and then, with their twenty-five-year-old telescopes. What good does that do anyone?"

He goes on like this for some time, stopping only to devour his food, a running monologue peppered with expletives and head shaking. The world, according to Darwin Speer, is seriously screwed up. And he will fix it, single-handedly if he has to.

"When the Romans wanted to keep the people from rising up, what did they give them? Bread and circuses! It's the same thing today. As long as people are well-fed and have the latest iPhone, they really don't care that the world around them is going to hell. They'll be too busy checking Facebook." He tosses a claw on the growing pile. "People are sheep."

Says the man who shot me up with drugs and held me captive.

"What are your plans for CERN?" I interrupt his diatribe. "Why are you expanding it? What do you hope to accomplish?"

"Oh, CERN. That's a giant toy factory for me. I love big machines, can't help it. You should see inside that place. I mean, it's beyond awesome. You look at it and go, how did human beings even build that?"

"So that's it? Just playing around with giant toys? Nothing more?"

"Well, maybe a *little* more. It's fascinating, quantum physics. Not really my area—it's more Bill's thing. He talked me into it. He's the theoretical physics nerd. But CERN is the key to everything in the universe. I couldn't keep my hands off it."

"You're playing with fire, Speer."

"It wouldn't be the first time. But don't worry, I always come out on top." He puts his fork down and picks up his wine glass. "Do you know what I find so fascinating about you, Jared? Aside from your genes, I mean. You never sold your soul. Here you are, this practically immortal man, and you never tried to capitalize on that. How old are you anyway? One hundred? Two hundred?"

"Something like that."

"When did you know for sure that you were…different?"

"I don't remember a time when I didn't know."

"What about your parents? Your father, Lucas—was he like you?"

"I don't know. He died when I was still young."

"Oh, right. Trapeze accident, wasn't it?"

"Yes."

"It seems strange that an experienced performer like your father would have died that way."

I shrug. "Accidents happen."

He smiles. "Not to people like us."

"What are you saying?"

"I'm saying maybe your birth father was more than you thought him to be."

"You think he was—like me?"

Speer shrugs. "How else do you explain your genetic

makeup? Oh, I've heard that story about the fallen angels and the Abyss. But everyone knows that's a fantasy."

"How does everyone know that?"

"C'mon, Jared, get real. You know as well as I do that it can't be true."

"What proof do you have that it can't be true?" Anger rises, heating my blood. "Are you the final arbiter of truth now?"

"Take it easy. I'm only saying that there's a difference between scientific discovery and fairy tales. Look, I get it. Quantum physics proves that what we thought were fixed rules of the universe really aren't. That what we see is not all there is. It's absolutely mind-blowing. We're on the cusp of discovering other dimensions and other universes, and the next step will be the ability to send messages back and forth, or even travel between them. I get where you're coming from with the whole angel thing. Science is getting closer and closer to—"

"God?"

He blinks. "To proving we don't *need* God to explain the stuff we don't understand."

"Like the creation of the universe."

"Exactly! We're halfway there with CERN. I'll simply give the place a power boost and take it over the finish line. Since the Higgs discovery, nothing has come out of there, with a whole lot of money going in. That seems wrong to me. And if I see a problem I can fix, I'm all about fixing it."

"You don't get the basic flaw in your premise," I say. "You are looking to the universe to explain how it created the universe. Do you see the problem? A thing can't create itself."

"I'm not saying we can know everything, but if we could figure out how it all started, that would give us some serious clues for the rest."

"Yet you believe we're living in a video game."

"Simulation. Is that really any different from your God

hypothesis?"

"What do you mean?"

"You believe an all-powerful divine being created and controls reality." He picks up his wine glass. "I believe we are in a giant simulation created by alien beings with superior intelligence. Same idea, different players."

"It's not the same," I say. "Where is morality?"

"Morality is a construct invented as a way to control people. All religion is about control, mainly through guilt."

"Yet you believe there are alien gamers controlling *you*."

"Controlling my *reality*, not me. How I deal with reality is my business."

"So you believe in free will, despite the fact that we exist in a computer simulation." I shake my head. "And you think I'm crazy for believing in God."

"Frankly, Jared, I don't care what you think about God. I think you *are* a god. To have lived for so long and still look like you're in your early twenties—you're like Wolverine or Thor come to life. I'm not interested in God. I'm interested in you." He downs his wine in one gulp and slams the empty glass on the table. "I mean, do you really believe there is a pit filled with fallen angels under the earth?"

"Yes."

"Why?"

"I've been there."

I expect him to laugh. To mock me. But his face is still. He takes a long time to respond.

"Prove it."

"What?"

His eyes narrow and a corner of his mouth turns up. "Take me there."

24

After You

Grace

We sit around the dinner table and watch Mace devour three servings of Emilia's meatloaf without stopping to take a breath. He acts as though he hasn't eaten in ten years. Maybe he hasn't.

The deliverance yesterday took over four hours, but it wasn't as dramatic as Shannon's or Crow's. Mace was eager to release the main spirit, which went by the name of the goat-demon Baphomet, well known for torturing young, lost men. It was difficult without Jared, but Penny came to help, and she turned out to be almost as good at discerning evil spirits. She ordered those demons around like they were nothing more than cockroaches.

Baphomet, it turned out, is a character in the game Dungeons & Dragons, which Mace had once played to obsession.

He was exhausted when it was over, so Ralph invited him to stay the night and gave him Jared's room. I couldn't bear that and had to leave. The deliverance had taken my mind off Jared for a few hours, but it all came roaring back.

When Silas, Penny, and I arrived at the Hobbit Hole today, we found Mace washed and in clean clothes with his hair neatly combed. Emilia had done a miracle—I hardly recognized him. Watching him eat, I try to reconcile this scrawny child-man to the drug-addicted wizard who had nearly killed me in a satanic ritual.

In between mouthfuls of food, he provides more information about his life. At the age of ten, he'd started playing D&D at a house owned by two men he referred to as Ned and Fred. A bunch of kids always hung out there. Engineers during the day, at night Ned and Fred were high wizards and practiced black magic that blew Mace's mind.

"They could make demon faces appear in mirrors and make things levitate and stuff like that. I wanted to learn, so they taught me. By the time I was eleven, I could do the spells myself. They said I had a gift. I thought this was what I was meant to do. The spells always required a sacrifice. We would lure stray cats in by leaving food outside in the yard. And when the cats came for the food, we'd nab them."

I push my plate away, sickened. Mace continues to eat, unfazed.

"I decided I would be a wizard too—a High Wizard. I started doing drugs with Ned and Fred because they said it would heighten my power. Crank, mostly. Man, there's no high like a crank high." He glances at us and sees that we don't know what he's talking about. "*Meth.* On meth, I could do anything—I was like Superman. Ned and Fred only let us shoot up during the rituals. It wasn't enough for me. I started sneaking around when they were asleep and stealing drugs. But they were wizards, so of course they knew what I was doing. They caught me and kicked me out. That's when I went to the silo."

"How old were you?" I ask.

"I don't know…fourteen, fifteen."

"You lived at the silo all that time?"

"On and off. I'd hang out at clubs where Blood Moon was playing, and I met all these fans who called themselves the Sodality. I wanted to be a part of that, a part of something. And 'cause I needed money for the meth, I started doing spells for people at the club and they would pay me. I'd put curses on people and they usually worked, so I got to be pretty popular. Sometimes I stole stuff. I went to my mom's house and stole her jewelry and even this gun she had, and sold them. Whatever I could find. Once, I put a hex on my father for leaving us, and a month later, I found out he had a heart attack and died."

Mace stops eating, clearly shamed by that memory.

"How did you get involved with Jam...I mean, Torega?" Penny asks.

His face twitches. "I met him at a Blood Moon gig. He found me and told me he'd heard about my sorcery skills. He worked for a cartel called *Rosa Negro*. Black Rose. The leader is La Parca—'Grim Reaper.' I thought that was a cool name. La Parca owned some seafood companies, fronts for his drug business. He was expanding his operation to Buffalo. Torega offered me and the Sodality all the crank and smack we could want in exchange for doing certain rituals. No brainer. I was like, bring it on."

"So you went into business with La Parca."

Mace nods. "Until that night at the silo. When I got caught, I confessed and told the cops all about Torega and the cartel. La Parca put out a hit on me." He leans back in his chair and rubs one arm obsessively. "They never give up. They will find me and kill me, only they won't do it quickly. They'll use me for a sacrifice. That's what happens to anyone who betrays them." His voice breaks. "I'm sure La Parca is the one who got me out of jail early. I don't know how he did it but I know that he has people everywhere, even in the government, the prison system, and the courts. They're *everywhere*."

Penny uses a tissue to dry her damp cheeks. I set my jaw. I do not want to feel sorry for this boy.

"You're safe here," Ralph says in a gentle voice. "But more importantly, you are *forgiven*. Always remember that."

"Forgiven," he repeats. "You mean, you can just ask God to forgive you...and He does it?"

"When there is a transgression, there is always a cost. Someone has to pay. That's what Jesus did, on the cross. He paid, because you could not, no matter how hard you tried."

"But the stuff I did, it's way worse than the stuff any of you did."

"It doesn't matter."

Mace's head moves slowly back and forth. "That don't make sense."

"You're right—it's completely illogical," Ralph replies. "But that's what makes it...wonderful."

"Satanism makes a lot more sense," Mace says. "At least, it used to. The way Ned and Fred taught me, if you give your life to Satan, you get power. Money. Total freedom. You can do anything."

"Anything Satan wants you to do," Silas murmurs.

"Everyone worships something," Ralph adds. "And whatever you worship owns your soul."

After dinner, while Mace and Penny clear the table, I take Ralph into the other room. "You aren't going to let him stay here, are you?"

"For the time being," Ralph says. "He has nowhere else to go. Besides, we have plenty of room these days." His voice chokes up. "Mace has a lot to learn about God. I can help him with that. It feels good to...help someone." He turns away so I won't see his tears.

"We'll find him." I put my arms around his waist and hold on.

"Of course we will."

25

Conversations

Jared

"You're kidding, right?"

"Nope," says Speer. "Look, I'm the kind of guy who believes in the power of possibility—that's how I live my life. If this Abyss really exists, and these Watchers you say are your—*our*—ancestors, I want to see for myself."

I shake my head. "Not possible. And even if it were, I would never go back."

His eyes bore into mine. I steel myself for a long argument. In the end he sighs. "Think about it anyway. We'll talk more." He picks his napkin up and begins folding it in an intricate pattern. I've noticed he can never keep his hands still. "We'll be docked in the morning."

"Where? Switzerland?"

"No. Reykjavík." He grins at my alarm. "I have some business in Iceland, and I own a nice little place there. You'll like it. It's off the grid. It'll give you time to think things over."

"I don't need time."

"If you change your mind, it's only a short flight to Norway—"

"I won't change my mind."

"Just saying. You might need some time anyway. All of this will be hard to explain to your family, won't it? Will you tell them about this? That you signed a contract?"

I say nothing. He smiles.

"That's what I thought. So I'm doing you a favor, see?"

"You need to book me on the first flight to New York."

He sighs, still folding the napkin. "Okey-dokey. If that's what you really want. First flight to New York."

"Fine," I stand and turn to leave.

"Wait…tell me something. Why did you go there in the first place?"

"Where?"

"The Abyss."

I hesitate, but I know he won't stop asking until I give him an answer. "To kill Azazel."

"Azazel?"

"One of the Watchers."

Speer finishes his napkin sculpture and sets it on the table between us. It's shaped like an angel, wings and all. "Tell me about this Azazel."

I take a breath. "He was one of the leaders of the Two Hundred, the Watchers who descended to earth on Mount Hermon and sinned with human women."

"So you're saying that angels have—body parts?"

"In this realm."

"This realm? You mean our own visible universe?"

"Yes."

"So they exist also in another, invisible realm?"

"Yes."

"And they can go back and forth?"

I nod. "Some of them have that power."

"Fascinating." He glances around. "Are there any in this room right now?"

"Angels? Maybe."

"Demons?"

"A few."

"Really?" His eyes widen. "What do they look like?"

"They look like…you and me."

Speer stares at me a moment, then throws his back and laughs. "You can be funny when you want to be."

"I'm not joking." But he doesn't hear me. He's too busy laughing.

~

I stand at the bow the rest of the night and watch the northern lights dance in the sky—an undulating curtain of blues and greens and purples. Seeing the lights awakens something inside me, something I'd thought long dormant. Fear. Longing. Dread. The irresistible pull of the Dark. Even here, on this boat a thousand miles from Seiland, I am much too close to the Abyss, that place of my origin and my curse.

We head into Reykjavík Harbor as the sun rises. The gentle peaks of western Iceland surround us. Clouds descend, making the air heavy with dew—mist settles like a blanket on the water. There is a mystical quality to this scene that makes me feel at home.

Many large fishing boats are at anchor as well as a small cruise ship. *Lucille*'s crew flies into action, guiding the yacht to its berth and tying in. The passengers come to the top deck to watch Iceland's capital city reveal itself. A sea of low, colorful buildings gives way to the breathtaking backdrop of stark gray mountains dusted with green.

"Great, isn't it?" Harry remarks.

I don't respond although I sense Shannon's eyes on me. I turn away and go to my room to get my things.

My passport is missing.

I find Speer and demand he return it. He says he knows nothing about it.

"You had my backpack all the time I was drugged," I say. "Someone took my passport out of my backpack."

"Jared, I will find out who did this, I promise." The crew

searches the yacht but my passport isn't found.

I still suspect this is one of his games—a way to keep me around a little longer. Speer assures me that we will go to the embassy and have my passport replaced at once. I have no other recourse but to agree.

"Let me call my family," I say. "I need to tell them I'll be home soon."

"Oh, sure, you can use the phone on the yacht."

I go to the bridge, and the captain hands me a ship phone. I dial the number, but the call won't go through. After several failed attempts, I give up.

"Must be the heavy cloud cover," says the captain. "But you can send an email." He gives me access to the yacht's computer. I sit down, wondering what I should say.

> I'm with Speer in Iceland. Need to replace my passport but will be home soon. Don't worry. I'm fine.

I should write more explain all that has happened. But Speer is right. I can't tell them what I've done. Not yet. I dread the moment when I get home and have to confess it all. I can already see Ralph's disappointment and Grace's disbelief in my mind's eye. It is enough, now, to let them know I'm alive.

Once we disembark, Speer says goodbye to the Ravels, who are flying directly to California. Harry shakes my hand and tells me again what a "great" thing I am doing for humanity.

Shannon gives me a knowing smile. "Give my love to Grace."

Marta supervises the offloading of several refrigerated crates, shouting at the crew to be careful. My blood is in those crates. I have a manic thought. What if I destroyed them? Walked over and casually tossed them into the harbor?

But I do nothing.

I wonder about Speer's plan to manufacture a serum from my DNA. Switzerland, he had told me, is one of the easiest places to get new medical treatments onto the general market. Still, it will take some time. Perhaps the trials will fail and the serum won't be approved. I perhaps the serum will prove ineffective on non-carriers. I can hope for that.

But Speer will not be deterred for long. He will put his treatment on the black market for those who can afford to pay millions for the gift of perfect health and perpetual youth. Shannon no doubt will be one of his first customers.

Speer directs Lucille and me to a car, and we drive to the embassy, stopping along the way at the passport center to have a new picture taken. Once they realize Darwin Speer is in the house, the embassy workers promise to fast-track the application. The passport will be ready tomorrow.

We drive to a private airfield outside the city. A black helicopter with the golden spear logo stands waiting, the rotors turning lazily.

"Let's go for a ride!" Speer's childlike enthusiasm is grating. We fly low under the layer of heavy cloud, and the mist below us breaks, revealing a barren, moon-like terrain, broken by deep craters and narrow rivers. Iceland, the land of fire and ice, a landscape out of some fairy tale universe. According to Speer's running commentary in my headset, this island is very young and still growing: volcanos erupt frequently, and earthquakes rip apart tectonic plates. A deep fissure runs through the entire island, like an open wound widening each year.

I keep my eyes on the scenery to avoid Lucille's unblinking stares.

"You'll like Iceland, Jared," Speer says. "They believe in invisible people too."

"Invisible people?"

"Elves. The people here are mad about them. I couldn't even build my house until I had it officially certified elf-free.

Cost me almost ten thousand dollars." He laughs. "Ask any-one in Iceland and they will have an elf story to tell. Iceland-ers are very good at telling stories. They're mostly descended from Vikings anyway, so you'll feel right at home."

A half hour later, we land on a high plateau ending at a dramatic cliff on the ocean's edge. The chopper shimmies, buffeted by gusty winds, as it settles into place. Speer jumps out and helps Lucille.

"Where's the house?" I duck to avoid the rotors and fol-low them away from the chopper.

"Right in front of you!"

I can't see anything but a blade of white concrete surging from the edge of the cliff. Speer leads us down a flight of stairs and through a narrow passage. As we enter the house, it reveals itself: a soaring structure of glass and concrete that sweeps out over the sea. The house stands poised on the precipice, like a knife handle sticking out of the rock, the blade imbedded in the earth.

"I saw the design for this house on an architectural web-site." Speer is clearly pleased with my reaction. "Everyone said it couldn't be built. So of course I had to build it." He takes me through the sparsely furnished main room with its wall of windows to the wide balcony. I glance over the rail-ing to the waves crashing against the cliff's edge, over-whelmed by an urge to jump. Swaying, I take a white-knuckled grip on the rail.

"What do you think?" Speer asks.

"It's…hard to put into words."

"I know, right?"

"I'm going to take a nap," says Lucille from the doorway. When she disappears from view, I glance at Speer.

"She seems…off."

"She's fine. You're something of a distraction—better lock your door tonight." He winks and heads inside. "Look around, make yourself at home. Dinner will be ready in a half hour."

"Are you cooking?"

"Of course! I love to cook. I don't know about you, but I'm starving."

~

A noise invades my senses, heavy with sleep. I'm surprised, as sleep is still an uncommon experience for me. I rise and look around, searching for the source of the sound—monotonous and rhythmic, like an army marching to war.

I leave my room and creep along the hallway to the concrete stairs. The bedrooms are underground, and the lack of windows creates a Stygian darkness. The thudding noises grow louder as I ascend to the main floor and go out to the deck. I hear a strange noise over the crashing sea, like chanting. I can't tell where it's coming from. I go inside and take another set of stairs to the upper level. Lights flicker in the windows—I follow them to the upper deck. The chanting grows. The lights become torches encircling a large bonfire near the cliff. Dark shapes twirl and dance around the fire. Demons.

A dream. I'm still asleep. I try to wake up, but I can't.

Something touches my shoulder. I whirl, then cough and sputter when a cloud of dust fills my nostrils, burns my eyes and bites into my throat.

"Come with me." The voice emanates from within the cloud. Female. I cannot tell if it's demon or human. A hand clutches my arm and leads me down the steps to the ground where the fire rages and the demons dance. I focus my burning eyes on the figure leading me—a flowing robe, a hood, teasing glimpses of pale skin, and eyes black as midnight.

The chanting pierces my brain and makes me dizzy and disoriented. Heat courses through my veins like rivers of molten lava bursting through my skin.

The dancers gather around me. The spawn of Azazel, exploding into kaleidoscopic patterns of color I never knew existed. The patterns are strangely symmetrical, far too per-fect, the faces hidden by masks. But the eyes blaze and waft, multiply and diminish, a hundred and then one and then a hundred again. They chant a single word.

Babble, babble, babble.

I stand before a large, flat stone. The robed figure tugs at my arm and then gives me a firm shove, so that I find myself lying down. The stone is hot from the fire and it sears my naked back. I'm naked? I don't remember undressing.

The chanting rises to a roar.

—*Flee! Flee!*

I try to rise—a hand pushes me back onto the stone. I comply as if I have no will to refuse.

I see red—lips, red as blood, and bright, familiar eyes. Something sharp touches me—a knife? The blade slides down my arms and my legs, igniting every inch of my body, until I am nothing but a raging flame that spreads to the edges of my fingers and into the stone itself, turning me to ash.

26

Figure it Out

Grace

Ripley forwards Jared's email to me. I read it over and over, unbelieving. *That's it? That's all we get?* It makes me spitting mad. *How dare he?* He disappears without telling us where he's going and doesn't even have the decency to call and then...this?

"Maybe he can't say anymore," says Penny. "Maybe they have him under surveillance and they are controlling what he says. Otherwise, he would have called, right? Not emailed."

Ripley does manage to trace the location of the email server. "He's in Iceland all right," he says. "Makes sense. Speer has a house there, although no one knows exactly where it is. They say you can only get there by helicopter."

But why didn't he say more? I concoct an elaborate scenario in my head—Jared acting as a spy, learning Speer's secrets and his intentions. He would come home soon and reveal all.

Another day passes with no further word. And then I get a call out of the blue. From Shannon.

"Grace..." Her voice is tentative, as if she's afraid I will hang up. "How are you?"

"Uh…okay. What's the matter? Is everything all right?" I wonder if Lilith is back but I hear no trace of the demon in her voice.

"Yes, fine. I'm in New York. I wondered if I could come and see you. I—I need to talk to you."

"You want to come here?" My mind scrambles for an excuse. *I'm traveling to Paris. I'm under quarantine. I'm going into witness protection.*

"Only for an hour. I can't stay."

"Oh, okay."

"Great. I'll be in Buffalo in two hours. Can we meet somewhere?"

I give her the name of a restaurant called the Flying Tigers, near the airport.

"See you soon." Then she's gone, the dead silence of an empty line filling my ear.

Silas is painting a mural on the tile backsplash in the kitchen, a surrealistic windswept tree that reminds me of the graffiti he used to paint at the silo.

"That was Shannon on the phone," I say.

He stops painting and looks at me, waiting.

"She's coming to Buffalo in a couple of hours. She wants me to meet her."

"Oh?" Hopeful rather than anxious. "What for?"

"She didn't say. But she sounded…different."

"Different?"

"From the usual Shannon. Nervous."

"Well, it's been a long time since you've seen each other."

"But for her to suddenly fly to Buffalo—"

"Do you want me to come with you?"

I shake my head. "I can handle it."

He gives me a half-smile. "Okay then." He returns to his painting. I can tell he's disappointed.

I drive the Mini to the restaurant and tell the hostess I'm meeting someone. She takes me to a table at the large windows looking out on the runway. A dad with two sons is at another table. The boys are plastered to the window, watching a taxiing plane while the dad explains how planes fly.

I flip through the menu and read the history of the Flying Tigers Fighter Squadron on the back cover. They were a volunteer squadron of American fighter pilots from WWII. A photo shows them with one of their planes, the nose painted to look like an angry shark. I wonder why they didn't call themselves the Flying Sharks.

"Grace."

I look up. Shannon is wearing jeans and a sweatshirt with a baseball cap covering her red hair. What's more, she's alone. No bodyguards or attendants. She certainly doesn't look like a movie star or a first lady. But she does look healthier than the last time I saw her.

"Hi," I say as she sits across from me.

"I hope I didn't keep you waiting."

"No" I say.

"I'm sorry for the short notice. My schedule is so packed these days. It's hard to get away."

"Yeah, I'm sure." So far so good. She seems flustered but not manic. Practically…*normal*.

"What's good here? I'm starving."

That's a new one for Shannon. The waitress comes and she orders a chicken Caesar salad. I nearly fall off my chair. I order chicken tenders and fries.

"You eat meat now?" I ask.

"On occasion." She smiles. "You gave me a taste for burgers, remember?"

How could I forget that night? I feel a blush coming on.

"Tell me, how is Charles? You mentioned he had lung cancer."

"He's doing okay." I'm surprised she remembers this. "It's in remission."

"Oh. Good." She sounds distracted.

"I'm sure he wrote you a letter."

"Did he? I never got it. But the mail—it's out of control.

I'll ask Melanie."

"Melanie is still with you?"

"Yes. She's a saint, that girl."

This is definitely not the Shannon Snow I used to know.

"I know it's been a while since we talked," she says. "After what happened at the house...well, I needed time."

"I know. It's fine."

"But something's happened recently. I thought you should know."

"Okay."

"It's about your friend Jared."

"Oh?" My heart does a flip.

"Yes. I saw him recently."

"What?"

The waitress appears with plates. Perfect timing. I hold my tongue until she's set them down and asked us if we need anything. Once she's gone, I lean over the table, my nuggets forgotten.

"You saw Jared?"

She nods. "On Darwin Speer's yacht."

I almost choke. "You were on Speer's yacht?"

Shannon picks her fork up and rummages in her salad as if looking for something. "Darwin and Harry have been friends for years. Darwin had told Harry that he had a wonderful investment opportunity for him, something that would really help with his work, both at the church and as governor. Naturally, Harry was intrigued. Darwin invited us for an excursion so he could tell us about it. Then Jared came aboard." She puts a small piece of lettuce in her mouth. "I had no idea Darwin and Jared knew each other. Then Darwin told us that Jared was donating his own DNA to some new genetic therapy Speer was working on. A miracle cure. He said that Jared's DNA had actually saved his life—"

"Wait—what? *Speer* was sick?" Confusion fills me.

"Not any more. That's what I'm telling you. Darwin used Jared's DNA to cure himself. Isn't that incredible?"

"Are you telling me that Jared was there of his own free will?"

"I couldn't believe it myself. But Jared was quite excited about the whole project. He signed a contract and everything."

My eyes blur and I can't swallow. I lean back heavily. "Contract?"

"He didn't tell you, did he?"

I shake my head. *No, no, no.*

Shannon reaches over the table and takes my hand. "I'm so sorry, Grace. But Jared is not who you think he is."

I pull my hand away. "You're lying. Just like you've always lied."

"Not this time. I came to tell you the truth. All the two of them talked about was how much money they would make. Millions of dollars. I was as shocked as you are."

I stare at her, searching for the deception in her eyes, but I don't see it.

"I'm so sorry. But I thought you should know."

A weight of tears builds behind my eyes. I put a hand to my throat to force down the rising bile.

Shannon comes around to my side of the table. She puts her arms around me and rocks me softly as a mother does an inconsolable child, telling me it will be all right.

But it won't. Never again.

27

Smoke and Mirrors

Jared

The horrific headache brings me out of the dream. My tongue is thick and fuzzy, my throat so dry I can barely swallow.

I get up and gulp water from the bathroom faucet. My head pounds as every capillary pulses with blood.

And I'm naked. What did I do? Sleepwalk?

I go back into the room, steadying myself along the wall. I never get sick and never have headaches. What's happening to me?

The dream…the dancing. Images flash through my brain like memories, except I have no real memory of them. A knife cutting my arms and my blood flowing… I look at my arms but see no wounds.

Another image comes to mind—a golden chalice, like the kind used in Communion Mass. I remember it tilting over me, pouring out—what was in it? Did I drink from it?

I shake the dream off and search for my clothes. When they are nowhere to be found, I drag a sheet from the bed and throw it over my shoulders, then search the other bedrooms. They are empty. My clothes are not in any of them. Not even Lucille's—that's a relief.

I take the stairs up to the main floor. It's morning. Morning? A thick mist lies over the outside world.

Disoriented, I shuffle through the house, searching, but find no one. The place is empty. A note lies on the dining table. I pick it up and read it.

> Jared: Hey, sleepyhead! Lucille and I are flying into the city for supplies. I'll pick up your passport. Be back soon. Help yourself to whatever you need. Also, the maid took your clothes to wash. There's a robe in the bathroom.

A robe. I hadn't seen one, but I hadn't been looking. I hadn't seen a maid either. I head to the stairs but turn when I hear something—a voice? Someone calling.

I go out to the balcony that juts out over the sea. The air is cold, the wind bitter. My breath comes out in clouds. The sound seems to be carried on the wind like the echo of a voice from far away. I move to the railing, searching for the source. The voice grows as I move. It's like strands of color jumbled together, a prism of sound, clear and strong.

—*Jared, my son.*

The voice washes over me like a bracing rain.

—*Come to me. Come. Now.*

I throw the sheet off and climb onto the railing.

—*Yes, yes! My boy, my love. Come to me! Come!*

I raise my arms out straight to the sides. The wind rises under me and the sea calls me home.

I jump.

PART FOUR

THE SECOND LAW

28

Human

Angel

An old fisherman winds his ropes on a rusty trawler that bobs against a weathered dock. Cod season is over, and he has failed to catch anything. He considers trying again to-morrow, but the coming storm might be a bad one. Late September means snow is not far off. He can smell it—that bleak, frosted scent. All the more reason to get his boat tied down before the wind kicks up.

I hover close, wrapped around his thoughts, twined into his vision.

A disturbance ripples the water, much like a large fish swimming just below the surface. The fisherman peers at it, hopeful. Could it be that the gods have delivered him a great cod, the prize he was seeking? Would it come right to the dock and offer itself as a sacrifice?

The fish breaks the surface. To his astonishment, the fisherman sees not a fish at all, but a human, although unlike any human he has seen in his life. He hoists himself up onto the dock, streaming water, his tall, naked body glowing as if lit from within, his hair snow-white.

The old man drops his ropes and stares in wonder. He knows what this creature is. One of the *Ljosalfar*, the Light

Elves, that come from the beautiful, mysterious land of Alf-heim. He has heard tales of the *Ljosalfar* as well as their coun-terparts, the Dark Elves or *Dokkalfar*, who were so ugly they lived underground in a place called Niflheim. No human would ever want to encounter a *Dokkalfar*, for to do so would mean certain death. But to see a true *Ljosalfar*, a being of light and magic and perfect beauty—he thinks he must be dreaming or has died and entered Valhalla.

He pulls his phone from his jacket—a gift from his daughter. He'd insisted he didn't need the contraption, es-pecially living in such a remote place, but in this moment, he is glad he has it. His hand trembles as he touches the video button as his daughter had shown him to do. He records for several seconds until the creature turns and begins to walk toward him.

The fisherman remains still as the Light Elf comes near. His heart races, his mind entangled in myths and legends. What was one to do when encountering a Ljosalfar? Bow? Ask for a wish to be granted? Beg for mercy? His thoughts race—I struggle to keep up.

"Ertu týndur?"

Are you lost?

The creature looks at him, not understanding. Does it not speak Icelandic?

"Ertu að fara í Aflheim?"

Are you going to Aflheim?

The creature nods but seems uncertain.

The fisherman glances at his boat and at the looming darkness. He shouldn't attempt it as a storm is coming. But he finds he cannot resist.

"Ég mun taka þig."

I will take you there."

29

Starlight

Jared

The fisherman drops me off at a port on the eastern coast of Iceland. He gave me clothes, canvas trousers and a heavy jacket he had in his trawler, as well as a knitted cap and boots. He did not speak to me on the journey and actually seemed afraid of me. I decided it was better that way.

Several container ships are loading when we dock. I thank the fisherman, wishing I knew some Icelandic. He nods and points, directing me to where I should go. I'm sorry I have nothing to give him for his trouble, but at least the storm held off.

I walk along the dock from ship to ship until I find one headed to Norway. A small container vessel named *Baldr*. A group of rough-looking seamen lounge on the dock, eating fried cod from paper bags. I ask them in English if I can get a berth in exchange for work. They look at me as though they don't understand. But then one of them answers.

"You in the union?" A woman. She has a feisty, weather-beaten face and a fleshy body with a number of piercings and tattoos, including a large dragon on one shoulder. A finger is missing on her right hand. She speaks good English.

"No," I say.

"No union, no job." But she smiles and looks at me the way women tend to. "You got any skills?"

"I'm...pretty strong."

"Oh yeah?" She smirks at her companions and says something in Norwegian. They laugh. "You're so strong, can you lift that?" She points to a crate sitting beside her on the deck. "These weaklings can't do it. We're waiting for a crane to take it on board."

I pick up the crate, hoist it on my shoulders, and carry it onto the ship. The sailors watch me, their mouths dropping open. When I return, the woman regards me with new interest. "How did you do that?"

"It wasn't heavy."

She translates for the others. Their laughter is not so mocking now.

"You might be useful," the woman says. "Maybe I will talk to the captain. See if we can do something for you. I'm Jonna." She holds out a four-fingered hand for me to shake.

I take it. "I'm...Danny."

"You have papers?"

"No."

"I didn't think so."

I wait while she goes to speak with the captain. The other sailors skirt away from me with suspicious looks. Jonna returns wearing a broad smile—in addition to a finger, she's missing a front tooth.

"Okay, you are good to go," she says. "I said you were a long-lost cousin. We look alike, don't we?" She chuckles. "We have an extra berth, lucky for you. Stick with me and you'll be fine."

The journey to Norway takes four days. All I do is pick up heavy stuff and move it around for Jonna, who treats me like her personal slave. I eat with the crew in the galley and sleep in the hold belowdecks, which is cramped but clean. The crew ignores me. Few can speak English anyway.

Jonna talks nonstop. She tells me how she lost her finger

to a codfish twenty years before while working on a fishing trawler in the Norwegian Sea. The other sailors treat her like one of the boys, and she can drink and swear with the best of them. I assume it is because of her tattoo that they have nicknamed her "Amma Dragon," which means "Granny Dragon."

"Nope," she says. "I got the tattoo to match the name."

Jonna is respected on the ship. No one messes with her. She's older than most of the men—mean and motherly at the same time.

"Where you from, Danny? America?" she asks one night. I'm on deck, leaning against the bulwark and staring at the stars reflected into the black sea. I do this most nights. A boat is confining, and anyway, I am sick of boats. Jonna joins me often, usually to smoke her pipe. It's freezing cold, but she doesn't seem to mind. She never wears a jacket, only her ubiquitous tank top.

"France, originally," I say.

"You don't sound French."

"My parents emigrated to Canada when I was young."

"Ah. So why do you want to go to Norway?"

"A sick uncle."

"Oh, right. Everyone has a sick uncle in Norway." She laughs, a throaty, slightly emphysemic sound.

"Where does the ship dock?" I ask.

"Bergen." That's all the way in the south. "Where's this sick uncle of yours?"

"In the Nordland."

"Then you have a long way to go. How will you get there?"

"Walk."

"Walk? Nonsense. Take a boat. Rent a car. You got any money?"

"No."

"What happened to your money? Your papers?"

"Stolen."

"Stolen! Why don't you go to the police? Or the embassy?"

"I was going to if you didn't give me a ride."

"Then how will you go back?"

I shake my head. "I'm not going back."

"Not going back? You really like this uncle of yours?"

"Not especially. But…I don't have anywhere else to go."

She falls silent for a moment, puffing on her pipe.

"Here," she says finally. She pulls a roll of bills from her pocket and shoves them at me. "Take it."

"I can't take your money."

"Then I'll make you." She looks momentarily ferocious before she breaks out into a wide grin. "You need money to get where you are going. And not everyone is as nice as me."

"Thank you," I accept her gift.

"You, boy." She reaches up to cup my chin in one hand. "There's something strange about you. But I like you. You're a good worker. Pretty too. If you change your mind, come back and find me. I'll get you a job. You will always have a place on my boat."

I smile, moved by her words. She pats my cheek a few times.

The next morning, the ship docks in Bergen. I help unload and then say goodbye to Jonna. She swats my cheek and reminds me there will always be a place on her boat for me. Her eyes look a little glassy.

"Go on now," she says gruffly. "I got work to do."

I head down the gangway, past border agents who don't give me a second look. I keep walking, though I'm not sure which way to go. Jonna had given me one of the maps that was tacked to the wall in the galley. I guess it will take me a few weeks to walk to Northern Norway and then sail to Seiland. I consider Jonna's idea of booking passage on a boat, assuming there is one. But I prefer walking. I need to move, to slough off the events of the past weeks, clear my head.

I decide to head up to the mountains. Norway is covered in good trails, and there will be few hikers this time of year. Jonna gave me nine hundred Krona, around a hundred dollars. At a supply shop, I buy a cheap backpack, a t-shirt that reads "Berserker Training," a plastic water bottle, protein bars, a map of the trail system, a lighter and an LED flashlight. That leaves me about sixty-five dollars, which I hope will be enough to rent a small boat to Seiland once I get to the north coast.

I put the shirt and hat on and start walking through the streets of Bergen. Brightly colored buildings line the waterway, dulled by the heavy mist of autumn. I could have taken the funicular railway up to the mountain but it's safer to walk—less chance of being recognized. Forlorn and Blood Moon had been popular in Norway, especially after our performance at the Northern Lights Festival in Tromsø. I can't take a chance.

I try not to think about Grace and Ralph and Silas. This is what I have to do. Grace is better off without me. She will recover and move on. She will find someone to love, someone who can give her a real life, a normal life. I wanted to be that man but it is not my role. I know that now. I'm ready to face my destiny, at last.

30

War of Hearts

Grace

I try to deny the things my mother had told me, sure that Jared will return soon and explain everything. But as the days and weeks pass, I have to face the fact that he isn't coming home. He's really gone this time.

Every morning, I get out of bed with this knowledge. *Jared is gone. He's dead to me. He betrayed me.* This is confirmed by what we learn about Darwin Speer. After his prolonged absence from the world stage, the reclusive billionaire has started making very public appearances. He shows up at swanky movie premiers and White House dinners, always with a different woman on his arm. It seems he's become an international playboy and daredevil overnight, heli-skiing in the Alps, surfing in Hawaii, racing Formula One cars, hang-gliding over the Grand Canyon, parachuting into the Mojave desert, piloting experimental planes he designed himself, and showing off his latest engineering feat, the prototype of a one-man rocket ship to Mars. Physically he's gone from a skinny, dark-haired dork to a muscular, toe-headed Apollo. The hair was what convinced me more than anything that Shannon had told me the truth. Darwin Speer had used Jared's DNA to turn himself into a Nephilim, or something close to it.

The media is obsessed with the change in him. How had he done it? Plastic surgery? Vitamins? He gives tantalizing hints about some "medical breakthrough" he's working on.

"The way I look at it, we're living in an age where the Sims world has become a reality. We can create ourselves, our bodies, our brains, everything about us. We can become whatever we want to be. It's fantastically exciting. We need to take advantage of this. What used to be a mere computer simulation of reality is now reality itself."

It sounds totally absurd to me, yet when Darwin Speer says it, people nod their heads and go along with it. He is, after all, the smartest man in the world.

Silas still refuses to believe Jared has willingly entered into a partnership with Speer. "Through all he endured with Crow, he never turned, never. It was hard, so hard. But he stayed true. He didn't give in. Why now? Why would he give in so easily this time?"

But I know the answer. Ralph always said it would happen, one day. It happens to all the Nephilim. They go crazy. They go to the dark side, or whatever. The angel part takes over, and the human part is too weak to resist. When Jared was with Crow, he had Silas to keep him grounded. And before that, he had Ralph. But in Speer's hands, he had no one to save him from himself.

Ripley rails against the Interlaken Group, which is the "influence" behind Speer's genome project, and the Hyde Foundation, which is the money. He paints a gloomy picture of what will happen next.

"Speer will market his gene cure to his groupies and other billionaires who can afford it. They'll open special clinics where anyone with enough cash can come and get the Nephilim Makeover. Once the USDA gives its blessing, the government will insist that insurance companies provide coverage. Hyde will figure out a way to extend its reach as a 'charitable' project to third-world countries. Then the government will pay billions for an exclusive contract and find some way to weaponize it."

We're living out the plot of a bad superhero movie.

No mention is ever made of Jared. He never appears in Speer's company, at least not on camera or in the media reports. This gives me a tiny bit of hope. Lucille doesn't appear either. Maybe she stayed in Iceland, a good place for the Ice Queen. Maybe she and Jared are *together*. She had a thing for him from the start. Maybe he couldn't resist her. Maybe—

I have to stop thinking about this stuff.

I've avoided the Hobbit Hole for a while, not only because Jared wasn't there but because Mace hadn't left. Ralph said he could stay until he "got back on his feet." But Mace didn't seem to be interested in using his feet at all. Whenever I stopped by to check on Ralph and Emilia or get an update from Ripley, Mace was sprawled on the couch, eating potato chips and reading from Ralph's extensive library.

I found his presence not only annoying, but suspicious. What if Torega was still hunting him? What if Mace inadvertently led Torega to the Hobbit Hole? Or worse, what if Mace was really a spy for Torega, and the story he told was a big fat lie? I've dealt with demons for far too long to trust anyone, no matter how sincere they seem.

I confided my fears to Penny, but she brushed them off.

"I think he's nice," she said.

"Nice? He almost killed you!"

"That was before. He's trying hard to change. You should give him a chance."

"So you've forgiven him?"

"Sure. After all, God forgave *me*."

I tried to put my mind to other things, like cooking in our newly finished kitchen. It turned out that I was a terrible cook, but I hoped if I practiced enough, I might get something to turn out halfway decent. Silas and Penny pretended to like my food, but always ended up being "not that hungry." For Silas, this was probably true. The cancer drugs ruined his taste buds, so eating was a chore for him.

Silas has started collecting broken-down bikes from around the city and fixing them up in the old light bulb shop on the first floor. With the loft complete, he needs something to fill his days. He's even managed to get Mace to help him, and now the two of them spend long days fixing bikes, with Mozart blaring on the ancient boom box they'd bought from a thrift shop. Silas plans to open a bike shop, selling or even giving away refurbished bikes to the kids in the neighborhood. Ralph has given him money for the renovation.

I admit, I'm jealous of them—of their sense of purpose and ability to move forward. Once again, I'm stuck. I still inhabit the world of No-Jared, unable to get on with it.

~

One morning, I get a message from Ripley.

Come. Now.

Scared, I grab Penny and Silas and race to the Hobbit Hole. Ralph, Mace, and Ripley are huddled around his computer in the Lair, staring at the screen. They don't even look up when I come in. My heart skips. Have they found him? Is he dead?

Ripley's playing a YouTube video entitled "The Elves Awaken in Iceland—MUST SEE!" It has three hundred thousand views.

"I was doing a random search, and I found this," he says. "I couldn't believe it."

The video is grainy and depicts a glowing figure standing on a dock, dripping water.

I suck in a breath.

"It's him."

"Yep," says Silas. "That's him all right. Where is that?"

"East coast of Iceland. I analyzed the video. No CGI or

doctoring. It's gone viral over there. It was even featured on the news."

"Look at the time stamp," Silas says. "October 1. Around the same time Jared would have been in Iceland with Speer. Maybe he escaped."

"Then why didn't he contact us?" I'm angry. "Why would he wander around in the wilderness like that, naked? Unless he's gone completely crazy?"

"There's more." Ripley switches to another video, this one of an old man wearing a fisherman's hat, speaking in Icelandic. Underneath is the translation. The fisherman says he saw a *Ljosalfar* come out of the sea onto his dock and that he took him to Alfheim in his boat.

"Ljosalfar?" I say.

"It's Norse mythology," says Ralph. "A magical being made of light."

"Kind of like angels," said Penny.

"Exactly."

"Can we contact that fisherman?" I ask.

"I got hold of the person who posted the video," Ripley says. "The fisherman's daughter. She said her father took the *Ljosalfar* to a port village, believing it was Alfheim. That's sort of the home town of the elves. It's possible Jared got on a ship from there."

"But why?" I almost scream. "What's he doing?" I turn to Ralph. "Do you know?"

Ralph's face is solemn and his eyes droop. "It is very likely he is headed to Norway—to the Abyss."

"What for? Will he try to kill Azazel again?"

"He's not going to kill him. He's going to join him."

31

Great Wide Open

Jared

I walk for days without stopping, except to drink water and eat a protein bar. I find I don't need the map. I know the way as if it's etched on my heart, a homing beacon.

Azazel speaks to me day and night, calling softly, *Come to me, my boy. Come.* He shows me the path, laid out for me like the yellow brick road. Sometimes, there is no actual trail, and I have to bushwhack through tangled brush, cross streams, climb vertical rock faces, or jump over cliffs. But it feels good to move, to walk and climb and jump again. I am getting stronger as my body dispels the weeks of drugs and idleness that wreaked havoc on my system. Each day I become more and more myself again.

On the third night, I stop at the top of a steep embankment above a small lake. The sky has cleared and I have a spectacular view of the Northern Lights. I rest for a moment under a tall pine and stare at the sky, lost in the play of dancing light. For the moment, I am at peace.

Suddenly, I hear was a cry from below near the lake. I can't see anything except the lights reflected on the surface of the water.

Ignore it. It's only some animal.

The cry comes again. It's definitely human. A cry for help.

I brace myself and jump, clear the embankment, and land in a tree at the edge of the lake. I scramble down, searching for the source. Nearer the lake I hear a low growl and another yelp of pain. As I move closer, a man comes into view, dangling from a tree branch while a young brown bear roars and swats at him with huge paws.

Thinking fast, I look around, pick up a long stick, and charge at the bear. I howl at the top of my lungs, drawing the bear's attention from the man in the tree. The animal swivels and swipes at me, roaring its anger. I yell even louder and bring the stick down squarely on its head. It lurches backward with a grunt and stares at me a moment, stunned. I raise the stick again—it growls but turns away and moves off into the darkness.

I throw the stick down and go back to see if the man is all right. He's dropped to the ground and cradles his leg, his pants ripped and bloody.

"Thank God you came," he says, gasping for breath. "I went to take a…you know, bathroom break, and I guess I scared him…and then I tried to run away. Not the smartest move." He's in his early fifties with dark brown skin, a scruff of black hair, and a short beard streaked with gray.

"Never run from a bear," I say. "Walk away slowly or stand your ground." I bend down and look at his leg, where a deep gash is bleeding profusely. "Do you have any first aid supplies?"

"Yeah. My camp is just that way."

I help him up and walk him to his campsite near the edge of the lake. His fire smolders, almost out. I set him down in front of his tent and throw a few more sticks on the blaze.

"Thanks, man. You saved my life. Where did you come from, anyway? I haven't seen a single person out here for days."

"It's late in the season," I say without answering his question. "Where are your supplies?"

"Backpack. In the tent."

I find the backpack and rummage through it to retrieve a first aid kit. Inside are bandages and a packet of Celox wound-sealing powder. I rip the packet open while the man tears the bottom of his pant leg away.

"How bad is it?" he asks.

"Not too bad. Got any water?"

He hands me a canteen. I clean the wound and pour in the Celox, then grab a gauze from the kit and press firmly. My whole body heats up with the weird sensation of light coursing through my veins. I turn my face away, so he'll think the glow is coming from the fire.

"Got a name?" I ask.

"Mike. You?"

"Danny. Good thing you had the Celox."

"I guess so. I bought the most expensive kit they had—didn't even know what was in it."

"Are you traveling alone?"

"Yeah. A buddy was supposed to come but cancelled at the last minute."

I catch sight of a pair of skis with his camping supplies. "You planning to use those?"

"I heard the snow comes pretty quick here. I've never been to Norway before. You?"

"Once." I pull my hand away but see no blood leaking from under the Celox. It's already healing. I wrap Mike's leg with the bandage before he notices. "This should hold until you can get to the hospital."

"Thanks, man, you're a lifesaver. Where'd you learn to fight a bear like that?"

"I read about it once. Do you have a phone? Can you call for help?"

"Nah. I'll be fine. It feels better already."

"Okay then. Good luck on your hike." I get up to leave.

"Wait a sec. Don't go yet. I owe you. How about some dinner? I got all this freeze-dried stuff. It's not too bad, really, and I brought way more than I need. You could help me get rid of it."

I hesitate. I don't want to stay and talk. But I sense it would not be a good idea to leave this guy alone yet. He seems fairly helpless and the bear may still be lurking nearby.

"Okay."

He fills a pan with water from his canteen and I set it on the fire. Then he takes a package of sunflower seeds from his backpack and starts eating them, spitting out shells, while he waits for the water to boil. He offers me some seeds, but I decline.

"It was a young one, though, wouldn't you say?" Mike chews while I tend the fire. "A juvenile. Had it been older or a mother, I'd probably be dead."

"Brown bears are usually shy around humans. I'm surprised it attacked you at all."

"Guess I'm just lucky."

Lucky. I think of Grace.

When the water boils, I add the food mix and stir until the mixture thickens.

"So, what are you doing out here in the middle of nowhere?" he asks. "Do you have a camp nearby?"

"Uh…not much of one. I'm sort of roughing it."

"Ha! I guess someone upstairs was looking out for me, huh?"

"I guess so." I take the pot off the grate and pour the food—chicken and rice—into two bowls. Mike pulls two plastic spoons from his kit and hands me one. He starts eating right away.

"So…you're American, right? What are you doing out here?"

"I'm going…to see my father."

"Where's that?"

"In the Nordland."

"Whoa. You've got a long way to go. Do you plan on walking?"

"Yeah."

"All the way? In winter? Are you nuts?" He says it jokingly, but from the look on my face, he realizes it isn't a joke after all. "Did you think about driving? Or taking a boat?"

"I prefer walking."

"I hate to tell you, but I don't think you'll get too far. Once the snows come, you'll be out of luck."

"Perhaps."

"Why don't I join you for a while? I could use the company. Would you mind?"

"Your leg…"

"It's nothing. Doesn't even hurt. That Celox is like magic." He chuckles. "I've got no place to go, anyway. Know what I mean?"

"Yeah," I murmur.

"So you don't mind if I tag along?"

"I like to move kind of fast—"

"If I can't keep up, you can go on without me. You'd be doing me a real favor, you know. And I have a map to where the huts are—the DNT cabins. Super nice. These Norwegians do it right." He takes a key from his pocket. "This key will get me into any of the self-service cabins on the trails. There'll be food and water and beds to sleep in. Pretty amazing, isn't it? You couldn't do that in America. The places would be ruined in no time. But these Scandinavians are so organized, so *civilized*, you know?"

I can't help but smile.

He offers me a drink from his canteen. "Where you from, back in the States?"

"New York."

"I'm from Chicago. Although I haven't lived there in a while. I've been traveling around, seeing the world."

"No family?"

"Not anymore." Mike takes a drink. I sense there is

something he's not telling me. "When's the last time you saw your dad?"

"About four years ago."

"Wow. Well, I can understand. Living so far north, it's not exactly on the way to anywhere, is it?"

"No."

He peers up through the trees. "I bet if we got up to the ridge, we could see the lights tonight. The Northern Lights. Always wanted to see them. I've seen pictures, but there's nothing like the original, right?"

"Want to go now?"

"What, up there?"

"It's not that far."

"I'm not sure my leg is good for climbing yet."

"I'll carry you."

He looks at me, one eyebrow cocked. "Carry me? Seriously?"

"Sure."

He chuckles under his breath. "Well, okay, if you think you can."

We get up and I help him to the bottom of the ridge. "Get on my back," I say. He hesitates. "Don't worry. I can handle it. Promise."

He puts his hands on my shoulders. I hoist him up so he can wrap his arms around my neck.

"You sure you're all right?"

"Fine. Hang on tight." I start the climb to the top of the ridge, which in some places, is nearly vertical. I grunt a bit to make him think this takes some effort. Neither of us speak until I reach the top. I climb over the edge and lower him to the ground.

"Man, you're strong. Stronger than you look."

We sit together on the ground and stare at the sky.

"It's awesome," Mike says after a moment. "This should be on everyone's bucket list."

I lie back, spread my arms, cross my ankles, and simply

gaze at the sky.

Mike's gaze is on me. I feel it.

"Did you leave someone behind?"

I glance at him. "What makes you think that?"

"I don't know. I can tell. It's a gift, I guess." He laughs. "A girl?"

"Yes," I murmur.

"Did she break up with you?"

"No. I...left." It seems okay to unburden myself to this man I don't know and will never see again. "I was no good for her. She deserved better."

"You seem like an okay sort."

"You don't know me."

"What are you? An axe murderer? Should I be worried?"

"Maybe."

"Oh, well, I'd better sleep with one eye open." I half hope Mike will change his mind about traveling with me, but he doesn't. "So, you think you aren't good enough for her?"

"I don't belong there anymore."

"Been there." He lies down beside me, staring at the lights. "Makes you feel sort of insignificant, doesn't it? The world is so big. The universe. And here we are, worried about our tiny selves. In the big picture, what does it matter, right? If we live or die. Or whatever."

"It matters," I say. "To someone."

"Does it? Even for guys like us who don't have anyone?" He pauses. "What about God? Do we matter to God? He made us, right? He must have had a reason."

I don't answer. I can't. God is not my father. Azazel is my father.

We fall silent, still staring at the sky.

32

Breaking Through

Grace

The Grand Opening for the Lighthouse Bike Shop is March 15. It snows. A few people do stop by despite the weather, including Bree and Ethan, who are home on spring break. I'm sure Ethan, who probably can't even ride a bike, is there for the free cookies. Still, it's good to see them.

"Why did you have the opening in March?" Bree shivers and sips our Grand Opening—i.e. Emilia's—hot chocolate while Ethan fills his pockets with Snickerdoodles. I don't tell him I made them myself.

"It's when the ice cream shops open." I quote Silas, because I'd asked the same question a hundred times. You never know in Buffalo. It could be seventy degrees, or it could be snowing on any given day.

"The shop is cool, anyway." Bree gazes around at the various bikes, all refurbished, hanging from the ceiling and lining the wall. I have to admit Silas and Mace did an amazing job. Silas painted the bikes in psychedelic colors and added cool, old-fashioned accessories like blaring horns, neon lights and streamers. One of them is tricked out with shiny metallic gizmos so it resembles a motorcycle. "I didn't know Silas could fix bikes."

"He can do pretty much anything."

"Are you selling them? These are more like art pieces."

"Silas mostly gives them away to anyone who needs them." There are a lot of those. The shop has become a haven for quite a few local kids who need someplace to simply hang out. Silas teaches them how to fix bikes and helps them figure out their lives along the way. "This shop won't be very profitable."

"He's like the Pied Piper." Now Bree is watching Silas show some kid how to inflate a tire.

"It helps keep his mind off being sick," I say. "And Shannon."

"Shannon? He still has a thing for her?"

"He doesn't talk about it."

"But she's married and having a baby. That makes her basically off limits."

"Yeah."

The news of Shannon's pregnancy blew up social media. Everyone seemed to think it was wonderful, a sign that she had recovered from her "lingering cold" and is thriving in her role as First Lady of California.

"I guess she's happy. I'm happy for her."

"You haven't spoken to her?"

"No. I've called but she never calls back. Guess she's busy."

"I guess." Bree shrugs. "Nothing from Jared either?"

I shake my head and try not to cry, which is what I usually do when someone says his name. As much as I want to forget him, I still can't. The mornings are the worst, lying in bed, searching for a reason to get up at all. Winter was long and dark and cold. But lately it's been a little easier. Maybe it's the bike shop, or the hope of spring, or that God and time have done some healing and I can move through the day with less pain. Jared is gone, but I'm still here, and I *will* get through this.

She sighs. "Where's Penny?"

"Upstairs. She has homework." Penny isn't happy that we've opened the bike shop to the public. She's still worried that Torega is lurking around, but we've seen no sign of him since Jared left.

Since Jared left. In fact, everything has been relatively normal since then. Maybe Jared took all the demons with him.

Ethan comes over, cookie crumbs on his chin.

"How's school?" I ask.

"You know. Same old, same old."

"He hates it," Bree translates.

"Working on any new games?"

"The company wants a *Wrath of the Watchers Two*." Ethan wipes his mouth. "The first one's already sold over fifty thousand units."

"Really?" I remember the night of the GAME-ON convention. Jared and Ethan in their goofy demon outfits. Bree and I dancing down the street. It seems like a million years ago.

"You should come over to my house tonight," Bree says. "We can watch *The Office*, like old times."

"Sure."

～

That night, over popcorn and *The Office* in Bree's basement, I tell my two oldest friends about Jared and Darwin Speer.

"You have *got* to be kidding," Bree says.

"I read about this so-called scientific breakthrough," says Ethan. "The Swiss Health Board already approved it for sale and GIBE has endorsed it."

"What's GIBE?" asks Bree.

"The Global Initiative for Biotechnology and Human Engineering. They're working to eradicate genetic diseases through gene therapy."

"So this is a good thing, right?" says Bree. "I mean, who doesn't want to eradicate genetic diseases? Jared does have some pretty awesome genes."

Ethan clicks away on his laptop. "Wow. It looks like Harry Ravel has already pushed through legislation to approve Speer's treatment for use in California, ahead of the USDA. I bet those Hollywood movie stars are lining up as we speak."

"Let me see that." I scroll through the post. "This is unreal. How can they do this so fast?"

As I am scrolling, the subhead of another story on the sidebar stops me cold.

Dana Martinez, 26, found dead, former girlfriend of Darwin Speer.

33

Everywhere I Go

Jared

I gaze down from the top of a high bluff. The town of Alta hugs the harbor below. Everything is layered in snow, although it's a clear day, for once, the first sunshine we've had in a very long time.

"What the heck is that?" Mike points to a silver, circular building that dominates the tiny town.

"The Northern Lights Cathedral." The structure looks like a ribbon of spiraling steel rising to the sky. An arctic Tower of Babel.

"I can't decide if it's beautiful or the ugliest building I've ever seen." He laughs. "It sure is different."

He stayed with me through the entire trip. His leg healed rapidly, thanks to the Celox and, perhaps, to me. I could have moved a lot faster without him, but in the end, I decided I wasn't really in that much of a hurry after all.

Mike was good company. He talked a lot, filling the nights and the still air between us with stories of his previous life as a Marine sergeant and then a police officer in Chicago. This suited me. Listening to his constant prattle kept me from my own dark thoughts.

It took a month to get to Trondheim, and then we had to stop when the mountain trails were closed due to a series of severe snowstorms. We spent days on end laid up in a DNT cabin as the snow piled up around us. We played rummy and Go Fish with a deck of cards we found in a drawer or read some of the well-thumbed English-language paperbacks previous hikers had left behind. Mike ate endless sunflower seeds and told me about his travels since his retirement from the force, the people he'd met, and the times he almost got himself killed. The bear had not been his first brush with death. He planned to visit every single country on earth before he died. He only had twelve more to go.

Once the weather cleared, I borrowed a pair of skis from the cabin and we set out again. I had never skied before, but Mike showed me what to do. Once I got the hang of it we made good time, although we stopped often to take in the scenery. Mike took lots of pictures with an old point-and-shoot camera he had in his backpack. I noticed that, like me, he didn't carry a phone.

The closer we got to the Nordland, the less in a hurry I felt. Had Grace and Ralph and everyone moved on with their lives? I thought of them often, especially Grace. Her absence weighed me down, like a stone I carried with me.

"Man, I hope there's a decent hotel down there. I could use a shower and a hot meal," Mike says. We haven't had either in weeks.

We trudge down the hill and stop at the first inn we find, a rambling farmhouse on the outskirts of town. Inside, an elderly woman gives us the key to a large room with a kitchenette and private shower. Mike is thrilled beyond speech with the hot water and clean sheets. I take a shower and Mike gives our clothes to the proprietor to wash. I wear a threadbare bathrobe I find in the closet while Mike cooks the rest of the canned food we'd carried. We eat at a small dinette by the large window as the sun sets.

"We've walked twenty-one hundred kilometers." Mike glances at his watch. He's been keeping track the whole trip. "Thirteen hundred miles. That's kind of crazy. Felt more like five thousand."

"How's the leg?"

"Fine. Good as new. Hey, want some coffee? I want to use up the last of it. And there's a machine here."

"Sure."

Mike makes coffee and comes back to sit at the table.

"What's next for you?" He sips from a mug of steaming liquid. "I mean, after you see your father."

"I think...I'll stay here for a while. It's...where I belong."

"There's no place like home." He puts his cup down. "I gotta tell you, though. I may be way off here, but something tells me you're running from more than just your girlfriend. What is it? Are you wanted by the law?"

"Not the law."

"You can be straight with me, you know. I'm not a cop anymore. We've been together for what...six months now? I've told you my whole life story. But you haven't told me anything about your life. Talk to me. And don't tell me this is all about a bad breakup, because I don't buy it."

I let out a long breath. "Okay. I'm going to see my father, who is a fallen angel chained up in the Abyss, deep in the earth under the island of Seiland, across that channel."

Mike stares at me for a long time. Then he opens his mouth and laughs with gusto.

"I get it," he says. "You don't want to talk about it. Well, I tried." He drinks his coffee. I stare out the window. "You need to know, though...no matter how far you run, you can never get away from yourself."

I look at him.

"That's what you're really running from, isn't it? It doesn't work. I've tried it. Believe me. I'm a lot older than you."

"I doubt that," I murmur.

"Look. Whatever you've got going on in your life, I know it seems bad to you. But running away will not fix it. The way I look at things, you have to accept who you are, what you are, and go from there."

"That's what I'm doing."

"Really? Look, Danny. I consider myself a fairly good judge of character, and I get the sense that you wish you were someone else. That you were a *mistake*, somehow. But can I tell you something? Something that's really, really true? You aren't a mistake. No matter what you think. No matter what you've done. You aren't...forsaken."

Why did he use that word? The word that runs through my mind like a never-ending song. Is he actually speaking a truth that I am unable to accept? No, it's true for everyone else in the world, but not for me. Mike doesn't know what I really am.

And yet, his words begin to replace that endless loop in my brain: *Not forsaken, not forsaken, not forsaken...* I want so badly for this to be true.

After he goes to bed, I stay up and stare at the sky. This is my last day on earth. Above it, anyway. The last time I will see these stars. The last time I'll have a chance to hear the voice of God, a voice that has been silent my entire life. But has the voice truly been silent, or have I not been listening?

But then I remember. I set my course when I collaborated with the enemy. I surrendered. I am an agent of the world's ruin, as have been all my ancestors. This is my fate.

I stay up all night, not wanting to miss a moment of the beauty still left in this world before it all fades to fire and darkness.

~

Early in the morning, I find my clothes, washed and pressed, outside the door of the room. I put them on and, leaving Mike sleeping peacefully, I tiptoe out, closing the door quietly. I slink down the creaky stairs. The front desk is empty so I go out the door unseen.

It's cold and gray as I walk down the road toward town.

The mist falls over everything like a harbinger of gloom. The town is larger than I expected, with neat rows of houses that seem the norm in this country. I head to the harbor and scan the few fishermen in the marina, getting ready to cast off for the day.

At the end of the pier, a small whaler with an outboard motor is tied up next to a larger fishing trawler. I approach the salty-looking fisherman on deck, preparing his nets.

"How much would you take for this boat?" I ask, pointing to the little whaler. I hope he speaks English.

"How much you got?" he replies in a crusty voice.

"Five hundred."

He shakes his head. "Two thousand."

"I don't have that. How about if I rent it?"

"No rent." The fisherman shakes his head. "Two thousand. Cheap."

He seems fairly immovable. I open my mouth to try a different tack when a voice booms from the pier.

"I got this!"

I turn to see Mike hastening toward me, lugging his backpack as well as the one I had left behind. "You forgot this," he says. He sets the backpack down and pulls a wad of kroner out of his pocket.

"No." I hold up a hand to stop him. "You can't come where I'm going."

"Without my money, you aren't going anywhere," he says with a sniff. He turns to the boat owner. "There. Can you add some gas?"

The man pockets the money with a grunt. "Where are you headed?"

"Seiland," I say.

"You want to take this little boat to Seiland? No, no. Why don't you drive to Storsandnes and take the ferry to the hotel?"

"There's a hotel on Seiland?"

"Yes, yes. Closed now. Open in the summer. Most for

the scientists, miners. But the ferry runs all year in good weather. You want to go?"

"No," I say. "I would rather go alone." I turn to Mike. "Thank you. I can't repay you."

"That's okay," he says with a wave. "It's been real, you know? Traveling with you. I wish you…joy, Danny No-Last-Name."

I smile. "You too." Sensing he might want to hug or something, I hasten to get into the boat, pull out the choke and yank on the starter. It turns over on the third try. I push the choke in slowly until the engine stops sputtering. Mike unties me from the dock.

"Do you know how to drive this thing?" he asks.

"I'll figure it out." I put the throttle in reverse and back carefully away from the pier. Mike soon disappears into the mist. I push the tiller to turn the boat and head off in the opposite direction.

I can barely make out the outlines of land on either side of me as I navigate the channel. As long as I don't run into one side or the other, I will eventually come to Seiland. The ailing engine drowns out any other sound on the water, even the hammering of my own heart.

Mike's words still rattle around in my head. *Not forsaken.*

There is still time to turn around, to go back. He might still be there, waiting. We could go get a big breakfast, and I would tell him everything.

I keep going.

A half-hour later, the water grows thick with ice, and I know I'm closer to land. The fjord I want is to the north, farther up the channel, so I motor along the icy edge for a time until I recognize the deepest fjord on this side of the island—so deep that the water doesn't freeze. My breath shortens as I steer the boat into it.

Staying close to the shore, I search along the steep, forbidding rockface for the waterfall that hides the cave entrance. That's how Grace and I went through the last time.

I motor back and forth twice, but I find no waterfall at all. Nor is there any opening in the rock, not even a sliver.

Finally, I stop searching and idle the engine. I bob in the water, wondering what went wrong. Is this the wrong fjord? After all these months, have I come to the wrong place?

Or is the portal to the Abyss now closed?

This is something I had not considered. My road ends here. I have no Plan B. No idea what to do now. I listen for the call of Azazel, but I hear nothing.

And then—something. A low rumble, gathering strength from above. The water shivers, rocking the boat. *He's here. Azazel. He's coming for me.* The rumble grows and the wind strengthens, creating a vortex in the water. The bow of my boat drops dangerously. I grab the throttle and throw it into gear, but the circling current is too strong. I feel the inexorable pull of the water dragging me under. This is Azazel, bringing me to him. I let go of the rudder.

A shadow passes over me. I glance up to see something breaking through the mist. It's black and multi-limbed, like a prehistoric spider. The rumble becomes a roar, but it sounds mechanical now, like an engine at full throttle.

This is not Azazel. This is a helicopter—shining black, with the golden spear emblem on its nose.

I grab the rudder and throw the motor into reverse, hoping to pull the boat out of the vortex. But the motor is not strong enough. The bow is already swamped and there's nothing I can do but jump into the icy water. The chopper lands only a few feet away from me and pontoons burst from its skids. An inflatable raft springs from the open door.

I swim toward the cliff, grab onto a handhold on the rockface, and start climbing. I glance behind me to see the powered raft racing toward me with two men aboard. One drives and the other raises a rifle. A pinging noise echoes off the cliff and something slams into my shoulder. Not a bullet—a dart. Heat spreads down my arm—it seems to weigh a hundred pounds. I keep climbing and force my arm up, although I rapidly begin to lose strength. The top of the cliff is still a hundred feet above. I have little chance of making it, but still I climb, determined to fight until the very end. Another dart pierces my leg. The numbness travels like fire through my body. My arm freezes and my fingers slip from the rock. My legs become like molten lead.

I close my eyes and let go.

34

Battlefield

Grace

I grab the laptop out of Ethan's hands and read the entire story aloud. Dana Martinez died by hanging in a hotel room in Los Angeles. Her death was ruled a suicide. While she had a history of drug use, friends said she'd been off drugs for over a year and she hadn't been depressed. In fact, she'd recently gone back to school. And there was evidence that she'd "changed her mind" and tried to get loose from the rope when it was too late.

I don't believe Dana Martinez killed herself. Darwin Speer killed her. Darwin Speer is a Nephilim, and he cannot control his new power. He will kill again. If more people undergo his treatment, it might happen to them too. It will be like a zombie apocalypse, only worse because these zombies will be strong and beautiful and fast. I'm reasonably certain even I could outrun a zombie. But I'd never outrun a Nephilim.

"You need to call the police," says Bree.

"And what will she tell them?" Ethan asks. "That Darwin Speer killed a woman because he's a Nephilim?"

"We can't let him get away with this."

"You don't even know for sure if the girl was murdered.

The report says suicide."

Bree tosses her hair. "We should get the case reopened."

"Who are you now? Veronica Mars?"

"She's right," I say. "I'll call Bradford, the detective I met in California. He might listen."

Bree claps. "Let's do it now. It's three hours earlier there, anyway. Maybe he's still at work."

We use Ethan's laptop to search for Lieutenant Bradford. It isn't as easy as I thought it would be—Bradford is a common name in California, and I don't remember his first name. I narrow it down to a couple of precincts and call around until I finally get the right place. His phone goes to voicemail, so I leave a message.

He calls me back five minutes later.

"Grace Fortune?"

"You remember me?"

"How could I forget? Craziest case I ever worked. How is everything? How's that friend of yours, the rock star?"

"Oh, he's fine." I swallow hard. "I'm calling to tell you something you might not believe."

"Why am I not surprised? What's up?"

"Well, you know that case about the woman who killed herself, Dana Martinez? Girlfriend of Darwin Speer?"

"Uh, yeah, sure. It's not my case but I read about it."

"I have good reason to believe that Speer murdered her."

I hear a faint cough. "The Mars guy? What makes you think that?"

"Because he recently underwent a procedure that changed his genetic structure in a way that might cause him to commit murder."

There's a pause on the line.

"Come again?"

"I know it sounds a little crazy, but could you at least take a look at the case? I mean, I am dead serious—Speer did this."

"That case is closed, Grace. Even if I did 'look into it,' it would take an act of God to have it re-opened."

Maybe we would get one of those.

"Can't you just say you got an anonymous tip and they should re-examine the evidence? Didn't the family say there was no way Dana would have killed herself?"

"I know, but they always—"

"There was no note. And there was a sign of struggle. Isn't that unusual in suicide cases?"

"You could be right." He pauses, breathing heavily. "Look, I'm in Special Crimes, but I have a buddy in Homicide. I'll run this by him. Now that I think about it, that case was wrapped up pretty fast. I'm not making any promises, but I'll see what I can find out and get back to you."

I thank him profusely and hang up.

"He said he'd do it," I say triumphantly. Bree cheers. Ethan rolls his eyes.

～

I drive home and park on the curb in front of the Lighthouse. A faint light and strains of classical music emanate from the bike shop. Silas must be working late. I hate when he does that. He needs rest and is pushing himself too hard—perhaps even becoming obsessed. I consider going in to tell him about Dana Martinez, but I'm too tired. It can wait until morning.

Halfway up the steps, I change my mind. I should tell him now. Right this minute. I go back down and out onto the street. The door to the shop is locked. I can't see Silas—he must be in the workshop in the back. I rattle the door and bang on the glass but there's no response. He probably has his music turned up too loud.

I give up and return to the stairs. As I start up to the loft, I hear the squeal of tires on the street and hurry back down to street level. A car weaves erratically down the middle of the road. A drunk driver, I immediately assume and duck into the doorway in case it lurches onto the sidewalk.

The car pulls to the curb and almost crashes into my car. My heart skips a beat. The rattling engine idles but no one gets out.

Burglars, casing the place? Bike burglars? Or merely a drunk who happened to pick our building to pass out in front of.

I should go back inside and up to the loft. Maybe call the police. That's what I should do.

But I don't.

I take a breath and step out into the open. At the same time, Silas comes out of the back room, rolling a bike. I dart for the door. He sees me and comes to open it. Out of the corner of my eye, I see the back window of the idling car roll down and a black object emerge that could only be the muzzle of a gun.

Make that a rifle, a semi-automatic. *Pop, pop, pop* explodes in my ears. The front windows of the shop shatter. Silas shouts, hauls the door open, and I dive through. We both sprawl on the floor amid shattered glass. Bullets splinter the back counter, the wall, and my every thought.

I scream. A lot. I lie on top of Silas and hold him down. He tries to get up, but I won't let him.

Then I sing.

35

Knights of Cydonia

Jared

I don't hit the water.

I'm stopped by…something. A counter force, defying gravity, attaches to my coat and wraps around my waist. Instead of falling, I now rise rapidly. The men in the boat shout and point. They probably see what has me, although I can't.

I struggle to turn my head but catch only glimpses of a chain of black fur reaching all the way to the top of the cliff. I am being reeled up as if with a fishing line, smooth and effortless. But by what? Bears?

At the top, I am flung onto the ice. I still can't move but something turns me over. I stare at the furred creatures gathered around me. Several pairs of bright blue eyes peer out from cloaks of black fur. The figures are huge, more than seven feet tall, their faces as white as snow, quite human and eerily beautiful.

Abominable snowmen—that is what they look like. Sasquatch. Yeti. Before I can speak, they pick me up by my arms and legs and run, virtually flying over the glacier at such speed that my stomach lurches into my throat.

And then I am falling—a dead drop into what I assume is a crevasse in the glacier. The white sky disappears. I land almost gently and am set down on a hard surface from which I stare up at a sea of blue waves like the underside of the ocean.

An ice cave inside the glacier.

The smell of fresh blood rises in my nostrils. The floor is littered with bones and ripped animal carcasses. Thick patches of red smear the rock floor and the ice walls. I try to move my arms and legs as the nerves ignite and the numbness wears off. The creatures make noises. I realize they are speaking a language I know—Archean, the language of angels.

These creatures are like no angels I've ever seen before.

They began to paw me with fur-covered hands, examining me.

Then I see teeth. Sharp, like fangs, as mouths open— blood-red mouths. I struggle to rise, to get away, but I am still too weak, and they are too many.

"Do not touch him!"

The voice commands in Archean. At once, they move away, making room for an even larger creature, this one at least nine feet tall. It bends down to inspect me, its blue eyes gleaming. The face, like the others, is very white, quite human.

It speaks in English.

"Welcome, Brother."

~

Brother?

"It is you," says the giant one. His voice is low, no more than a whisper. The others begin to chatter excitedly. "We had hoped for you to come. Jared Lorn. Our brother."

I strain to find my voice. "Who are you?"

"I am Rael." With that, he straightens and removes his fur hood. I gasp. Though his face is human, his head is elongated and covered in silvery-green scales, like that of some prehistoric reptile. "Do you know me now?"

I shake my head.

"Then I must tell you." He sighs and sits on a block of ice that has been carved into a kind of throne. The others disperse—some pick bones up from the floor and gnaw at them, their eyes still on me, curious and hungry. I count fifteen. Several have removed their hoods to reveal the same elongated heads and scaly skin.

I sit up, flexing my fingers in an effort to get sensation back. I am in danger here. I search for an escape, but the crevasse is too high for me to jump, especially in my present condition.

"How did you know my name?" I ask.

"We have known of you for some time. Because you are one of us," Rael says.

"One of you?"

He nods. "You don't recognize us? Of course you don't. We are supposed to be extinct. We should not have survived. But you—you have given us hope. That you were born into this world, that you have survived. They haven't killed you. How is that possible?"

I am thoroughly confused. These creatures looks like nothing I have ever seen before, yet their leader seems to know all about me.

"What are you?" I ask. "Aliens?"

Rael laughs—the others join in. Their laughter is like nails streaking across steel. "We have been called that. And worse. Monsters. Trolls. Elves. Abominations. Giants."

Giants? My heart slows and I feel the blood drain from my face.

"You are…" I cannot even say the word.

"We are *you*, Jared Lorn. The giants, the fallen ones, the gibborim, the rephaim…the *Nephilim*."

Whatever strength I have leaves me. I slump forward, sickened.

Rael laughs again. "Now you see? You thought you were

alone, didn't you? The only one of your kind. You were wrong. It is true that not many of us remain. Our kind tends to kill each other if there's no one else to kill. We must stay in the shadows, in the empty places. We must hide ourselves until the proper time." He pauses and his gaze floats to the ceiling. "Once, we were like you—strong, beautiful, unconquerable. I was born when our ancestors the Merovingians still ruled Europe. When Mohammed first claimed to hear the voice of the angel Gabriel. When the Byzantines controlled the empire, and the Mayans ruled the far corners of the world."

Fourteen hundred years ago.

"We are children of gods." Rael sighs wistfully. "Our fathers, the Watchers, were princes of the divine. They shared their understandings with the humans of earth—the workings of the stars, the bending of metals, the secrets of the plants. The women loved our fathers and our fathers took them for wives and made them great with children. For this, they were condemned and imprisoned in Du'dael. Tartarus. The Abyss. But we survived. We the children of gods. We the Titans. Even the Flood could not destroy us completely. We built empires and forged kingdoms. The God of Israel hated us. His chosen people drove us from the land and murdered our kings. They stole our cities and empires. But we did not all die. We sought new lands, new kingdoms, built new empires—"

"And ravaged the earth," I say. "I read the book. I know how it ends."

"That was our curse," says Rael. "The curse that made us slaves to our own power. We warred against our own. We killed our own. I am of the line of Samyaza, the greatest, the leader of the Enlightenment, when the gods gave their gifts to the humans."

Samyaza. He was the co-leader with Azazel of the Watchers.

"You have lived here all this time?" I ask.

"We have traveled from all the corners of the world to this place. Called by our fathers, as you were called for the time of the Unleashing comes near."

"The Unleashing?"

"You say you read the book," Rael says with a sneer. "It is prophesied that in the seventieth generation, the Watchers will be released. They will rule again. The time is now at hand. You know this. You heard your father calling you."

"You're dreaming," I say. "The Watchers cannot escape from the Abyss. I should know. I've been there."

"You are wrong, Jared Lorn. It was you who made the Unleashing possible."

"No!"

"You gave yourself to the world as a living sacrifice. It is your blood that now works in the hearts of the men who rule the world. You are the messiah of the Unleashing. We have waited for you for over a thousand years."

Living sacrifice. My deal with Darwin Speer. A deal with the devil.

"That is why Darwin Speer comes for you," Rael goes on. "You are his messiah too. He wants you for his own."

I try to think. The helicopter. Speer's henchmen. How did they know where I was?

Mike. It hits me like a thunderbolt. Mike wasn't some random hiker. He's a spy. For Speer. I should have known. He'd said we were brothers. He lied.

These creatures are my true brothers.

"Speer doesn't even believe in the Abyss," I say.

"That was before."

"Before?"

"Before he became one of us."

I shake my head, more to convince myself than Rael. "It's still impossible. The portal is no longer here. It's gone."

"That does not matter." Rael's grotesque smile distorts the beauty of his face. "All he needed was the general location. Now, he will aim his machine at precisely the right place. He will break through."

The collider.

I shake my head. "The collider can't do that."

"You know there is something between the seen and unseen, yes? The barrier between dimensions? Scientists call it the Wall. But we have another name. The Veil." Rael rises to tower over me. "The machine will break the Veil."

He is so close to me now, I can feel his breath, hot like a vapor on my face. He switches to Archean.

"When that happens, our fathers will be free."

A sharp pain pierces my chest and radiates outward to electrify every nerve in my body. No, this is *not* what I had planned. I intended to go into the Abyss, into my punishment, deserving of that end. I never meant to allow the Watchers to come out.

Rael withdraws, his expression puzzled. His head tilts to one side.

"Why are you not pleased, Jared Lorn? Is not this what you wanted?"

"No," I say. "No." I look up. I have to jump, have to try, at least. "I must go back. To warn them. To stop Speer—"

"Stop him?" Rael's voice rises to a bellow. "Stop him? What are you talking about? You made this, Jared Lorn! You sacrificed your own body for us. You are our messiah, Son of Azazel!"

The others chant, *Messiah, Son of Azazel* in the Archean tongue. They pick up the bones scattered about and beat them against the ice, which shivers from the hideous racket. I put my hands over my ears, but still it cuts into my brain like a hot blade.

"Hey, Danny!"

The chanting breaks off. I look up to see a small brown head braced against the light spilling down from the crevasse. I frown. Mike?

He waves. "Need some help?"

Mike. The traitor has come to deliver me to Speer. But

he is no match for these creatures.

"No," I yell. "Go away, Mike! Don't—"

But it's too late. He's already jumped.

36

Game of Survival

Grace

I sing the AngelSong, the song that is always in my head, even now. Notes and words in a language I don't even know, and yet it vibrates through every corner of me, so that my body disappears and I become nothing but sound.

The shooting stops. I close my mouth and the Song dissolves. There is a moment, as brief as the space between heartbeats, when I sense my life hanging in the balance.

I see them, then—angels all around us, bright as morning stars, a room full of suns filling every empty space. It is beautiful and frightening, a light so complete that no Dark would stand a chance.

The engine revs and the car peels away.

The Light begins to fade. Objects come into view—bikes, broken glass, and Silas. I stand and as my lungs expand, there is no pain in my chest or anywhere else. I glance at my body, my arms and hands. No blood. No bullet holes.

I have survived another shooting. This is getting ridiculous.

Silas groans and rolls over, holding his chest. I bend down to help him up.

"Hey, are you okay?"

He rises slowly, his face pale with shock. He nods cautiously.

"Thank God," I say. "I was afraid you'd been shot—"

He turns me to face him and studies me carefully. Then he pulls me into his arms and hugs me so fiercely, I can barely breathe.

"Thank God," he says, his voice like a sob. "Thank God."

His body trembles, and I am aware of his love pouring out of him into my soul.

"What the—" From the other side of the shattered window, Penny gazes in horror at the destruction.

Silas releases me and I almost fall down again. Every inch of my body trembles.

"Call nine-one-one," he says, although we can already hear the distant sirens.

Here we go again. I am a little tired of this *Britney Spears.*

"This was a professional hit," I say. "No way was it random."

"Torega," Penny whispers.

And then the building is bathed in flashing red lights.

～

How is it that I managed to find myself in the middle of yet another debacle? Just lucky, I guess.

I remember the name my mother had originally given me. *Mallory.* Misfortune. My curse.

Silas and I ride in a police cruiser to the station to give our statements. The detective assigned to the case is the same one who had covered the school shooting. Detective Marconi.

"Grace Fortune," he says when he sees me. "Are you still getting shot at?"

Buffalo detectives are hilarious.

I tell him I had barely arrived home when the car pulled

up and opened fire.

"Are you sure this wasn't random?"

"I'm sure. It has something to do with the drug bust at Silo City." I don't mention the whole Satanic ritual part—that had been left out of the media reports.

"Okay, well, I'll look into it and inform Narcotics that we might have cartel involvement. They'll want to talk to you at some point. Do you have someplace safe to go? Otherwise, I can put you in protective custody."

"Thanks. I have a place."

Ripley and Penny are in the waiting area with Silas when I'm released.

"We came in the van," Ripley says. "To make sure you were okay."

"I'm okay."

Silas gives me a long hug. "Maybe the bike shop wasn't such a good idea."

"It was a great idea. We'll fix it. We'll open it again. In time for summer." His smile is bleak. "They will not win," I say through gritted teeth. And I wasn't only talking about the cartel. I mean *them*. Every evil force that is trying to mess with our lives.

～

We climb into the PsychoVan and Ripley drives off, taking a route to the Hobbit Hole I can only call "circuitous."

"Mace told someone," I say.

"No way," Penny says. "He wouldn't."

"You don't know him as well as you think you do. He could be secretly working for the cartel. He knows about the bike shop. He knows where we live."

"No way. And I told you not to open the shop. Anyone could have seen you. The cartel has eyes everywhere. Mason didn't do this."

Mace is equally emphatic. As soon as we get to the Hobbit Hole, I accuse him of being a mole. He denies it and starts crying.

"He didn't do anything." Penny continues to defend him. "There are all kinds of kids hanging out at the bike shop. One of them probably ratted you out."

"Why are you always taking his side?" I yell.

"I will turn myself in to him. I'd let him kill me if it would stop this," Mace says. "If it will prove to you I had nothing to do with it!"

"Fine. Do it!"

"Calm down." Silas puts an arm around me.

"Let's all sit and discuss this." Even Ralph is rattled. "Emilia, hot chocolate is in order."

I sit with Silas on the couch, still shaking. Ripley sits on the edge of an ottoman. Penny and Mace are on the floor, way too close together. She puts her arm around him, comforting him. How bizarre this is. I can't help but think of the night I walked into my apartment and saw Penny on the floor, bleeding, with Torega standing over her. And Mace's knife at my throat, his voice in my ear—

I remember something.

Emilia hands out cups of hot chocolate.

"Now." Ralph settles into his chair. "Mason swears he has had no contact with Torega. He has rejected Satan and been forgiven. That much we know."

"Then let him prove it," I say.

"How?" Mace says. "I'll do anything."

"Okay, then. That night you and Torega attacked us, he told you something about me. He said, 'with her blood, we will have all the power we need.' Do you remember that?"

A guilty look creeps across Mace's face. "Yeah. He needed the blood…for an offering." He pauses and glances at Penny. "That's why we kidnapped you."

"But why *my* blood? Why me?"

"It was required by Ogun."

"Ogun?" says Silas.

"All the cartel bosses offer sacrifices to their gods. There are many gods of Santeria. Ogun is the patron god of criminals."

"There's a patron god for criminals?" Disgust edges Penny's voice.

"What's Santeria?" I ask.

"It's their religion. Kind of a cross between Catholicism and voodoo," says Mace. "You have to make offerings in exchange for protection and power. Ogun demands blood offerings. Animals. Goats, chickens. And sometimes...humans."

"Human sacrifices?" Penny whispers.

"In Mexico, people disappear, mostly children, and no one looks for them. They're just gone. La Parca believes his sacrifices are the reason for his success. He's never been caught."

"Have you heard of Ogun?" I ask Ralph.

He nods grimly. "Ogun is the god of iron...and rum. The proponent of war and metal-making. Swords in particular. Who does that sound like?"

"Azazel," I say.

"Exactly."

"So Ogun and Azazel are the same?" asks Penny.

"We don't know the exact relationship between the pagan gods and the Watchers," says Ralph. "But it seems they are closely linked. Remember, Ogun is also a god of rum— a drug. A natural fit for drug dealers."

"But Torega said he wanted *my* blood," I say. "Not Penny's. Penny was already knocked out. They could have taken her. But they waited for me."

"Obviously, they believe your blood has some sort of special power," says Ralph. "Often, the cartels target people with special gifts. College students, for instance, because they are considered smart. The higher the status of the victim, the greater the power gained. Right, Mason?"

Mace nods.

"You have such a gift, Grace. Your Song. Azazel knows about it. So do all the demons associated with Torega. And therefore, Torega himself. And La Parca."

"We have to stop this." Penny raises her tear-streaked face, her eyes shining like glass. "We need to find his shrine and destroy it."

"His shrine?" I say.

"If we destroy the shrine, we destroy his power."

"She's right," says Mace. "Most of the drug lords have shrines where they do their rituals. But I don't know where Torega's shrine to Ogun is. He never let me go there."

"So we find it and destroy it," says Penny.

"We cannot be a party to the destruction of private property No matter how evil." Ralph folds his hands as if in prayer. "This is a job for the police."

"I agree," I say. "So, Mace, if you really want to prove your innocence, call him."

"What?" Mace straightens, alarmed.

"Call Torega. Tell him you know how to find me."

"Are you crazy?" Penny blurts.

"It's me Torega wants," I say. "Not Mace. Not Penny. Me. So let's give him what he wants. I'll talk to Marconi. We'll set up a sting like they do on TV."

"No way," says Silas. "You can't do this—put yourself in the hands of the enemy."

"Paul testified before emperors and kings," I say.

"Paul was executed!"

"This is a job for law enforcement—" Ralph begins.

I cut him off. "Mace, you can still contact Torega, can't you?"

Mace looks around nervously. "I don't know if he has changed his phone…"

"Call him. Tell him you want to give him an offering in exchange for your own life. Tell him that if he will cancel the hit on you, you will give him me."

"This is madness." Ralph frowns.

"Absolutely not!" Silas coughs with the effort to raise his voice.

But my mind is made up.

37

Lion

Jared

Horror seizes my insides as I watch Mike descend through the crevasse. Yet, as he falls, his body changes, lengthens, takes on mass and muscle. His cropped dark hair grows and lightens to a sunburst around his head. He lands on his feet, his brown skin shimmering like polished bronze.

Michael.

I gasp. How could I not have known him?

He draws his sword. It flares in the ice, blazing with fire and light. The Nephilim scatter in fear, shielding their eyes. Michael aims the sword at Rael, who stands his ground.

"What are you doing here, Angel?" he bellows, although his body trembles with fear. The fur of his cloak begins to smoke and curl.

"I came for the kid." Michael's voice is a curious mix of archangel and human Mike. I wonder how I never heard it before. His power to conceal his true nature for months on end—it's astonishing. As is the reason for it. To protect *me*.

Rael roars like a wounded bear. His arm shoots out, impossibly long, and his fingers encircle my neck. He forces me to my knees and his claws dig into my flesh, cutting my breath off.

"Stay back or he dies!"

I try to dislodge his grip, but his strength overpowers me. I hang helplessly, my eyes on Michael, who continues to advance. The flaming sword makes the ice around us pop and crack.

"Let him go," the archangel says.

"I will kill him!"

"No, you won't."

I'm pretty sure he would. Rael's grip tightens and his claws puncture my neck. My breath gurgles as blood trickles into my lungs.

"Elohim has claimed him." Michael continues his slow advance. *Faster! I'm dying here.* Rael stumbles backward, dragging me with him.

"Liar."

My vision becomes a flashing aura as sharp daggers of pain shot through my body. I have known pain before, but it has never touched me greatly, not like this. This is the prelude to death.

And yet, through this haze of agony, the words Michael spoke begin to penetrate. *Elohim has claimed him.* Could this be true? For I am no different from Rael, no different from any other monster in that cave.

"*Let him go!*" Michael's voice rises to thunder. The sword flares and a tongue of flame leaps toward us. Rael gasps and releases me as his fur cloak bursts into flame. He screams in rage.

I collapse, breathing blood as a numbness spreads to my limbs. I close my eyes—there is no difference now, everything is gray and black. Then something presses against my throat, a heat like a brand. My body jerks and flinches as air floods into my lungs. I open my eyes to see Michael standing over me, his free hand wrapped around my neck.

"Better?" He pulls me up and tosses me onto his back. "Hang on."

The others rush in, screeching in fury, their claws out and

teeth bared. They are no match for Michael's sword which swings in a wide, lethal arc and ignites their cloaks with streaks of flame. They shriek and fall back, rolling on the ground.

"Jared!" Rael rushes toward us, his cloak gone, burned to ash. I see his body for the first time—the massive, muscular torso, the legs and arms twice the length of a man. Silvery green scales have replaced his skin, and snake-like tentacles protrude from his shoulders and sides, giving the appearance of wings. A spiked, serpent tail sweeps around his powerful legs. His fingers and toes are long and sharp, like talons.

Part man, part monster.

Rael's voice rises to a hoarse roar. "Jared, we are your destiny. You look human now, but one day, you will be like us. Condemned to the shadows and cursed by God. But all that will change when we are joined with our fathers. We will become our true selves again. We will be free and you will be our king, Jared. You will rule the New Earth—"

"Enough!" Michael bellows, raising the sword. Melting ice drips on my head and puddles on the floor.

"Do you want to know why I came to rescue this one?" Michael says. "Because long ago, even after he knew what he was and what he would become, he chose a different path. Not because he feared death but because he feared a life without love. Without peace. Without joy. You, cursed ones, were born without love or peace or joy. Your only craving is for power. Dominion. Blood. But you too can choose another path, the Way of Elohim. Most of you won't. This one is the first of your kind to do it—and probably the last."

Michael sheathes the sword. The cave darkens. He carries me to the spot directly beneath the opening. I remember then how I carried him on my back when we climbed to the ridge to see the Northern Lights. His muscles compress as they gather strength, and with an explosion of power, he springs upward, to the top of the crevasse. He lands on the ice five feet from the opening.

I slide off his back and peer down at the scene below. The Nephilim gather, chattering like lunatic birds while chunks of ice fall upon their heads. Rael mournfully wails my name, drawing it out into a lament.

"Jaaaareeed…"

I look at Michael. He is Mike again. Sitting opposite me on the ice, he rubs the top of his head and smiles. "Surprised?"

"I should have known."

"Yes. You should have."

I take another breath. Breathing has become a new experience. "Is it true? What you said?"

He sighs. "Elohim sent me to take you from the fire once before, remember? I admit I argued against it. I thought you would be nothing but trouble, and frankly, I was right."

"After what I did—"

"You should know by now that nothing you do is a surprise to Elohim. And there is nothing you can do to thwart His will. He is still in control. He will have the final say."

I glance below, at the screaming Nephilim. "Will you leave them to die?"

"They will not die. Not yet."

I nod and raise a hand to my throat. The skin is unbroken. Healed.

"Oh, one more thing." Mike grabs the back of my neck. A sharp pain knifes the base of my skull and I gasp. He withdraws his hand to reveal a small metal disk in his palm.

"It's a tracking device. They inserted it when you were on the yacht. That's how they found you."

"I thought it was—"

"You thought it was me." He shakes his head, disappointed. "I was sent to protect you. But Speer is still after you. He needs more blood."

"Why doesn't he simply use his own? He's a Nephilim now."

"He's discovered that there are complications. The new cells are mutating. He needs constant infusions. And they've been unable to synthesize your DNA. He's begun to realize that your genes don't work like ordinary genes so he needs you back. You signed a contract. Legally, he can milk you like a cow for the rest of your life. You should have read the fine print."

"What do I do now?"

"Go home," he says, getting to his feet. "Your family needs you."

I stand up and glance once more into the crevasse. "How long does it take—to become like them?"

He laughs. "Don't worry, you won't live that long." He grips my shoulder, and suddenly I am surrounded in a light so bright it seems as though I have fallen into the center of the sun.

When the brightness fades, I stand on the street before the burned hulk of the Mansion.

And spring has come.

PART FIVE

ABSOLUTION

38

Pressure

Angel

Speer hurls his beloved pinball machines into the bulkhead of the yacht, irreparably damaging both. He rages at the man standing before him—the leader of the team that tried to capture Jared in Seiland. The man's body is rigid with fear, his hands clasped in front of him as if facing a firing squad.

"How could you let him get away?"

We had him." The man speaks with a German accent. "But he was rescued."

"By whom?"

"I…don't know. They looked like…abominable snow-men."

"What?" The veins in Speer's neck pop dangerously

"We have pictures." The man produces a smart phone from his jacket pocket. He searches for images then holds the phone up for his boss. The images are fuzzy and indistinct, a chain of furred blobs linked together, hauling Jared Lorn up the cliff.

Speer stares at the phone, then snatches it away and flings it into the broken pile of pinball machines.

"Take your crew back there," he says. "Find those things. Whatever they are. Maybe they still have him."

"Do you think he's still…alive?"

"He'd better be."

"Darwin." Lucille's voice floats from a doorway. She wears a black kimono, her hair undone as if she'd just woken up. "What's all the noise about?"

"They lost him," Speer says. "They had him, then they lost him. And the tracker's gone too." He sinks onto the couch, balls his fists, and smashes them onto his knees so hard he makes bruises.

"You need to get a grip on yourself." Lucille waves her hand to dismiss the man. She sits beside Speer on the couch, pulls one of his fists away and holds it tight.

"If we don't find him…I can't…"

"I know, but we will find him. You have the best people in the world working for you."

"I should have taken more." Speer throws his head against the back of the couch with such violence it rocks backward. "I should have bled him dry. I should have chained him to the bed. I thought I had him, you know? He was so docile. He'd given up. I thought he was all mine."

"Darling, you're cured. You've seen the test results yourself. The disease has not come back, no matter the side effects. Isn't that enough for you?"

"No." He speaks through clenched teeth. "No. It's not enough now. I like being this—who I am now. I need it. I *crave* it. I can't live without it."

Lucille's eyes widen slightly and her head tilts. Her mouth turns down at the corners. "You *can* live without it," she whispers. There is fear in her voice.

"You don't understand," Speer says. "You've never understood. You've always been beautiful. You've always had men falling at your feet. It's so easy for you. I can't go back to what I was, don't you understand that? All I've done, all I've built, was to become this. I'm not going back."

"I see something!"

The spotter tells the chopper pilot to hover and shines the spotlight down on a clump of something that appears to be moving across the ice.

"Bears, maybe" says the spotter. "No. Two-legged, upright. People in fur coats. Huge people. They're headed for the mountain."

"Is the kid with them?"

"Can't tell."

"Don't shoot them. Use the net gun."

The chopper drops low and follows the figures, who suddenly break apart and scatter. The spotter draws a net gun, aims, and shouts at the pilot.

"Bank left!"

The aircraft swerves and the spotter launches the net. One of the running figures falls, entangled.

"Got one!"

He launches again and another goes down. But the first one has already torn the net open and escaped.

"Nets won't hold 'em. Switch to rifles!"

"Don't kill any of them but keep them away from the mountain," the pilot orders.

The three men in the back of the chopper fire a haze of bullets around the running Nephilim. Some are hit, but they are up in a flash and race away again.

"It's not working," the spotter shouts. "Try the grenades."

The chopper banks sharply and the men launch three grenades at the mountain, over the heads of the Nephilim, who have already started to climb. They are blown backward, momentarily stunned. A few are on fire. They bellow in fear, and their cries echo hellishly against the rockface.

"Now! Net 'em!"

The spotter launches more nets to trap a few of the

stunned Nephilim. One of them rises before the hovering chopper and raises his arms in surrender.

"Set down," he says. "They're surrendering."

The men jump to the ice and quickly surround the creatures huddled around the one with his arms up—Rael. The men gasp at the sight of this huge, outlandish being.

"Let them go," Rael shouts. "Take me."

"What the heck?" says one of them under his breath. "What are these things?"

"Aliens," says another.

"Where is Jared Lorn?" the leader shouts.

"If you let the others go, I will find him for you."

"How?"

"Take me to Speer. I will speak only to him."

"He won't fit in the chopper," says the spotter. He tells the pilot to radio for another aircraft—the biggest one they can find.

39

Miracle

Grace

He walks in the door. Just like that.

No one heard the door open or close. Ripley never saw him on the surveillance feed. It's like he materialized out of thin air.

I stare at him, convinced he is a ghost. He's so pale, his skin is almost as white as his hair. His eyes blaze blowtorch blue, the only color about him. He wears canvas pants and a coat over a gray t-shirt that reads, "Berserker Training."

I take in all these details in a frozen instant, unsure what to do or say.

He speaks. "Can I come in?"

I don't remember walking or even running but am suddenly wrapped in his arms. His body is cool, even cold, perpetuating the ghost theory. But he's real. Totally, completely real. I can see him, smell him, and touch him. I never want to let go.

I pull myself away and beat my fists against his chest so hard he actually stumbles back.

"Where the *Fred Flintstone* have you been?"

"Jared!" Penny screams from across the room. She runs and leaps into his arms. Everyone else comes running, even

Ripley, all talking at once, shouting, and crying. Ralph's eyes are misty and he babbles like a child, unable to put two words together. Silas, who had been napping, comes out of his room and blinks. He wraps an arm round Jared's neck as tears stream down his face. It's some kind of crazy miracle.

"So," I say once all the hugging is over with. "You'd better start explaining right now."

He tells us some of his story, with me and Ralph and everyone else interrupting constantly to ask questions and make loud exclamations like *Holden Caulfield* and other literary favorites. Emilia practically spoon-feeds him hot chocolate and then beef stroganoff, which he tries without success to refuse. A few times, I think he'll be sick. As he talks, he relaxes and a trace of color returns to his barren cheeks. He stops twitching at every random noise.

Iceland. Norway. A remnant of thousand-year old Nephilim. Michael the archangel appearing as a human to travel with him, watch over him, rescue him. It's too much to take in. And yet there is much he hasn't explained. Why he went on that boat in the first place. As the first blush of joy at seeing him again starts to fade, I am suddenly overwhelmed by unanswered questions.

"But do they really believe Speer will open the Abyss?" Penny asks.

"They believe it," Jared says.

"It's like the mother of all conspiracy theories." Ripley is, of course, ecstatic. "I knew it was true all along."

This must be a dream. It can't be real that he's here, in the Hobbit Hole. Back from the dead...again. Shannon's accusations hover at the corner of my mind. I need to know the truth. But at this moment, all I care about is that he's back and he's alive.

"Uh, hey—" I turn to see Mace standing in the kitchen entrance, looking uncomfortable. "Don't mean to interrupt but I should probably be going now."

"No," says Penny.

"What is he—?" Jared jumps up, his skin flaring. He rounds on Mace, who steps back with eyes wide, hands raised in surrender.

"It's okay," Penny says. "He's with us now." She goes to Mace. "You aren't leaving."

Jared looks at me, questioning. I coax him back to his seat and explain all about Mace. He relaxes, the glow dying away.

"Look," Mace says, "I appreciate all you folks have done for me, but it's really time for me to go. I don't want to take your room—"

"No," Jared says. "It's…fine. I don't sleep that much, anyway."

Mace lets out a breath he's probably been holding for an hour.

Later, after everyone else goes to bed, Jared and I sit together on the couch. I wrap myself around him, trying to touch every part of him at once. He holds me like he's holding a life belt in the middle of a raging ocean. We don't speak for a long time. So much remains unsaid between us.

"I missed you," he says.

"Duh." I sound like I'm sixteen again, meeting him for the first time, when I was overwhelmed by his beauty, his presence, and his power over my body and my soul. Yet there is something irrevocably different about him—like he has shed some of his angel-ness. He seems depleted, finite. *Human.*

"How did you get back here so fast?" I ask. "Michael did some kind of angel-thing?"

"I guess so." He breathes and his chest moves against mine. "I'm sorry, Grace. For leaving you. For not…believing."

"I forgive you. Well, I *will* forgive you, eventually. How's that?"

"Good enough."

I kiss him. He doesn't pull away. This, at least, hasn't

changed.

"I need to know something." I sit up to put space between us. "Shannon told me you were working with Speer, that you'd partnered with him to make millions of dollars selling your DNA. She said you...*wanted* to do it, that you signed a contract."

Jared averts his eyes. "I did agree to it. They tied me up, they drugged me...but that's no excuse. At the time, I didn't think I had a choice. I thought it was my destiny."

"Your destiny?"

"It's who I am. I couldn't escape it."

"And that's why you went to the Abyss."

"Yes."

"And Darwin Speer is really a Nephilim now."

He closes his eyes, unable to answer.

I tell him about Dana Martinez and my suspicions regarding her 'suicide.' He leans forward and buries his face in his hands. His body trembles and I hear a muffled sob. It's the worst sound I've ever heard.

"Once he gets a taste for it—" He seems to want to shake the thought away. "I should have died. Why didn't I die? Why did Michael—"

"Maybe you aren't as forsaken as you thought." I push a lock of hair out of his eyes. "Maybe God has a plan even for you."

"What can I do? Only damage. Anyone who comes near me ends up dead."

"Hey, I'm still here. Not dead yet." I grin.

He doesn't laugh.

"Jared...there's more."

He raises his head to look at me. I tell him about the attack on the Lighthouse. His eyes widen, his skin flickers.

"That's why we're living here. The loft is still a crime scene." Before he can speak, I launch into our plan to destroy Torega's shrine. "We think if we destroy the shrine, he'll believe he's lost his protection and leave town, close up shop. Apparently it's happened before. But we don't know where the shrine is."

"How will you find it?"

I tell him, and he shakes his head. "Ralph agreed to this?"

"Not exactly, but he knows he can't stop me. I'm twenty-one and a legal adult. Besides, he knows there's no other way. But don't worry. I have the bracelet." I hold up my wrist, still encircled by the tracker bracelet Ralph gave me two years ago. "I still can't figure out how to get it off. Anyway, no matter where they take me, Ripley will be able to find me. The plan is foolproof."

"When is this happening?"

"The day after tomorrow."

"So soon?"

"Yeah."

His head drops back. "That's what he meant."

"Who?"

"Michael. This is why he sent me home."

I sigh and put a hand on the side of his face. "I'm glad he did."

40

Start Again

Jared

I want to rest, talk more with Grace, and get everything off my chest—to unburden my soul about the journey I've taken. But I don't have time to do that. The next morning, she and Silas go to the police station for a briefing and final instructions about the sting operation they have planned. I want to go with them, but she won't let me.

Penny goes to church to pray. She's found an old church in the Broadway district called The Church of the Transformation. It's been abandoned, as so many churches in this city have been, but a small group of former parishioners continue to go there to pray. Mace goes with her. It's weird seeing him all cleaned up and filled out, thanks to Emilia's beef stroganoff, no doubt. And his genuine affection for Penny, a girl he almost killed, is mind-boggling. God does work in mysterious ways.

With Ripley in the Lair and Emilia in the kitchen, I decide to talk to Ralph. The Hobbit Hole isn't likely to be this quiet again.

He reads in his favorite chair, as usual, a cup of tea on the table beside him. I sit opposite him. He looks at me, closes his book, and takes off his glasses.

"What's up?" He picks up his teacup and takes a sip. "Is everything okay?"

"I had this dream. In Iceland."

"Oh?" Ralph's eyebrows wiggle a little. "Tell me about it."

I tell him about the ritual, the fire and the dancing and the chanting of the word "babble." "Since then, I've had more memories. In one of them, there was a woman wearing a red cloak, and her skin was red too. She was riding—a goat."

"A goat?"

"It looked like it was covered in blood. Or maybe it was the firelight. I'm not sure."

"Was the woman in red holding anything?"

"A cup. Like a chalice."

Ralph sets down his tea. "It could be a reference to Revelation 17, when the Scarlet Woman, sometimes called the Whore of Babylon, appears riding a horned beast."

"Why would I dream this?"

"Jared...what happened before the ritual began. Do you remember?"

I think back to being inside the house and following the noises to the balcony. And then I recall something else.

"Powder." I frown at the memory. "White powder. Someone...or something...blew it in my face."

"I see." Ralph is silent a moment. When he speaks, his voice is gentle yet tinged with doom. "Jared, I don't believe that what you experienced was a dream."

My stomach tightens like I've been punched. This is what I feared.

"The powder could have been Burandanga, better known as Devil's Breath. A potent hallucinogenic drug. It renders a person incapacitated, although still conscious, and highly suggestible. It's popular with street thugs, who use it to get their victims to hand over their valuables. It also causes amnesia, so the victims rarely remember what happened to them. Did you see who blew the powder in your face?"

"It was a woman. Maybe Lucille."

"You're sure it was a woman?"

"Yes. It wasn't Speer, that I know. But I don't get it. What was this ritual about? What did it have to do with me?"

Ralph leans back in his chair. I don't like the expression on his face.

"It sounds like the occult religion Thelema, once very fashionable among the intellectual elites. The purpose is to unite the woman they call Babalon—that was most likely the word *babble* that you heard—with the Great Beast or Dragon in order to bring about the birth of a so-called Moonchild. In other words, the Antichrist."

"Unite?" I said. "You mean…"

"Think hard, Jared. Who was she? The woman with the goat? Was it Lucille?"

I shake my head as if I can loosen the memories. I see her clearly in my mind—the red skin, the red lips, the red hood, and the shadowed eyes. But suddenly, there is a new detail, a strand of hair plastered to her cheek. Red hair, not dark like Lucille's.

The blood drains from my face and pools in my throat.

"It was Shannon Snow."

~

Ralph is too stunned to say anything. I'm glad, because I can barely think anymore. I want to go to sleep and wake up to find that none of this really happened.

"How is it possible?" I whisper. "She couldn't have been there. She'd left Iceland the day before."

"Are you sure of that? Did you see her leave?"

"No."

"What day was that?"

"I don't remember. The day I sent that email to you."

"Ah, yes. I remember now. But it was a day or two later

that Shannon called Grace and asked to meet with her. So perhaps she didn't leave Iceland right away, after all."

A coldness seeps into my bones. "Why would she do this? We got rid of Lilith—"

"This is not Lilith we're dealing with. This is, I believe, the Whore of Babylon. A far worse demon. Our getting rid of Lilith merely paved the way for this one. Or maybe it was there all the time, waiting for Lilith to leave so it could take over. It might even have helped us push Lilith out."

I lean back on the sofa, my hands over my face. "Okay, so they used me for their ritual. Shannon and Lucille. But it doesn't mean anything. It's a stupid, occult ritual that has no power—"

"Jared."

I look at him.

Ralph takes a long moment before speaking again. "She's pregnant."

The word takes a long time to penetrate my brain.

"Who?"

"Shannon."

Cords of grief wrap around my chest and tighten so I can't breathe. This is my worst nightmare. My ruination.

"We can't tell Grace about this," I say, when finally I am able to speak at all.

Ralph shakes his head. "You must tell her, Jared. Not only for her sake, but for yours."

"I can't do that. It will destroy her. It will destroy…everything. Besides, she has enough to deal with right now."

"Do you prefer to live a lie? There is no future in that."

"Ralph, please. Promise me you won't tell her. What does it matter anyway? The woman has a husband. He's most likely the father, isn't he?"

He sighs, and in that moment, he seems to age ten years. "Yes, it's certainly possible. I won't tell her. But you are making a mistake."

"I've already made so many. One more will not make that much difference."

41

Fighting Furies

Grace

It's cold the day I drive to Silo City. I wear a heavy green cardigan and red boots, but I'm still freezing. I've replaced my angel necklace with a small, black, heart-shaped pendant the cops gave me. It contains a microphone and recorder so the detective in charge, Don Beranski, can hear what's going on—assuming they can get the radio van close enough. Beranski tells me not to lose it, because he borrowed it from a precinct in Queens and it cost a fortune. Under the circumstances, I find that hilarious.

I insist that Jared be allowed in the surveillance van. Beranski is against it, but he goes along because I won't back down and neither will Jared. I need to know that he is nearby if something goes wrong.

Silo City looks deserted, except I know it isn't. Cops in unmarked cars are parked all around the entrance and along the road. If Torega comes for me, they plan to follow him back to his "lair" where we assume the shrine is located. And a whole big stash of drugs, we hope.

Mace has told Torega that I go to Silo City every Friday afternoon. It's a ritual for me, like visiting a gravesite on an appointed day—and it's how Mace found me in the first place. He kept his voice reasonably calm on the phone, although he sweated and fidgeted and practically hyperventilated. He was terrified Torega would want to meet in person and make him shoot up to prove he was still an addict. We gathered around and prayed him through that call. Torega bought it, in the end. Maybe his desire to get to me overcame his caution.

If Mace is putting on an act, he's a stellar actor...yet I'm still not sure we can trust him. But Silas, Ralph and Penny are praying for me, Ripley is tracking my bracelet, Jared is close by and, as Ralph loves to remind me, God is in control.

I leave the Mini in the gravel parking lot and walk past the chain-link fence to the embankment that leads to the river. This is the same route I took when I met Mace. The grass is dead with pockets of old snow. The wind howls, rippling the water. Spring in Buffalo.

I sit on a block of concrete—the same one I sat on the last time. My heart beats so fast I think it will burst through my ribs. Can Jared hear it? It's a weird thing between us, how we hear each other's heartbeats at the strangest times. My legs shake and my breath comes in short bursts. I stick earbuds in my ears. They aren't connected to anything but it has to look as though I can't hear anything around me.

Shadows lengthen on the river. The wind penetrates my sweater and prickles my skin. I hug my knees to my chest in an attempt to block out the cold, then press my face to my knees and pray.

Finally, I hear the crunch of snow and the faint crackle of footsteps on dead grass. I keep my head down, pretending I'm unaware, lost in my own thoughts. Fear constricts my throat.

Lord, make me brave.

It's quick and sudden like a car crash, only quieter. I'm jerked backward, a bag slides over my head, my arms are pinned. I scream and twist, trying to fight off my unseen assailants. They stuff part of the bag in my mouth and wrap tape around my head. My arms and ankles are bound. I am immobile.

It all happens as expected, and yet it's surreal, like a nightmare. They carry me roughly up the embankment and throw me into what I presume is the trunk of a car. I've been in this situation before. What little light I can see filtering through the bag disappears as the trunk closes. Doors slam. An engine rumbles and the car lurches into motion.

I pray.

Though I walk through the valley of the shadow of death…
I will fear no evil, for You are with me.

This is what the shadow of death feels like.

It's a long ride—too long—with many twists and turns. Evasive driving, I realize. Do they know they're being followed? This worries me. My body rolls from one side of the trunk to the other and I gag at the strong, acrid stench of gasoline. I focus on breathing through the bag, pursuing every molecule of air I can. Panic will make it harder. Every intake of breath is a prayer. I asked for this. I willingly stepped into this pit and can do nothing now but trust. Trust the cops to find me. Trust that Mace isn't lying. Trust God to rescue me.

It seems an eternity before the car swerves and screeches to a halt. The doors open and slam shut again. Hurried voices speak Spanish and then the trunk clicks. I'm pulled out and hauled up several steps into someplace warmer. I smell incense, and very loud African drum music rattles my ribs. My captors drop me on the floor, then unwind the tape and remove the bag from my head.

I blink as my eyes adjust. I'm in a cramped, smoke-filled living room, crammed with strange figurines and idols and skulls, all elaborately decorated. A woman scurries by carrying small jars. She glances at me but looks away quickly and says something to the men who stand over me, arms folded, smiling in satisfaction.

"It's her." I recognize Torega's voice above the drum music. He looks so different from the school boy I knew. He has a mustache, and his hair is long and stringy. He wears a heavy gold cross on a chain around his neck. Ironic. "At last." He kneels and puts his hand on my neck, tracing the scar left by Azazel. "The mark of Ogun," he whispers. "So it is true. She has been touched by the god. This is why her voice has magic."

Wrong, moron.

"Did you see the other one? The white-haired one?" Torega questions his men.

"No. He's gone. Disappeared. That's why she goes to the Silos. To mourn him."

"What about the cops?"

"We lost them."

A weight presses into my chest, squeezing my heart. *Lost them?*

"I knew that *culero* Mace was setting me up." Torega gets to his feet. "Put her downstairs and watch her. We must wait until La Parca gets here."

"La Parca is coming?" The others buzz with excitement.

"Yes. I told him we would have her. He wants to see for himself."

La Parca is coming. Does Beranski know? Or did Torega's men really lose him? Is my bracelet working? If it isn't, I will spend the last few hours of my life in this house of horrors.

I'm lifted again and carried downstairs to a basement. It's dark but for a string of colored bulbs hanging from the ceiling and a few smoking candles. It smells like blood and death. This must be the shrine, where they do their sacrifices. Skulls—animal and human—line the walls. Candles and bowls filled with powders and liquids crowd the tops of small tables. In one corner, a life-sized skeleton is dressed in a multicolored robe and flower garlands, a crown on its ghastly skull head.

The woman I'd seen upstairs squats before a cauldron in the middle of the room. She sprinkles something onto its contents—blackened sticks and bones. She glances at me, her eyes dark and piercing. She whispers incantations in Spanish and rocks in rhythm.

At her side, a teenage boy sings and rocks as well. His hands are folded in prayer and his eyes downcast.

The men toss me on the floor. One of them speaks to the woman in rapid Spanish. She nods and replies. Then, the man speaks to the boy in English.

"Watch her. We will be back soon. *¿Tú entiendes?*"

The boy nods and produces a long knife from his belt. I catch my breath.

God, help me.

The men and the woman leave me alone with the boy. After the door at the top of the stairs slams shut, he fingers the knife handle and watches me. Something lurks behind his gaze. Drugs? Fear? Hunger? Maybe all three. He continues to chant as he turns the blade in his hands.

At least I know they will wait for La Parca before performing the ritual. That gives me a little time. But I don't know for sure if the cops, or even Ripley, know where I am. I need some sort of plan, in case they don't come. I look around, searching for something—anything—that can give me hope, and spot a small window near the ceiling, above some shelves.

My gaze settles on the boy, who continues to rock and chant to himself. I notice a plastic water bottle on the floor beside him. It seems such a strange, incongruent thing in this room of ancient magic.

"Could…I have a drink of water…please?"

He stops chanting and looks at me. His eyes flicker with

uncertainty. He glances at the bottle then picks it up and puts it to my lips. I barely get a sip before he takes it away again and drinks the rest himself.

"Thank you. *Gracias.*" I struggle to sit up. My arms and legs ache. "What is your name?"

"Pedro."

"I'm Grace. How old are you?"

"Fifteen."

"What is that?" I indicate the robed skull.

He looks at me like I must be an idiot. "Santa Muerte."

Santa Muerte. I remember my high school Spanish. Saint Death.

"So she's a saint?"

He frowns.

"Sorry, but I'm scared to death right now, and it helps to talk. Do you mind? Just talking?"

He shrugs. I wonder if anyone ever talks to him. It seems like they just yell or give orders.

"So tell me about your religion." I keep my voice friendly, so he won't be alarmed. "What does Santa Muerte do for you?"

"She protects us."

"From the police?"

He nods, his gaze on the floor. "And our enemies."

"Like your...business rivals?"

Another nod.

"So you make offerings to her? What kind of offerings?"

"Anything. Candy. Flowers. Tequila. Wine. Cigarettes."

I glance at the cauldron. "Bones?"

He follows my gaze. "Sometimes."

"But upstairs they were talking about Ogun...do you pray to him too?"

"Ogun is an *orisha*. A spirit in human form. We make offerings to Ogun to gain strength and power for war." Pedro points to another corner of the basement, where old tools and scrap metal lie in a heap, overlain with dried palm fronds. "That is his shrine."

"And what kind of offerings does he like?"

"Tobacco. Coffee. Meat."

"Meat? What kind of meat?"

Pedro hesitates. "Dogs," he murmurs.

I feel a wave of nausea. But I need to keep him talking. Even if I die, the pendant will record his words, assuming it's working.

"That woman who was here—is she your mother?"

"Yes."

"And Manuel?"

"He is my brother."

A family affair.

"And this is where your brother runs his drug operation?"

Pedro looks at me, alarmed.

"You might as well tell me," I say. "Who will I tell? They are going to kill me anyway."

"Kill you? No, no." Pedro shakes his head. "They won't kill you. Just take some blood. Enough for the offering."

"You don't expect me to believe that, do you?"

"It's true."

"Look around. Look at these skulls. Those bones. Where did they come from?"

"The cemetery." But his voice wavers. "They take the bodies from the graves. No one cares."

"Pedro." I level my gaze on him. "Do you really believe your brother doesn't kill people here?"

He jumps up and goes to the stairs but stops. He sits on the bottom step. I swivel around to look at him.

"Do you believe in God, Pedro?"

He doesn't look at me but he fiddles constantly with the knife. "Yes."

"You know that worshipping other gods is a sin?"

"No, no. They are not gods, they are saints. Spirits. We pray to them. We honor them."

"God doesn't honor kidnapping and murder. Or hurting people to get what you want. He condemns such things." I pause and take a breath, gathering courage. "That skeleton over there doesn't have power. It's only a skeleton."

Pedro shoots to his feet, the knife pointed at me. "You can't say those things about Santa Muerte!"

I stare at the knife as a shockwave of fear slides through me. But the boy who wields it is more afraid than I am. I swallow and press harder. Nothing to lose now.

"*Think*, Pedro, think for yourself. For once, stop listening to the lies your mother and brother tell you. You know these idols have no power. You know they are false gods. Will any of them stand by you on the final day? Will any of them be able to defend you against the True Judge? Look at that skeleton dressed up in flowers and a crown. What is that compared to the God of the Universe—"

"No more talk! Shut up." He paces as he slams the flat of the blade against his palm.

"You don't want to live like this, do you? You want to get out. You want to be free."

"Shut up!"

"Cut my bonds, Pedro." I hold my hands up. "Let me go and I will help you be free."

"*Cállate!*"

The basement door opens and heavy footsteps thud on the creaking stairs. One of the men barks at Pedro, probably wondering what is going on. He responds, shrugs, and points to me. The man crosses the room, puts his boot on my shoulder, and presses me back to the floor.

"You. Quiet. Or I take your tongue." He snaps an order to Pedro and disappears up the stairs.

"See? You got me in trouble," the young man says.

"I'm sorry," I whisper. "But Pedro, please…help me. You can come with me. We can get out that window—" I tilt my head to the small basement window above the shelves. "But we have to do it now before they come back.

I'll help you, I promise. The police will help you too, if you tell them what you know. They'll give you a new name, a new identity, a new family…" My voice falters. "You can be free of all this. You want to be free, don't you?"

"Shut up!" He lunges at me, fury in his eyes. His arm raises high, the knife pointed at my head. I fall flat and shut my eyes—and my mouth.

42

Get Up and Fight

Jared

The radio picks up only static.

"I don't know what's wrong," says Jason, the radio operator, as Beranski and I look on anxiously. "All I get is interference."

"Can we get closer?"

We're a block away from the house. Beranski doesn't want to get closer for fear Torega's men will spot us.

A SWAT team has deployed, hidden in the bushes and on rooftops of adjoining houses. They are waiting for the signal to move but Beranski refuses to give it.

"It could be the wrong house," he says. "Maybe she's not even in there."

The whole operation has been a massive screw-up. Torega must have suspected Mace would double-cross him, because the drug dealers showed up in three cars, all the same model, all black. After they grabbed Grace, the vehicles left together and then went in different directions, forcing the cops to split up too. They led the police on a wild goose chase for nearly an hour, taking random turns down one-way streets and alleys. Grace's tracker wasn't working either. The drug dealers must have had jammers in the cars.

Torega knew he would be followed. He'd taken precautions. All of our carefully planned measures had failed.

Beranski screamed into the microphone the whole time. He's a big man with a bald head and a red face, the lead detective in Vice, so this is his game. But even he was losing his cool. A young woman's life was on the line.

I felt utterly helpless. Grace was in the hands of violent drug dealers who wanted to use her for a ritual sacrifice, and there was nothing I, with all my power, could do about it.

Michael, why did you send me here for this?

Then a name came to me, like a billboard in my mind. *Babcock.*

"Babcock," I said aloud.

Beranski looked at me. "How do you know?"

"I know."

The detective rolled his eyes but spoke into the mic.

"All units head to Babcock. Now."

A few minutes later, one of the cruisers called in a confirmation—one of the black cars was located at a house on Babcock Street.

Beranski eyed me suspiciously, but ordered the van driver to head to that location. We cruised past rows of small, neat houses, some boarded up and abandoned, others with trimmed grass and fresh paint. An unmarked police car sat on the curb across from a white two-story row house with peeling paint and a detached garage. Colored lights glowed through the curtains in the main window. A black sedan was parked in the narrow driveway, practically invisible in the dusk.

I let out a silent breath. We'd found her. *Thanks Mike.*

～

But Jason gets nothing from Grace's pendant except random static punctured by African drum music.

"Something's blocking the signal," he says. "They've got

jammers in the house. Or maybe she's in the basement. Concrete walls."

"You need to get her out," I tell the detective.

"We don't even know if Torega is in there."

"Go in there and get her out!"

"You are not in charge of this operation," Beranski says.
"Sit down and be quiet. Look, the SWAT guys can be in
there in twenty seconds. We'll give it another few minutes
and see if we can get anything on the radio. If we bust the
wrong house, we're dead in the water."

"But the ritual—"

"Rituals are not illegal."

"What if they kill her?"

"That would be illegal. But if we go in now, we have
nothing."

"I don't care." I throw the back door of the van open.

"Hey! Get back here! What the—"

Ignoring his protests, I run across the street toward the
house.

I hope the SWAT guys don't shoot me.

A strong odor of incense wafts from inside. I knock on
the door.

No one answers, but I hear scuffling and voices. I knock
again. The door opens a crack. An older woman's face appears. She peruses me with suspicion and says something in
Spanish.

I don't bother to answer. I push the door open and shove
her aside. She yells and two men appear behind her, their
assault rifles trained on me. One is big and muscular, the
other shorter with bad skin. Before they can pull the triggers
I advance on them, I grab the barrels and rip the rifles out
of their hands. Startled, they come at me with their fists and
I fling them into the wall, knocking down pictures and shat-
tering furniture. The woman screams again. I pick up the
rifles, break them in half and toss them to the men, who
don't get up.

I turn to find another man advancing on me, holding a machete. He's smiling.

"You must be Jared," he says.

Manuel Torega. I've never met him, never seen him. If I had, I could have warned Penny before she got involved with him. The man is infested with demons.

"They said you were gone, but I knew you weren't." He grins. "Ogun told me you would come."

"Where's Grace?"

"She's alive—for now. But if you make one move, I will order her killed. You won't get to her in time."

I stare at him, reading his demons.

"I don't believe you."

Without warning, I lunge at him, grab the wrist that holds the machete, and snap it. Torega screams and falls to his knees. The woman runs past us into the kitchen. I follow her, taking the machete with me. She stands before a closed door and shouts in Spanish with one hand raised in a devil sign, obviously putting a curse on me. I almost laugh.

"You can't curse someone who's already cursed."

I push her aside and throw the door open.

Stairs to a basement. A bad smell. *Oh, God, no. She's dead already.* I can't feel her and can't hear her heart. I barrel down the stairs.

The evil in this place is nearly stifling. I pause on the bottom step, unable to move further—the oppression and the stench overpower my senses. I scan the room—shelves lined with skulls, tables of bizarre artifacts and candles, and a cauldron filled with bones. A dressed-up skeleton with a crown dominates a scene that resembles a horror movie.

But I don't see Grace.

She isn't here.

The woman rushes down the stairs, yelling and still cursing me.

"Where is Grace?" I demand.

Her mouth falls open when she sees the basement is

empty, and she begins to rant in Spanish. I make out a name—Pedro.

Torega stumbles down the steps, holding his broken arm. He takes one look, gasps, and races back up. I drop the machete and storm after him. I tackle him as he tries to escape out the back door, take hold of his broken arm and twist. He screams in agony.

"Where is she?"

Torega answers with a stream of Spanish curses. Suddenly, the front door bursts open and the SWAT team swarms in, shouting. I release the man and put my hands in the air as they charge into the kitchen, their guns trained on us. An officer knocks me to the floor and presses his knee into my back.

"I'm with you guys," I say.

Beranski arrives and barks at the SWAT guy to let me up. Another has Torega pinned down.

"What the heck happened?" Beranski asks me.

"She's not here," I say.

His face reddens. "I told you, didn't I?"

"She *was* here. This is the right house. She must have escaped."

"From a basement?"

"There's a broken window. Find her. More men out there. Torega wouldn't be here with only two guys."

Beranski barks orders to the SWAT team leader. "Search the other houses and that garage out back. The girl is 10-57. Find her before they do."

43

Brave

Grace

Pedro and I crawl along the back of the house where tangled, leafless thorn bushes scratch our faces. Bits of glass from the broken window are embedded in my skin and hair. The warmth of seeping blood trickles down my cheek, but I cannot pause to wipe it away. I have to focus—*focus*.

The boy's breath comes loud and fast and I want to tell him to be quiet. The fear is almost paralyzing. I pause to peer into the backyard. It's fairly empty except for a firepit. A tall fence surrounds the property and a dilapidated garage takes up one corner.

"We need to get over the fence," I whisper.

"They will see us!"

"We have to take the risk. There's no other way out. Follow me."

He shakes his head, frozen in terror. "No. No."

"Pedro, if they find you—"

"There are guards…everywhere," he mutters. "They will see us."

"Then we move fast. The police are nearby. I promise!"

He refuses. I must do this alone. I crawl on my belly across the scant, muddy grass, passing the fire pit, which is filled with ash and the remains of bones. The fence suddenly seems a long way off but at least it's darker around the edge of the property. I continue my low crawl, focused only on my freedom, praying for invisibility.

"Don't move, witch."

I freeze when something cold and hard presses into my neck. A heavy boot kicks me onto my back. I stare into the face of a young, bearded man holding an assault rifle.

"Where do you think you're going?" His accent is American. "Get up." I rise slowly to my feet, my hands open. He looks me over and his eyes narrow as he gives me a leering grin. "Move." He tilts his head toward the house and shoves me hard. I exaggerate my stumble, desperate to prolong this death march. I turn to him, drop to my knees, clasp my hands together.

"Please," I say. "If you let me go, I'll pay you. My father is very rich. I'll give you whatever you want."

I keep babbling in an attempt to stall him and to keep his eyes away from Pedro hiding in the thorn bushes.

To my relief, the man pauses to consider my offer. Holding my breath, I wait for him to decide my fate.

"You're lying," he says finally. "Move." He pulls me to my feet and spins me around to face the house.

Suddenly, there's light everywhere, shining in my eyes and almost blinding me. Angels? But no—searchlights rove the yard. A voice bellows over bullhorns. "Throw down your weapon!" Commotion erupts inside the house—screams and shouts and breaking doors.

The man grabs me by my shirt and hauls me toward the garage. He pulls the door up halfway and drags me inside. I break free and throw myself against the slowly descending door but he's stronger. He pushes me to the floor, slams the door closed, and turns the locking handle.

I lie on the floor, panting. A lightbulb swings on a chain overhead, illuminating the space. The garage is filled with crates and boxes.

I hear a whimper and turn to see two small children huddled in the corner, sitting on a filthy blanket. Their clothes are ragged and their bare legs are covered in bruises. When I look at them, they shrink back and hide their faces.

The man with the rifle is pressed to the garage door, listening to the shouting outside. Clearly, a raid is going on. I say a prayer of thanks. They found me.

"Who are these children?" I ask the man. "What are they doing here?"

"Shut up." He brandishes the rifle at me. But he doesn't need to answer. I know exactly what he's been doing. I forget my fear in the rage that builds inside me.

"They will find you," I say. "You should surrender now. They'll go easier on you if you do that."

"Shut up!"

"Of course, when they realize what you've done with these children, they'll lock you up for the rest of your life and throw away the key. But that's nothing compared to what God has in store for you."

"I said shut up or I'll kill you!" The man trembles and wipes his mouth.

I crawl over to the girls, who huddle together, trembling, eyes wild.

"It's okay," I whisper. "They're coming to help you. They will take you home…"

Scuffles outside are followed by a rattle as someone tries to open the door. Muffled dialogue ensues. "Locked!" "Stand back. We're breaking it down!" A second later, something huge and heavy slams into the door from the other side. The girls whimper as it splinters.

I get to my feet, ready to run. My captor rushes over, grabs me around the neck and holds the gun one-handed against my head.

"Get back or I'll shoot!" he shouts as a SWAT officer climbs through the hole. The officer aims his rifle at the man who holds me, shouting at him to release me. The muzzle of my captor's gun bores into my neck, choking off my windpipe. He threatens to kill me if the SWAT officer comes any closer. They continue to yell back and forth, neither one conceding. My body goes limp with fear. Stars spangle my vision. The little girls cry.

I pray. *God save me.* A simple plea. *Give me strength. Courage. One last time.* I gather whatever strength I can muster and I stomp on the man's foot while I reach up and shove the gun barrel upward. An explosion rips into my ear. Everything turns white, then red, then black.

~

I'm not dead.

I know this because I see the face of the SWAT officer looming over me. He definitely doesn't look like an angel.

"You okay?"

His words are muddled by a loud ringing in my ear. I nod.

"That was the stupidest move I've ever seen," he says. "And the bravest."

He helps me to my feet. My head swoons, a warmth runs down the side of my head. My ear is bleeding. Pain knifes my skull. My captor is on the ground, hands cuffed behind his back. Other officers are tending to the two children.

"Let's get you fixed up." The SWAT officer escorts me to an ambulance. Jared is already there. He gasps when he sees me—I must look pretty bad.

"I'm fine," I say. I'm shaking, I'm bloody, I'm in shock, but I'm fine.

He pulls me into his arms, and I know by the fierce trembling of his body that he'd feared I was dead.

I lie on the gurney in the ambulance while a paramedic dresses my wounded ear and tends to the scratches and cuts on my face and arms. She seems too young for her job, with multi-colored hair and many piercings. Jared sits beside me, holding my hand, answering her non-stop questions.

"Your ear's going to ring for a few days," she shouts, snapping her gum. "Don't worry about it. You'll be fine."

Detective Beranski comes in to see how I'm doing.

"Heard you took down a guy with a gun to your head," he says. He has to repeat himself when Jared tells him to speak up. "Marconi said you were pretty good at dodging bullets."

"I've had a lot of practice," I reply. "Did you find Pedro?"

"Yeah, he's fine. We have him in custody. He's talking. Turns out it's the woman who's the head of the operation."

"What? You're kidding."

"Nope. They call her Mama Rosita. She's not talking. Neither is Torega. Not that they have to. We've seen enough. The product stashed in that garage will put her and her son away for life. And shut down the cartel, at least for a time."

"They said La Parca was coming to witness…the ritual."

"Really? Interesting." The detective smirks. "Although I doubt it. Maybe one of your friends called Torega and told him that? To stall him?"

I glance at Jared, who shrugs. "Could be."

"What about those two little girls?" I ask.

"We're looking for their families," says Beranski. "It's a thing with these cartels, kidnapping children."

"Grace!" Penny appears at the back of the ambulance with Silas in tow. She tries to get in but the paramedic stops her.

"Hang on, there's no room in here. She'll be out in a minute."

As soon as I step down from the ambulance Penny and Silas throw their arms around me.

"Thank God you're all right," Silas says. "Ripley said he lost your signal. We thought—"

"How *did* you find me?" I ask Beranski.

"Ask your boyfriend," the detective says with a derisive

chuckle. "Cause I have no idea."

"You need to tear this house down," Penny tells him. "Bulldoze it."

He regards her, one eyebrow arched. "I'll see what I can do."

～

It was Ralph's idea to call Torega. He had Mace pretend to be one of La Parca's henchmen. Torega fell for it. Maybe Mace isn't a traitor after all. The detective told us later that Rosa Negro shut down their operation in Buffalo virtually overnight. One cartel down, a dozen to go. But it's a beginning.

The drug sting made the papers, but Beranski kept my name out of it, as promised. Torega and his mother are being held without bail. Pedro was given immunity in exchange for his testimony. Beranski put in a request to have the house condemned and demolished—surprisingly, it was granted. We took the PsychoVan over to Babcock to watch the bulldozers destroy Torega's shrine forever.

In the weeks after, we return to some semblance of normal. We move back into the Lighthouse and re-open the bike shop. Penny goes back to school. The weather warms. The last of the crusty, blackened snow disappears. The raid becomes a dusty nightmare in the back of my mind, stacked with all the others that lurk there. Even the ringing in my ear has stopped.

One warm evening, Jared and I take a blanket up to the Mansion and have a picnic in what once was Ralph's library. We spread the blanket and eat cheese and crackers and drink Loganberry—well, I do. Jared tells me more about his journey with Mike, about Jonna and the ship, and about the bizarre and beautiful house in Iceland. I sense he leaves a lot of stuff out. But I figure that in time, he will be able to tell me all of it.

"Jared," I say. "I want to get married."

He nearly chokes on his cracker. "What?"

"You heard me."

"Grace, you know we can't."

"Why not? You love me, right? And I love you. That's what people in love do. They get married."

"Not us."

"You don't want to marry me?"

"I do. I mean, I would if—"

"If you weren't a Nephilim."

He sighs, lies back on the blanket, and stares at the moon. I watch his face, the subtle clenches in his jaw, and the faint glow of his eyes. He has told me what the Nephilim he encountered in Norway looked like, and that he would eventually become like them. But it doesn't matter to me. I won't live to see it. And maybe he won't either. I don't care about the future. Or the past. I only want the now.

"Ralph won't go along with it."

"We're adults, Jared. We don't need his consent. Not that we shouldn't ask him. I love Ralph. He's been a guardian, a father to both of us. I respect his opinion but…this is our decision." He doesn't respond. "Look at me." I knee my way over to him. "My legs are fine now. Since the Abyss. Something *did* happen to me there. I'm not sure what, but my legs are healed. And you've been healed too. We're different than we were."

He rolls over on his side and looks me in the eyes. "Are you sure you want to do this?"

"Yes! I want it more than anything. Jared, will you marry me?"

He smiles. "Aren't I supposed to ask you that?"

"Okay, then, ask me. I'll pretend I wasn't expecting it." I gaze up at the moon and whistle under my breath.

"Grace Fortune, will you marry me?"

"What? Are you kidding? I thought you'd never ask!" I tackle him, wind my arms around his neck, and kiss him hard. "Tomorrow."

"Tomorrow? Isn't that a little soon?"

"Okay, then, the day after tomorrow. What are you doing on Saturday?"

He hesitates, and perhaps that should have made me wonder. About the things he still hasn't told me. Does he love me like I do him? *Can* he love me? After all, Nephilim aren't supposed to have feelings. At least, not feelings that are unselfish, like love. I keep telling myself he isn't what he used to be. He's changed. My love changed him. And God's love.

"I...need to get a ring..." he murmurs, stumbling over the words.

I laugh. "I have it covered." I pull two rubber band rings out of my pocket. "I made them myself. Penny showed me how." I put one of them on his finger. It's yellow and purple and mine is blue and pink. He stares at his ring, silent. I frown. "What's wrong?"

"You know...we can't...really be married, don't you? Like..."

"I know that," I say. "I mean, I know it won't be like a normal marriage. But it's okay. I won't ask that of you."

"But...don't you want to do this properly? Like with a party and a wedding dress? Are you really sure—"

"I'm sure. I'm sure I'm sure. I'm sure I'm sure I'm sure. Is that enough sureness for you? We need to do this, Jared."

"What if God disagrees?"

"Let's ask him." I clasp my hands together. "Heavenly Father, if you don't want us to get married, say so. In a big way. Amen." I open one eye and look at Jared. "How was that?"

"Okay, I guess." He grins despite himself.

"I love you, Jared. Love can't be wrong, can it?"

44

Us

Jared

I have agreed to marry Grace.

Of course, I should have said no. There is so much she doesn't know. And yet I want to believe, as she does, that this will make everything all right. That despite what I am and what I will become, we can have a life together.

We go back to the Hobbit Hole and she makes the announcement.

"When did all this come about?" Ralph asks. His gaze falls on me, but I can't meet it.

"Just now," Grace says. "Well, it's been on my mind for a long time. After Jared came back, I started to worry that something might happen and we'd be separated. And then with the Torega thing—I don't want to waste any more time."

"Well," Emilia says with a happy sigh. "I'll finally get to use my wedding cake recipe. I do love wedding cake."

"Have you talked to your father?" Ralph asks.

"I will when I get home."

"You realize that a wedding is a public event."

"Celebrities get married all the time without anyone knowing until after," Grace points out. "We'll go to the courthouse tomorrow and fill out the paperwork. And then get married the next day before word gets out."

"You forget that Jared is a citizen of Canada, which means he has to file for a change of status. That could take weeks."

Grace seems deflated by this information. "Then we won't bother with the paperwork part. It doesn't matter what New York State thinks, anyway. It's not like we'll file joint taxes or have kids or anything." She glances at me when she says this. A heaviness fills my chest.

"Marriage is a sacred commitment." Ralph stammers a little. He's really flummoxed. "With or without a license. It is more than a promise. It is a covenant that requires a great deal of thought and preparation and—"

"Of course," Grace says. "We understand that. But we are both adults, and we know what we're doing."

Do we?

"Why don't you talk to Silas," Ralph says. "We can discuss this in the morning."

She sighs. "Fine, but I'm not changing my mind."

~

I go to the Lighthouse early the next morning to talk to Silas. He's working alone in the bike shop.

"Congratulations," he says. I can't tell if he means it.

"I think I was supposed to ask for your permission," I say. "We've gotten this all backward."

"No worries." He stifles a cough. "We're not exactly a traditional family, are we?"

"Are you okay?" I ask. The cough always makes me nervous.

"I got the results yesterday. The cancer's back."

I draw in a breath. "Have you told Grace?"

"No. I'm not going to either. Not until after the wedding, anyway." He grins faintly. "I'm happy for the two of you.

It's about time."

"You don't think we're making a terrible mistake?"

"You mean 'cause of the whole Nephilim thing? I don't know much about that, but I know that life is short—for some of us, anyway. When you find love, you need to hang onto it. That's what the Hallmark cards say."

There is deep sorrow behind the joke. He's thinking of Shannon.

"Well, thank you."

"No problem."

"Can I ask you a question? About…Shannon."

He stops working and looks at me. "What about Shannon?"

"I'm wondering if back when you knew her…before…well, if she ever participated in any occult rituals."

He's quiet for a moment as he considers this. "Yeah. She belonged to a group with some other LA actresses. They called themselves the Daughters of Babalon. She would go to meetings every month. That kind of thing was big in LA back then."

"Do you know what they did?"

"Not exactly, but she asked me to come to a meeting once. They did some sort of bizarre ritual. I was pretty wasted so don't remember much, except for Lily in this red dress. There was a lot of chanting and incantations and incense—honestly I thought I was on a bad trip."

"Silas, think. When did she get pregnant? Was it…*after* that?"

His brow furrows. "It must have been, because then she went to France." His eyes search mine. "What are you getting at?"

I take a breath. "Whatever the ritual she did back then—with you—I think she did the same ritual with me," I say. "In Iceland."

Silas' face goes still. He walks over to a stool and sits

down.

"What's the point of the ritual? What's it for?"

"To unite the Scarlet Woman and the Great Beast, like in Revelation. To produce…a Moon Child. The Antichrist."

His eyes widen. "She's pregnant now," he says.

"Yes."

"And you think—"

"It's possible. I hope not. But…yes."

He straightens, a look of horror crosses his face. "But if she did that same ritual with me, then Grace is…"

I shake my head. "She's not. The ritual didn't work back then."

"It didn't?"

"No. Because you were not the Beast." I pause and struggle to form the next words. I had read the scriptures before coming to talk to him. One line had chilled me:

The beast that you saw was, and is not, and is about
to rise from the bottomless pit and go to destruction.

"I am the Beast."

45

Forever On Your Side

Grace

I wear the long white dress I wore for my high school graduation, and Penny made me a crown of baby's breath for my hair. She wears a purple dress, the first time in a long time that I've seen her in anything except black. She has Mace dressed up in a suit that's too big for him. I'm not crazy about him attending my wedding, but Penny won't go without him. Besides, I do owe him something, for helping catch Torega. I apologized for doubting him, but I still don't like him hanging around.

Ralph has on a black button-down shirt with a checked bowtie—a new look for him. Silas wears a jacket I didn't know he owned. Emilia looks like a seventies bridesmaid in pink frills and floppy hat. She clutches a cake box in her arms and shoos anyone away who tries to take a peek.

Jared wears a new white button-down shirt with a blue tie that matches his eyes. I reach up and adjust his tie, although it doesn't need adjusting.

"You look very handsome." An understatement.

"You look...beautiful."

"No touching before the wedding!" Penny grabs my arm, and pulls me into the van.

It's early May, the sun is shining, and the crab-apple and cherry trees are blossoming. Ralph drives, although he refuses to tell us where we're going. It's a "surprise." I wanted the wedding to take place outside, somewhere pretty. It will be nice to be outside again. We're out of hiding at last.

We pick up Ethan and Bree at a shopping center just outside of town. As soon as the door slides open, Bree takes one look at me and screams at the top of her lungs. Ethan follows her into the van, closes the door, and slings his backpack on the floor. He looks vaguely annoyed as usual. Ralph told them to not bring their phones and Ethan always gets antsy without a device in his hand.

I give him a hug. "Thanks for coming."

"Like I had a choice." He rolls his eyes at Bree, who scoffs.

"Are you kidding? He wouldn't miss it. Ethan, make sure the two heroes get married in your sequel to *Wrath of the Watchers*. That would be awesome."

"Oh, yeah, thirteen-year-old boys are sure to be ecstatic over that one. Although…" He pauses, looking up like some new idea has popped into his head. "Maybe a Watcher attack on the wedding would be cool…kind of a revenge thing…this time it's personal…"

"Oh, brother."

We all burst out laughing.

Bree talks nonstop as Ralph drives into the countryside. Jared is quiet and nervous, his leg bouncing up and down. He stares out the window like he's searching for something.

"Looking for demons?" I laugh.

He doesn't. "Drones, maybe."

I take his hand. "Speer's not still looking for you, is he?"

"You never know with Speer."

"He got what he wanted from you. You're done with him. Done with all of it."

After an hour, the terrain grows hilly and forested. Ralph turns onto a narrower, country road that soon becomes a dirt track, which we follow for a couple of miles. The ancient shocks of the PsychoVan bounce us all over each other.

"I really don't want to have to throw up on Grace's wedding day," Bree calls out to Ralph.

"Sorry! We'll be there soon."

He finally pulls over and cuts the engine. "We have to walk from here."

We exit the van. Silas takes a small table from the back and hands Mace a large picnic basket to carry. We hike up a footpath several hundred feet through the woods, swatting gnats all the way. Mud splatters on my white dress. Bree complains loudly that no one told her to wear sensible shoes.

Finally, we arrive at a level clearing to find a tiny stone building with a tower in one corner.

A chapel.

I gasp. "Oh, my gosh…it's adorable. How did you know about this?"

"I read about this place in a book on the history of this region," Ralph says. "This land was once owned by a prominent businessman who used it for hunting more than a hundred years ago. He built a house here as well, but the house burned down. The chapel was a memorial for his wife."

"It's perfect," says Bree.

I go in first. The place is musty but recently swept. There are no pews and no altar, just a granite memorial in the center with two names: "Gladys Merriman, Beloved Wife" and "Grace Merriman, Beloved Daughter."

"Daughter? Did she die too?" I ask.

"The mother died in childbirth," Ralph says.

Below the dates of birth and death is a scripture verse: *I have loved you with an everlasting love.*

"Her name was Grace," I say. "The baby."

"Yes, I thought that was interesting too."

Bree runs her fingers over the inscription. "So sad."

Ralph pulls a Bible from his coat pocket. "Are you two ready?"

I turn to Jared, who stands stiffly in the doorway as if he needs permission to enter. I go to him, take his hand, and lead him to where Ralph waits, near the memorials. The others gather around us and put their hands on our shoulders like we're all getting married together.

"This is my first wedding ceremony, so forgive me." Ralph clears his throat—did he seem a little choked up? "We know that the first couple, Adam and Eve, were joined in the presence of God alone, according to His will. So we ask our heavenly Father for His permission, this day, for the joining in marriage of Grace and Jared. We ask You, Lord, to bless these two or to make Your will known if this marriage about to take place is contrary to Your purpose."

Ralph falls silent. We all listen for a peal of thunder, a crack of lightning, or a sudden earthquake. Emilia sniffs. Silas coughs. Bree giggles.

"Very well." Ralph sighs. I think he's disappointed that God didn't intervene. "Listen to the words of the apostle Paul: *If I speak in the tongues of men or of angels, but do not have love, I am only a resounding gong or a clanging cymbal...*"

He reads the entire chapter, slowly and with dramatic flair. Then he looks up, his gaze focused on Jared and me. "This is the most difficult chapter in all the Bible because it is nearly impossible to live up to. My prayer for you two is that you will remember always the love you have declared this day, that you make this covenant not only with each other but with God, and that you break it on pain of death. Do you understand?"

We both nod and a lump forms in my throat. I grip Jared's hand. It's burning hot. He reaches up with his other hand to loosen his tie.

"We are the witnesses to this covenant." Now Ralph addresses the others. "Our job is to hold these two to the promise they have made—a promise more serious and binding than any legal document devised by man." He closes the Bible and refocuses his gaze on the two of us. "I believe you have some vows to give to each other."

"Yes." Jared turns to me. He looks so serious I almost burst out laughing.

"Grace, as God is my witness, I vow to love you forever, as I love you in this moment. I will be forever by your side. I will defend you with my life, and I will never abandon you, no matter what."

I try to keep my voice steady as I repeat the same vow. We'd stayed up practically all night working on vows, but in the end, decided that simpler was better.

"Well, then," says Ralph, "I guess you are now...husband and wife."

～

Husband and wife.

I love those words.

It's right, I know it is.

I want to remember every moment of it, to have it seared into my memory so no matter what happens in the future, I will always have this. The way he takes my face in his hands, his kiss like a soft breeze on my mouth. The way his breath catches, and mine too, and then we breathe together. The way our hearts beat in unison, for now we are truly joined as one. Nothing and no one will ever separate us again.

And then, there's music.

I glance up, startled. Ethan holds up a cassette recorder and smiles. The song is a gorgeous solo guitar version of Amazing Grace.

I look at Jared. "That's you!"

He nods. "For you." And for the first time all day, his smile reaches his eyes.

We stand still, singing along with the guitar and letting this moment of grace hover over us like protecting angels. And I am certain God is with us.

The song ends and the stillness is broken by applause and

Bree's gleeful shrieking. Emilia and Penny are weeping. Jared sweeps me up in his arms and carries me out of the chapel, into the dappled sun.

I can't stop laughing.

Silas and Mace set some chairs up around the portable table laden with the cake, two bottles of sparkling cider and, of course, several cans of Loganberry. The cake is a multi-layered explosion of pink trimmed with perfectly formed angel wings. Emilia outdid herself. I hate to cut into it, but we do anyway. Bree insists on following the usual wedding traditions—a first dance, a father-daughter dance with both Ralph and Silas and throwing the bouquet, which is a bunch of wildflowers Jared picked for me. Unfortunately the flowers aren't bound together so when I throw them they scatter in all directions. Bree manages to grab one of the stalks and declares herself the victor. Ethan's face reddens.

We eat and drink and dance and laugh so hard my ribs hurt. Bree and Ethan, who had decided they were Maid of Honor and Best Man, make rambling, hilarious speeches about us. Bree can hardly get through hers without breaking up in giggles followed by tears. Ethan, totally straight faced, reads his from a three-by-five card. "Having a friend who is a superhero can be a real pain in the butt. But he does come in handy when you have a giant bullet hole in your gut. Or you need to open a jar of pickles."

Then Jared takes my hand and announces we're going for a walk. We leave the others and head into the woods. The whole bottom of my dress is brown by the time we come to a small lake, perfectly nestled in the surrounding woodland. We sit down together on the bank.

"This may be the only time we can be alone." He smiles and kisses me again, lingering longer than usual.

"Are you okay?" I ask.

"Yeah. I'm fine."

We lie down, side by side in the tall wet grass, holding hands.

"Thanks for the song," I say.

"It's a good thing Ralph is so retro and still had a cassette player. He wouldn't even let Ethan bring a Bluetooth speaker."

I laugh and turn over to face him. His heart trips when I put my hand on his chest, and his breath catches. "I know this isn't a normal marriage so…I don't quite know what to do now."

"Let's not do anything."

"Good idea."

"I love you, Grace."

My heart trills at the words.

"I love you back times a thousand."

It's dark when we get back to the Hobbit Hole. It occurs to me that we haven't a single picture of our wedding. But every frame is locked in my memory, more permanent than any camera roll.

I kiss Jared goodbye before returning to the Lighthouse. This is the hard part. We don't even live in the same house. But we're still married and he promised never to leave me again.

~

The next morning, I find a message from Lieutenant Bradford on my voicemail. "Call me."

I've been so consumed by the wedding that I'd almost forgotten about Bradford and the investigation When I call, he picks up right away.

"What took you so long?"

"I was getting married," I say.

"What? Seriously? To the rock star?"

"Yeah."

"Congratulations."

"Thanks. So, did you find anything?"

"Maybe," he says. "The detective on the case told me

some unknown DNA was found under the victim's finger-nails. He'd assumed it was due to cross-contamination. I told him I had a tip, and so he rechecked the evidence. The same DNA was found on the rope Dana hung herself with."

"So someone else handled the rope."

"It's possible. He had the DNA analyzed."

"Was it Speer's?"

"We got no hits."

"So his DNA isn't in the system."

"Actually, it is. Speer was arrested for trespassing when he was a teenager. At the time, anyone arrested in California was swabbed. That was before the ACLU got involved. Anyway, we did a comparison. It's close, but not a match."

My heart sinks. How could this be? But then I remember.

"His DNA has changed."

"DNA doesn't change."

"Yes, it does. That's what this is all about. The treatment he did modified his DNA. It won't be a match to when he was a teenager."

Bradford heaves a big sigh. "I'm not sure how we'll prove that. We'd have to get a new sample of his DNA, which would require a compulsion order since the guy hasn't been arrested and isn't even a suspect. Even if we could do that, he has lawyers out the ying yang. Not going to happen, I can guarantee it."

"We have to stop him. Before he kills again."

"Grace, I have to tell you—there's not a lot to go on here. I think maybe you're barking up the wrong—"

"I'm not. I promise. Look—find out if any other recent victims have ties to Speer. Dana might not be the only one."

Another heavy sigh. "Aye, aye, Captain."

I tell Silas and Penny about the conversation. "Without a fresh DNA sample, we have nothing, basically." I sit at the breakfast bar and grab a box of cereal. It suddenly doesn't feel so much like the morning after my wedding anymore. My groom isn't even in the house.

46

Shadows

Jared

The world—and all my problems—comes roaring back the day after the wedding. I can't ignore them, as hard as I try.

Darwin Speer is all over social media promoting his breakthrough genetic therapy, speaking on college campuses, and doing interviews on television. He's even writing a book that has already been picked up by a large publishing house, with a six-figure advance. He made the cover of Time, Newsweek, and People Magazine all in the same week. Time named him "Person of the Year." On top of that, the new collider is almost ready to go online. It's nearly twice as long and able to collide protons at thirty trillion volts of energy to generate a magnetic field two hundred thousand times that of the Earth's atmosphere. Ripley still believes it'll cause a worldwide cataclysm—earthquakes, strange matter, black holes, or simply an explosion greater than all the nuclear bombs in the world put together.

Not to mention opening a portal to the Abyss.

And then there's Shannon's baby, due in a few weeks.

I can't change any of this, nor can I fix it. Only God can right the wrongs I have set in motion.

I try to forget all of this and focus on Grace, on being

with her in the studio, writing songs, taking walks, or talking late into the night. She's the only peace I have, and now she's my wife. I experience a fierce need to protect her from whatever is to come.

Maybe I was wrong to marry her. But I did it for the right reasons—for love and for hope.

Among my many hopes is that Darwin Speer has forgotten all about me.

But, of course, he hasn't.

～

It's nearly midnight. Grace and I are playing in the studio when everything goes dark.

"What happened?" she says. I can't see her at all. "Power outage?"

"It shouldn't be. We run on a generator."

"Maybe it broke."

"Yeah, maybe."

"Can you turn your glow on so we can get out of here?"

I laugh a little. "Turning on my glow" is not something I have that much control over.

"Sing a little," I say.

As soon as she starts singing, my body heats up and the room lightens.

"Not bad," she says. "The human flashlight."

I take her hand and we find our way out the door to the Lair. All the computer screens are blank. I practically trip over Ripley, who's asleep on the floor, wrapped in his tauntaun sleeping bag.

"Rip, wake up!"

I shake him and he startles awake.

"Huh?"

"The power's out," I say.

"That's impossible." He lurches over to a computer and bangs on the keyboard. "What the—"

"Maybe the generator blew a fuse. Where is it?"

"It's topside in the shed. Maybe it got hit by lightning or ran out of gas. Wait, let me find a flashlight." Ripley searches through his piles of stuff and overloaded drawers until he finds a red plastic flashlight with a dim, wavering beam. "There must be a dozen LEDs in this place. How come this is the only flashlight I can find?" He grumbles to himself.

We follow him outside. My glow dims until the flashlight is the only light we have. It's pitch black. No lights shine from nearby houses and no glow in the sky from the lights of the city.

"Weird," says Ripley. "It looks widespread. There haven't been any storms in the area. Maybe it's a computer glitch, like the one that knocked out the whole east coast in 2003." He leads us behind the burned-out mansion to a corrugated steel shed and fishes in his pocket for the keys. We wait impatiently as he fumbles around and finally unlocks the padlock.

He opens the door and shines the beam of the flashlight all around the generator. He checks the gas level, the spark plugs, the batteries. "Can't see anything wrong—" He opens a compartment and pulls out the control board. "*Holden Caulfied.* It's fried."

"Fried? How could that happen?" I ask.

"Only one way. EMP."

"A what?"

"Electromagnetic Pulse. I always knew this could happen. We should have put the generator in a Faraday cage—"

"What causes that?"

"Solar storm or nuclear blast—it wipes out electronics. That means the whole city grid is probably down. Check your phone."

Grace pulls her phone from her pocket.

"It works, but there's no signal."

"The towers are down," Ripley says. "This is it. We're

dead."

"Take it easy," I say. "There might be another explanation. I'll go check it out."

"I'll come too," Grace says.

"There's no need—"

"We're married, remember? Wherever you go, I go."

"Take the PsychoVan," says Ripley. "It's old enough that it should still work."

"You mean, the EMP affects cars too?" Grace asks.

"Anything with unshielded electronics."

We go back to the Hobbit Hole. I take the flashlight and grab the van keys from the hook in the kitchen. I also pull some candles out of a drawer and bring them back to Ripley.

"In case you don't find your LEDs," I say.

"Thanks."

Grace and I go to the garage and start up the PsychoVan. The engine turns over. Grace exhales in relief.

I pull out of the garage and drive slowly down the street. It's deathly quiet. A few blocks later, we see a driver peering anxiously under the hood of a stalled car. He's trying to make a call on a cell phone.

"This is eerie," Grace whispers.

As we draw closer to downtown, we catch glimpses of more disabled cars. People roam the street and mill in clusters, shining the lights from their cell phones, obviously confused and frightened. Abandoned cars block our way to the main thoroughfare.

A sudden loud *thwump* on the roof elicits a scream from Grace. The van is surrounded.

"Hey, man, give me your cool ride," a young man yells through the windshield.

"Get away from my car." I try to keep my voice steady.

"I said give it up!" The man raises a baseball bat and aims for the windshield.

I work the anger through my veins and throw the door open, slamming into him. He grunts and buckles and I grab the bat. Another one jumps me, but I throw him off, send him flying into two more of them. The others desert quickly, looking for easier prey. I toss the bat after them.

"You okay?" Grace reaches through the window for my arm which glows brightly.

"Yeah."

Demons are everywhere—big demons, bigger than I've ever seen. They are darker than the darkness, enveloping everything around us.

I get back in the car but we can't drive any further. Dead cars and debris block the road. No point anyway. I will my heart to slow, my breathing to even out.

Grace speaks softly, her hand still on my arm. "Jared, we should go back and tell Ripley."

"Yeah." I put the car in reverse.

Then I hear my name.

"Jared!"

"What's the matter?" Her grip on me strengthens.

"Did you hear that?"

"Jared!"

"I don't hear anything. Jared, let's go back. Now!"

I get out of the car and start walking.

47

Bad Dreams

Grace

"Jared!"

I yell at him to stop but it's like he doesn't hear me—like he's in a trance. I jump out of the van, follow him, and grab his arm.

"Jared! What's the matter?"

He doesn't answer but continues purposefully up Delaware toward Niagara Square. I run to keep up with him, begging him to tell me what's going on.

At the square, mayhem rules, with people running and screaming as if they've seen ghosts—or demons. Cars are not only dead, they're flipped over and some are on fire. The trees lining the square are all broken, some pulled out by their roots. It looks like a war zone.

Suddenly, Jared stops walking and stares. His eyes pulse and his body lights up, but I can't see what he's seeing. He seems to be listening intently.

Then I hear it too.

"Son of Azazel!"

Azazel? Was Azazel here? Has the Abyss opened? A thousand horrible thoughts run through my mind all at once.

A crash precedes more screams. I gasp as the huge marble obelisk that stands in the center of the square smashes to the ground. In its place on the stone slab stands a huge figure—half man and half reptile—with a white face and electric blue eyes that glow in the dark night. Its whole body glows, even brighter than Jared's. The creature spreads its long arms to display a fan of snake-like tentacles and sharp talons.

It has to be some kind of demon. A demon I can *see*.

This is a dream. That's what I tell myself. Dreams often do this. They start out reasonably and then descend into total chaos. I try desperately to wake myself, to force my consciousness through the layers of sleep, one after the other. No matter what I do, I can't get all the way to the surface.

Jared shouts. "Rael!"

Rael. The Nephilim who had captured him in the ice cave.

This is the worst dream ever.

The creature turns to Jared. "Son of Azazel!" The voice is whispery and deafening at the same time, weirdly distorted as if it's been run through an Autotune gone haywire. "I have searched for you in many places."

"What do you want?"

"Come with me and I will show you."

"No!" I grab Jared and turn him to face me. "Look at me, Jared. *Look at me!* You are not going with him."

His eyes glow white, strangely vacant. "I have to."

"Why?"

"I just do."

"Then I'm coming too."

"No."

"You promised me."

He sighs. "I'm sorry."

Jared pushes me away and walks toward the giant.

"No!" I try to pull him back. He shrugs me off, but I won't be stopped. At the stone slab, the giant wraps one of its long tentacles around him. I grab the thick appendage, feebly attempting to pull it off him. I'm sobbing now. And then I am torn away, pulled out of Jared's reach by a tremendous force. Another tentacle encircles me, so tight I am nearly suffocated. I scream, but I am drowned out by a chorus of screams all around me. Others watch in horror.

Rael jumps. My stomach lurches into my throat as we launch into the air and slam into the side of a building. I'm sure we will be crushed or plummet to the ground, but Rael's other tentacles cling to the surface like Spiderman. He climbs the building, using his many limbs as anchors until we reach the top.

He hauls himself over the edge and flings us away from him. I careen forward and smack my head into something hard—a concrete block. Everything goes black.

"Grace! Can you hear me?"

Hazy shapes waver in the dark. Jared's eyes glow bright.

"Yeah." I try to rise and pain shoots through my skull. "My head hurts."

"Who is this insect?" Rael looms over both of us. One of his tentacles snakes toward me and Jared slaps it away.

"Don't touch her," he orders and the Nephilim withdraws.

"She was not invited."

"I don't go without her."

Rael moves away from us and crouches on his haunches, his serpentine tail coiling around him.

Jared bends to examine my head. "No blood, but you hit pretty hard," he says. "Just stay still."

I obey as every tiny movement causes a spear of pain to slice through my skull. Presently, I hear a rhythmic thumping and see the twinkling lights of a helicopter overhead.

"How come that thing works?" I manage to say.

Jared watches the chopper. "Either it came from outside the EMP's range, or it's been somehow shielded." The wind kicks up and Jared hovers over me to protect me from the blast of air. The chopper lands on the roof like a giant locust. The Speer Enterprises logo flashes on its side.

A man wearing a headset opens the door and beckons to us.

"Get in!" Rael orders.

I gasp in pain as Jared picks me up and carries me into the chopper, ducking to avoid the spinning rotors. He sets me gently on the seat and climbs in after me. The man with the headset shuts the door and clambers back into the pilot's seat.

No way will Rael fit inside the chopper. But as we lift off, he grabs hold of the landing skid. The whole craft wobbles and I'm sure we will crash. Somehow, the chopper continues to rise into the black sky with Rael dangling below.

I lie with my head in Jared's lap. He cradles me and strokes my forehead.

Part of me still refuses to accept this as anything more than a bad dream. Soon, I will wake up and it will be morning, and everything will be all right.

Or not.

48

Courage

Jared

"Hang on, kids. We'll be there in a jiff."

The pilot has a laconic, Texas accent. The chopper wobbles mercilessly with the weight of the Nephilim clinging to the skid. It flies low, barely clearing the tops of buildings. I glance out the window. The center of the city is one giant black hole but the outskirts are still lit. So it had been a limited strike, enough to get my attention.

The pilot speaks over the radio. "Angel in the net," he says.

There's a burst of static and another voice responds, "Fantastic! FatBoy is on standby."

"Got a Smurfette too."

"What? Who?"

"Girlfriend, maybe."

There's some garbled swearing.

Grace opens her eyes. "Smurfette?"

"It's only a code name."

"Great. You get to be an angel and I get to be a blue-skinned cartoon."

I smile. "You're way prettier."

She grips her head and presses her face into my stomach

as the chopper dips and wavers. Grace hates flying, even in regular planes. This is far worse, but I can see she's in too much pain to care.

We land a half hour later at the Rochester airport where a cargo jet waits on the tarmac with a side door open. Rael has already jumped off. The pilot tells us to get into the plane. The Nephilim watches our every move—we won't be able to make a break for it. Grace clutches my arm as she walks.

"How are you feeling?" I ask.

"Dizzy. Nauseous. Like I'm going to die. Otherwise, awesome."

The interior of the plane is empty but for two rows of seats at the back. A pilot appears holding a bag of cheese puffs. He chews as he points to the back. "Sit down and buckle up." He seems unsurprised when Rael climbs aboard. The Nephilim doesn't try to sit. Instead, he crouches in the center area and wraps himself in his tentacles.

Once we're buckled in, the new pilot closes and locks the door and disappears into the cockpit. A moment later, the engine whines and revs up. Grace covers her ears and squeezes her eyes shut. I touch her leg. The plane shudders as it takes off, bobs around in the unsteady air, then finally levels out. Grace puts her hands down and closes her fingers over mine.

"Why are we in this stupid cargo plane?" she whispers.

"Because of him, probably." I point to Rael.

"Where are we going?"

"My guess would be Switzerland."

"You are correct." Rael speaks in Archean so Grace won't understand.

"So you work for Speer now?" I ask in English.

He seems to bridle at the suggestion. *"I made a bargain."*

"What kind of bargain?"

"He promised to let my people go free if I found you."

"And you believe he will keep his promise?"

"It doesn't matter. Soon, our fathers will be released. All humans will be at their mercy."

"God will not allow Speer or anyone to open the Abyss." I've switched to Archean. I don't want Grace to hear this part.

"Is that so? Did God stop scientists from building nuclear weapons? Did He stop Adolf Hitler from killing six million people? Has He stopped governments from committing ethnic cleansing or condoning the murder of unborn humans? No, God has left the world to its own devices. And its own destruction."

"You're wrong," I say. *"The world will end one day, but only when He decides to end it."*

"And are you not the agent of that? You gave your own body for it. God has forsaken you. It is time you forsook Him as well."

"What are you talking about?" Grace asks.

"Nothing. Just…nothing."

The flight takes six hours. Grace sleeps most of the time, which seems to be her only relief from the pain and the terror. I remember something about having to keep concussion victims awake. I watch her carefully and listen to her breathing and her heartbeat. It's strong and regular. Sleep, I decide, is what she needs.

Although I might never sleep again.

A loud banging noise fills the cabin. Grace awakens with a yelp.

"Landing gear," I say.

She blinks. "Oh." Her fingers take a white-knuckled grasp on the arm rests. "I hate landings."

"How are you feeling?" I ask.

"My head hurts. My body hurts. Everything hurts." I know she isn't only talking about physical pain. "I'm giving this airline a bad review on TripAdvisor."

I smile.

The plane lands hard and bounces twice before reversing the engines. Grace groans, holding her head as if she's afraid it might explode.

After an eternity of taxiing, the planes stops and the engine powers down. The pilot appears, without the cheese puffs this time. He opens the door and lowers the steps.

The sun is out when we emerge, although the air is chilly. A snow-capped mountain range rises up along one side of us with a lake on the other.

"Where are we?" Grace asks.

"Geneva," says the pilot. "Watch your step."

A car idles on the tarmac. Two men stand beside it, watching us from behind dark sunglasses. From the bulk of their coats, I know they're armed. Beside the car is a large panel van. For Rael, probably.

I help Grace down the stairs—she's still unsteady. One of the men approaches and holds out two pieces of black fabric. "Put these on. Don't take them off."

Blindfolds.

I take them, then help Grace into the car. The doors slam behind us. The two men take the front seats. I tie one of the blindfolds around Grace's head and she winces. After I do mine, I take her hand. She grips my fingers hard. The car starts moving although I never hear the engine start. Electric.

"It will only be a short ride," the driver says. "Mr. Speer is waiting."

PART SIX

DRONES

49

Algorithm

Angel

One day before Grace and Jared land in Geneva, a large crowd gathers in the courtyard of the CERN campus. They sit in stands erected for the occasion—the celebration of the re-opening of the new and improved Large Hadron Collider. All the members of the Interlaken Group are present, as well as heads of state of forty countries, including the President of the United States. The Governor of California, Harry Ravel is also present, his expectant wife Shannon at his side. Rows of white-coated scientists surround the dignitaries, all waiting in eager anticipation for the ceremony to begin.

It is strange that Darwin Speer himself is absent.

Piped-in orchestral music thunders from a hundred speakers. They surround a gigantic screen that has been erected behind a statue of the multi-limbed god, Shiva. An image of the god is superimposed over the façade of the newest detector known as APOLLYON, a massive magnetic coil that shines bright orange so it resembles Shiva's circle of fire.

As the music builds, figures emerge from the curtained area below the screen—dancers in white coats with zombie-like expressions. They march in lock-step, curve around

Shiva, and form three lines before the audience. The music stops and a drum—part ritual, part militaristic—beats loudly as the dancers separate. They fling their coats off to reveal skin-colored bodysuits so they appear to be naked. The drumming intensifies as the dancers move to its rhythm— they gyrate wildly, flinging themselves in a frenzy like protons in an atom. More dancers emerge from the curtains wearing black masks and flapping huge white wings. They surround the naked dancers as if they are attacking them, cover them with their wings, and some of them perform mock sexual acts.

Soon the "angels" and the naked dancers form a huge, writhing cluster. Out of their midst is launched a man wearing a costume of white fur with horns on his head. This man is Darwin Speer—except it isn't. It is a very tall, muscular dancer with a shock of white hair, his face painted to look like a skull. He is carried forth by the mass of dancers, human and angel, his arms spread wide. The audience erupts into cheers. The Speer character is placed before the statue of Shiva, and all the dancers bow down to him. One of them throws a white robe over his shoulders. They begin to chant *"La roi du mode est ici!"* over and over.

The king of the world is here.

The music builds as the dancers seem to tear each other apart in ecstasy. Giants appear from behind the screen, walking on stilts with goat horns attached to their heads. Some of the angel dancers are raised on harnesses so they appear to be flying.

The ceremony ends with a crash of symbols and the entire company, all but Speer the goat-god, fall to the ground as if dead.

The audience erupts into a standing ovation that lasts several minutes.

"What does it mean?" I ask Uriel.

"It means Darwin Speer has made himself a god. And this collider is his stairway to heaven."

50

Castle

Grace

We drive for over two hours. I try to peek beneath the bottom of the blindfold like we used to do in second grade playing Pin the Tail on the Donkey. Blindfolds are really stupid. They should have used a bag. Don't these people know I'm an old pro at being kidnapped?

Not that I see anything except grass and trees and distant mountains. My vision becomes increasingly blurry, so attempting to focus makes my head throb. I keep touching the back of my skull, sure there's a big crack there and my brains might be falling out.

"I need to go to the bathroom," I announce as loudly as I can. There's no response from the front seat.

I seriously do have to pee, on top of everything.

Vaguely, I wonder why I'm not more scared. Is it the result of being hit so hard that I can't even process my situation rationally? Or my belief that I am still in the dream and I will wake up before I am actually killed?

The car picks up speed around curves. My stomach roils and I put a hand over my mouth to keep from throwing up.

"Are you okay?" Jared asks for the seventh or eighth time.

No, definitely not.

"Sure."

Only a week ago, we celebrated our wedding in a little stone chapel in the woods. There'd been cake and Logan-berry and dancing. And I had started to think everything would be okay.

Little Mis-Fortune.

The car starts to climb, taking several curvy switchbacks. Just when I can't hold the nausea anymore, the vehicle comes to a stop. Our door opens and someone hauls me out of the car. The air feels blessedly cool. My head spins and I lean on the car for support.

"Welcome, Jared. Grace. You can take those off now," says a German-accented female voice I remember all too well.

I take the blindfold off. High stone walls with medieval towers surround us. It's a castle courtyard. Normally, I would find it pretty cool.

"Wow, a castle," I say. "Good for you, Lucille. You're a true evil queen now."

She raises one eyebrow.

"She's injured," Jared says.

The woman gives me a last, withering look. "We will have her examined."

I don't like the sound of that. She gestures for us to follow her. I hang onto Jared as we walk, and struggle to not throw up all over Lucille's shiny shoes.

She approaches a massive door and two guards in black military outfits swing it open. We find ourselves in a vast medieval foyer lined with suits of armor and colorful shields.

Darwin Speer stands among them.

"Jared! Grace! Welcome to the Ark!"

He wears blue jeans and a black turtleneck. He looks thinner than the recent magazine covers, hollow-cheeked and pale. His white hair is streaked with black. Something is clearly wrong with him.

We follow him into another large room furnished with couches and tables but equally medieval. Not a single modern convenience in sight, only stone and wood and candlelit chandeliers.

I wonder if this castle has a modern bathroom because I really need one.

"I'm really sorry about the way this all went down," Speer says. "I know you've had a long night. Do you want to eat and get some sleep first? Whatever you want to do."

I don't get this guy. He nearly took out an entire city to find Jared and force him back to Switzerland, and now, he acts like the genial host? He must be totally deranged.

"Bathroom," I blurt. Even saying the word makes my head shatter.

"Grace has a concussion," Jared says. "She needs attention."

"What? Oh, gee, I'm sorry about that." Speer speaks into his watch like a super spy. "Owen, can you come up? We have a situation."

Owen appears instantly. He is the attendant with the baby face and slick haircut I remember from the yacht.

"Can you take Miss Fortune to the restroom? And then the clinic. Have her checked out."

"I'm staying here," I say and lean heavily on Jared.

"No, you need to go," Jared's voice is firm, and he removes my hand from his arm. "I'll see you later. Promise."

I hate his brusqueness and how he practically pushes me away. But I do really have to go.

"Follow me, Miss Fortune," Owen says.

"It's Mrs. Lorn," I snap.

"What?" says Speer. "You two? Well, congratulations! We'll have some champagne and celebrate when you're feeling better."

Seriously?

"We don't drink champagne," I say as Owen leads me away. I strain toward Jared, but he doesn't look at me. His eyes are locked on Speer.

We pass through several more grand, medieval rooms and then to a set of stone stairs. I have to stop on almost every step as the act of stepping down makes my brain slosh around in my skull. Owen waits patiently.

At the bottom, he swipes a badge to unlock a large, modern, steel door. He opens it and gestures for me to enter first.

The hallway is dimly lit with actual electric lights. Owen points to a door marked with a WC sign. "Can you manage alone?"

"Of course." I wrench away from him, and grab the wall to keep from falling.

I get through the door and shut it but there's no lock. The bathroom is modern, thankfully—I was afraid I'd find only a chamber pot. I take care of my business, despite the gradual darkening of my vision and the way my blood seems to flood my temples like a tsunami. When I open the door, Owen is standing there with a pleasant smile on his face. He has something in his hand I can't quite see.

"I need to...lie down."

That's the last thing I remember.

51

Mercy

Jared

"Do you mind if I have a drink?"

Speer looks terrible. His skin is splotchy although he has tried to cover it with the turtleneck and what looks like makeup. He's jittery too, reminding me of Lester Crow in withdrawal. His eyes are a dull gray as if they have been drained of color.

He goes to his bar and pours himself a large glass of whiskey.

"How did you do it this time?" I ask. "The EMP."

"Pretty cool, huh? It's called CHAMP. A non-nuclear device currently in its testing phase by the United States government."

"You stole a government weapon?"

"I didn't need to. The Chairman of the Joint Chiefs is in the Group. We've become buddies, as you Americans say."

"And a client?"

"It seemed like a fair trade." He downs the glass and pours another. "After you ditched me in Iceland *and* Norway…well, I had to figure out a new way to draw you out. This was the perfect solution to achieve my goal without any loss of life. I hoped that would make you happy, at least."

"Except for all the destruction you caused. What were you thinking, using Rael for this?"

"Don't worry—he's been contained. Anyway, I can't be held responsible. Collateral damage. It happens." He takes another gulp of whiskey. "Man, you really had me going. How did you get out of Norway, anyway?"

"I'm here," I say. "What do you want?"

Speer sits in a chair. He crosses and then uncrosses his legs, drinks some more, and wipes sweat from his brow.

"I seem to have a glitch or something." His voice thickens like he's having trouble forming the words. "I did more tests. There's no evidence that the Huntington's has come back. It's just…I don't know. Doctors can't figure it out." He swallows the rest of his drink. "I need to know, Jared. What are you?"

"You've seen Rael. That's what I am. That's what you are too, now."

"No." He shakes his head. "No, there has to be something I missed."

I take a breath. "How many people have already had the treatment?"

"Not many. A few dozen. But there will be many more very soon." He jumps up and goes to refill his glass, talking fast. "That's why I need to get more blood. Our lab experiments show that new infusions alleviate the negative symptoms in mice. But we can't make the serum fast enough, and we can't replicate the strands. I tried extracting from Rael, but his strands are too corrupted. The mice merely turn into zombies. Look, I'm sorry for doing it like this but you didn't give me a choice. You disappeared."

"You never intended to let me go, did you? The whole thing with stealing my passport and pretending to get a new one—that was all lies."

"No, no! It was only a delaying tactic. Admittedly, a little crude. I wanted you to stay with me until we'd finished the serum to make sure it worked. But then you…look. The

State of California will approve my treatment for use in a matter of weeks. We have doctors from California and all over the world here learning how to perform the procedure. What did you expect? I had to find you."

I sigh. "I guess neither of us has much of a choice."

Owen appears in the archway. "Sir?"

"What?" Speer snaps.

Owen glances at me. "The girl...fainted. We took her into medical. The doctor says she will be fine but she's very dehydrated and has a severe concussion—"

"I want to see her," I say.

"Don't worry, Jared, we'll take good care of your wife." Speer downs his third drink. He chuckles.

The anger comes in a rush, overwhelming any shred of sense. I lunge for him and knock him back against the bar. His glass flies free and I punch him in the face. He falls to the floor and covers his face with his hands. Blood pours from his nose and drips onto his shirt. I tackle him and tear at his clothes, lost in a rampage.

Shouting and scuffling ensues. Hands pull me away but I flick them off easily. In the next moment, there is the familiar prick in my neck. I let go and drop to the floor.

"Take him..." Speer says, choking on blood. Two men haul me to my feet. My strength runs out of me like air from my lungs. I tuck the piece of Speer's shirt in the waistband of my jeans before I lose the ability to move at all.

~

I awaken strapped to a gurney. A thick steel collar rims my neck. Manacles on my arms and legs are attached to chains anchored into the floor.

A bright light shines in my eyes. It's then blocked by the face of Len Wilder staring down at me.

"Welcome back, Jared. Good to see you again. Although I did hope we wouldn't have to do it this way." He sighs as if he's disappointed. "I'm not sure what you were trying to prove by attacking Darwin."

"I'm a Nephilim," I say. "I can't control myself."

"I suppose that's true." He straps the tourniquet on, swabs my arm, and sticks the needle in. I wince at his roughness.

"I want to see my wife."

"I'm afraid that won't be possible for a while. But we are taking good care of her. Please don't make trouble. The sooner we get what we need, the sooner you can be reunited with her. Assuming Darwin allows it. We thought you'd killed him."

If I wanted to kill him, he'd be dead.

I grit my teeth and ball my fists as I struggle against myself. Everything in me is ready to explode. I lie still as the blood drains from me. One bag, then two. He should stop, but he keeps going. Three…four…six. Half the blood in my body. Either he's trying to weaken me so I can't fight or escape, or Speer is so desperate for more blood that he doesn't care what danger he puts me in.

When the doctor is finished, the guards unhook the chains and all four of them lead me out of the room. They practically have to carry me, I'm so weak from loss of blood. They bring me down a long hallway to another set of stairs and we descend further underground. The air grows cool.

We arrive at a dark, musty-smelling space, lit by a single red-tinged light bulb. I blink, my eyes adjusting, my vision blurred from loss of blood. Iron rings are embedded in the dank stone wall, dripping with mildew. A ledge juts from the wall on which lies a thin blanket. A bucket stands in the corner.

A dungeon.

The guards drag me across the dirt floor and attach my chains to the rings. The chains are long enough that I can lie down or stand, but I can't move more than two feet in any direction. They helpfully move the bucket within my reach.

"Let's see if he can get out of this," one of them says in French.

"I can't wait for him to try."

They laugh and head up the stairs. The steel door slams with one final, damning echo.

52

Awaken

Grace

I don't know where I am.

Pain jackknifes through my skull and I remember.

Jared.

I left him with Speer. Where is he? I see him in my mind in some Frankenstein-like laboratory, hooked up to machines, screaming as bolts of electricity run through his body.

I need to get up and find him, but I can't move.

My body doesn't seem to be connected to my brain. Am I awake or asleep? Alive or dead?

I glance down and notice my left hand resting on my stomach. I focus on one finger until it flinches. Then the others, one by one. Finally, my hand. I raise it to form a fist.

Okay, so I *can* move.

A fancy, red-velvet canopy hangs over my head, like the kind on old-fashioned beds. A wooden chair with velvet padding and gold trim sits nearby. Beyond that, a tapestry hangs on a whitewashed stone wall. The window is tall but narrow and the room is circular.

It's like the tower of the castle.

Ralph would love this place. It's definitely old-school—

Dark Ages-school.

It takes a while to rise to a sitting position. Every time I move, my brain slams into my skull. I swing my legs over the edge of the bed and wait for the nausea to pass. A glass of water and a bottle of Tylenol sit on the bedside table. The bottle contains two tablets. I take them both. That won't even make a dent, but it's better than nothing.

When the room finally settles, I straighten and look around in search of a door.

There isn't one.

I'm locked in a tower like Rapunzel, except without the cool hair.

I feel for the bracelet—it's still on my wrist. *Can you find me, Ralph?* Probably not, since the power is most likely still out in Buffalo, even if the bracelet worked at this range. Does anyone know where we are?

Someone knows.

Ariel knows.

God knows.

Get us out of here, I whisper. I try to stand. The room spins and spins and I drop back to the bed, my head between my knees.

A loud, scraping noise comes from under the floor. I jerk upright. A trap door opens in the floor and a tall man in a white coat appears like the devil emerging from the underworld.

"Ah! You're awake."

He hoists himself up from a ladder and approaches me. He's smiling, but his eyes are beady and intent. "I'm Doctor Wilder." He takes something from his pocket and I tense. A gun? A needle?

No, a flashlight.

"Grace, right?"

I don't bother answering. He shines the light in my eyes. I squint and see red.

"Can you tell me what month it is?" he asks.

"Uh…May."

"Good. And where do you live?"

"Buffalo."

"Do you know where you are now?"

"I'm being held prisoner in the castle of an evil ogre."

"Ha-ha. Good. Your memory seems fine. Are you experiencing dizziness? Nausea? Headaches?"

"Yes."

"That should ease in time. What you need is rest and fluids. No strenuous movement for a while."

"This Tylenol won't cut it."

"Ibuprofen will be more upsetting to your stomach."

"Where's Jared?"

"Jared is fine."

"I want to see him."

"That won't be possible right now. You should know, he attacked Mr. Speer and almost killed him."

"What?" The shock of this hurts worse than the headache.

"Yes, we've had to…secure him. Thankfully, Mr. Speer got away with only a broken nose. It could have been far worse."

If Jared had wanted it to be 'far worse,' it would have been. He must have held back.

But why attack Speer at all? Can he really no longer control his anger?

"Perhaps in a few days, when you're feeling better, we can arrange something. It's best for you to rest and take it easy. You don't want to risk re-injury." He straightens and heads for the trap door. "I'll be back to check on you. In the meantime, Borg will look after your needs." He climbs down the ladder and pulls the trap door shut. I hear the sliding of a bolt and a scraping noise as the ladder is pulled away.

Now what?

I lie back and wait for the room to stop spinning.

A plan. I need a plan, but what? This castle is huge. Even

if I could get out of this room, how would I find Jared? How would we get out of here?

Don't worry about tomorrow. Tomorrow has worries of its own.

True. I have enough worries to last me for today.

I close my eyes and pray.

Lord, protect us and save us.

The same prayer I prayed when I clung to the side of a waterfall on Jared's back. Levin's prayer from *Anna Karenina*.

Lord, protect us and save us.

And then another.

Though I walk through the valley of the shadow of death...I will fear no evil.

For You are with me.

53

The Fire Remains

Jared

It's been five days. At least, I think so but I am starting to lose track.

I can't move much because of the chains. Not that I want to move at all.

Every day, I am taken to the Blood Room, as I think of it, by the four guards. The needle is inserted and the blood drained—five pints, sometimes six, until I pass out. I awaken back in the cell, chained and alone.

Like Azazel.

Perhaps this is my fate. To be chained in a pit and treated like an animal. I am as guilty as Azazel. Maybe more so. I knew what I did was wrong and I did it anyway. I allowed myself to be used by men who thought they ruled the world.

There is no excuse.

My blood is not regenerating fast enough to keep up with my "donations." Wilder leaves me only enough blood to keep my heart pumping and my brain functioning. I am barely alive.

When I refuse to eat, they force-feed me thick shakes made of pureed vegetables enhanced with large amounts of turmeric. For blood-enhancement, Wilder says. They give me plenty of water to drink, which I crave. The thirst is maddening.

I lie on the ledge, half-sleeping and half-dreaming. I have visions of Grace in her wedding dress, the crown of flowers in her hair, whispering those words—our vows. Of kissing her—dancing, laughing, and free.

"Hey kid."

I open my eyes to see Mike before me. He leans against the wall, eats sunflower seeds, and spits out the shells. I'm reasonably sure I'm hallucinating.

"Mike?"

"It's me."

"Did you come to get me out of here?"

"No. I've come to distract you from your own thoughts. You're going down the rabbit hole, aren't you?"

"Yeah."

"I thought so. You have to hang in there a little longer."

"Why?"

"A little longer." He comes closer and puts a hand on my head. His Light surges through my body like an electric shock. My heart races and nerves fire as blood pumps through my veins into the tips of my fingers.

Maybe I'm not hallucinating.

Mike withdraws his hand. "That should keep you for a while." He steps back. "I have a message for you. From Elohim."

"What is it?"

"You're not alone."

"Grace—"

"We have Grace."

A shining stillness overtakes my body and slows my heart. Peace.

When I open my eyes again, Mike is gone.

But a sack of sunflower seeds lies on the floor.

~

Footsteps. I roll over and groan. Already? Has a day passed since the last blood-letting? Mike restored me somewhat, but I'm not ready to be drained again. I need more time— to sleep without dreams and to hope.

"Time to wake up, Vampire Boy."

They have all sorts of names for me.

The main guard's name is Stefan. He only speaks French and doesn't know I can understand him. I pretend I can't. "I hear you're an angel," he said the first day. "Where are you hiding your wings? Or are they invisible?"

The others laughed.

The next day: "Are you still here? I thought you would have broken out by now, that you could melt these bars with your laser eyesight. Or is that Superman? I can never remember."

The day after: "Whoa. You really do look like a vampire now. Better watch out, fellows. He might want to bite your neck! He needs some blood, that's for sure."

Today, he seems surprised at my condition.

"Look at you. Back from the dead?"

The guards unhook the chains and lead me up the stairs. But instead of the Blood Room, they take me to a bathroom.

"Take a shower," says the one who speaks English, Claude. "Put the clothes on. Knock when you are done." Stefan pushes me in and shuts the door and the lock clicks.

They have a point. I guess I am starting to stink.

I look around. There are no windows, only one vent but that's too small to fit through. I sigh, peel the clothes from my body, and take a long, hot shower, although it's difficult with the manacles. I put on the clothes laid out for me— black pants and a black hooded sweatshirt with the golden spear logo on the breast. I stick the piece of bloody fabric in the pocket of the pants. They still haven't found it. I suppose that if they were going to strip-search me, they would have done it already.

I knock on the door when I'm done. Stefan opens it and immediately puts the chains back on me and pulls the hood over my head. They take me up the stairway to the main floor of the castle.

I hear voices, commotion. I am led down a hallway to a curtained archway. Stefan pushes the curtain aside to reveal a medieval chapel lined with ornate arched windows and dark marble columns. About a hundred people are seated in chairs facing the altar. They all turn to stare at me.

Darwin Speer stands on the altar platform in front of a large, blank video screen. He looks fully restored—there's not even a bandage on his nose and no trace of a bruise. He must have had a new infusion.

"Ladies and Gentlemen! Mesdames and Messieurs!" He continues speaking in both English and French. "This is the moment you have waited for. We have here with us the donor of our serum himself, the 'superman' I've told you so much about. He hasn't been very cooperative of late, so we've been forced to take some precautions. Nothing to be alarmed about."

Speer motions to Stefan, who pushes me forward. The two guards holding my chains follow. Another lingers close by with a rifle. I feel all the eyes in the room on me in the shocked silence. It's like being led to the gallows.

I recognize a few of the faces. William Hyde. Marta What's-her-name, the scientist. Lucille. Harry and Shannon.

This must be the Interlaken Group.

Speer watches me, his mouth set in triumph. I shuffle onto the platform. Stefan pulls my hood away. A murmur of curiosity sweeps the room.

"Here he is, our patient zero. We call him "Abaddon." Speer grabs hold of the chain attached to my neck and yanks playfully. "Abaddon is over one hundred and fifty years old. Yet see how young he looks. Hardly more than twenty-five."

Gasps and murmurs follow.

I focus on Shannon Snow. She sits still, a smile painted on her face and her green eyes fixed on me. She puts a hand to her rounded belly and rubs it absently.

Questions are fired at Speer one after the other. Many still doubt his story. Speer becomes agitated, his face flushed, and his eyes pulse. Apparently, his groupies are not that impressed with me.

"He doesn't look all that remarkable," says one woman. "How do we know this is real? How do we know he is what you say he is?"

"I will prove it to you!" Speer shouts, clearly agitated. Things have not gone as he hoped. He turns to an armed guard, grabs the rifle, and swings it at me. I have no time to think or act. He fires, the shots echoing in the vast space. Bullets slam into my stomach and my side and I drop to the floor. Screams and gasps join the echoes, although I can hardly hear anything now. My world has become suddenly small, a spinning vortex of pain.

"Don't worry, he'll be fine!" Speer shouts over the rising din. "His regenerative power is remarkable. So it is for all those who have the treatment. Think what this could mean for our military. Our soldiers would not be killed as long as we protected their hearts and heads. They would recover in hours rather than months." He stands over me. "Get up!" he snarls.

I whisper, "You promised...no government..."

"Get up!" He turns back to his audience. "As soon as we are able to mass-produce the serum, the cost per treatment will come down dramatically. And I can assure you—especially my military friends—that the cost would be far, far less than all that body armor and medical care you pay for now.

"California, thanks to our friend Governor Ravel and his lovely wife Shannon, is about to approve our treatment. Clinics will soon be open all over the state. And you know what they say, as California goes, so goes the country. And then, the world."

Speer pushes the mic away and whispers to Stefan: "Get him up."

The guards grab me under my arms and haul me to my feet. Speer comes over and rips open the front of my shirt to display the bullet holes in my body.

"You see? The bleeding has already stopped. In a few minutes, the wounds will be completely healed. This is more than a breakthrough, ladies and gentlemen. This is the future! And you have seen it happen right before your eyes!"

Faces gape at me in disbelief. I want to shout, *Do you see what he just did? Do you see the monster he's become?* No one moves. No one speaks. Then Harry Ravel stands and begins to clap. Others join in and the applause spreads as people jump to their feet. The sound reverberates through the vaulted space and drowns out the braying laughter of demons.

Speer whispers to Stefan. "Get him out of here."

54

Carry You

Grace

I've been in this tower for six days.

I'm going crazy with boredom. I stare out the window at the serene Swiss countryside, the lake, and the mountains. I leaf through the piles of science magazines left on the nightstand, most at least ten years old.

And I search for a way out.

I've tried to open the trap door but there's no handle on the top and it's bolted on the other side. The room contains nothing that I could use to pry it open. All my fingernails are broken from trying.

Every day is the same. Borg arrives with breakfast and fresh towels. He's young, blond, and looks extremely healthy. I wonder if he's had the treatment and is like a mini-Jared. He looks as though he could lob me out the window with very little effort. He gave me a package of clean under-wear, thank goodness, and a dress that probably came from Lucille's closet—it's clingy, black and short. I hated putting it on, but my clothes were rank.

After a breakfast of fruit and oatmeal that Borg calls Muesli, the doctor appears. He shines his flashlight in my eyes and asks dumb questions. "What is the capital of New

York State?" "How many fingers am I holding up?" Sometimes, I say the wrong answers and he gives me a worried
look and writes something down in his chart. Even though
I feel better—the dizziness is gone and the headaches are
only intermittent—I decide not to tell him so.

"I want to see my husband," I say every time.

"You will soon. Your husband is fine. He's in good
health and well taken care of."

Britney Spears.

Borg returns at noon and five p.m. sharp with lunch and
dinner, mostly salads, vegetables, and steamed fish. "Brain
food," he tells me. "High in antioxidants to help replenish
brain cells." It isn't bad, exactly, but I long for a chicken
nugget.

I long for Jared.

Something is wrong, I feel it in my bones. Jared is in deep
trouble.

I have considered trying to escape out the window, but
the panes are permanently soldered into the wall. Besides,
the drop to the ground is at least a hundred feet. Even my
bedsheets wouldn't get me close enough to make it without
injury, assuming I could break a window and squeeze
through.

And then I got to thinking that if this is a real castle, it
might have a secret passage. So I searched the room and
looked under carpets and behind furniture. I felt along the
walls and tried to pull away loose stones. I found nothing.

How much longer will they keep me here? What will they
do with me?

Six days.

I get out of bed, stretch, and look at the clock. Borg is
due in fifteen minutes. He's extremely punctual. I go into
the bathroom, which is tiny and probably converted from a
storage closet. The toilet is actually right under the shower-
head, which makes doing either of those activities rather
awkward. I strip my clothes off, take a shower and attempt

to wash my hair, although getting my arms over my head is a risky maneuver. As I turn to rinse out the shampoo, I slip and almost fall into the toilet. I grab the shower head for support, but it comes loose from the wall. Water sprays everywhere and I manage to shut it off and then examine the hole in the wall. I'll have to tell Borg I broke the shower.

I realize I can see all the way through. Behind the fiberglass shower stall there is—nothing.

I stand on the toilet and stick my head as far as possible into the hole. I see a rounded shaft about three feet in diameter. The crumbling stones tell me it's part of the original castle. Water pipes and electric cables run up and down its length. I can't see the bottom.

Maybe it had been used originally to dispose of the contents of chamber pots.

Or maybe it was once an escape hatch.

My heart starts to race. I dry off and wipe the soaked bathroom down with the towels. I stick the shower head back into the wall as best I can and close the curtain, hoping Borg won't open it to check. I quickly brush my teeth and comb my wet hair, still a bit slick with shampoo. That done, I leave the towels on the sink, go back into the room, and put the black dress on.

Then, I lie on the bed with a washcloth over my forehead as the hatch in the floor swings open.

"Guten morgen, Fräulein."

"Hey, Borg. What's up?"

"No, no. Say, *Was is los?"* He's trying to teach me German.

"Was is los?"

"Nicht viel."

"Cool." I have no idea what he said.

"You should learn German. You Americans only speak English."

"'Cause everyone speaks English." This is another conversation we always have.

He comes over and peers at me. "*Bist du krank?* Sick?"

"Only a headache."

"I give you some *Medizin.*"

"Thanks."

He puts two orange tablets on the nightstand, then goes into the bathroom. I hold my breath.

A moment later, he comes out carrying the sopping wet towels. I wait for an interrogation, but he doesn't remark on them, just sticks them in the laundry bag he's brought with him.

"I bring you more clothes." He pulls a pair of black yoga pants and a white T-shirt from another bag. "You like?"

"Awesome."

"Anything else I can do for you?"

I let out the breath. "You can take me to see my husband."

"*Es tut mir lied*, I can't do that."

"I figured you'd say that."

"Bis später, Fräulein."

"Whatever."

I wait until the trap door is closed and bolted and the ladder scrapes away from the opening before I get up and put on the new clothes. Much better. *Good timing, Borg. You're a prince.* I go to the bathroom, stand on the toilet, and carefully pull the shower head out. Working as quietly as I can, I rip away pieces of the wall until the hole is big enough to fit through.

I test the water pipe, hoping it's sturdy enough to hold me. The stones of the shaft are uneven and look crumbly, but at least they will give me some footholds. It takes time to hoist myself up to the hole. I stand with one foot on the toilet and the other on the wall and squirm and wiggle my way in until I can grab onto the water pipe and pull my hips and legs through. I gasp, thoroughly sweaty, and pray I don't get stuck. Finally, I free one leg and jam it against the shaft wall to steady myself. I take several long breaths and pull the other leg through.

Balanced as best I can, I take a break until my heart rate slows. My head swims with the exertion. I glance down, and see nothing but blackness. The air inside the shaft is stale and hot. I slide my hands down a few inches, pull one foot from its perch, and drop lower, sliding before I find another foothold. My heart thuds in my ears. I do it again and move a few inches at a time. The pipe wobbles and loose stones fall down the shaft. I don't hear them hit bottom. Sweat pours into my eyes but I can't wipe it away. The muscles of my arms start to burn and my hands cramp. Cobwebs catch in my hair and I swear spiders are crawling down my neck.

If I fall and die, no one will ever find me.

I keep going, while my mind questions everything. How much farther? How much longer? What if Borg comes back and finds me gone? What if Wilder shows up early? What if someone hears me rattling around in the shaft? Will they be waiting for me at the bottom?

My foot slips off a crumbled stone. I lose my grip on the pipe and drop like a literal rock. My heart nearly stops but the bottom comes up quickly.

The drop is only a few feet.

Maybe my luck is changing.

Breathing a thank you to God, I check to make sure nothing is broken. Then I stand and peer into the utter darkness. I stick my hands out and move until I hit the wall, then I slide along it, creeping slowly in the hope that I will come upon some sort of doorway or opening. There has to be some way out, or else why bother making a secret passage in the first place? I finally discover a break in the stones—a small opening. It seems to be a wooden door, only about three feet high, but it won't budge—probably hasn't been opened in centuries. I get down on my hands and knees and throw my weight against it again and again. I try punching it with my feet, but all I get is pain.

Panic fills my chest. Hot, breathless fear nearly suffocates me. I'm trapped.

Though I walk through the valley...

I start to sing, softly, only to myself.

Keep going.

Was that my voice, or God's?

They will come looking for me once they realize what I've done. They will find me—

Keep going!

That nagging voice. *Ariel, is that you?*

I heave out a breath and haul myself upright. On shaky legs, I slide along the wall, hoping against hope that there is another way.

And then I nearly fall over a step.

I drop to my knees and clasp my hands together, almost crying with gratitude before I crawl up the steps—there are only four—to another door.

In the gloom, I feel around but there is no door handle. My heart hammers. *Please please please...* I press both my palms against it and push as hard as I can.

It gives. I let out a gasp of relief and push harder. The door scrapes against the stone floor. I thrust against it and manage to open it a little more each time. A rattle on the other side indicates that it has hit something. I reach in to figure out what's blocking it.

Shelves.

I throw my back against the door and shove as hard as I can. Blood pulses in my head, awakening the concussion. My vision turns red and my body shakes with strain. What I wouldn't give for Jared's superhuman strength right now.

The door moves enough that I can squeeze through into the tight space between the shelving units and the wall.

Thank you thank you thank you...

I feel around on the shelves—boxes and jars, bottles of

pills. It appears to be a storage closet of—drugs? Medical supplies?

I work my way along the wall until the shelving stops at a door—regular sized, and modern, with a knob. I open it a crack and stick my head through.

I'm greeted by light and noise—people talking and moving around a long hallway with a curved ceiling, like a subway tunnel, the stone walls painted white. Old-fashioned fixtures at intervals overhead cast pools of light on the tile floor.

There's a great deal of hurried activity—people in white coats moving from one passage to another, some pushing gurneys. Excited chatter echoes through the halls. It seems to be a medical facility or a hospital. Is it possible that Jared might be here somewhere?

I step through the door and dash into the first room I find. It's another closet with a few white coats hanging on hooks on the wall. I put one on and walk out again, careful to hold my head high and act like I'm supposed to be there.

I saunter down the hall. People rush by without noticing me. Everyone seems extremely busy. I peek into rooms and see patients in hospital beds, hooked up to IV's. Many have bandages on their heads. They must have already had the treatment.

I pass two operating rooms—one empty, another in use—as I turn corners and go down more hallways. Curious, I peer in the window. The patient lies on the table. A weird contraption is attached to his head, like in some old science-fiction movie. Is this how they administer the treatment?

Part of me wants to watch longer to see how this works, but I have to keep moving. I have to find Jared. After a while I realize I'm lost. The hallways extend in every direction like a rabbit warren. I'm going around in circles.

Help me.

I see a guard approaching, a rifle strapped to his chest. I duck into a room and wait until he passes. Then, maybe by instinct or divine guidance, I follow him.

The guard takes several turns before he stops at a set of double steel doors. He scans his badge and a buzzer sounds. The door closes behind him when he goes through. I race forward and try to grab it, but it clicks shut. I lean against it, my heart pounding in my chest.

But not only *my* heart. A second beat echoes like a distant drum—slower and more labored, an echo of my own.

Jared.

He's here. Somewhere beyond these doors.

A hand falls on my shoulder and a voice barks in my ear, "What are you doing here?"

I turn to face another armed guard, his face hard and mocking. I swallow. *Think fast.*

"Let me see my husband," I yell. All activity in the hall stops and everyone turns to look at us. Heat rushes to my face. This is my only play. "You can't keep me locked up forever. I demand to see Jared. Now!"

The guard releases me, uncertain. I press forward to address the onlookers who are murmuring to each other.

"Darwin Speer has kept me prisoner here. He's not who you think he is. He's a—"

"What's going on?"

Lucille appears from nowhere and pushes the guard aside. Her eyes burn into mine.

"Grace, you're ill. You shouldn't be out of bed. Come, let us take you back—"

"I want to see Jared." I force myself to stand straight and face her without blinking. "You people have lied to me. I need to know he's okay."

She glances around at the curious crowd and pastes on a fake smile. "No problem at all. I'll take you to him. But you need to calm down now." She puts her arm around my shoulder. "Everything's fine, go back to work." She waves the guard off and scans her badge at the door. "This way."

As soon as we're through the door, she pushes me into the wall, her face inches from mine.

"Don't you ever do something like that again," she snarls.

"You can't hold me prisoner here—"

"You are not a prisoner. You are a *patient*. You came here with a severe concussion. We offered you medical treatment. That's all."

"And Jared? What are you doing to him?"

She hesitates. "I have nothing to do with that."

"And I suppose you know nothing about Dana Martinez either."

"Who?"

"Your brother's girlfriend. The one he murdered."

"You're crazy."

"Am I really? So how come *you* haven't done the treatment yet?"

She opens her mouth but closes it again.

"You know what it's doing to him. He's a monster. He's a Nephilim."

She backs away. "You have no idea what you're saying. You've had a severe concussion and have probably sustained some brain injury. However, despite your opinion of me, I do have a heart. I will take you to Jared if you promise to go back to your room and not speak of this to anyone."

"Sorry. I can't do that. But you *will* take me to Jared. Now. Or I will find him myself."

"The guards are armed."

"Then they will have to shoot me. Is that what you want? To explain to the authorities how a girl your brother *kidnapped* ended up dead?"

She bites her lower lip. "Come with me." She takes my arm and leads me down the dark hallway, her high heels echoing in the curved space. After several turns, we end up at another steel door. A guard sits on the chair beside it.

"Open it," she orders. He looks at me, then her, and does as he's told.

"Down there." She points down a long stone staircase.

"You first."

She glares at me and starts down the steps. I follow. The dim light changes from white to red. The stairs end in a large cellar-like space with a single red light bulb hanging from the low ceiling. It smells of mildew and human waste.

I wrinkle my nose. "What is this place?"

"It's…a holding facility."

"You mean it's a dungeon."

She doesn't respond.

It looks unoccupied, and I'm certain I've walked into a trap. Then Lucille steps a little farther into the room, and I make out a human form lying on a stone ledge built into the far wall.

He faces away from me, his body shrouded in black. He doesn't move. I step closer, fearful.

"Jared?"

Slowly, he turns over and peers at me. His shirt is ripped open, revealing several ugly wounds. Blood smears his skin. I hear a loud clanking sound and realize he's chained up, his arms and legs manacled. A thick steel collar is fastened around his neck.

I clasp my hand over my mouth to keep from screaming.

"Grace?" His voice is very faint. He squints into the dark—I don't think he can see me.

I stumble toward him and fall to my knees at his side.

"What did they do to you?"

"He…shot me."

"Who? Speer?"

"He was…showing off. For his friends."

I gasp and turn to Lucille.

"Are you people insane?"

"It was only a demonstration for the Group," Lucille says. "No major arteries were hit. He'll be fine."

I touch Jared's face. His skin is hot and clammy but not in his normal way. His glow is completely gone. His eyes are darker and almost black.

He's sick.

That's impossible. Jared can't get sick.

I examine his wounds. They've healed over but are an ugly shade of purple. I touch one of them and he winces.

"He's not healing," I say to Lucille. "His wounds are infected. Can't you see that?"

"It's only taking a little longer because of the blood loss. But he'll recover."

"He needs medical help. You need to let him go."

"We can't. He attacked Darwin."

I remember the doctor telling me this. I turn to Jared. "Why?"

"Because I...couldn't do this anymore..." He reaches into his pocket, pulls something out, and presses it into the palm of my hand. "Take this...keep it safe..."

My fingers close over the fabric. Is this some sort of memento? I have no idea. I only know it has to be kept hidden.

I bend over him and start to cry, shaking my shoulders and rocking so Lucille won't see me stuff the fabric in my waistband. I stand up and face her.

"He'll die if you keep him here."

"It's not my call," Lucille says.

"Then tell your brother—"

"He's not here. He's at CERN. The collider goes online today."

Today?

"It's time to go," says Lucille. "You got what you wanted."

Jared will die. They've taken too much from him, but there's nothing I can do to help him.

Except...

God, please, help. Please.

I take Jared's face in my hands and force him to focus on me.

When he does, I sing.

55

The Light

Jared

She sings the AngelSong.

It's like the first time I heard it in the school atrium, when it shot through my body like liquid fire to ignite every muscle, every nerve, and every molecule of my being.

The Dark has descended so thoroughly in the last days, I have not even tried to fight. It's the first time in my life I can remember feeling real, soul-killing pain. Pain so intense and pervasive, it's become my very existence, renewed with every breath.

This is your destiny, said the voice in my head, Azazel's voice, over and over. *I warned you this would happen if you rejected me.* I would die in chains but I welcomed it. It was like penance. It would be an end.

But suddenly, there is Grace.

And Light—a light only I can see, pure and Dark-defeating.

I grip her hand and try to absorb every note through my skin. The music washes over me and through me, exposing all the dark places and suppressing the pain like a narcotic.

"Stop it!" Lucille shrieks. She covers her ears, the Song

like a knife in her soul, piercing and terrible. I see her demons twisting and contorting in agony, screaming for silence.

But the Song only grows louder until the very stones of the prison vibrate and shift.

Lucille flees up the steps. I rise from the ledge, compelled by Grace's voice as if I'm levitating. She puts her arm around my waist—whether to help me up or to keep me from floating to the ceiling, I'm not quite sure. I raise my arms and wrench the chains from the wall. Dirt and stones shower us. I strip the cuffs off and then the collar—it's so easy, like tearing paper. I yank the leg chains from the crumbling wall.

"Jared…" She stares at me in breathless wonder, as if she can't believe what just happened. I glance down at the packet of sunflower seeds still on the floor where Mike left them. I was not abandoned. Not forsaken. Maybe I was even forgiven.

I hold her. It's all I've dreamt of, having my arms free so I could hold her again.

Thank you.

She wraps her arms around my waist, sobbing into my chest. I'd stay there forever if it weren't for the fact that the walls of this prison are crumbling around us.

"I think we need to get out of here," I say.

"Good idea."

We run for the stairs. A guard blocks our way and points his rifle at us.

"Stop!"

There's a flash of Light before me, compressed into a single blade, and that blade is Michael.

The gun jams.

We push past the confused guard and run down the passage, searching for a way out. A discordant alarm sounds, and the hallway is suddenly choked with people rushing around and yelling in panicked voices. This can't be about us. Something else is going on.

"Jared!" Grace points down another hallway, where people careen toward us. They're running away from something. Then, I see the source of their terror.

Rael.

He barrels down the passage, knocks light fixtures from the ceiling, smashes holes in the wall, and tramples anyone not fast enough to get out of his way.

It's Rael, but only parts of him.

He has no tail. The tentacles have been severed to stumps and one of his hands is missing. He's more of a horror now than he had been before.

I pull Grace away from the flow of people and duck into a doorway. Rael continues past us. He sees nothing and no one—he only wants to destroy. Like Godzilla decimating Tokyo. Blood looms in his wild blue eyes.

Whatever they have done to him, it's worse than what they did to me.

The halls are mostly empty now, except for the injured. A lone guard darts out of a room and fires at Rael. The bullets only aggravate him. He swats the gun away and hurls the man into the wall—his body makes a sickening crack and falls in a heap of plaster.

"Come on," I say.

We follow the Nephilim down another passage that dead ends at a blank wall. There is no way out. He slams his fists against the wall, over and over. Plaster cracks and breaks off. The lights overhead shiver and fall to spray sparks everywhere. I look behind us and see three guards with tranq rifles creeping toward us, followed by two men in white coats. We're trapped, but Rael continues to punch the wall.

"Rael, stop. We need to fight now. They're coming."

But he doesn't stop. To my amazement, daylight shines through the holes he's made amid the clouds of plaster dust. The stones of the thousand-year-old castle wall give way to his punishing assault. The guards are almost upon us when the Nephilim lunges through the opening. Grace and I stumble after him while the guards scream at us to stop.

This is my first glimpse of sun and my first intake of uncirculated air in many days. I savor the moment, but it doesn't last long.

We're at the base of the castle, on a steep, grassy slope that leads down to the lake. Drones whir overhead. Darts sail past and somehow miss us.

Rael hurtles down the slope. I follow, half-carrying Grace. We make it to the edge of the water by the time several ATVs roar down the hill. Gunshots echo in our ears—warning shots, I assume. They won't kill us. Rael is in the water, wading across the lake.

"We're trapped," Grace whispers.

A voice on a megaphone commands, "Stop at once!"

Grace sheds the white lab coat and I take off the ripped hoodie. We look at each other, grab hands, jump into the water and start swimming.

From within the small motorboats that zoom toward us, men shoot at Rael. He roars and slaps the water, stirring up great waves. Grace is swamped and disappears under the surface. I dive to search for her. The huge waves churn the bottom up, making the water murky. I can't see her so I dive deeper, fighting the pull of the current Rael has created as he turns the peaceful lake into a turbulent ocean.

She's been under too long.

When I find her, she's drifting, limp, eyes closed. I pull her to me and fight my way to the surface, although it keeps shifting away as I swim toward it. Bubbles escape from her mouth and nose. I kick harder, thrusting my body upward against the force of the undertow.

Just when it seems I will never make it to the surface, something clamps onto my shoulder and hurtles me out of the water, Grace still in my arms. We slam against a slimy surface—it's Rael's stumped back. I cling to him, holding Grace with one hand as he wades across the lake, only his head and shoulders above the water. The gunfire stops. I assume the boats have probably been swamped, but the drones still buzz overhead.

We reach the opposite bank and Rael runs up the slope and deep into the trees.

"Stop!" I speak the word like a command, not expecting him to obey. "Hide. Grace isn't breathing."

I'm a little shocked when he ducks under a thicket of trees, and crouches low. I slide off his back, taking Grace with me. The water will have calmed and the boats will soon get to the shore. We have little time. I lay her on the ground, give her mouth-to-mouth, and thump her chest until she vomits water. While she coughs and gasps, I turn her onto her side. She's alive.

"Sorry about this," I say, and hoist her onto my back again. Rael and I continue up the slope, remaining under the cover of the trees, but the drones keep up with us. When I hear crashing in the underbrush below us, I know that our pursuers are closing in.

We reach the end of the tree line. The top of the ridge is all grass, no cover.

"We need to get over the ridge," I say. They'll be here any second. There's no place to go but up.

Rael only nods in reply. We run to the top of the ridge and look down. The ground drops steeply into a deep ravine.

"Grace," I whisper. "Hang on."

We jump over the edge.

I've done this before, a hundred times. Jumping is my freedom, my release. For a moment I am airborne, Grace on my back, soaring as if I really do have wings. Rael is not so aerodynamic. He lands halfway down and tumbles the rest of the way. I land on the slope and jump again, leaping toward the a stream bed at the bottom. Rael comes to rest beside me a moment later.

"What just happened?" Grace's groggy voice cheers my soul.

"You don't want to know."

I run through the stream to a rock ledge and duck under it, letting her down from my back gently. Rael joins me, though his bulk is still largely exposed. I wait, but I don't see any drones overhead. Nor do I see any of Speer's men on the ridge.

"Maybe we lost them," I say. "We should keep going and get to the other side of the next ridge. Just to make sure."

Rael says nothing. I wonder if Speer took his tongue as well.

"What did he do to you?"

He takes a long time before he speaks. "He tried to...fix me."

"So he lied to you too, didn't he?"

Rael looks away. "He fears what he has done. To himself."

"What's he saying?" Grace murmurs.

I kneel beside her. "Nothing. Are you okay?"

"You say that way too much."

"I know."

"Are *you* okay?" She touches my stomach and my side. The bullet wounds that are now barely visible. "Would you look at that." She smiles.

"Thank you for coming for me."

"Wait 'til you hear how that went down."

"Do you still have it? What I gave you?"

"Yes." She reaches into her waistband and retrieves the strip of fabric. It's soaked but the blood stains are still there. "What is it?"

"It's Speer's."

Her brow knits as she stares at the fabric. Then she takes a breath, understanding.

"That's why you attacked him."

I nod.

"You almost died."

"Make sure Bradford gets it. When you get home."

She shakes her head and tucks the fabric away again. "When *we* get home."

"Can you walk?"

"I'd rather not."

"Then get on my back."

We start up the next mountain, Grace on my back and Rael leading the way. The terrain is steep and rocky and there are few trees, but no one follows us anymore. We're alone.

Eventually, we reach a sheer rock face and start to climb, scaling the nearly vertical cliff. Grace clutches my neck and her breath rasps in my ear. Rael gets to the top first and reaches down to pull us up. Grace slides down my body and lies flat on the rock shelf, closing her eyes.

"That wasn't...fun."

We're on the summit of a mountain under a perfect blue sky. The wind is soft and chill. It's quiet. I look around, searching for a town, a farm, a chalet, something. I see nothing.

We need to get to a phone and call Ralph. The thought of him comforts me. Ralph. The Hobbit Hole...home.

I leave Grace where she is and climb a little farther up, to the very top. It's windier here. I realize I'm not the first person to do this. Before me is a large mound of rocks, and at the very top, a wooden cross.

I smile. It seems fitting, to find this cross at the end of this journey.

I drop to my knees and fold my hands. A prayer touches my lips, a simple prayer, but the first I've ever prayed.

Thank you.

Suddenly, the air seems to shatter, shot through with sound. A massive boom like a hundred trains colliding, a thousand earthquakes, the earth itself falling out of orbit and crashing into a void. The mountain under my feet trembles so violently, I'm knocked off my knees. The cross on the rock pile shivers and tumbles. And then, I see it.

A blade of pure light rising like a golden spear into the sky.

56

Descent

Angel

The massive energy breach breaks the collider open and sends waves of nuclear heat soaring like a blade of light into the sky. But most of the explosion goes underground. It tears through the earth like a meteor, melting solid rock, obliterating everything in its rush to the core.

This was not a surprise to Elohim.

It is time for the princes to gather the armies. To assemble on the mountain of the Lord and face the consequences of the folly of men. For the heaven has fallen away, and the earth is sinking into the void. The Dark ascends.

THE PLAYLIST

All the chapter titles in this novel are song titles from the *Forgiven* novel playlist, available on Spotify and iTunes. Music plays a big role in the Forlorn series, so I develop a playlist for each book, which guides me through the writing. The Part titles are all names of albums from the band Muse, whose music often evokes the effect of technology on the human condition.

"Going to Mars" Judah and the Lion
"Where We Come Alive" Ruelle
"God Only Knows" for KING & COUNTRY
"Poison in the Water" Von Grey
"Play With Fire" WAR*HALL
"Dangerous Game" Klergy
"New Born" Muse
"A Beginner's Guide to Destroying the Moon" Foster the People
"Who Will Save You" Katie Garfield
"Hard Love" NEEDTOBREATHE
"Control" Halsey
"Rescue Me" Thirty Seconds to Mars
"Spiritual War" Emily Brimlow
"Demon in Profile" The Afghan Whigs
"Unstoppable" Sia
"Don't Dream It's Over" The Head and the Heart
"Feeling Good" Muse
"Clearly" Grace VanderWaal
"On Fire" Firewood Island
"Giant" Matrimony
"Houdini" Foster the People
"A Demon's Fate" Within Temptation
"Gold Plated Lie" Scott Mulvahill

"After You" Meghan Trainor
"Conversations" Judah and the Lion
"figure it out" Faith Marie
"Smoke and Mirrors" Imagine Dragons
"Human" Of Monsters and Men
"Starlight" Muse
"War of Hearts" Ruelle
"Great Wide Open" Thirty Seconds to Mars
"Breaking Through" Audrey Assad
"Everywhere I Go" Sleeping at Last
"Battlefield" Svrcina
"Knights of Cydonia" Muse
"Game of Survival" Ruelle
"Lion" Saint Mesa
"Pressure" Muse
"Miracle" CHVRCHES
"Start Again" OneRepublic
"Fighting Furies" Charmaine
"Get up and Fight" Muse
"Brave" Moriah Peters
"Us" James Bay
"Forever On Your Side" NEEDTOBREATHE
"Shadows" The Afters
"Bad Dreams" Faouzia
"Courage" Peter Gabriel
"Algorithm" Muse
"Castle" Halsey
"Mercy" Muse
"Awaken" Klergy
"The Fire (Remains)" The Dear Hunter
"Carry You" Ruelle
"The Light" Disturbed
"Descent" Lawless

SPECIAL THANKS

To publisher Dawn Carrington and everyone at Vinspire for their excellence and support.

To Judah Raines and Delia Latham for expert editing.

To agent Julie Gwinn for opening doors and being a wonderful friend.

To my husband Steve for supporting my writing habit through the years.

To my daughters Danielle, Dominique, and Samantha for explaining to me how teenagers really talk.

To D.L. Rosensteel, Mark Buzard, T.L. Sherwood, and Mary Akers for reading, commenting, and generally making this book better.

To readers young and old for taking a chance on my books.

And of course, to God, for everything.

~

This story isn't over...

ABOUT THE AUTHOR

Gina Detwiler is the co-author of the bestselling *The Prince Warriors* series in addition to the *Forlorn* series. She also writes about angels, Nephilim, and other bizarre Bible stuff on her blog at www.ginadetwiler.com.

Follow on Instagram and Facebook @ginadetwilerauthor. She also loves to hear from readers, so write to her at 61 Ponderosa Court, Orchard Park, NY 14127.

TRADEMARK
ACKNOWLEDGEMENTS

The author gratefully acknowledges the use of the following trademarks in this work:

Facebook, Inc. CORPORATION DELAWARE 1601 Willow Road Menlo Park CALIFORNIA 94025

Instagram, LLC LIMITED LIABILITY COMPANY DELAWARE 1601 Willow Road Menlo Park CALIFORNIA 94025

iPhone and iPad Apple Inc. CORPORATION CALIFORNIA One Apple Park Way Cupertino CALIFORNIA 95014

CADILLAC General Motors LLC LIMITED LIABILITY COMPANY DELAWARE 300 Renaissance Center Detroit MICHIGAN 482653000

Dungeons and Dragons (REGISTRANT) Wizards of the Coast LLC LIMITED LIABILITY COMPANY DELAWARE 1027 Newport Avenue Pawtucket RHODE ISLAND 02861

Superman (REGISTRANT) DC COMICS E.C. PUBLICATIONS, INC., a New York corporation and WARNER COMMUNICATIONS INC., a Delaware corporation PARTNERSHIP NEW YORK 1700 Broadway New York NEW YORK 10019

The Sims Electronic Arts Inc, 209 Redwood Shores Pkwy, Redwood City, CA 94065-1175

Dear Reader

If you enjoyed reading Forgiven, I would appreciate it if you would help others enjoy this book, too. Here are some of the ways you can help spread the word:

Lend it. This book is lending enabled so please share it with a friend.

Recommend it. Help other readers find this book by recommending it to friends, readers' groups, book clubs, and discussion forums.

Share it. Let other readers know you've read the book by positing a note to your social media account and/or your Goodreads account.

Review it. Please tell others why you liked this book by reviewing it on your favorite ebook site.

Everything you do to help others learn about my book is greatly appreciated!

Gina Detwiler

Plan Your Next Escape!

What's Your Reading Pleasure?

Whether it's captivating historical romance, intriguing mysteries, young adult romance, illustrated children's books, or uplifting love stories, Vinspire Publishing has the adventure for you!

For a complete listing of books available, visit our website at www.vinspirepublishing.com.

Like us on Facebook at
www.facebook.com/VinspirePublishing

Follow us on Twitter at
www.twitter.com/vinspire2004

and follow our blog for details of our upcoming releases, giveaways, author insights, and more!
http://www.vinspirepublishingblog.com.

We are your travel guide to your next adventure!

CPSIA information can be obtained
at www.ICGtesting.com
Printed in the USA
FFHW021114180719
53710382-59400FF

9 781732 711273